Salvatore

JEFF DELBEL

This book is a work of fiction. Names, characters, incidents, events and places are either the product of the author's imagination, or used fictitiously. Any resemblance to persons living or deceased is purely coincidental.

ISBN 978-0-69297-246-5

For more information visit JeffDelbel.com

For

Becky and Natty

Namaste

CHAPTER I

New deal

"Get out of the way!" Salvatore commanded.

A tall big-bellied man wearing an oversized Hawaiian shirt and knee-length madras shorts stood mindlessly blocking the hotel doors. Reading glasses rested on the tip of his nose as he perused the racing form circling his bets with a pencil. An elderly woman pulling an oversized suitcase struggled to maneuver around him.

"I SAID GET OUT OF THE WAY!"

The gambler lowered the pencil, licked his upper lip, exhaled, and turned to confront the man who dared try to boss him. His face sobered. He folded the paper, strolled to a nearby corner, and glanced back.

At six-foot-four with the build of a gladiator, Salvatore Esposito was not one to mess with; even a numbskull could see that. Salvatore glared into the gambler's eyes. The man casually placed the pencil behind his ear. He paused and cracked a smile, then tipped his purple Panama hat and swaggered off.

"Let me help you with that," Salvatore said to the elderly woman and reached for her bag.

The woman smacked his hand. "I can handle it myself, young man. But you could step aside if it's not *too* much trouble. I hope you didn't get rid of that big lug just to stand in his place."

Sal grinned and moved.

Seeing the woman for the first time, a porter rushed over.

"This place is full of Boy Scouts," the woman said. "I'll take care of my own luggage. You go help someone who needs it."

The porter stood aside. The woman shook her head and hauled her suitcase to the counter.

"Come on, Sal. Let's go; we're running late." Angelo Costello hadn't worked for Sal long, but he was a good fit and had quickly learned how seriously Salvatore took his schedules.

"Yeah, Ange, let's go," Sal said.

The dense air was smothering as they pushed open the glass doors and walked outside onto a large marble court. Sal never liked summer in Florida, even with his Mediterranean genes and many years at college in Miami. Tampa Bay was sweltering, and he wouldn't be here if he didn't need to see Stosh.

"Your car is ready Mr. Esposito," the porter said. As they walked to the drive, a Lincoln stretch limousine pulled up.

"Think you could have found something bigger?" Sal said.

"I know you like a smaller ride, but it's what I could get," Angelo said. "Come on, Sal; you only told me about this last night."

"At least it should have a well-stocked bar."

"It does."

The air conditioning chilled them momentarily and then brought relief. Angelo handed Sal a Crown Royal XR on the rocks and poured himself a glass of wine.

"I've seen that guy before, Ange."

"Who?"

"The guy blocking the door. I know I've seen him, but I can't place him. There's something different about him."

"Maybe it will come to you later."

"You don't get it. I don't forget things like that."

Sal sipped while his mental rolodex spun. Then he shrugged. "Maybe you're right. It will pop into my mind later."

"Yeah—listen, Sal. You've talked about Stosh before, but fill me in again. This is a complicated deal, and any information will help me understand the layout."

"I've known him since we were kids. Stosh is a worker—the kind of guy who had three jobs at one time in high school. He made a ton of money in the plumbing supply business before he sold it last year. He's a guy I would trust with my life.

"So, we need him—if he's willing. You know this real estate thing, Ange, you've got to pounce, and that means you've got to be where the deal is—and he will be. I see excellent potential in this region.

"I talked to Stosh about it; he said he needed a face-to-face, and here we are. In the summer, he spends most of his time on his boat with his wife. You'll like Deb. She's a straight shooter, no bullshit."

The limo glided along the side of the bay. Sal watched the slight chop of the waves. A great blue heron slowly flapped its broad wings as it glided high over a cluster of nose-diving cormorants. The sky mixed bits of bright blue between dark gray clouds. Sal knew there would be a downpour that afternoon—there always was in August—but this was coming early. The palms began to sway, and jumbo raindrops dimpled the water.

"This weather is bizarre, Ange."

The sprinkling suddenly changed to a drenching downpour. The windshield wipers couldn't compete, and the driver pulled to the shoulder. Sal listened to the roar of rain on the metal roof and sipped his whiskey.

"This is like a monsoon," Angelo said.

"When were you in a monsoon?" Sal asked.

"Years ago. I was in India for a while in college; never seen rain like that. This kind—off and on, day after day until it just shuts off. But the green, Sal, you've never seen such green—unbelievable. You'd like it."

Sal's face soured.

"I mean it, Sal; I think you'd like it."

"The last place on earth I care to see is India, Ange. I can't stand the smell of curry, and being crowded just pisses me off."

"I think you'd like it if you actually saw the place."

"You're not listening, Ange. I've got no use for anything Indian."

"Why?"

"I've got my reasons."

Ange knew he'd hit a nerve and let it go.

The driver pulled back onto the boulevard and soon found the marina.

"Now listen," Sal said as they walked down the docks toward Stosh's berth. "There are going to be some very attractive women around here. They're Stosh's neighbors. Remember, these people live here."

"So, keep my eyes forward."

"Yeah. I know your style, and this isn't the place."

"Understood, Boss."

Angelo stood five-foot-nine, with a slightly athletic build. He was balding. With his glasses, he looked harmless. But Sal had watched him draw women like a stray puppy. And Ange liked it. Sal also saw him become obnoxious when he drank too much. But he was an excellent accountant. Sal was starting to trust him.

The marina harbored hundreds of boats. The limo dropped Sal and Ange at the sailboat section. The elaborate system of wide planked docks supported by fat round piles seemed to go on for miles. Boats of all sizes rested in their slips. Ange looked through a forest of rigged masts, some over a hundred feet high. Proud sailors scrubbed and hosed their floating homes while sipping beer. Ange and Sal stopped and watched a man as he held a pelican down on the dock and wrestled its mouth open.

"What happened?" Ange asked.

"Aw, he grabbed a fish with a hook in it and got it in his bill," the man said.

"Don't those birds bite?"

"Sometimes, but they're not as tough as they look. See how thin the bill is?"

The man pushed the pouch down showing its flexibility and

worked the hook loose. The freed bird flew to the nearest pylon, stared back at his savior, and then left to find a fresh fish.

The man looked at the sky. "I don't like the looks of this weather."

"Looks OK to me," Ange said.

"You a sailor?"

"No."

"That's why."

"Do you know where *Rainbow's End* is?" Sal asked.

"Right down there." The man pointed.

Sal spotted a huge man waiting by a fifty-one-foot Morgan near the end of a pier.

"HEY, YOU SON OF A LOON!" Stosh yelled.

"HOW ARE YOU, BIG GUY?!" Sal shouted back.

Angelo's eyes widened. At six-foot-five, Stosh was slightly taller than Sal and built like a mountain man. Sal and Ange marched to Stosh's boat where the old friends bear hugged.

"I'd like you to meet my colleague, Angelo Costello. Ange, this is Yashu Stanislaus Stoshowicz. We call him Stosh."

"Nice to meet you, Angelo."

"Nice to meet you too, Stosh."

"Come on, Deb's waitin' on the boat, and there's some drinkin' and eatin' to be done. I hope you brought your appetites."

Sal smiled. He knew Deb would insist on feeding them though he'd asked her not to go to any bother.

Deb was waiting in the large cockpit with the libation. Sal introduced Ange as she filled the drink orders.

"Chins up," Stosh said.

They all raised their glasses and repeated, "Chins up."

"I think a Jimmy every time I say that toast," Stosh said.

"Yeah, me too," Sal said.

"I watched a dolphin the other day. I thought a how good Jimmy swam. He was a frickin' champion, remember? You used to call him Fins, Sal." Stosh chuckled. "Yeah, Fins. I always liked that nickname."

"I'll leave you gentleman alone to conduct your business," Deb said. "Don't be too long. It's been a long time, and we have a lot to catch up on, Sal." Salvatore nodded.

"Now let's get down to business before we get too puddled up. Ange has been my accountant for almost two years. I've had investments in many places, but nothing to speak of down here. In my view, Florida real estate is destabilizing. Many builders are overextended. I think we could close in on some of the new complexes at excellent prices.

"Stosh, I know you didn't retire to take on a second career, but if you could help me get started, I'd be indebted to you. I've decided to divest my assets in New Mexico and Arizona. We haven't sold it all, but most are gone, and the rest will follow soon. Right, Ange?" Angelo nodded. "So, we think we have enough cash."

"Just what do ya want me to do? I don't know nothin' about frickin' real estate, Sal."

"Yeah, but you know how to spot quality construction. And, Stosh, you've got exceptional instincts, and you know what you don't know. That's extremely valuable, Stosh. You'll be great at this. I know I can trust you. You'll make good moves, and within a few months, I'll be out of your hair."

"Look, Sallie," Stosh said. Angelo's head jerked. He'd never heard anyone use that name and survive. "I don't think this real estate thing can last much longer. That's one a the reasons I sold the company. I set the boys up in good manageable businesses and sold off the big stuff cuz I think the whole frickin' things gonna crap the bed. There're too many houses already. And the frickin' things cost too much. On top a that, the banks are givin' money to people who can't pay it back. This can't go on much longer."

Sal shook his head. "Stosh, I've been listening to this for years. I could have gotten out many millions ago, but here we are over half way through 2008, and the system still keeps cranking out the cash. I love your skepticism—I really do. That's one of the reasons I need your help; I know you'll be cautious. Will you try this for me? I promise I won't second-guess any decisions you make."

"I think you're goin' down the wrong road, but I'll help ya any way I can. But, no second-guessin', right?"

"Absolutely, no second-guessing."

Stosh nodded and shook Sal's hand.

"Just how much money are we talkin' 'bout Sallie?"

"Ange, would you fill Stosh in?"

Ange took a notebook from his pocket. "OK, we're looking at seventy-three and change."

"Are you talking millions?" Sal and Ange nodded. "You want me to handle that kinda money?" They nodded again. "Shoot Sallie ... I said I'll do it for ya. But ya shoulda told me how big this was."

Stosh shook his head and chugged his beer.

"Ange will have it set up in a bank down here. Only you and I will be able to access it, and I won't touch it without consulting with you first. Agreed?"

Stosh nodded. "I need another beer," he said. "But first, I'm gonna visit the head."

Angelo stared at a woman in a bikini on the next boat.

"Eyes front," Sal ordered.

"You weren't kidding when you said they'd be hot. Let me ask you something."

"What," Sal said.

"Why doesn't your buddy just swear? Why—"

"He used to swear like a drunken sailor. It was bad for business, and Deb got sick of it. So, he reformed—sort of."

"OK, and did he go to college with you?"

"No, he never wanted to go to college. He wanted to work. Listen, Ange, he may seem rough around the edges, but he's very smart and very honest."

"I get it."

"And Ange, I mean it about your eyes." Ange nodded.

Sal surveyed the sky. The cloud cover still looked ominous. He lowered his eyes and watched a man on a smaller boat nearby filling his fuel tank while smoking a cigarette. The man flicked his ashes an inch from the flowing gasoline. Sal flinched, but there was no flame.

"What an idiot," Sal whispered.

"Who's ready?" Stosh yelled from below.

"I'm in," Sal said.

"I'll pass for now," Ange said. Sal smiled.

Deb appeared with a platter of deli sandwiches. “Time to eat,” she said.

Sal took a loaded Italian special. Angelo found a turkey. “Do you mind if I take a few things off?” he asked. “I’m trying to watch my waistline.”

“No problem, make yourself at home,” Deb said and chuckled. “Big Stosh here could use a little of your moderation.”

“Say, Stosh, who’s the guy over there?” Sal asked and pointed to the smoker.

“Oh, him. He’s one a them guys who’s always temptin’ fate. I’ve seen him do the stupidest crap. But he’s the luckiest turd you’ve ever met. Smokin’ around gas is nothin’ compared to some of the bonehead things he’s pulled.”

Sal smiled and nodded. “What do you think of these skies?”

“Hard to tell for sure. But they ain’t good.”

As they sat and drank, stories from the past began to flow. Ange listened carefully. This was his first trip with Sal, and he was on a mission to learn as much as he could. The name Jimmy kept popping up.

“Did you ever get your stick, Sallie?” Stosh asked.

“I did better than that; I bought the whole property. Kate must have told you.” Stosh nodded. “I’ve only been there once, though. Kate was away, and I didn’t go into Jimmy’s study. Just doesn’t feel right yet.”

“Jesum Crow, Sallie, he’s been gone for five years.”

“Yeah, five fucking years.” Sal looked at Deb. “Sorry, Deb,” he said.

“Swear away, Sallie; you wouldn’t be the same without it.”

“Thanks, Deb. You know I didn’t even miss him for the

first year or so. Then I went to call him about a legal problem; I'd completely forgotten he was dead."

Sal chuckled and paused.

"Buying Jimmy's place was a good move for me, and Kate too," Sal continued. "It's way too big for a single woman—shit, Stosh, in total it's over five-thousand square feet. Kate bought the cottage next door from Ray. It's a beautiful house, three bedrooms, great views, much more manageable for her. And Ray moved to an old farm in the Adirondacks where he always wanted to be anyway. He still keeps an eye on things, though. I don't know him well, but I suspect I'll be seeing more of him."

Ange was learning. He had never seen Sal so relaxed and open. He made mental notes of the new names he heard. He'd ask about them and the stick later.

"Say, could I use the restroom?" Ange asked.

"Sure," Deb said. "I'll show you the way. Then I'll give you a little tour of *Rainbow's End* if you like."

Ange smiled, nodded and followed Deb below.

"Sallie, look, now that we got a minute alone, I don't get why you want me to do this. You're the smartest guy I know. No one's ever been as good at turnin' a buck as you. None of us ever knew how you did it. Why me, why now?"

"I need someone I can trust. Angelo is new. I think he'll be good. But you're the man. I'm at the point where I don't want to manage everything myself anymore. And I need time away. I'm going back to London next week, you know."

"Yeah, good for you. But who's goin' to watch that nightclub you opened? You usually go for at least a month, don't ya?"

"My partners have assured me they'll step up while I'm gone. I doubt it, but if they fuck up, Ange will be back after a week or so. And how about you? I keep inviting you and Deb. You'd love the beer in England."

"I bet. One of these years I'll surprise ya."

"I'm not holding my breath. Listen, Stosh; I really need you. Not for too long. But right now, I need to make changes."

"OK, I already promised ya. But I'm nervous."

"Don't be, Stosh. My instincts tell me this is the thing to do. They're seldom wrong."

Deb and Ange returned chuckling.

"I've never seen Asian carpets on a boat before," Ange said.

"Yeah, Deb and me met this great little gal who sells em at a place in Tampa. I didn't know if I'd like em, but they look real good. And the gal said we could always take em back if we wanted."

"You know," said Deb, "I should introduce her to you, Sallie. I think you'd like her."

"Deb, please, no matchmaking. I'm a lost cause in that area, remember?"

Deb smiled and nodded.

"Hey, Angelo," Stosh said. "Want to see a little more of the marina? I'll show ya around."

"Sure," Ange said.

"OK, I'll lead the way."

"Wherever you go, I'm going.

"Eyes front, Ange," Sal reminded.

Ange and Stosh took their drinks and wandered down the dock.

"I'm glad I had a chance to talk to you alone, Sallie."

"What's up, Deb?"

"It's Stosh. I'm embarrassed to talk about this."

"Spit it out, Deb. No need to hold back from me."

"Well, since he retired he's been ... well, drinking a little too much."

"He seems OK today," Sal said. "And he always drank a lot of beer. He's a big man, Deb. I've never seen him not able to hold it."

"He is OK today, and it isn't all the time. He's taken a liking to vodka. When he doesn't have anything to do, he drinks it almost like beer. And he's starting to forget things. Don't get me wrong; he's not mean. He doesn't even seem drunk. He just doesn't think."

"Well, he'll have plenty to do for a while with the work I've got for him."

"And that's a godsend, Sallie. He won't let you down; don't worry about a thing on that end. But I'm still worried about the long run. I've mentioned it to him, but he doesn't want to talk about it."

"Do you want me to say something?"

"Oh no, not now anyway. I just wanted you to know. There's no one else I could talk to about it. Maybe I'm telling you more for my sake than his. Between the vodka and that cussed bomb shelter—well let's just say I have my days."

"You've still got the bomb shelter?"

"I thought when we bought the house we'd take the stupid thing out. The crackpot who built it was supposed to get rid of it before we closed. But then Stosh thought it might be useful for something—you know how he is about getting rid of anything. Who in their right mind keeps an old bomb shelter? In Florida? No one even has a basement here. And now he's starting to hang out down in the damned thing. He almost fell on those steep stairs a few weeks ago."

Deb sipped her drink.

"He said I could fill it in if I want. But I think he'd be upset, maybe even drink more. I'm sorry, Sallie. I'm just worried, and I know I've blown everything out of proportion. Things will work themselves out."

Sal nodded. "The best thing is to get him back to work," he said. "Now I'm even gladder we're going to work together awhile. Let me know if things don't improve. I'll find a way to talk to him."

Deb relaxed as they chatted. Old stories and a few jokes got her laughing. She smiled as she pointed to Ange and Stosh walking toward them and then up at the dark sky.

"They're lucky it didn't start raining," she said. "I think we're in for a storm."

"What did you think, Ange?" Sal asked.

"This is one hell of an operation."

As they boarded, a sudden gust thrust Ange and Stosh against the cockpit's side wall.

"THIS AINT GOOD!" Stosh yelled.

The group rushed to stow loose gear and cushions. The gusts turned to a steady, gale force wind, and torrential rain pelted the marina. Deb and Ange hurried below while Stosh and Sal grabbed onto the safety line and watched to see if other boats needed help.

A deafening crack of lightning struck the mainmast of a sloop two slips over. Stosh and Sal grabbed their heads and ducked. Stosh pointed and yelled over the hollowing storm, "THE FRICKIN LIGHTNIN' HIT MY BUDDY DAVE!"

Sal squinted and saw a man lying in the cockpit of the sloop. He leaped off *Rainbow's End.* He scrambled through the squall swatting flying debris from his head. He hurdled on board Dave's boat. He grabbed Dave, pulled his face from a puddle, raised him to his feet and shook him. Dave regained his wits and nodded.

Sal saw smoke in the cabin and pulled a fire extinguisher from its mount. He covered his face with a wet towel and rushed below. A couch near the mast's base was in flames. Sal aimed and blasted until the fire was out and then hurried out of the smoke to rejoined Dave. They clenched the safety line, and Sal threw the wet towel over their heads. They held on for several minutes.

As quickly as it had started, the microburst vanished, and the sun reappeared. Sal and Dave tossed the towel and waved to Stosh. "EVERYTHING OK?" Stosh yelled.

"CALL AN AMBULANCE!" Sal hollered back. "HE SEEMS ALL RIGHT, BUT HE TOOK A HELL OF A JOLT!"

Dave waved to Stosh. He shook his head and pointed to his mouth. Sal helped him to the dock, and they plodded to *Rainbow's End.*

Ange and Deb joined Stosh in the cockpit as Sal and Dave boarded. "You OK, Dave?" Stosh said.

"I think so, but some fillings in my teeth melted. Damnedest feeling having that kind of juice flowing through you, Stosh."

"He's real fucking lucky," Sal said. "Under most circumstances, he'd be toast. But lightning is fickle—it will give you the rush of your life one day, and incinerate you the next."

"Good thing you had a doctor on board, Stosh. I was out cold."

"Doctor?" Ange said.

"We'll talk about it later," Sal replied. "I think the fire is out, Stosh, but you should call the fire guys anyway."

"They'll come along with the ambulance."

"That's right," Sal said and nodded as he sat and took a deep breath.

The ambulance and fire patrol quickly arrived. Sal gave the paramedics a summary report before they took Dave for a full examination. The firemen checked Dave's boat and confirmed the fire was out. Stosh offered Sal dry clothes, and the two changed while Ange and Deb put the cockpit back in order. Stosh brought fresh drinks, and they all laughed and jabbered about the near catastrophe.

"You ever been that close to a lightning strike, Stosh?" Sal asked.

"Nope and I hope I never am again. Did you see how all that juice lit up Dave's boat? Jesum Crow, Sallie, the whole thing was outlined in the brightest frickin' flash I ever saw."

After several minutes, the conversation changed, and they all sat relaxed, almost as if nothing had happened.

Sal looked at Stosh's smoking neighbor standing at his boat's stern, cursing. He'd left his gas can teetering on the transom's lip, and the storm had dumped it overboard. He pinched his cigarette and stared at the color spectrum from the leaking gasoline swirling on the water. He sucked on the filter. The cigarette's tip glowed, and he flicked it into the center of the spill. The butt sparkled and then fizzled out.

"You're right, Stosh. That asshole just loves to press his luck," Sal said.

"Yup, it's a funny world, Sallie. A guy like Dave—greatest guy you'll ever meet—minds his own business and gets zapped by a lightnin' bolt. Then ya take that jerk. I know a fella who used to work for 'im. Says he's nothin' but a stingy, mean a-hole. He's *tryin'* to fry himself, and nothin' happens. But no matter. The fire always cooks an S-O-B like him, when it's time."

Deb turned on the ship's stereo to an easy listening station and poured refills. The opening bars of a song made Sal smile. A woman with a smooth mellow voice began to sing "Moon River." Sal's eyes glazed as he looked at the bay.

"Wow Sallie," Deb said. "What a coincidence. Angelo, did you know that Sal's mom was a singer. She was magnificent, could have been big time. And 'Moon River' was her signature song, just before she quit."

"Why did she quit?"

"She married my pop," Sal said. "He was a tailor, a damn good tailor too. She had a kid from a previous husband when they met, but Pop didn't care. He was nuts about her, said they were a perfect match. Unfortunately, the deal came with my fucked-up brother, Johnny. Pop adopted him. After I came along, the family became her primary concern, and she rarely performed. When I was twelve, she gave it up altogether."

Ange's eyes widened. "So, Johnny Esposito *is* your brother?" he asked. Stosh and Deb winced.

"Yeah," Sal said.

Ange realized he'd gone somewhere forbidden and changed direction. "Are your folks still alive?"

"Pop passed ten-or-so years ago. Ma's in a home near Albany. She has Alzheimer's. Doesn't know who I am sometimes. But she can still sing with the best."

The group was quiet while the song finished.

"That was lovely," Deb said.

"Yeah," Sal whispered.

After another round, Sal suggested it was time to go.

"You know," Ange said, "I didn't write anything down. Do you think we should go over things one more time just for memory sake?"

Sal smiled; Deb and Stosh chuckled. "Sal won't forget," Stosh said. "Sal remembers everything."

Angelo looked at Sal, smiled and nodded. He was starting to get the picture.

***

Sal and Ange walked through the crowded hotel bar, found two vacant stools and ordered drinks. Most heads were craned up at the televisions. It looked like the Democrats would be running an African-American candidate for president.

"What do you think of Obama, Sal?"

"I don't give a shit who's president, Ange. Nothing in the financial world will be affected."

"Do you think he can win?"

"No. I don't see the same people who reelected G.W. going for a liberal black guy. But, as I said, it doesn't make any difference."

Sal and Ange chatted about the storm and their afternoon on the boat.

"I like your friends, Sal. I can see why you trust Stosh."

"Yeah, they're the best. Listen, Ange; I want to talk to you about something"—Sal took a sip of whiskey— "just this one time." Ange nodded. "It's about my brother Johnny."

"I don't need to know, Sal."

"Just shut up and listen. Johnny's one of those guys who is rotten from birth. He was twelve when I was born. We'd just moved to Plattsburgh. Even then he had a racket." Sal snickered. "The bastard was selling protection to the shoeshine kids downtown before he was a teenager. He quit school as soon as he could. Ma was heartbroken.

"When he could drive, he started fucking around in Montreal—first small-time theft, a little extortion. He did one big job with a guy named Buzzy Klein."

Sal stopped and looked off a moment.

"It was a total clusterfuck, so he went back to the chicken shit he was good at. He got away with it for years. Then he was busted—big time. He'd started moving drugs across the border—before 9/11, it was easy if you knew the area. But he was a braggart, and everyone knew.

"By the time he was busted, he was wanted in both Canada

and the U.S. He probably would have been extradited if he hadn't been put away in New York. They got him on a murder charge.

"He killed a guy who was messing around with his girl—or at least he thought she was *his* girl. Fucked him up with a knife, even sliced off his package—cock, nuts, the whole enchilada—a lesson for you and your wandering eyes."

Ange nodded. "Where is he now?"

"Dannemora. Been in a long time."

"And the Buzzy Klein guy?"

"Don't know; I never saw him again."

"You knew him?"

"Met him once. He was a cutthroat son of a bitch."

Sal took a deep breath and another sip.

"Any chance Johnny will get out of prison?"

"Not alive. Lung cancer. He'll leave there in a box."

"Sal … I'm sorry."

"I'm not. Listen, the legend of Johnny Esposito is bullshit. He's nothing but a low-life punk. He's fucked up everything he's touched and hurt my folks like you can't imagine. And, now you know why I insist on legitimate operations. I've made much more money without—well, by doing things my way. I only crossed the line once, and that was from a lack of information. It won't happen again."

"When?"

"A deal in Arizona five years ago. I didn't know who was working behind the scenes. By the time I found out, it was too late. Damnedest thing, though. Somehow the deal still went my way and with no retaliation. I still can't figure out why. Shit, Ange! That's who that guy was!"

"What guy, Sal?"

"The guy blocking the door this afternoon. That was Dominic Scardaccione; they call him Pencil Nick.

"He's a bookie. Used to be around Saratoga, but he moved to Phoenix. He was a beanpole, must have gained a hundred-fifty pounds. That's why I didn't recognize him. What the fuck is he doing here?"

"Pencil Nick?"

"Yeah, I know it sounds stupid. He always keeps a pencil behind his ear. Lots of those guys picked up kiddish names from some quirk."

"Maybe his being here is a coincidence?"

Sal smirked and looked at Ange. "No fucking way, Ange. He's here for a reason." Sal paused. "No sense worrying about it now. If those guys wanted me, they would have moved on it long ago."

Sal rubbed his lips together and shrugged.

"Back to Johnny, Ange. I don't know how many of our guys know he's my brother; I don't care as long as it's not discussed. He's total shit. And now we will close this conversation. We won't talk about him again."

Ange nodded and sipped his wine. "Can I ask you a couple of other questions?"

"Ask away."

"That guy said you were a doctor? So, you're a doctor and a lawyer?"

"Yeah, I graduated from medical and law school. Next?"

Ange paused. "OK, I met Kate at the closing on your lodge—"

"Camp, Ange, it's called Camp."

"Yeah, Camp. What does Kate do?"

"She's a psychologist, finished her Ph.D. just a couple of years ago—and good for her. When you're our age, reaching a goal like that is fantastic."

"And Ray?"

"Kind of a recluse tree hugger type. He guides in the Adirondacks once in a while, but mostly he reads."

"Who's Jimmy, the guy you called Fins?"

Sal paused and exhaled. "Jimmy Eagleson. He died a few years ago."

Sal looked off, face blank. His usually busy hand lay flat on his thigh.

"How did he die?"

Sal turned and stared into Ange's eyes. "He fell off a fucking cliff."

"Sorry, Sal, didn't mean to pry. I get it. No need to be sarcastic."

Ange let some time pass.

"And 'the stick'?"

Sal smiled. "When Jimmy and I were kids, we had this fort—great place; you should have seen it, a tent we made from an old canvas tarp, fire pit—fabulous place. We slept over when we could, cooked hot dogs, had a hell of a time. Stosh was there a few times when he wasn't at one of his fifty or so jobs."

Sal grinned.

"You see, Jimmy's old man would never let him have

guns—toys or real, didn't matter—no one ever knew why. One day, Jimmy found this stick. Dead ringer for an old polished musket—I mean the thing is beautiful. I wanted it so much. But Jimmy wouldn't part with it. Hell, I made him an offer a few months before he died—by that time, it was more of a joke, you know.

"Well, he left it to me in his will. It's the damnedest thing; I think about it all the time. I've bought tons of shit over the years, but there's something about that stick. You know, it might be the best thing I own, a fucking stick."

The conversation changed to some plans for the Saratoga Club when Angelo turned, and his eyes performed a thorough examination of a full-figured woman in a summer dress strolling to the end of the bar.

"Get a good look, asshole?" a man said as he took her hand.

"Shit, Ange. Didn't you hear anything I said?"

"I did; I did. I just couldn't help it. She's gorgeous."

Ange glanced back; the woman smiled and winked. Her date saw, smacked down his drink, and started toward Ange. Sal shook his head and stood. The man grabbed a pepper shaker and twisted off the top. Sal took a step forward.

"If you're going to do that, you'd better hurry," Sal said. "Once I have your hand, I'll crush that fucking thing into your palm. Or you can twist the top back on, sit down, and save it for your steak. Your choice."

"I see, this little fuck keeps a big stooge to fight his battles."

"And a shithead like you needs a hand full of pepper. As I said, your choice."

The man's date hurried to him and put her hands on his shoulders. "Come on, Honey; the guy didn't mean anything."

The man stood firm. Then he grabbed her arm and pulled her to their seats for her purse. He threw the shaker on the floor and stormed out.

"Sir, please sit down if you are going to stay," the bartender said to Sal. "You're making other guests uncomfortable. I know you didn't start this, but if there's any further trouble you will have to leave."

Sal smiled and sat. "Please give everyone a drink on me with my apologies."

The bartender nodded and delivered the drinks. Customers looked over and gave Sal thumbs up.

"Well, Ange, I was almost tossed out of a bar. That hasn't happened in a long time. And a damn nice bar too—although not as nice as my club."

"I'm sorry, Sal. That was my fault."

"No Shit. Along with that asshole's date."

"It won't happen again."

"Never promise me what you can't deliver, Ange."

***

Sal's room came with a gulf view. He popped a beer and sat on the terrace. The day's thoughts flowed into his head. He hadn't spoken about Johnny for a long time, although he saw his face every morning when he worked out on the heavy bag.

And Angelo had been to India. Where did that come from?

He chuckled as he thought of Deb's concerns about Stosh. She'd always been a bit neurotic. Sal had no worries about his new partner.

He looked at the seascape. The sky was speckled with stars and the water spotted with boats. He could hear a party on the floor below with loud talk and lots of laughter. He remembered times like that with friends in Plattsburgh. He thought of times with Jimmy, and his stick.

The thick, salty air became uncomfortable, and he decided to turn in.

Sal emptied his pockets on the bureau. Out came his thick wallet, loaded money clip, and a gold brooch in the shape of a lotus petal. He picked up the brooch and polished it with his handkerchief.

"Why do I still carry you around?" he whispered.

He took a few pills, undressed, and lay on the bed. Soon he began to doze.

The dream came quickly.

Salvatore's mother stood on stage in a smoke-filled barroom. Sal's father pumped an old player piano, accompanying her as she sang "Moon River." Sal sat at a table sipping whiskey with Johnny. Sal was twelve, but one of the men. Johnny wore a Superman t-shirt and played with a switchblade.

Johnny pointed to a door. Sal stood and walked through into a foggy alley. He squinted. In a garbage can, he made out a short piece of two-by-four covered with rice. The rice started wiggling and turned into maggots. He opened his shirt. The maggots were on his chest squirming and making him itch.

He tried to brush them away with an old bandanna, but they wouldn't fall off.

Instantly, he was in the back of a delivery van, driving itself. Inside was nothing but the two-by-four and him, with the now maggot-covered bandanna tied around his face. The walls of the van slowly contracted. He gasped for air while struggling not to inhale maggots.

The van swirled and transformed into a ventilation duct. Clenching the two-by-four, he started crawling. In intense heat, the maggots withered and the bandanna fell from his face. A pungent smell of curry filled the sweltering space.

He looked down through an open vent onto a boiling cauldron of lentil dhal. The two-by-four morphed into a short black cobra and slithered over his arm through the opening. A powerful force started pulling him toward the cauldron.

Drenched in sweat, he fought to grasp the vent's hot, slick edge and push himself back. His wet hands were slipping. The dhal churned and transformed into molten gold. The boiling gold bubbled and spat at him. He lost hold, felt his body sucked head first through the portal and free-fell toward the gurgling cauldron.

Sal sprung up saturated in sweat and dry-mouthed. He adjusted to the unfamiliar room, swung out of bed, and staggered to the bathroom for a drink of water. His clammy hands barely held the glass. He twisted on the shower to cold and stepped in.

It had been months since the dream had visited. He tried to

analyze what invited it. Maybe all the talk? That must have been it, the talk about Ma, India, Johnny.

The shower cleared his head. He changed the water to warm and gradually relaxed. He'd become adept at this ritual; it didn't take long.

He dried off, poured a drink, returned to the terrace and imagined himself at the fort with Jimmy, his safe place. The dreams couldn't get him there; nothing could get him there. He sipped his drink and felt good.

Soon, he'd return to bed. He knew the dream wouldn't come again that night.

***

"How'd you sleep?" Ange asked.

"Just fine," Sal said.

"You work out?"

"Always, Ange, and the heavy bag took one hell of a beating this morning."

"I'm going to the bank to set up the accounts. I'll need you and Stosh this afternoon to sign. You want to fly out after that?"

"Yeah, the sooner, the better. I've got some things to do before we can leave for London. I didn't really think we needed our own jet, but now I see the advantages."

"Yeah. And about London. Where do you want to fly from? I'll need to tell the pilot."

"Plattsburgh. You fly there a few days after we get back

to Saratoga. I'll meet you. I want to see Kate and check out a few things at Camp. I'll stop and see Ma first. The airport up there is going to be handy for us. Have you taken care of all the details?"

"Yeah, we're all set. Nothing like a closed Air Force base looking for a new life. Great runways and cheap hangar space. And real convenient, now that you'll be in the North Country more often."

Ange picked at his whole-grain cereal as Salvatore loaded a plate with sausage and eggs. They talked about the day before. Ange sipped tea; Sal gulped black coffee.

"Have you decided on a bank?" Sal asked.

"Yeah, we'll go with one I found in Bradenton. Given the amount we're depositing, a bank that size should bend over backward for us."

"Whatever you think, just try not to draw too much attention."

"Sal, I can guarantee we will draw plenty of attention."

"Yeah, I guess so."

"I'll call the pilot. You want the plane ready for—let's say—three o' clock?"

"Yeah."

"OK." Ange took a last sip. "I'm out of here."

Sal refilled his coffee and moved to a patio overlooking the Gulf. He thought of the dream—one of a set, all recurring, all with the same theme. He remembered how they began when he was in high school and then escalated. In college, he became obsessed with dream analysis—picking every detail apart, identifying multiple possibilities for the meaning of each segment.

Then he realized he was wasting his time. He knew what they meant and why they came. And he knew he could do nothing but learn to live with them.

As he watched the birds fly, he looked forward to London. A good road trip always cleared his head, and he'd made friends in England who would be good to see. But first, his mother and the North Country required his attention. Being "the good son" came with responsibilities.

He smiled. He'd also get to see Kate—and his stick.

CHAPTER II

Moon River

Salvatore pulled into his driveway. Remembering the garage was full of boxes for Camp, he parked his Mercedes near the front door. He threw his keys on the marble table in the vestibule. He looked in the mirror and shook his head. He used to be good on the road for weeks, but now only three days and he was beat. He stepped into the living room, shaded his eyes and flipped a switch lowering the blinds on the floor-to-ceiling picture windows. The western glare faded out. He looked eastward onto the Hudson and watched the flowing water.

He poured a whiskey in the kitchen, skimmed through a stack of mail, and returned his attention to the river. He loved gazing at fast moving water. He often sat alone watching the rapids tumble over the rocks.

The house had four bedrooms, each with a bath. But no one ever stayed. He liked it that way; Sal saw people on his terms. He looked to the south wall at his pop's classic player piano. He could hear his father scolding, "Don't pump so hard, Salvatore, you'll blow out the bellows."

Sal chuckled. Pop loved the thing. He couldn't play piano but wanted desperately to accompany Ma. The old player was the perfect solution. He remembered evenings when the house was full of guests and music.

He thought of the trip and how good it was to see Stosh. He thought of the changes in the making. Moving assets was always risky, but he needed to slow down. He hadn't told Ange or Stosh that he was thinking of getting out completely. He'd spent most of his life making money, but it didn't do much for him anymore. One or two more years would be enough.

He wondered again why Pencil Nick was in Tampa and remembered the deal in Phoenix. He knew he'd fucked up—crossed a line with the wrong people. But he came through without a scratch. He'd racked his brain trying to figure why. He knew he wouldn't be so lucky a second time.

Sal's cell phone rang. He blinked and flipped it open. "Yeah, Ange."

"Sal, I'm finishing the transfers to the bank in Bradenton. We need to talk about the rest. We have a buyer for the Phoenix property."

"Which property?"

"All of it."

Sal smiled. "Good."

"Look, this is a lot of money, and the deal is moving fast. We need to make some decisions."

"We already have."

"Yeah—in general. Listen, I think we should reconsider stocks."

"We've been over that, Ange."

"Sal, it doesn't make sense to leave that kind of cash sitting in banks."

"Why? Not much interest? So what?"

"I think we should at least move some of it to the market. I know stocks can look shaky, but they're always good over time. We're not talking about day trading here, just good conservative long-term investing. Shit, Sal, it's 2008. Think of the return you could have in 2018."

Sal pondered. "I suppose selling all at once nets a lot more cash-on-hand than I planned. It's one hell of a lot of money. But, what stocks? I don't know shit about the market, and I don't like what I don't know."

"I'll get a broker. I'll find someone you can trust—someone who'll work just for us. Let's at least listen."

"OK. We'll listen and *just* listen for now. You got someone in mind?"

"A few guys. I'll check them out and get back to you to see when we can meet. OK?"

"Yeah." Fucking stocks, Sal thought, hanging up.

As he refilled his drink, he gazed through a west window, watching the sunset. The morning sun would rise over the river. Sal hoped to see it. He glanced up at a picture, Linda, his last ex. Sal hadn't done well with romance. Both of his marriages failed. Both wives said the same thing: he was self-centered, unavailable, and painfully private—especially when it came to the dreams.

How concerned Linda had been when he'd wake in a cold sweat. He could never tell her why; never found the courage.

Sal regretted their breakup. She was totally devoted to her

new husband but checked in from time to time. Sal came to like the guy—even had a drink with him once in a while. But Sal still missed her concern for him.

Caroline, his first, didn't care much. He hadn't heard from her in years. She bolted as soon as the divorce was final—somewhere in the Midwest, he thought. Didn't miss her at all.

He'd had a few relationships since Linda, but as soon as a woman got close, he would shut down. He'd always been the big tough guy. Weakness wasn't going to happen.

Besides, there would always be the dreams; they were his alone.

In a few days, he'd see Kate. Kate had been through a lot. Jimmy's death hit her hard at first. Sal always thought of her as a little sister. He looked forward to seeing her, and Camp.

This trip he'd sleep there for the first time since Jimmy died. Then off to England for a while—no agenda this year. He'd stay as long as he liked.

The moon appeared from behind a cloud and cast a rippling reflection on the river. He thought of Ma. The way she was before the Alzheimer's, and he smiled. Tomorrow he'd face her *present* condition, but tonight he'd be content. He absorbed the view. His thoughts were quiet. The dream wouldn't be visiting.

***

Sal sat in the car before checking in at the nursing home's front desk. He'd paid for the finest in the area, but it still had the smell. Every home he'd looked into had it, urine mixed with feces and Lysol—the unmistakable scent of infirmed old people. No cleaning could eliminate it. His mother had a private room with a sitting area, large television, and bathroom fitted with multiple safety bars. She had a small stereo with plenty of music. When Sal walked in, she was in a lounge chair gazing out the window at a kingfisher perched on the limb of a young oak tree.

"How are you today, Ma?" Sal asked.

"Just ducky," she replied. "You can empty the waste basket in the bathroom before you change the bed. And the sink needs to be scrubbed. And don't call me Ma. You don't even know what it means."

"Ma, it's me, Sal, your son."

"Oh, you know my son? Johnny's a good boy. He's a doctor you know. He makes a lot of money and has a house on the river. He visits me almost every day. He'll be taking me home just as soon as the pneumonia is gone."

Ma had entered the home two years before with a chest cold that was now long gone. He looked at his shoes and shook his head. Her memory was even worse than the week before. "Johnny's at his office right now. He's a good boy."

"Ma, it's me, Sal. I'm the doctor."

"Well, if you're a doctor you must know Johnny. He'll probably be here soon if you'd like to see him. You should hear his father play the saxophone. We have a band you know. We're at the Palladium tonight if you'd like to come. I'm the singer." Sal's eyes misted. She was much worse.

"Casey will be coming too. He's a great hitter—the best the Yankees have. He's very busy, but he finds time to see me."

For the past few months, Ma had come to believe a baseball player named Casey was visiting. Sal thought she was probably remembering parts of an old poem she used to recite—she and Pop loved baseball in the day, especially the Yankees. And Sal had become so used to her fantasies that he hadn't bothered to ask the staff about it. For what reason? Alzheimer's wasn't something that came with many answers.

As Sal and Ma chatted, he felt better. He asked questions without trying to correct her and listened to stories about the past. It was good to hear her talk. A nurse practitioner visited awhile. She told Sal his mother was physically well, but her mental condition had worsened. No shit, Sal thought. He didn't tell her he was technically an MD.

Sal looked at his watch; he'd been with Ma for over an hour. He smiled at her.

"Hey, Ma, would you like to sing?"

"Sure."

Sal walked to the stereo, pushed in a CD of classic ballads, and selected the fourth song. "Moon River" began to play, and Ma sang. The doorway filled with spectators and Sal wiped his eyes.

"I love it when she sings this song," a nurse said. "You know, she'll only sing 'Moon River' for you, Mr. Esposito." Sal smiled; at least he still had one connection.

When she finished, all applauded. "Thank you, thank you," Ma said.

Sal was immersed in memories as he walked to his car. He

tried to envision Ma when she was young with her long black hair, dark eyes, and tan Mediterranean skin. The visits were becoming harder, particularly her confusion with Johnny. She used to say that Sal was a good boy. What he would give to hear that one more time. Now it was Johnny she called a good boy. What a fucking irony. He knew this was the nature of Alzheimer's. There was no longer reason in her memory, no predicting where it might take her. But she remembered all the lyrics, and she could still sing like a pro.

***

Sal's black Mercedes sedan weaved through the late afternoon traffic blasting past cars, trucks, and RVs. Interstate 87 was like a NASCAR track at this time of day, but Sal always had the right wheels to win the race. The meeting would be at the high-end nightspot his associates convinced him to invest in a year ago. Sal had intended to keep his involvement confidential. But as word quickly got out and spread, he became the not-so-silent partner. As it turned out, it was good for business, lending a little mystique.

Sal parked in his reserved spot next to the club's entrance. He'd always wanted an authentic Italian restaurant, designed and decorated to make the customer believe they were in Palermo. He settled for a renovated drugstore but insisted it be done with class. The outside was refinished in dark wood, and small, high-placed windows insured the ambiance would be controlled from the inside. Sal strolled down the slate walkway, through the large front door, and into the vestibule. As always, he stopped to inspect the spacious premises.

The black industrial ceiling offset the light gray walls. A stage with professional sound and lighting dominated the far end. Next to it was the door to Sal's office. At the other end, a horseshoe-shaped bar offering forty beers on tap had swivel stools with leather backs for forty-eight guests. It was surrounded by high tops and tables to accommodate over one hundred more.

Booths designed for privacy lined one wall, and scores of small pendant lights hung strategically, all with dimmers for fading away facial flaws. A cherry dance floor separated the spaces. The room could easily accommodate a large banquet or reception and occasionally offered top area bands—although a house DJ had proven to be more popular.

The menu was basic. The most expensive entree was a New York steak, and the closest Sal got to his Italian cuisine was brick fired pizza. Sal didn't care; the money was in the booze, and the place sold tons.

As soon as Sal was seen, the welcomes began. "Hello, Mr. Esposito—Nice to see you, Mr. Esposito—You're looking well, Mr. Esposito," and the occasional brave, "How are you, Sal." Sal snapped back quick salutations to each greeter, then spotted Ange at the far side of the bar with a stranger and worked his way to them.

"Salvatore Esposito, meet Roger Clark," Ange said.

"It's nice to meet you, Mr. Esposito; I've heard a lot about you."

I'll bet you have, Sal thought. "Ange tells me you know the market. Let's sit and talk."

The late afternoon crowd dressed in business professional swarmed around the bar. Frank Sinatra and Dean Martin sang in the background. In a few hours, designer jeans would take their place, and the music would segue to Justin Timberlake and Rihanna, blasting and booming the packed dance floor.

A customer signaled his two seated friends, and all three quickly moved while smiling and nodding. Sal nodded back, thanked them, and took his usual place on one of the stools they'd vacated in his honor.

The bartender ran through the happy-hour specials for Roger while instinctively pouring a Crown Royal XR on the rocks for the boss and wine for Ange. Roger chose Guinness. The bartender pulled a frosted glass from a cooler and worked the pump, carefully draughting the dark brew. Once the stout had settled, he quickly swirled his spoon over the head drawing a perfect shamrock. Roger grinned and took a sip.

"All right, Roger, let's get down to it," Sal said over the crowd noise as Roger moved his ear closer.

"I've made my money in real estate," Sal said. "That's what I know. We've done well. From 1997 to 2006, property values increased by nearly one hundred twenty-five percent. That's slowed in the last couple of years, but complexes can still turn high profits. A lot of builders are maxed out or over-extended, and when they find they can't handle the sub-prime balloon deals they've gotten themselves in, they'll need to downsize at almost any cost.

"On the residential side, the ratio of debt to disposable

personal income is one hundred twenty-seven percent; in short, people can't afford their houses—how the banks let that happen is beyond me. There's already a lot of action. Piles of foreign money have been injected into the market, but there's still a glut of high-end properties available at a steal.

"Now, the worry has been the possibility of a major downward readjustment in true assessments, but any significant decrease in property values would cause a financial crash." Sal sipped and paused. "The powers that be won't let that happen."

"So, Roger, after all that, and even though I still see potential in real estate, I'm moving assets. I'll stay with real estate only in Florida and New York. All our holdings in the Southwest have been liquidated, and I now want to simplify and back off from the dealing process.

"Ange has been with me for two years. He knows the layout almost as well as I do. We're here because he likes the stock market. I don't. It's that simple. Make your sale."

Roger nodded and placed a sheet of paper in front of Sal.

"Here it is, in a nutshell," Roger said. "I've been investing for fifteen years. You can see my average annual returns. Ange tells me you're not interested in day trading. That's good. If you're in for the long-haul, the market has always been the best place for maximizing profit. I have a system for building portfolios to fit several levels of risk. And they've all produced—you can see my track record." Roger pointed to a section of his summary.

"Why shouldn't I just put my money in offshore accounts?"

"Higher returns. If you want your money to make money,

the market is the place. You're a well-informed man, Mr. Esposito. Your summation of the real-estate market is right on. I don't think we'd be talking if you hadn't already done your homework."

Sal smiled. He was starting to like Roger.

"I have always worked with a limited clientele," Roger continued. "While I can't promise to work for you only, I will agree not to add clients beyond my present obligations. I can assure you I will have the time to manage your investments carefully."

Sal nodded. "I'll think about it a day or two, but tell me more."

Sal listened carefully as Roger presented a preliminary plan. Ange took notes though he now knew it wasn't necessary. After a half-hour, the business ended, and talk became casual. A stylishly dressed woman walked up to Ange and gave him a kiss on his balding head.

"Thought I'd find you here," she said. Ange looked surprised and made a nervous introduction.

"So, this is the famous Salvatore Esposito," she said. "Very pleased to finally meet you. Angie has told me a lot about you." Sal smiled politely. "Honey, will you watch my purse while I freshen up?" Ange nodded, and she left for the ladies' room.

"Are you out of your fucking mind?" Sal said. "Do you know whose wife that is? Do you have a death wish?"

"It's not what it looks like," Ange said. Roger stared at his drink.

"Bullshit 'Angie, Honey'; who the fuck do you think you're

trying to snow? If Frankie saw this, I'd be finding parts of you in the dumpster."

"They're not together anymore, Sal. He dumped her. They're divorcing."

"And you think that matters to a guy like Frankie Napoli? Just because he doesn't want her doesn't mean he's going to let anyone else in. Jesus, Ange, the guy's a fucking, sadistic maniac for hire. He'll take any dirty job the big boys send him. His favorite pastime is maiming his prey. They don't call him 'Frankie the Crippler' for nothing. He'll beat you senseless and leave just enough of you to think about it while your bedpan's being changed. And I don't want him coming around here."

Sal paused. "Shit, that's what Pencil Nick was doing in Tampa. He wasn't watching me; he was watching you! Don't you see what's happening?"

"Listen, Sal, in a few days we'll be in London, and this will all fade away."

"You're playing with fire this time, Ange. Fuck it; it's your skin."

"It's OK, Sal."

Sal looked at Roger. "What do you think?"

"I'm just a broker; I know nothing." Sal laughed and looked at Ange. "I like this guy."

***

Sal turned down the long driveway to Camp, shading

his eyes from the bright midmorning sun. He instinctively pulled into the second bay of the four-car garage. He parked, stepped out, and instantly felt alone; his Mercedes sat next to the vacant spot where Jimmy had always parked his classic Lincoln. Sal had the Lincoln in storage. Maybe it was time to bring it home.

Sal entered the two-thousand-square-foot great room and looked around. The furniture Kate chose for Jimmy when Camp was built sat comfortably in its place. He smiled as he looked out the enormous picture window at Lake Champlain. He surveyed Jimmy's bar, still fully stocked with liquor, though the beer taps were pulled forward and covered with mugs. The room looked like an exclusive lodge ready to reopen.

Sal walked to the south wing and checked each of the four bedrooms and their baths. He remembered how they were often filled. He went room to room and shook his head. No wonder Kate didn't want to keep this place up.

He ventured to the north side, Jimmy's private area. The bedroom was clean and ready for him. He opened the door to the study. He gazed at the dozen or more jam-packed bookcases surrounding Jimmy's cleared desk, leather furniture, and rocking chair. He reached up and gently rubbed the treasured stick, cradled in its rack on the wall.

Stosh was right; it had been five years and well past time to move on. He sat in the rocker and relaxed a few minutes.

Sal stood and walked to the commercial-style kitchen. It had been cleaned and organized. In the refrigerator, he found cold cuts, unopened condiments, and Diet Coke. A loaf of his favorite bread was on the counter. He snapped open a can of soda and went to the wraparound porch.

As he sipped, he looked at the lake and down at the rock he and Jimmy so often sat on. They'd called it Turtle Rock because of its shape. At seven feet across it had often held several happy partiers. Those were good days.

The splash of something jumping into the water surprised him, and his head snapped to the right. Kate stood on her beach watching a black Labrador retriever swim vigorously toward something floating. She laughed and slapped her knees, encouraging him. Sal opened the door and waved.

"You're here!" she shouted. "Come down. I have someone for you to meet."

Sal put his soda down and stepped outside, pausing to survey the north woods. He made his way down the stairs leading to Turtle Rock and trod over the stone beach to Kate's dock. Kate gave him a long hug and a kiss on the cheek.

"Oh, Sallie, it's so good to see you. Welcome. I put a few things in the fridge for you."

"Thank you. I found them. Who's this?"

"Sallie, meet Boozer. Boozer, sit."

Boozer's tail wagged frantically as he stepped toward Sal and then obediently went to Kate's side and sat. Kate bent and rubbed his ears.

"Who's a good boy? Are you a good boy? Boozer's the best boy. Isn't Boozer the best boy?"

Sal grinned. He hadn't heard talk like this in years. Boozer rolled over on his back and panted as Sal reached down and rubbed his belly. Then he popped up, licked Sal's hand, and stood beside him.

"Wow," Kate declared. "Not everyone gets that reception. He likes *you*, Sallie."

Sal looked around the beach for a stick. Boozer stood rigid in expectation. Sal found and threw a piece of birch as far as he could into the lake. Boozer sat and with his head tilted, looked up at Sal.

"What's wrong, Boozer?" Sal asked.

Kate laughed. "It's the funniest thing, Sallie. He'll only chase *his* stick. He's had it since he was a puppy. He never gnaws it, just carries it around and plays with it. I guess he's a one-stick dog."

Sal looked at the stick lying between Boozer's paws. "Go ahead; I think he'll let you take it."

Boozer's tail swung in a frenzy as Sal threw Boozer's stick far into the lake. Boozer ran to the dock's end, leaped into the water, paddled out to his prize, snatched it in his mouth, and turned back. Sal and Kate laughed.

"I didn't know you liked dogs; when did you get him?"

"When Ray moved. He was worried about me being alone. So, I looked for a dog. I think Boozer chose me." Kate chuckled. "I went to a farm, just to look; he left his litter, sat on my foot, and gazed up at me. It was as if he'd said, 'I'm the one; just take me home.'"

Kate smiled. "He's been with me ever since. About a year and a half now."

Boozer returned, dropped his stick in front of Sal, shook, and splattered water in all directions. Sal jumped back.

Kate laughed and bent forward. Again, she slapped her knees and smiled at Boozer. "Who's a silly boy?"

Kate and Sal played with Boozer and chatted. Kate told him Ray would be coming later, and they decided to have dinner in town that night. Kate asked him to visit her place in the afternoon. Sal happily agreed. As he turned to leave, Boozer nudged his leg.

"Yup, he really likes you," Kate said.

Sal grinned. "OK, see you in a little while," he said and made his way back to Camp.

Sal sat in one of the rockers on the porch and looked at Lake Champlain. He took a sip of his warming soda. Kate looked good, he thought. She smiled a lot and had a bounce to her. He looked forward to seeing Ray, although he didn't know him well.

He fumbled for his cell and made reservations at a restaurant he liked. Then he realized he had nothing to do until the afternoon. He slowly rocked and relaxed. Champlain was calm. Sal knew how treacherous it could be—but not today. He let out a long exhale.

***

Kate answered the door dressed in a light blue blouse and a floor-length white skirt.

"Hi, Sallie," she said. "Come in. Your buddy's waiting for you."

Wagging his tail and sniffing, Boozer scooted in. Sal rubbed Boozer's ears and smiled.

Kate had decorated her cottage in Far-Eastern décor. Brightly colored tapestries hung from the walls, and several Hindu deities and Buddhas sat strategically throughout the rooms. Two soft floral couches faced each other by the picture window, with a large oak table between. Inviting chairs and a simple hardwood dining set finished the furnishings. Dozens of healthy plants grew from decorative pots on tables and floors, and hung from the ceiling. Persian rugs complimented the light maple parquet. Sal had always admired Kate's eye for detail.

"How about a drink, Sallie? Beer or rye or whatever?"

"A beer would be fine."

Kate opened a Molson Canadian and poured herself a white wine.

"Let's sit on the porch," she said.

The porch continued the Asian theme with the addition of wicker furniture. The view of the lake was nearly as magnificent as Camp's. Sal sat, and Boozer curled up on the floor beside him.

"You've done a fabulous job with this place, Kate. When did you become so interested in the East?"

"Oh, a long time ago. I started yoga when I was married. It helped—you remember how it was then. Now I'm an instructor. I'm fascinated with the East—particularly India."

Sal looked toward the lake. Here we go again, he thought.

"I worked some Asian concepts into my Ph.D. studies and dissertation. It's fascinating how well they address stress. But it's not something I'd shove down anyone's throat, Sallie. I know how you feel about things that might seem touchy-feely. And I don't buy all of it. I'm still grounded in many Western precepts—particularly logic and scientific inquiry. Still, there are times when Eastern explanations make more sense. Well, I'm rambling on."

"No, Kate, it must work for you. You seem happy."

"I am, Sallie. How does Camp feel to you? This is really your first visit. Last time was just for a few minutes, and no one was here."

"It feels good, a little strange without Jimmy, but good."

"Are you still feeling a lot of stress?"

"About what?"

"Work, Jimmy, anything?"

"It comes and goes."

"Let me show you something that might help—don't worry, as a psychologist, not a guru."

Sal chuckled and nodded, "Sure."

"Sit up straight and close your eyes. Now breathe slowly through your nose letting your belly fill with air."

Sal breathed in slightly longer than normal and exhaled.

"Don't stop. Keep inhaling until your belly is filled. Count slowly to ten if it helps."

Sal tried again, this time he felt his belly fill and expand.

"Now comfortably breathe out through your lips and empty your belly."

Sal followed Kate's instructions.

"OK, try again."

Sal complied, and after several deep breaths, he began to feel calm.

"I think this works," Sal said.

"It's not smoke and mirrors, Sallie. There's a lot of supporting research on the physiological benefits of breathing exercises."

"Breathing techniques were just being introduced when I was finishing med school. I missed most of it."

Sal took several more deep breaths and smiled. He sat back and sipped his beer. "Thanks, Kate, I think I'll be using that."

"You're welcome. I'll show you some other things another time if you like."

Sal smiled.

"Hey, speaking of showing you something, follow me."

Kate led Sal to the garage.

"What do you think?"

Sal grinned as he inspected her reconstructed VW microbus complete with a flowered and Paisley paint job.

"It's not a big Mercedes, but it still gets almost thirty miles per gallon—well, when there isn't much wind."

"This thing is great," Sal said. "Wow Kate, you're a Hippy again."

"Yup, but this time I can afford it."

They chuckled and returned to the porch.

"I'm glad you moved to this cottage," Sal said. "You've made it *yours,* and it's the right size for you."

"Yup, and now you're next door. How often will you be here?"

"Don't know exactly. I'm leaving for London in a day or

two. It's an annual thing now. I'm changing the business around when I get back. I'll be up here more then. And, Camp does feel good now."

Kate smiled and nodded.

"When I first walked in today, I felt strange," Sal continued. "But that's gone. It's funny how I'm the last one to let Jimmy go. You know it didn't bother me at first. Then I missed him. He was my conscience."

Sal paused. "OK, that's enough of that shit."

"It's OK, Sallie. Get it out."

"Yeah, I know. But that's not my way, Kate. Listen, thanks for getting the place ready, and the food, and everything."

Kate showed Sal the bedrooms and kitchen, and they walked around the property. He continued to praise her taste. Boozer walked beside them with his stick.

"I'm going to head back over and put a few things away," Sal said.

"I'll see you at about four," Kate said nodding. "Ray should be here by then, and we'll come over."

"Perfect."

Boozer followed Sal to the property line, dropped his stick.

"See you later, Boozer," Sal said.

Boozer woofed a goodbye.

***

After a quick knock, Sal heard the porch door screech open.

"Hello," Kate yelled.

"Come in!" Sal hollered back. "You know the place better than I do."

Kate entered the great room with a plate of fresh shrimp. Ray followed carrying a case of Molson Canadian.

"You guys look like you're ready to party," Sal said. "Ray, how the hell are you; it's been a long time."

Ray nodded. "Should I put this in the fridge, Sal?"

"Absolutely."

It had been years since the last gathering around Camp's bar, and it was long overdue. Sal opened a bottle of wine and poured a rocks glass of Crown Royal XO. Ray returned with a full beer mug.

"Say, Ray, would you get me one of those too?" Sal asked. Ray smiled and nodded.

Ray had always been a man of few words—something Sal always liked.

"How was the rest of your afternoon?" Kate asked.

"Quiet, nice and quiet," Sal said. "Ray, what have you been up to?"

"Not much. I'm in Peasleeville now. Found a little place. Used to be a lumber farm. Got a couple of ponds and some old barns. It's right on the Little Ausable River. Lots of trout."

"Say, what did you do with the boat, you know the old Lyman Jimmy had?"

"It's in storage, in one of the barns, in fact."

"That was a beautiful old classic."

"Still is. I'd put the hoist in and keep it here again, but nobody uses it." Kate and Sal nodded. "Well, maybe next year, if you guys want. It's hard to believe it's almost September already."

The talk flowed. Ray told Sal about some Adirondack excursions. Kate filled him in on old friends and changes in town. Sal gave a nutshell explanation of his business changes.

"Does this mean you'll be around more?" Ray asked.

"I think so," Sal said. "There are no worries here; they begin about a hundred miles south."

"Let me know when you'll be staying awhile; I'll fire up the beer taps," Ray said.

"Yeah," Sal said with a grin.

The three friends had chatted for nearly two hours when Sal suggested they get going. Their lakeside restaurant was on the other end of town, and they were running late. They piled into Sal's Mercedes and cruised down Route 9, watching the lake and gabbing. Sal parked in the back of the lot out of the way, and they strolled to the entrance. A young hostess welcomed and seated them at a table on the deck with a broad view of Lake Champlain and Vermont.

"So, Sal, Kate said you're off to London?" Ray asked.

"Yeah, Angelo Costello—my business associate—is flying up tomorrow. We'll leave the next day."

"Flying?" Kate asked.

"Yeah, I bought a plane last year—got a fantastic deal—part of a bankruptcy."

"You've got your own plane?" Ray said. "That's big time, Sal."

"It's been handy, a lot better than fucking around with the airlines—sorry Kate."

"For what?" Kate grinned. "I was wondering when you'd start sounding like yourself."

"Well, it's a jet. I can take eight, very comfortably, and I fitted it with seats that convert to beds. Let's see; it's got two heads—one with a shower—and all the entertainment gear. And you know it's nice to have your own bar. I'll be keeping the plane here now. That's why Ange is flying up; he'll take care of the details."

"It will be nice to go wherever you want, Sallie," Kate said.

Sal smiled. That would be nice, he thought.

The hostess seated three tipsy young men in cut-off shorts and sleeveless shirts. One wearing a crumpled fishing hat checked Kate out. "Not bad for her age," he said to his friends and snickered. Sal let it go.

"So, what will you do in London?" Kate asked.

"The museums, parks, pubs. I've been going there to clear my head for years. Made a few friends."

"Good for you Sal," Ray said.

Kate took a deep breath. "Listen, I know it might be a sore point, but have you seen Johnny?"

"No, no need. With Ma's situation, I've got nothing to say to him."

"Too bad; I know how you feel, but he is your brother."

"Half-brother and the half I got is complete shit. Kate, please, I appreciate your concern, but let there be no misunderstanding. I hate my brother."

"Sallie ... does anyone *hate* their brother?"

"I do."

Sal looked away and tapped his hand on his knee. He noticed the kid in the hat studying Kate again.

"Excuse me," Sal said as he stood and casually stepped over to the young men's table. "I've had enough of your eyes. Look at the lake if you need something to stare at."

The kid in the hat remained slumped in his chair and looked up with a smirk.

"OK dude, no reason to get hot."

Sal glared at the kid and turned back.

"But," The kid said, "you gotta admit, that's nice."

Sal whipped around, grabbed the kid's shirt and pulled his face eye to eye. The kid turned white. As his friends moved their chairs to stand, Sal faced them. They read his fury and sat still.

Sal turned back to the wiseass. "As much as I'd like to rearrange your fucked-up features, my friends wouldn't like it. Your presence has become an irritant. It's time for you to leave."

Sal took his hand away and stood over the table. As the three sheepishly stood, their waitress brought a tray of drinks. "I'll take care of those," Sal said.

The boys staggered toward the exit. Once at a safe distance, the pest in the hat turned back and held up a middle finger. Sal took a step toward him; the wiseass quickly swung around, knocked over a chair and scampered out.

"Sorry, Kate," Sal said as he stepped back to the table. "Now I not only sound like myself, I'm acting that way too."

Kate smiled and shook her head.

The group settled back in. The chat flowed with the drinks.

Dinner was excellent. The waitress thanked Sal for getting rid of the troublemakers. They'd come in before and caused problems, and they never tipped. The kids' drinks were not added to the bill.

"Say, Sal," Ray said. "You probably told Kate, but—if you don't mind my asking— I was wondering about your medical background. Why didn't you go into practice?"

Sal exhaled and looked down. He smiled and raised his head.

"Med school was for Ma. She always wanted a doctor in the family—maybe to compensate for Johnny's quitting high school—and all the rest of his bullshit. I graduated, was an intern; then in residency, I was placed under a real son of a bitch—a know-it-all surgeon.

"This guy had it for me—rode my ass from the first day—tried to find any mistake. I figured I could stick it out—shit I was almost finished—it was my second-to-last rotation.

"One night near the end of a sixteen-hour shift he started in. I sucked it up until he put his hand on my ass and told me how all my problems with him could go away. He really did want to fuck me—I mean literally!

"I lost it, put him against the wall, gave him a slap, and told him if he ever touched me again I'd break his hands. The next morning, I was called in and dismissed."

"Sallie, I never heard this," Kate said. "Why didn't you file a complaint?"

"I was given the letter by a secretary. No one on the staff would see me. You see, the asshole had been there forever; he was on the inside of the system. I saw real fast that I couldn't win, and tattling isn't my style.

"No, that was that. But I learned a lot. Never work from the outside. You've got to be on the inside to make it happen."

"You couldn't go somewhere else?"

"Didn't try. You see, Ray, I didn't want to be a doctor. That was all for Ma. Frankly, there's not enough money in it. So, law school made more sense—not to be a lawyer—to learn how to get information, to be on the inside. Another residency would have meant a full three years—the same bullshit all over again—and law school was three years. And I still had an MD—you know, for Ma."

Ray sat back and nodded. Kate sat with her elbows on the table and hands on her cheeks. Her eyes were wide as she shook her head.

"That wasn't an easy thing to talk about. Thank you for trusting us. And I believe that doctor will get his. His behavior will catch up with him."

"You mean the old 'what goes around comes around'?" Sal laughed. "I hope not, or I'm in deep shit."

The waitress politely interrupted and then brought after-dinner drinks.

"Sal, what made you leave the North Country?" Ray said.

"Well, it's quite simple really. When I was in college, Pop retired, and my folks decided to move. Ma always liked New York City, but Pop wasn't crazy for it. They settled on half way and went to the Saratoga area. Pop liked to play the ponies a little, and Ma could take the day train to the city when she wanted. They found a perfect spot on the Hudson and built their dream house. They saved for years for that place."

"Is that where you live?"

"Yeah—well I guess one of the places. I think I'll be here more than there now."

Sal took a sip and looked at Kate, "OK, Kate, now let me ask you something. Why'd you name your dog Boozer?"

Kate grinned. "When I brought him home, I had a welcoming party for him. One of my friends knocked over a glass of beer. Before I could get to it, the little bugger was lapping it up. He managed to get most of it before I picked him up. He burped and smiled at me. Then his tongue stuck out; he panted, and he wriggled to get down and have some more.

"My friend said I had a little boozer on my hands. And there you have it. You know, he reminded me of us, especially 'in the day.' We sure knew how to have fun."

Sal smiled. "Yeah, we did."

***

Sal sat by the picture window watching the lights on the Vermont shoreline. His mind drifted. Tomorrow Ange would come with the boxes. They'd spend most of the day unpacking things for Camp. The London bags were ready to go.

It was good to talk with friends. He'd overheard Kate tell Ray that she'd never seen "Sallie" so open. He looked at the bar and thought of the old days. He could see it filled with Camp compatriots, beer and booze flowing, and everyone safely settled in for the night. Now, all seemed serene. He moved to the den, sat, and gazed on his prized stick. Boozer had a stick too, and liked beer. Yeah, he had much in common with his new buddy.

Sal stood and surveyed the library, going shelf to shelf, head tilted while reading titles. Jimmy sure had eclectic taste, he thought. He touched the stick. It felt as smooth as he remembered. He took it down, aimed it, pretended to pull the trigger, and thought of his brother Johnny. How that slug fucked up his life. Soon Johnny would just be a memory. Not soon enough.

Sal put the stick back and moved to the bedroom. His pills were on the bureau where he'd left them. He unloaded his pockets and looked at the brooch. Maybe it's time to get rid of this fucking thing. Not tonight.

Sal popped his pills. He climbed into his sweat pants and flopped backward onto the bed. He soon fell asleep, and the dream came.

Sal was sitting in a rocker, looking at Champlain. The lake swelled and turned violent with rain, lightning, and twenty-foot swells. A tidal wave swept toward him. He was terrified but couldn't move. The wave consumed Camp, *and he was underwater. He gasped for breath.*

The water subsided, *and the picture window's glass* disappeared. He *stumbled out onto Turtle Rock. The lake had transformed in*to a broad, *flowing river. A Buddha sat on the opposite side and slowly waved to him. Sal raised his hand to wave* back, *but the Buddha had vanished.*

A two-by-four covered with leeches *washed on shore. Sal was compelled to pick it up. Once in his* hand, *the* leeches *were* gone, *and the two-by-four morphed into a fat black stick.*

Sal itched and ripped *open his shirt. He found the* leeches *attached to his chest and furiously clawed at them. As he tore at each, they flew into the river spurting blood and leaving open sores.*

Instantly, the leeches *were* gone, *and* he *was in a wet, stone tunnel crawling toward a light and grasping the black stick.* As he got closer, the tunnel narrowed, and he shrank. *He reached an opening* in *the floor and felt intense heat. He peered down at the familiar* cauldron *of* boiling lentil dhal and was overwhelmed by the smell of curry.

As always, the dhal *churned to gold. It bubbled and spat as* he *fought not to fall* in. The opening grew, his hands wildly slapped, and his fingers powerfully pressed to catch a ridge in the stone, the stone became wetter and hotter, his fingertips burned and slipped, and he was in free-fall.

Sal lurched up, drenched. His chest was covered with scratches. This one was new, but still the same theme.

He showered, sat in the great room, and gazed at Lake Champlain. A half-moon cast a bright narrow path across the water to the east side. He thought of Ma, how she'd loved the moonlight on the Hudson. She didn't have to worry about her memories any longer. He wondered what that was like.

He led his thoughts to the fort. He was camping with Jimmy. He smelled and touched the rough surface of the musty old canvas tarp. He breathed as Kate had taught him. Relief came—like the euphoria following intense pain. He was at ease.

In two days he'd be in London. He smiled; the dream never followed him across the Atlantic. He liked London. This would be Ange's first trip. Sal hoped Ange's roving eye didn't get them in much trouble. But, then a little trouble was OK too.

The moon disappeared, covered by a cloud—maybe a sign. Time to sleep.

CHAPTER III

Being Rich

"Drink Sal?" Ange asked as Sal settled into his large leather seat.

"Yeah, why not," Sal said.

The weather was good and the flight plan in order. In a few hours, they would be in London. The roar of the revved engines drowned Ange's voice as he said something and handed Sal a rye. Hearing nothing, Sal nodded anyway. A large-screen monitor mounted in front popped on and started a movie. This must be what Ange was trying to explain, Sal thought. He didn't care what film played; anything would be an improvement from the safety-script he'd been forced to watch for so many years.

The plane taxied to the runway, dwarfed by the commercial jets in front and behind. Once cleared, it smoothly ascended. As it banked, Sal took in a panoramic view of Lake Champlain. He could see the ferry from Vermont inching along half-way across its journey to Plattsburgh. They leveled off above the clouds.

"We're crossing in style today," Ange said.

Sal nodded. Time to relax and sip some Canadian whiskey.

Sal opened a book. After two pages, he realized he hadn't seen a word. He took a letter from his pocket and reread a part. He and Ange had been invited by his friend Colin Oakman to an event at his club the next evening. Sal had vacillated about it. Old money seldom mixed well with new. Sal's bankroll was larger than ninety percent of the British elite, but a European title was a different matter. Colin's father had been knighted, and the family still carried the prestige. Sal finally decided it might be fun, and Ange would enjoy the flirtatious ladies. And Sal liked Colin; he wasn't as stuffy as some of the other rich Brits Sal had met. Yeah, it could be an interesting evening.

"Which airport?" Sal asked Ange.

"London City." Sal nodded. Of the five London airports, London City was the smallest. It was perfect for private planes and processing was fast.

"Which hotel did you decide on?" Sal asked.

"Your favorite. They had the rooms you wanted."

"Good," Sal said. The hotel was like old England, located by Green Park, and it had an American style bar.

"Rooms?"

"You've got an executive suite, full layout with a large living room and all the extras you wanted. I'm in a junior. That'll be enough for me. I'm only here for a week or so anyway. You're booked through October—if you want to stay that long. I talked to the bar manager—no problem with the whiskey. And there'll be Canadian ale in your fridge. Let's see—no kids in the rooms over, under, or on your floor, a driver on an hour's notice, the laundry is all arranged—I think that's it."

"All right, sounds good, Ange." Sal closed his eyes. He remembered his first stay in London fifteen years ago. It started as business. He was interested in property near Notting Hill. He almost bought it, but he wasn't comfortable with the legal complications. Then he looked at a condo in a reconstructed church a block from Hyde Park. This was a place he could live in—the setup was phenomenal, and it was close to several pubs he'd come to know. His offer was too late. Probably for the best—no sense in owning when there are excellent hotels. He'd found himself going back at least once a year. He met a girl one time—but it was a one-trip deal for her. Too bad, he thought, he liked her—she knew how to keep her distance. Now, after sixteen or seventeen stays, he came for therapy. In London, he felt both at home and away. He could get his head together here. Almost no one knew him. Nobody expected anything from him. And the dreams didn't like the east-side of the Atlantic.

The plane shook and dropped in altitude. Sal's drink splattered on his pants. "Looks a little bumpy out there," the pilot announced. "We're going to have some turbulence for about a half hour."

"No shit," Sal said wiping his leg. Oh well, he thought; there's still plenty of whiskey.

***

The limousine halted directly in front of the hotel entrance. English country landscaping in full bloom accented the grounds. The large glass doors were impressively subtle, identifying the establishment as elite, not gaudy. The driver signaled a porter to unload the luggage and stood with arms folded at the opened trunk. Sal and Ange stepped into the lobby and stepped back a hundred years. Every detail of nineteenth century London had been worked into the decor. Crystal chandeliers glistened in the September sun. Victorian furniture and paintings filled the floors and walls. A formally dressed man greeted them, graciously presented envelopes with the room necessities, and offered tea. Sal and Ange declined, and Ange asked for directions to their rooms. Sal said an escort wouldn't be necessary, so the greeter drew a simple map on the back of each envelope before explaining that inside was a detailed diagram of the hotel with their rooms highlighted.

"Why didn't he tell us that in the first place?" Ange asked as they made their way to the elevator.

"Because you asked for directions, he was obligated to give them, not to tell you where to find them. Welcome to upscale England, Ange."

Ange smiled and nodded. "How 'bout we clean up and meet in the bar?" he asked.

"Yeah," Sal said as they stepped into the elevator.

Sal strolled into his living room. Two couches and three matching chairs were arranged around a fireplace with a carved mantel. An oak table with four chairs sat between two large corner windows near a small kitchen. In the fridge, Sal found a stock of Molson Ale and smiled. He popped the cap off one and took a swig. The bathroom had a walk-in shower, Jacuzzi, and another small refrigerator. Sal peeked in: more Molson. This is good, he thought. A king bed, three bureaus, and a large walk-in closet completed the bedroom. It looked like the suite would be the right place for a good long stay.

Sal walked back to the living room and sat in one of the leather chairs. He looked above the fireplace's mantel. For the first time, he noticed an oil painting. A giant, muscular man with a monkey's head and tail, wore a loincloth and red sash. He lifted a mountain high in the air with his left hand and held a club over his shoulder with his right.

"Hanuman, my friend. What the fuck are you doing here?" Sal said. "I haven't seen your picture since I was a kid."

He sipped his beer and smiled. His thoughts wandered to his boyhood listening to Ma read from the Ramayana, an ancient Hindu story. He gazed at Lord Hanuman, the monkey god, Ram's loyal companion in his adventures to free Rama's kidnapped wife, the fair Sita, from the evil King Ravana.

Ma had read from all the great epics to Sal–and Johnny. He learned of the exploits of Odysseus, Anness, and dozens of other mythical heroes. Ma seemed to like the *Ramayana* best, and Lord Hanuman was Sal's favorite.

Hanuman was powerful. A shapeshifter who could grow to massive size. He'd scoop up mountains and wipe out hundreds of the enemy with a single swipe of his odd shaped club the Indians call a gada.

Ma said she saw Hanuman's brute strength in Sal, but not his wisdom. She often said the gifts of the heart would come later, and some day Lord Hanuman himself would let Sal know when the ferocious side of Salvatore Esposito was no longer necessary.

Sal chuckled. Nothing from Hanuman yet, he thought.

Sal heard a knock and went to the door. One porter wheeled in his bags, and another carried a welcome basket with fruit, English biscuits, cheeses and—strategically arranged in the center—a bottle of Crown Royal XO. Sal nodded and tipped well. Before the door closed, he heard Ange call from the hall.

"Hey Sal, what do you think?" Ange said as he walked in.

"It's all good."

"You mind if I look around?"

"Yeah, sure, Ange. Want a beer?" Ange nodded.

After a quick inspection, Ange returned to the living room.

"It all looks good. Just want to make sure you're getting what you paid for."

"Yeah."

"Say, look at that Sal," Ange said and pointed. "That's Lord Hanuman. I haven't seen anything like that since India. He's a character from *the Ramayana*. The Indians love him."

"I know who it is, Ange; we go way back." Sal closed his eyes and shook his head.

"What? Is this a problem? I know how you feel about India. Do you want a different room?"

"No, Ange. It's kind of funny, in fact. An inside thing, you know? It's fine, just a surprise."

Sal smiled. No sense in trying to avoid it—fucking fatalistic

India was going to find him one way or another. Sal gulped down his ale. "One more Ange, then to the bar?"

"Good plan, I'll get them." As Ange left, Sal looked at the painting and grinned. This really is funny, he thought.

***

The hotel tavern was decorated from floor to ceiling with framed photographs. One wall displayed a random collection of American college football helmets, and hundreds of ball team caps hung from an overhead grid. The furniture varied from brown upholstery to light green leather; couches, chairs, and cocktail tables were planted throughout the room. A long oak bar faced the guests and offered any imaginable libation—all priced over ten pounds sterling per pour. Sal and Ange took leather barstools.

"Hello, gentlemen," the bartender said. "Mr. Esposito, I presume?" he added and looked at Sal.

"How did you know?" Sal asked.

"Your description precedes you, sir. May I pour you a glass of your reserve whiskey on the rocks?"

"You may, Sir."

"And for Mr. Costello, I've not been given any directions. What's your pleasure, sir?"

"A good Chardonnay." The bartender started to list his stock, and Ange interrupted. "I'll take your recommendation, sir." The bartender smiled and nodded.

"Quite the place," Ange said.

"Yeah. In an hour or so it will fill up; we're ahead of the crowd."

Ange took a sip and nodded. "Who comes here besides guests?"

"Oh, a few other Americans, Brits who feel like acting American, some single ladies looking for a rich American. Mostly wannabes who can't afford to stay here and envy those who do."

Ange smiled. "Single ladies?"

"Well, not all of them. Some will be stepping out. Over here it's all fair game, Ange, if that's what you're asking?"

Ange nodded. "Just don't want to cross a line, Sal."

"Tomorrow you might see some real action. A few of the married ladies at these clubs like to prowl. Not many, but a few."

"How do you know which ones they are?"

"Oh, they'll let you know. Usually, their husbands don't care—as long as it's low-key and they're not made to be embarrassed. Colin might be able to point one or two out; he gets hit on occasionally."

"Yeah, so what's the story with Colin?"

"Colin is an interesting combination. Some old money—some new. His grandfather was a Member of Parliament before the war. Made some money in the north—I think in coal or iron or some shit. His father was a businessman—left Colin some stores I think. He sold everything before I met him and went into real estate, the markets, and other ventures."

"Sounds familiar," Ange said.

"Oh, with two major differences. Colin will jump into

anything. He makes and loses money at a whim. I've watched him piss away fortunes on the most stupid fucking things, then turn around and make it all back on something even more boneheaded. Not my style—as you well know, Ange. While he's rich, he's never put together anything close to my assets. It's all in the method."

Ange nodded. "And the other difference?"

"Yeah, this is very important for you to keep in mind. Over here, no one knows what I do. My business is not their business—get it?" Ange nodded. "Over here I'm just some rich guy from the States who comes over to play. And that's the way it stays. Don't let anyone pull anything out of you—male or female. You see, Ange, this is a place I can come without the shit. It's like a retreat. It didn't start that way; I didn't plan it. But now I like the privacy. Over here I can enjoy being rich without thinking about all the fucking baggage that comes with it." Sal finished his drink and waved for another. "Let's keep it that way. You and I will discuss our business as necessary. You and I *only*, and *only* as necessary."

"You got it, Sal." Ange took a long sip and changed direction. "So, what's on for tonight?"

"We'll have a few more here, then wander around—hit a few pubs, get some fish and chips—you know, do some British shit. I've got plenty of places to show you." Sal clicked Ange's glass. "Welcome to London," he said.

An attractive blonde took a stool at the end of the bar. Ange caught her eye and smiled. She winked.

"Forget it, she's not coming with us," Sal said. "Say ... what did you do about Frankie Napoli's wife?"

"She's gone."

"Good."

"Yeah, she's back with Frankie."

Sal's eyes widened. "What?" He stared at Ange.

"Yeah, they decided to give it another shot. Good break for me. Got her out of my hair."

"Good for you? Are you out of your fucking head? Now you're the guy who was doing her when they were apart. Do you know what that means to a son-of-a-bitch like Frankie? To him, it's the same as fucking her in his own bed."

Ange looked puzzled. "But why, Sal? He'd dumped her; they were done."

"Jesus Christ, for a guy with your experience you can be really fucking stupid. Take my word: he'll care. You'd better stay clear of him when you get back."

"Shit, Sal, I don't even know what he looks like."

"Well, he'll know you—Pencil Nick will have taken care of that. Stay low, and stay away from her for good."

Ange looked at his drink and nodded. Sal shook his head and chuckled. The bartender turned on the television to a cricket match. Sal explained the game and cheered occasionally. Ange had business to talk about but decided to wait until morning. He was rethinking the thing with Frankie Napoli's wife and hoped Sal was exaggerating. Soon he let it go and joined Sal's enthusiasm for the game.

The concierge asked if he should call for their driver. Sal shook his head. "We'll walk tonight. Say, Ange, you did bring a tux?"

"Shit, Sal, I don't own a tux. I brought a black suit—"

"Nope, that won't work." Sal called the concierge over. "Mr. Costello will need a tuxedo by midday tomorrow."

The concierge nodded. "I'll have a tailor at your room at eleven tomorrow morning, Mr. Costello?" he asked.

Ange nodded and smiled. "Thanks, Sal—Jesus, a tailor by appointment on Sunday morning." Sal grinned.

As they walked through the doors to the street, Ange looked at his watch. "It's almost seven; we don't have much light left."

"There'll be plenty, Ange; we're farther north here."

They strolled down St. James Street to Piccadilly. "I always wondered where that name came from," Ange said.

"In London, they argue over such things," Sal said. "But I can give you my favorite explanation."

"Explain on."

"Well, in the nineteenth century the slang for a prostitute was a dilly. They would stand on this street as carriages passed waiting until they were picked by a gentleman." Sal chuckled. "So, it became Pick a dilly. It's probably bullshit, but the tour guides love the story."

"No shit? And where's the circus?"

"We're coming to it. Over here circus just means a traffic circle. And the Tower of London isn't a tower; it's a castle."

Sal pointed to a pub. "Let's try this place." Ange stopped and looked at the intricate sign swinging over the front door. Inside was a long bar with a dozen large colorful taps and a mixed selection of whiskeys. A collection of odd-lot wooden tables, chairs, and short stools was arranged to maximize seating. Kids ran around, stopping only to sneak a sip from an unwatched beer. The bartender took orders and handed each customer a wooden spoon with a hand-written number. A young woman with dyed orange hair darted about spotting numbers and delivering overfilled plates of fried fish, large cut fried potatoes, and mushy green peas. Sal and Ange stood in a short line, ordered, and received their spoon and pints. They took a table near a small unlit gas fireplace.

"This is just like some of those BBC shows," Ange said.

"Yeah. Years ago, they were even better. Now they're almost all owned by chains. Look at the menu, that *special* burger is all over town. But the pubs are still kept authentic looking—mostly for the tourists."

"Do they ever get rowdy? I've seen some scenes in movies."

"If there's a soccer match on TV, some guys might get it going, but there's not much action around here. I'll show you some of that in a few days ... maybe. If I feel like a good fight." Sal smiled and laughed. Ange knew he wasn't joking.

The girl brought their fish, winked at Ange, and left for the kitchen.

"Just what the fuck is it with you?" Sal asked.

"Don't know. It started in high school. One girl told me I was kind of cute and no threat—her words, whatever that meant. It's not all of them, you know. It just happens enough that it seems like a lot."

"You got that right."

"Anything on for tomorrow, before the club?"

"We'll talk in the morning—I know you've got business you're anxious about—then you get fitted, and I'm going out for a walk in the park. Then, we'll just take it easy until we leave for the club. Colin will meet us there. I think you'll get a kick out of him." Sal pointed at Ange's fish. "Hey, try the malt vinegar on that—on the chips too. It's good."

***

Sal slept well. After coffee with Hanuman in his room, he joined Ange for a full English breakfast. Ange filled part of a small plate with fruit and asked for tea. Sal piled on the Windsor bacon, added three eggs sunny side, fried toast, and more strong black coffee.

"OK, fill me in," Sal said.

"Roger designed a portfolio. It's mostly stocks, with a few commodities. The stocks look good to me, a combination of blue-chips and new options with solid potential. The commodities will come and go, but the stocks were picked for long-term holding. I told him no day-trading and—from what I can see—he listened. I think it looks good, Sal. And I sent a cash reserve off-shore, like you said. There's not a lot there, just a few million for a safety net. Now look, the market is strange right now. But I still think this it's the right move long term.

"I've got to tell you, Sal, I'm not sure exactly what you want. I've never seen you try to be conservative. I mean, you're like a demon when it comes to making money. Anyway—the western property is cleaned out, the accounts in Bradenton are there for Stosh, Roger seems to have the other assets in good order, and my gut's churning from it all."

"What's the matter, Ange?"

"Nothing really. It's just, this is a lot of money, and it's what

I would do if it were mine—well maybe not the Florida shit, but that's up to you. But, Sal, the money *isn't* mine."

Sal smiled, "I'd be nervous if you weren't nervous, Ange."

Ange handed Sal a leather portfolio case. "It's all here, organized the way you asked."

"Good," Sal said. "I'll check it before you go back. Now relax. You've done what you think is best. I'm not sure about the market, but if we've got a mix with real estate, I think we're covered. Now enjoy your breakfast."

Ange finished his fruit, got up and left for his appointment with the tailor. Sal sat, sipped and thought. He hoped he hadn't asked too much of Stosh—if Ange was this wound up, he couldn't imagine the stress the Florida deal was laying on the gentle giant. But he had a premonition. It was all going to be OK. His affairs were more unsettled than any other time in his life, but he wasn't concerned. He'd always been obsessed with his deals. But London was doing the trick. Ange had also missed one point—the money-making demon could always return from his sabbatical. Sal finished his coffee and headed for the room to drop off his papers and grab his jacket—late Sunday morning and time to hit the park. He bid adieu to Hanuman and took the elevator to the lobby.

"Do you need anything, Mr. Esposito?" the concierge asked as Sal headed for the door.

"I'm fine. Oh, one thing, make sure Mr. Costello's tux is on the company bill. Don't let him try to pay for it."

"Yes sir," the concierge said with a nod.

Sal walked to the hotel courtyard. White stucco buildings with dark wood accents and balconies surrounded a smooth gray-stoned patio with blooming planters and umbrellaed tables. A few guests peeked at him through their windows as he walked through to the street.

Green Park was quiet, just a few people wandering, feeding birds, and killing time. Sal crossed at the Wellington Arch to Hyde Park Corner and strolled through the gate. A jogger smacked Sal's arm as he huffed by. "Sorry," he said. Sal smiled. Not long ago that could have been enough for a showdown—still could be if Sal were in the right mood.

A deaf couple rushed toward him quarreling in sign language. The young man buzzed around the girl forcing his hands in her face as he passionately tried to communicate. She stopped and turned away. He repositioned, and she turned again. Again, he moved, and she waved him off. She folded her arms and stared upward. Then she lowered her head, covered her eyes, and cried. He tried to hold her, but she stamped her feet, and he stepped back. She composed herself and with a stern face signed a message and flashed a vee at his face with knuckle side of her middle and first finger. Sal smiled. The British way of flipping off always amused him, the only sign he'd understood. The young man's head tilted, his eyes widened, he opened his arms, and she hugged him. They kissed and walked hand-in-hand carelessly moving into the bicycle lane. A cyclist nearly hit them and yelled profanities. They silently laughed as they stepped back onto the walkway. Sal envied them. Their silence was their bond; they didn't miss what they didn't hear.

Two sauntering Arab men with hands clasped behind their back wore casual suits and talked gravely. Several steps behind them, barely able to see through the eyelets in their black burqas, their wives waddled along struggling to keep their proper distance. The men stopped to stress a point. One wife froze in place, the other stepped too far and cautiously snuck backward into position. The men resumed their walk. Their wives followed. The men abruptly stopped again. Again, the wives halted, this time in unison. The men laughed to each other, turned, and casually moved on. Now synchronized, the women followed suit. This wasn't the American way, Sal thought. He remembered the respect Ma and Pop had for each other. But it was clear *she* wore the pants. Pop didn't mind.

He thought of his first wife. No burqa for her, she tried to orchestrate everything and Sal *did* mind. She was completely self-centered—a spoiled daddy's little girl. She wanted children and was constantly cackling at him that he wasn't accommodating her life-schedule. She hated when the dreams awakened him. Told him to just get over them. Sal realized the marriage would eventually tank and was petrified of the thought of a split family. But he couldn't give up the sex; it was the only good thing in the relationship. So, on a business trip, he arranged a vasectomy. She never knew, and when she left, she threw his impotence in his face, making fun of his manhood. Sal got a kick out of that.

Sal sat at a snake-shaped pond named The Serpentine. Birds swam, and dogs chased balls. Sal wondered how his buddy Boozer was doing. He thought of Camp and Lake Champlain. He cracked a smile. In Champlain, there was a serpent in the water; here they put water in the serpent. He thought of Kate.

He'd be back in late October, still in time for the fresh apples. She made a hell of a pie.

A pair of Scottish Terriers with rhinestone collars and Frasier plaid sweaters approached Sal's feet, cautiously sniffing, tails wagging. Sal reached to pet them, and they backed away. One slowly crept to the side of the bench. Never removing her eyes from Sal, she slowly reclaimed a designer dog toy, and they scampered off to their master. Boozer didn't need upscale toys, Sal thought. He had a stick. Sal grinned.

Sal hiked over to Speaker's Corner and thought of its history. Once the site of executions, it became the first location where free speech was allowed in England, although only on Sundays. The tradition continued for hundreds of years. At first, those with a political or religious ax to grind stood on soapboxes. Now they used short step-ladders, much more practical for the twenty-first century and easier to fold and carry for a quick getaway. A crowd stood around a thin man ranting about the evils of women.

"All you need to do is look at the Bible. All sin is the making of womankind. Eve, Delilah, Bathsheba, it goes on and on."

"You're full of it." a woman in a short summer dress retorted. "You're a bigot and a sexist pig."

"Do you all see my point? This woman stands here in front of you as the personification of temptation. She shows her body to lure men into wicked acts. She is proof of the tainted nature of the female."

"Your problem is you couldn't get a woman for a million pounds. You stink, and you lie." The woman turned to the crowd. "This man stands in front of you all as the *personification of* a bloody wanker."

The gathering roared with laughter.

"The proof is again provided by this harlot," the man smirked. "Such language, such dress; she is clearly filled with sin."

The woman smiled back. "Fuck off, asshole," she said and walked on.

Sal had seen this guy before. He never seemed serious, more like a street performer, and Sal wondered if the woman was a plant, just to get things going.

On the next ladder, a woman berated George Bush "the war mongering capitalist." She touted the assets of "Obama, the savior." Sal moved on. He had no use for either, and—even at their best—he found the English bad at analyzing American politics.

At the end of the line stood an East Indian man in a long white kurta shirt. A bright red tilak glistened from the center of his forehead. His hands pressed together in prayer as he bowed to the crowd and repeated, "Namaste, namaste …." Soothingly, he began speaking about love. Most of the crowd respectfully listened and smiled. A few snickered. Sal stopped. This was different from the others' ranting. But just as much bullshit. Into Sal's mind flashed a vision of Hanuman standing with his club poised to crush the Indian man's skull. The speaker's words became distorted. Sal shook his head and looked down. The image lingered for several seconds before fading away. Sal's palms were clammy, and his forehead beaded with sweat. He wiped his brow with his shirtsleeve and looked up, away from the crowd. The speaker's voice was clear again, but Sal had heard enough. He worked his way through the growing audience and started his long trek back.

***

The sight of Salvatore Esposito in a tuxedo turned every head in the bustling hotel tavern. Ange had already arrived and grabbed two stools. The bartender automatically poured a double Crown Royal XO.

"You look sharp, Ange," Sal said.

"Thanks, Sal. The tailor had this done by three o'clock."

"They'll all be formal tonight, but we'll stand out. That will be good. It puts the pompous ones on edge." Sal took a long sip and looked around. "Something must be happening here. This is a big crowd." Sal asked the bartender what was up.

"A group of American lawyers is having a gathering. Only one is staying in the hotel, but he booked a conference room this afternoon. They've all spilled into here."

Sal smiled. Thirty lawyers and only one could afford the hotel. He liked being rich in London.

The limo pulled in exactly at seven. The club was near the hotel on a street off Trafalgar Square. The driver sped down Pall Mall and turned right at Cockspur. Ange's eyes grew as he surveyed Nelson's column.

"You know, if that guy hadn't won the battle of Trafalgar, they'd all be speaking French here," Ange said.

"What's wrong with French?" Sal asked.

"Well, you know what I mean. Sometimes everything swings on one event."

"That's our business, Ange. One fucking turn and everything's different. That's the rush of it."

The driver pulled up in front of a traditional English building. A small bronze placard near the door identified the club.

"Jesus, you wouldn't want to be looking for this place in the dark," Ange said.

A tall, thin man in a tuxedo with a shaved head and handlebar mustache stood on the stairs.

"He's just like the doormen in the movies," Ange said.

Sal laughed. "That's Colin."

Sal and Ange stepped out of the limo looking no less striking. Sal stood on the street and stretched.

"How the bloody hell are you, Salvatore," Colin yelled.

"Fantastic, Colin. And you?"

Sal introduced Ange, and the three paraded into one of Britain's finest establishments. A horde of gentlemen strategically maneuvered throughout the lavish hall patting shoulders and shaking hands. The ladies chatted and made pleasant gestures to one another. Colin led Sal and Ange to the bar.

"Do you have Canadian whiskey?" Sal asked.

The bartender looked around dumbfounded. "I'm sorry, sir. I don't see any," he said.

"All right, I would like a Czech beer and a whiskey glass with ice."

"Certainly, Sir. What whiskey would you like?"

"No whiskey, just a glass with ice."

The bartender's eyebrows rose as he prepared Sal's order. "Here you are, sir," he said.

Sal nodded, moved into the hall, found an inconspicuous spot, took a flask from his breast pocket, and carefully filled the glass with Crown Royal XR.

"There you are," Colin said. "Did you get what you needed?"

"Yup, I'm good," Sal said.

"I'd like you to meet Stephen. His family is highly respected. They built a large business in Birmingham—you know steel and the like—and now he resides here in London."

"Nice to meet you, Stephen," Sal said.

"Yes," Stephen replied. "And what do you do Mr. Esposito?"

"Oh, a little real estate. Nothing on your scale."

"Yes … well … real estate—houses and the like I suspect."

"Yes, that's real estate."

"Yes … well … how's your drink, Old Chap? I hope the barkeep didn't pour you an inferior scotch." Stephen took Sal's whiskey from his hand and sniffed. "Yes … this won't do. Let me get you something drinkable. I'll be back in a second."

Sal pursed his lips, shook his head and looked at Colin. "Steel?" he said.

"Used to. The company turned cockup some years back. He's living from a trust now. Not what he was used to. He's something of a skive—you know, a bloke not fond of work."

Sal nodded and smiled. "I get it."

Stephen returned with a new drink. "Here, Old Chap. This will be much better than the swill you were given. Would you excuse me? I must speak to that fellow." Stephen pointed to the corner. "Business, you know. It never ends."

Sal bowed and smiled.

"Let's move over this way," Colin suggested.

"Just a second," Sal put two fingers over his ice drained the scotch in a planter, and reloaded his Crown Royal. Colin grinned.

"It looks like we lost Ange," Sal said.

"He's over there," Colin replied and glanced toward two ladies smiling with glistening teeth and nodding. Ange was telling stories and making charade-like gestures.

Sal watched tuxedos of all shapes and sizes wandered about trumpeting their importance and wealth and egos. With meticulously applied makeup, the ladies wore colorful gowns and ornate jewelry. An attractive woman stood next to an elderly man leaning on a cane. Guests waited their turn to be greeted and awarded a word.

"Who's that?" Sal asked.

"Oh, that's Lord Geoffrey. Nice enough. He's from old title and money. You'd probably call him the real deal. The younger lady with him is his wife. He likes having a fit bird on his arm—though he's far beyond sexual activities and she's quite open about that." Colin snickered. "Yes, she's been thought to step out from time to time—always with discretion. He doesn't seem to mind as long as it's not in front of him or anyone of his select crowd."

"What's her name?"

"Estelle. Most just call her Este, but here she's Estelle."

Sal looked back and found Lord Geoffrey looking him over. The lord smiled and returned his attention to the crowd. A man slapped Colin's shoulder.

"And who's this fellow?" the man asked Colin.

"John, this is Salvatore Esposito from the United States."

"Ah, over from the colonies, eh?" The man extended his hand. "John Smith, sir," he said. "Now let's see … Esposito, that sounds a bit Italian, would that be right?"

"Yes, sir, you're very perceptive," Sal said and smiled.

"Good now, what is that you're drinking?"

Shit, not again, Sal thought. "The beer is German, but I prefer Czech."

"Well let me take care of that immediately, sir. And the whiskey?"

"It's an excellent scotch that one of your colleagues just suggested."

"Oh … well … not to second guess a colleague." John left for the bar.

"That was bloody slick, Sal," Colin said. "You're getting good at this."

The introductions and short, meaningless conversations continued for over an hour. Sal kept his eye on Ange as he wandered about and charmed the ladies at will. At eight thirty, Colin pointed to the dining room and suggested they sit. Sal turned to collect Ange and grinned. Ange stood face to face with Este, Lord Geoffrey's wife. Ange took her gloved hand and kissed it. Lord Geoffrey looked away unconcerned. The old man clearly doesn't care—so shit, why not go for nobility, Sal thought.

"Take a gander at that," Colin said gesturing toward Ange.

"Yeah, I see," Sal replied.

"He's a cheeky little chap, isn't he?"

"Yeah, the cheekiest in the joint. Let's sit."

A server intercepted them. "Sirs, if you will, we've been asked to change your places. One of the guests has requested that you join his party." Colin nodded, and the server led them to a round table for eight in the middle of the room. It had been reset for five. Sal's eyes were wide; all other seating was crowded. He felt a tap on his shoulder.

"Thank you for joining us," he heard. Lord Geoffrey was standing behind him. "Shall we sit?"

Sal was placed to Lord Geoffrey's right, Estelle at his left, and Ange beside her. Colin looked perplexed as he settled in next to Sal. The members of the exclusive party made their introductions and ordered fresh drinks.

After small talk, Lord Geoffrey signaled for Sal to come close. "Mr. Esposito, may I speak frankly?" he asked quietly.

Sal nodded. "Of course, sir."

"I'm a man of first impressions. When we are young, we are told not to judge a book by its cover. But that is bloody nonsense. I learned that in the military in India. Everything I need to know is right in front of me; explanations serve only to contaminate truth. Looking at you, I see a hard man whom, instinctively, I trust. Your scars look to be well earned, and I'm certain there are more. You project a complicated man of talent and have—how would you Americans say it?—a 'no bullshit' way about you. I presume that Mr. Costello is your assistant." Sal nodded. "Good. I would ask that you ensure that my wife is safe, and he is discreet in his time with her. This kind of acknowledgment may seem forward—perhaps even shocking. But you see, Estelle was twenty-nine when we married ten years ago. I was seventy-eight and well beyond participating in carnal activities. She has been a brilliant companion. I wish for her not to unnaturally suppress her libido. I can assure you the assignations will not continue for long. I hope that is understood by your colleague."

Sal sat stunned. He'd seen Ange hook up many times, but Sal had never been assigned as a chaperone.

"Yes, that would be understood by Mr. Costello," Sal said. "He's not new to these things."

"Yes. I thought as much. Thank you for your understanding. Few in this room possess your astuteness."

The talk turned to business and politics. The guests commented on the perfection of the beef Wellington. Drinks flowed, and Colin had his first, ever, discussion with Lord Geoffrey. It led to a lunch appointment for the next week. Sal watched as Este charmed Ange. Lord Geoffrey insisted on telling stories from his days in India. Sal respectfully listened—what the hell, if Hanuman couldn't bring the dreams, nothing could. Lord Geoffrey repeatedly said, "You must go to India, Salvatore." Each time Sal politely nodded and held his tongue. As midnight approached, the goodbyes began.

"Well, Salvatore, this has been most delightful," Lord Geoffrey said. "I hope our stuffy group hasn't bored you."

"No, sir, quite the opposite. Thank you for honoring us at your table."

"Don't lay such tosh on me; you were the only people here I cared to be around tonight. And, Salvatore, please remember what we spoke of." Sal smiled and nodded.

***

Sal sat alone in the dining room. A waiter snatched Sal's empty breakfast plate. As he sipped coffee, someone said, "Over there." Ange and Este walked through the vacant room and sat next to him. Ange was in jeans and a cardigan. Este wore her gown from the night before.

"The buffet is closed, but you can still order from the kitchen," Sal said.

"We ate in the room," Ange said. "We just wanted to say hello before I take Este home."

"Yeah, thank you, hello. Listen ..." Sal searched for words.

"Don't worry Salvatore," Este said. She whispered in his ear, "I know the rules."

Sal smiled. "What's up for today?"

"Well, how 'bout we give Este some time to change," Ange said, "then she can show us some of London?"

Sal nodded. "Let's meet at, say, one o'clock."

"Perfect," Este said.

Ange and Este stood, stretched and left. Sal shook his.

At one on the dot, the three climbed into their limousine.

"Where to?" Este asked. With dark skies and drizzle, the day wasn't for walking.

"Let's hit the British Museum," Sal said.

"Good choice. Have you been there?" Este asked.

"Many times, but it will be a first for Ange, and I heard about a good Persian exhibit."

"Yes, it's quite brilliant. The British Museum it is."

They walked up the steep stairs and shook their umbrellas before entering through the thick glass doors. Este led the way to the monumental interior court, once an outside garden, now with a modern glass roof and marble floors. A library occupied the center area. Exhibit halls surrounded them on all sides.

Este pointed to stairs leading to a third-floor restaurant and reception center. "This is where I met my husband," Este said. "He was standing there waiting. I offered to help him to the elevator. He laughed and pointed to his younger friend who was dragging behind. Once the chap arrived, the Lord bounded up ahead of us. He was already sipping his first drink at the top as we were catching our breath. I had no idea who he was until a rather famous actor approached him for an introduction. As it turned out, we had much in common, and three years later we wed."

Ange listened politely and nodded. In all his escapades, he'd never heard such praise for a husband from an adulterous wife.

"The Persian exhibit should be this way," Este said.

"When we've seen it, why don't you take Ange around and I'll meet you over there," Sal said pointing to the far corner café.

Este shepherded the men through the east hall past the Rosetta Stone to the special exhibit area. The impressive Persian exhibit kept them for nearly ninety minutes. Este and Ange left for a tour, and Sal visited some of his favorite rooms. He spent most of his time in the ancient Greek areas with the Elgin marbles and other Athenian artifacts. By the time he entered the Egyptian halls, the crowd had grown. School kids in uniforms and tunics lay on the floor mapping their observations. Others ran around playing tag and bantering while their teachers affably tried to keep order. A group of touring Asians butted others to get preferred camera angles. A Russian tour stood firmly with stern faces listening to a guide. Sal made his way past Ramses the Second through the entrance back to the center court. At the café, he ordered a beer and sat at a long metal table. He took a sip and exhaled; three hours of any museum was enough.

"There he is," Este said as she and Ange joined Sal, each with a glass of wine. They sipped and discussed their impressions before Este said, "There is one more hall I'd like you to see." Tired, Sal and Ange looked at each other and exhaled.

"OK, let's go," Sal said.

Sal had second thoughts as he saw the sign reading, *The Joseph H. Hotung Gallery—ASIA*. He entered the hall greeted by a six-foot Gautama Buddha. Este turned left toward the India exhibit. Sal had never visited this room but recognized many of the artifacts. He felt queasy and sat on a bench.

"Are you OK?" Este asked.

"No problem, just an old injury, pops up from time to time. I'll be fine." Sal took a sip from his water bottle and stood. "All right, let's do it."

Este strolled to a five-foot bronze statue of *Shiva Nataraja* dancing in a ring of flames. She described his features and explained the meaning of each gesture. Sal stared at the Dwarf of Ignorance squashed under Shiva's foot. Yeah, little buddy, I wish he'd get off my fucking back too, he thought.

Este pointed out figures of Shiva's consorts, Parvati the good wife, and Kali the bitch. She told the story how Shiva had returned home one night to find a boy blocking the way. Parvati was bathing and had told the boy not to let anyone into her chamber. In a rage, Shiva cut off the child's head. Parvati told him he had just killed the son she had made from the earth for them, and insisted Shiva bring the boy back to life. Shiva could not find the severed head and knew he must replace it with the head of the next living thing he saw, which was an elephant. He sliced off the elephant's head and placed it on the boy's shoulder. His son returned to life as Lord Ganesha, the overcomer of obstacles.

"I've been to India many times," Este said. "I'm fascinated by the culture. My husband took me before we were married. I've studied it ever since."

"I've been there also," Ange said.

"We've more in common than I realized," Este said giving him a quick peck.

"And you, Salvatore, have you been to India?"

"No, it's not on my list."

"That's a pity. You would find much more there than you imagine. You must go."

Sal smiled.

Este pointed out more artifacts. Sal looked for Hanuman but didn't see him—and didn't ask. Maybe the big ape only hangs around the hotel, he thought.

"I suspect we are overloading a bit by now," Este said. They made their way back to the museum entrance. Ange called for the limo, and Este announced she would treat the men to afternoon tea.

"We're not dressed for the Ritz, but we can go to one of the other hotels," Este said. She directed the driver to a place on Cromwell, and the three were seated next to an ornate fireplace in a room decorated with traditional English paintings. The waiter wore formal black and white and offered wine as well as tea. In all of Sal's stays in London, he'd never attended a tea. He never wanted to. He didn't like tea, and the idea of picking at tiny sandwiches, scones, and cakes while sipping Earl Grey made him feel stupid. But Ange's eyes were wide in expectation, and Este reveled in the opportunity to explain this British tradition. Sal thought he could suck it up this one time. The server brought a three-tiered tray with the food arranged in the "proper" order of consumption. He poured tea.

"Now, we'll start with the treats on the top tray and then nibble our way downward. Would you like some cream, Salvatore?"

Sal shook his head. "No thanks, I'll just take it straight."

"And for you Angelo?"

"Yes, please." Ange was into it.

The chit chat included recipes for each tidbit on every tray and continued for a half-hour. Sal spent most of the time looking out the window at the traffic.

"Well, if you will excuse me I'll be right back," Este said. The men stood politely and reseated.

"All right, Ange, drink this," Sal said and handed Ange his half-finished cup.

"No thanks, Sal. I don't like it straight, and there's plenty in the pot."

"I said drink this fucking piss, now!"

Ange got the message and gulped down Sal's tea. Sal pulled out his flask and half-filled the cup. The waiter watched and smiled.

"There, now maybe I'll make it through this shit. Listen, from here on you and Este plan on doing your own thing. I don't do the third wheel well, and I think you'll enjoy yourselves more alone."

Ange nodded. "Yeah, I figured you'd take yourself out as soon as you could ... and thanks, Sal."

At the hotel, Sal said goodbye to Este and Ange, making an excuse for missing dinner. He called Colin and joined him at a pub. Ange and Este spent the week together. Sal became worried that Ange was getting too involved and might get smacked. But Ange said he had it all under control. He'd be leaving soon anyway.

CHAPTER IV

Being Bad

"Have you bothered telling Este you're going back in two days?" Sal asked.

"Not yet. I was going to tonight, but she canceled. Something she's got to do with her husband."

"Imagine that," Sal said.

"We're meeting up sometime tomorrow. I'll tell her then."

"Yeah, good idea. OK, you're off tonight—Colin's busy too—you're coming with me."

"Where?"

"I promised I'd show you a little of London's underbelly. Tonight's the night."

The limo driver's eyes widened when Sal directed him to a pub in White Chapel. He told Sal he could drop off and pick up, but the company wouldn't allow him to wait in that part of the city. Sal shrugged. "OK, no big deal."

Sal and Ange dressed down the best they could but would still stand out. Ange watched out the window as they drove through the slum. Barred windows looked out at heaved concrete sidewalks with chunks missing. Unkempt men sat on doorsteps holding paper bag-covered bottles, arms resting on their knees. Others stood plotting near street lights. Spray-painted protests splattered street signs and walls. Piles of loose garbage sat at the curb. Litter was scattered everywhere.

"I didn't know London had this kind of shit," Ange said.

"Everyplace has this kind of shit, the real shit," Sal said. "This is where Jack the Ripper did his best work. We could get a guide some other time if you like."

"I'll pass. I'm a lover, not a—"

"Yeah, yeah I know."

The driver stopped at a corner pub with a faded sign and cracked front windows patched with duct tape. As soon as they stepped in, the rough looking crowd, most in sleeveless t-shirts, put Sal and Ange under surveillance. The room stank of stale beer and sweat. It was dim, lit mostly by the street and lamps over a threadbare pool table and horsehair dart board. Peeling green wallpaper spotted with fist-sized holes covered the walls. The old oak bar was gouged from knives and broken bottles. A worn brass foot rail rested in places on bricks. Six taps offered Guinness and five other Irish brews. The booze selection also offered nothing British. An Irish flag hung from the water-stained ceiling. Scattered about stood a few high-top tables. There were no stools or chairs.

"Ya want ta drink *here*?" the bartender asked.

"Yeah, two of those," Sal said, pointing to a tap head.

The bartender shook his head and poured the beers. "Three quid," he said and slapped the overflowing pints down.

"Are you sure this is a good idea?" Ange asked.

"We'll find out."

"Well, at least it's cheap here," Ange said.

A freckled ruffian with flaming red hair stood near with elbows on the bar and face to his beer. He eyeballed the new arrivals, snickered, smirked, and returned to his beer. Other roughnecks strolled by, staring and chuckling to one another. Ange saw one gawking at him. His hand began to quiver.

"Let's go," Ange pleaded. "I think this place isn't for us, Sal."

"Sal? Did this little shitlet call ya Sal?" the redhead at the bar said in a strong Irish brogue. "That's no name for a big boy like ya. Were ya supposed ta be a girl?"

Shit, Sal thought. It's starting already, and I haven't finished one beer. He ignored the Irishman and turned to Ange.

"Did yer mother put ya in a pretty dress? I bet she called ya Sally. Did she call ya Sally? Sally come on in from the rain, ya might get yer new tunic a mess. Sallie, the shitter needs cleanin'. Then yer brother wants ta fuck ya."

Eyes widened, Ange knew what was coming. His hand continued shaking, and he took a deep breath. Sal's face was blank. He took a sip from his beer, put it on the bar, casually massaged his right fist, and turned to the Irishman. "You are talking to me?"

"Ya mean to Sallie? How'd yer brother's cock feel up yer arse, Sally?"

Sal heard brother; brother meant Johnny; the right nerve was squeezed. He strode over until his face was an inch from the Irishman's. The Irishman belched in Sal's face and laughed. Sal pulled back in disgust. The Irishman smirked and slapped

Sal's cheek. Sal grinned and slammed his fist into the Irishman's jaw, sending him to the floor. Three men gathered to join in, but the bartender shook his head, and they stood back.

"Is that all ya got, Sally?" the Irishman said from the floor. "Yeah, ya liked yer brother's flute up ya, didn't ya?"

Sal raised his foot to stomp the Irishman's face. Then he stopped. He grabbed the redhead by the collar, lifted him to his feet, and placed him face to face. "Now you," he said.

"What?" the Irishman said.

"Now you. Take your best shot you suck-faced fucking mick. Say, I heard your mother loved nothing more than wrapping her lips around a sweaty English bone."

The Irishman eyes turned red. He twisted his body, and with all he had, punched Sal's face. Sal rocked back onto one foot, but stood.

"One more round?" Sal said, shaking his head.

The Irishman looked at his friends who stood watching silently. He looked at Sal and shook no. "Yer a tough fucker, Yank. I'll drink with ya anytime."

The others nodded, grinned and returned to their business.

"Finn, get these two a pint on me," the Irishman said.

The bartender delivered three beers, filled two small bags of ice and dropped one in front of each combatant.

"Savage, Yank, yer a gouger," Finn the barkeep said. "Ya hockeyed Flanagan here, and he's a true hardchaw—nice puck in the gob. The sprattle was a bit short for me liking, but fair play."

Sal pieced together the bartender's meaning and smiled.

Flanagan pushed his ice against his jaw. Sal slapped his on his left eye.

"Danny Flanagan," the Irishman said extending his hand.

"Sal Esposito." Sal shook Danny's hand. "This is Ange Costello."

"Ah, a couple a greasy Ginnies, that explains it. Me fist just slid off, couldn't properly take hold."

"Yeah, that's our secret weapon. You've got that layer of fat between your brain and your skull—blocks the pain."

"Suffrin' Jaysus, nothin' blockin' no pain right now," Danny laughed, rubbing the side of his face. "I'm thinkin' me feckin' jaw's banjaxed," he said and shook his head. "What the fuck brings ya ta this shit-hole?"

"Why, you. Where else could I find a Danny Flanagan to fuck up my eye?"

The three talked for an hour. Danny was over from Dublin. He frequently visited to see relatives. The bar was one of the last Irish hold-outs in the area. White Chapel was mostly Muslim now, and many of the old dives had closed. Sal told Danny that he and Ange were visiting on holiday, and he'd felt Ange should see a little of the London tourists don't know.

Danny laughed. "Ya sure picked the right pub fer that," he said.

Danny introduced Sal and Ange to the bartender and a few others. One invited Sal to throw some darts, but Sal declined, saying he would if he could see with both eyes. Some patrons patted backs saying, "Good go and savage hook."

"There are no women in here," Ange remarked.

"Yeah, it's a good night," Danny said. "There's a few come

in from time ta time, but the place is for the boys. The girls just cause trouble. If a fine thing's 'round, the men start ta cut the effin' and blindin', then they put on the holy show and start actin' a gobdaw. Naw, much better without em round."

Danny spoke about Dublin and his family's connection with White Chapel. Sal explained northern New York—as best he could. Danny wasn't aware there was anything but New York City, and at first, thought Sal's description of the Adirondack Mountains was a "horse's hoof." Sal convinced him it was true.

Sal invited Danny to join them tomorrow at Covent Garden—Sundays were always a gas there. Danny knew it well and gladly accepted. A downpour started.

"Suffrin' Jaysus it's bucketin' down," Danny said.

"Yeah, good time to keep drinking," Sal said.

"Now you're suckin' diesel," Danny said.

After several rounds, the rain stopped, and Ange called the limo. Sal and Ange ambled to the door, turned and yelled a goodbye. Their new friends responded loudly.

"Tomora' mo chara," Danny slurred out loudly.

"Yes, tomorrow my friend," Sal said.

***

"I don't know how you can eat all this shit at breakfast and still be in such good shape," Ange said.

"I don't know how you can eat that rabbit food and survive," Sal replied, eyes glued to the newspaper.

"Listen, Sal, I've got a question."

Sal looked up. "What?"

"Last night, why did you let Danny punch you? I mean, he was down and done. It looked like you wanted to be slammed."

"I did. Sometimes I like it. I told you I played hockey. Getting hit's what makes it fun. It's like penance ... absolution . . . you go to confession, and instead of a few Hail Marys, you take some shots. Then you feel purged, relieved, just good."

"What do you have to confess?"

"Now you're pushing it, Ange. Listen, what are you going to do about Este?"

"She's meeting us at Covent Garden. I'll tell her there."

"Good, you don't want to leave something like that undone. You never know when a woman left hanging will come back to haunt."

Sal finished his bacon, eggs, and potatoes. Ange sipped Earl Gray. They reviewed Ange's tasks for the next few weeks.

"The stock market is all over the place," Sal said. "Be sure you sit down—face to face—with Roger. We've got a shitload of money on the line."

"As soon as I get back. But, don't worry, it's just the way it works. You can't watch the market short term, or it looks nuts. It's only the long haul that matters."

Sal's eyebrows raised, and he tilted his head. "Yeah? Well, I hope you're right. I'm getting a bad feeling."

As they left the hotel, the concierge asked Sal if he was all right. Sal nodded and covered his black eye with dark glasses. "Almost forgot," he said to Ange. They walked across the park to Speaker's Corner and listened awhile. The sexist guy was there; the others were new. At noon, they left for the Marble Arch underground station. Today would be Ange's first ride on The Tube. They took the Central Line to Holborn and changed to the Piccadilly line for one more stop. The crowd increased at every station until it was shoulder to shoulder. At the Covent Garden stop, three-quarters of the train exited and rushed to the elevators. Signs reading "Warning Pick Pockets at Work" caught Ange's eye. They packed into a lift crammed with people of all nationalities, many with baby-strollers, large shopping bags, or oversized backpacks. When the door opened, all rushed out and turned right onto the busy street for the short shuffle to the building complex.

"What's the scoop on this place?" Ange asked.

"You ever see *My Fair Lady*?"

"Yeah."

"My ma used to sing some songs from that musical. This is where Henry Higgins finds Liza Doolittle. It was a center for flowers, fruit, and other agricultural shit—real poor. Now it's music, street performers, shopping, food, and drink. And speaking of drink, Danny's meeting us at a pub down this way." Sal pointed to the main entrance and started walking.

Ange flipped open his cell phone, called Este and told her where they'd be. They strolled by several actors dressed in 19th-century costume, and their skin covered in gold or silver paint. One with an accordion arm extended eight feet and touched a little girl on the shoulder. Startled, she began to cry. Her mother comforted her, showing the man's funny face. The actor smiled and made a mechanical noise. He reached out again and touched her mother's hand. The little girl giggled and clapped.

Across the street, a silver-painted mime in formal Victorian vestments stood perfectly still. Children teased, futilely trying for a response. A man—face painted like a friendly old pooch—had his head through a hole in a table covered by a small dog house. As he bantered with the crowd, the audience laughed and tossed coins into his dog dish.

On the corner, a guitarist with a battery powered amplifier sang and played protest songs with intense sincerity. A small group of fans listened and encouraged him on. Flower ladies in Dickens dress wandered about, pinning mini-corsages on tourists and asking for a pound or two in exchange. Sal led Ange through the main entrance around a side aisle and up the stairs to a second-floor pub overlooking Saint Paul's church. One the courtyard below, an acrobat performed for a large crowd.

"He's a fierce one," Sal heard from the outside balcony. He turned to see Danny watching the show, beer in hand. "What kept ya? Grab a pint and come out. This fella's a gas."

Ange and Sal got beers and joined Danny.

"Still feelin' yer puck," Danny said and pointed to his swollen jaw.

"Yeah, I'm blinking funny too." Sal lifted his glasses to show the purple half-moon below his left eye.

"Este!" Ange announced.

Este gave Ange a hug and kiss and looked at Danny. "Who's this?" she asked. "And what happened to you two?"

"Ah ya should see the other fellas," Danny said and introduced himself.

"Listen, Ange; we need to talk," Este said.

"Yeah, let me get you some wine. We'll sit inside."

As Ange ordered at the bar, Este said to Sal, "I can't stay long. We're leaving for Scotland in the morning, and I've got much to do. I've enjoyed our time, Salvatore, and hope to see you again. And you—Danny was it? —perhaps at another time, your jaw will be normal and I'll see what you really look like."

The three laughed, and Este left to join Ange.

"That his mot?" Danny asked.

"What?"

"Girlfriend."

Sal smiled. "No, not really. They've been together for nearly two weeks, but she's married."

Danny's eyes widened, and he smiled. "The little fella didn't look like he had it in 'im."

"You don't know the half."

Sal peeked in the barroom. Ange and Este sat face to face. She held both his hands and gazed into his eyes with concern and compassion. Ange's face was blank. He silently listened and occasionally nodded. After a few minutes, she stood, took a sip of her nearly full glass of wine, waved at Sal, turned, and left. Looking dumbfounded, Ange stayed seated.

"Looks like a jilt," Danny said. "Let's give the little fella a minute. Say, gander the acrobat. Sufferin' Jaysus, he's savage."

Ange guzzled his beer, dropped Este's glass at the bar, and got his refilled.

"Well?" Sal said as Ange rejoined them.

"She dumped me. *She* fucking dumped *me*. Oh, she said all the right things—she was beginning to feel too much, if she didn't go now she'd get hurt, I was too dangerous for her—all that bullshit. But, Sal, she fucking dumped me. That's never happened. I mean, sometimes they just disappear, or I get a note that things need to stop for a while. But she just sat me down face to face and dumped me. What the fuck?"

Sal grinned to himself. "It's all for the best," he said turning back. "And she got you off the hook—you didn't have to do it. You didn't have to hurt her."

"Sal ... she fucking dumped me!"

"Don't worry, Ange," Danny said. "There'll be plenty more puddin' fer yer mickey. Don't fret; it'll come along."

"You guys aren't fucking listening. She fucking dumped me!"

Sal and Danny fought back laughter but both broke out. Ange looked mad and then shook his head and finally smiled. "OK, time to do some serious drinking. My last day in London, let's enjoy it."

"Now yer talkin', time ta get pissed up."

After a few rounds, Sal left Ange and Danny to complete their mission and went off to wander. At the bottom of the stairs, he stepped out to rows of vendors selling arts and crafts. He glanced at jewelry, watercolors, and leather goods while maneuvering through the crowd to the main promenade. Light flooded into the second building from high vertical windows and glass roof panels, highlighting the structure's bright green and red beams. Two exposed basement level courtyards lay on each side of the breezeway, fully visible from railinged walkways and accessible from wide concrete stairs. Shops lined the upper level's inner walls. Below, a pub, restaurant, and specialty stores filled all available space.

Near the bottom of one stairway, a string quintet performed popular songs. Sal stood holding a rail and listened as they played "The Girl from Ipanema" while jumping and dancing for the audience. He crossed a blocked-off street to the back building. Artists sold photographs, sculpture, and calligraphy between booths and stands loaded with cheap London souvenirs. He shook his head and walked back across the street. In the distance, he heard the cellist's pluck the slow rhythm line for the next song. The viola began to bow "Moon River."

Sal returned to the rail. Behind his dark glasses, his eyes misted. He hummed along, occasionally mumbling lyrics. He thought of Ma when she was young—how angelic her voice, how proud of her son. He thought of his pop working hard to save for their dream house. Things were good then. His thoughts turned to Johnny—how he fucked everything up.

A man tapped Sal on the back and asked if he'd like to donate to the musicians. Sal put a hundred-pound note in the basket.

"Sir, this is too much," the man said.

"Twenty for each? That's not much. Not this day."

The man smiled and handed Sal a CD. Sal worked it into his pocket and clapped vigorously as they finished.

"There you are," Sal heard behind him. "I thought you'd be down this way," Sal turned to see Colin. "I ran into Angelo and the Irish fellow in the upper pub. They said you'd gone off."

"How were they?" Sal asked.

"Well on their way to pissed. Where'd you find the Mick?"

"His name is Danny. He's OK. I get a kick out of him."

"That's quite a jaw he's wearing." Sal removed his glasses. "Oh, yes, I see, well they're meeting us at the bar down below in a bit. Let's get a pint and sit on the court."

Sal smiled and nodded. The music would still be clear from there.

The quintet played "Spring" from Vivaldi's "Four Seasons." Sal and Colin sat and sipped.

"They're quite brilliant," Colin remarked.

"Yes, right now, the best," Sal said.

"Listen, Salvatore; I've got a proposal. Have you ever visited Amsterdam?"

"Years ago."

"Let's have a Dutch holiday. Let's see, what's the date?" Colin checked the calendar on his phone.

"Yes, today is fourteen, September. Let's say we go on the twenty-third or -fourth."

"Why the fuck do you want to go to Amsterdam?"

"To get away. It's smashing; you'll love it."

Ange and Danny stumbled out from the pub spilling beer and laughing.

"Hey, Sal. Was yer dander any use?" Danny asked.

Sal looked at Colin. Colin translated, "Did you enjoy your stroll?"

"Shit, 'tis goin' ta be handy with this fella 'round."

"Yeah, Danny. Listen, Colin wants to go to Amsterdam."

"Fierce, when do we leave?"

Colin's eyebrows rose. "We have yet to decide that," he said sternly.

"OK, I'm not in the mix, fine, I'll legger out."

"No, no," Sal said. "We haven't decided who's going, what we're doing, or any of that shit. I'm just wondering if it's a good idea."

"'Tis a feckin' grand idea," Danny said.

Colin's face mellowed, and he smiled. "Well, my Irish mate is in, how about you, Sal?"

"Yeah, what the fuck. Let's set it up for the twenty-fourth."

"I leave tomorrow," Ange slurred.

"Yes, Ange, we're aware of that," Sal said.

"My Lord, don't let Estelle see you like this, Angelo," Colin said. "She'll likely give you the boot."

The others broke into hysterics.

"Little late for that," Ange said laughing. "Shit, I always wanted to go to Amsterdam."

"You're going back tomorrow. Back to work—remember? You've got a lot to take care of."

"Yeah, I know. Want me to send the plane back?"

Colin's and Danny's eyes grew. "You've got a plane?" Colin asked.

"Yeah," Ange continued, "a fucking jet, you should see the thing. Sal had it—"

"Enough, Ange. He exaggerates when he drinks. It's just a corporate plane. A lot of us use it. I doubt it will be available." Ange got the message and looked down at his beer.

"No bother," Colin said, "commercial flights are cheap and

quick. Less than forty minutes. So, should I make reservations for three? I know a brilliant hotel. All in?"

The three travelers toasted to their adventure, and Colin and Danny left to fetch another round.

"I'm sorry. Sal," Ange said.

"It's OK. You've had a lot to drink. Listen, I know you want to go, but I need you stateside. There's a lot to do, and no one's held the fort for almost two weeks. I trust only two guys, and you're one.

Ange smiled. "Thanks, Sal. I won't fuck up."

"I know you won't." Sal and Ange shook and toasted.

"To making money," Sal said.

"To making money," Ange repeated.

***

After Ange had flown out, Sal visited a few sights and pubs and met Colin at his club for dinner.

"Yes," Colin said answering his cell. "What? ... Let's see, it's—" Colin looked at his watch, "—just after three o,clock in New York. This is not good. Yes, keep me up on it. Shit, Salvatore, your U.S. markets are bloody shambolic. Lehman Brothers filed for bankruptcy at 1:45. Dominos are falling all over."

Sal put down his fork. "Doesn't this happen from time to time?"

"Not like this—no one's seen anything like this. One needs

to be in the market to understand. I thought I knew my onions, but this could destroy me."

Sal nodded and tried to hide his concern.

"The market is still open, and it's looking like an avalanche," Colin said.

After rushing through dinner, Colin scampered off to his office. Sal returned to the hotel. He knew Ange would call with the full story once the markets closed. He planted himself in the bar—his phone and Crown XR in front of him—and waited. At eleven o,clock the call came.

"Yeah, Ange. What the fuck's going on over there."

"Nobody knows, Sal. The Dow tanked. It's down about five hundred points—around four and a half percent. But it's tomorrow they're shitting about."

"I heard about Lehman."

"Yeah, and Bank of America took over Merrill Lynch, too. It's all fucking crazy. The feds are looking at some kind of bailout, but what that's about or if it will work is anybody's guess. I'm sorry I talked you into this shit."

"Let it go, Ange. I'm a big boy. I make my own decisions. What does Roger say?"

"He's baffled too, but he says, whatever happens, don't sell off. I don't know why."

"He's probably right. Panic is the worst time to make a move. Let's watch and see. Keep me informed from your end."

"Yeah, Sal, and I'm sorry."

"Cut the shit, Ange. I'll talk to you tomorrow."

Ange called the next evening. "Good news, Sal. The feds bought eighty percent of AIG, the State of New York put in some stimulus, and Congress actually moved on some interventions. The market recovered one hundred fifty points."

"I want you to start sending me all of your reports so I can follow along—including the ones from the past two days."

"Will do."

***

Sal read his Wednesday reports. Major banks doubled their interest, and some bigger brokerage houses lost value and started talking merger. Even with the Securities and Exchange Commission's slowing down the short selling, the market lost over four hundred points—only gold looked good, increasing by eight percent. By Thursday, it looked like the fall had stopped. The Fed and major banks moved to free up the money supply. The market gained four hundred points. On Friday, President Bush announced an intervention plan, the SEC temporally banned short selling, and stocks rose by three-hundred fifty points. The market closed forty points up for the week.

Colin called Sal and—not knowing Sal's involvement—gave a short layman's explanation of the financial week. Sal listened politely as he reviewed his stack of faxes from Ange.

"I thought for a few days we would have to cancel Amsterdam," Colin said. "But all looks chipper now. In fact, it's 'bee's knees.' I hope things are well with you."

"Just fine," Sal said.

"Good, then we're off on Tuesday?"

"Yes, we are. Danny and I are raring to go."

"See you at the airport."

On Sunday, Sal and Ange talked for more than an hour.

"We don't know exactly what to expect," Ange said. "But the word on the street is, it's over and back to business tomorrow. The day-traders are pissed, but fuck them—they're a big part of the problem. Anyway, I think we're OK."

"For now," Sal said. "I still think things are fucked up. I've got a bad feeling in my gut about what's down the road."

CHAPTER V

The Amstel

The smooth flight to Schiphol Airport lasted forty minutes.

"This area was a shallow lake," Colin said, "most dangerous in wind. Scores of ships sank here. Hence, it's named Schiphol— 'ship grave' in English. I'll detail selected features as we pop about—if that's to your liking." Sal and Danny nodded.

A quick train ride to the Northern Station dropped Colin, Danny, and Sal at the crest of Amsterdam.

"Everything flows south from this location. The city's effortless to navigate, and most everyone speaks English. Let's get strip tickets for the tram and journey on to the Leidseplein. Many splendid restaurants and clubs are there. I booked a hotel nearby."

"The tram?" Danny asked.

"Yes, like a trolley—you know, tracks and electric wires and the like. It travels all about the city.

The packed tram barely had room for the three adventurers and their bags. A conductor stamped their tickets, and they crammed into the front corner. They rolled by rows of colorful, well-kept townhouses, all still in eighteenth-century style with ornate wood trim and large tall windows.

"Them buildin's are feckin' skinny," Danny said.

"Yes, hundreds of years ago, when the government started taxing property, they assessed by a structure's width. Accordingly, Amsterdamers built thin and tall. Most buildings are four or five stories. Staircases are much like ladders—if one moves things like furniture in, it is hauled up through windows. That's the purpose of the beams near the roof top. And the buildings lean forward to avoid scraping. It's quite ingenious. Land becomes a precious commodity when one must harvest it from the sea. One uses every centimeter."

They passed over canal after canal all perfectly aligned. Barges converted to homes lined the banks—each with a unique design and potted gardens. Sidewalks, narrow streets, bicycle lanes, and green space lay in strips in front of more rows of classic houses.

"Not many cars—hey, look at that little sucker," Danny said pointing to a midget-sized vehicle.

"Driving in the city is discouraged. Those who do, tend to have the smallest autos they can find. Most people ride bicycles. Watch out, too—the bloody bastards *will* run you over."

"Look at that idiot," Sal said.

"Yes, he's wild pissing—you'll see much of it."

"You mean they just piss in public?"

"Yes, no one gives it much thought. You see those small green structures? They're public 'pissoirs.' They reek of urine, but the Dutch don't mind. Strange, given everything else is so clean. Oh, with one other exception. Beware of dog shit. It's not as unruly as in years past, but it's still a menace. The old rule is first to step in it buys the first round."

The tram stopped near the hotel. Within a few steps, Sal slipped on a fresh pile.

"Son of a bitch," Sal said.

"That was quite quick," Colin commented.

The three stood and laughed as Sal wiped his shoe on the grass.

By the time the crew finished the short walk to the hotel, Sal's shoe was almost clean. The rooms were ready. They checked in and met in the bar.

"Try the Heineken," Colin said.

"Naw, it always tastes skunky to me," Sal replied.

"Yes, I've experienced the same in the States, but try it here. It's brewed locally. It's completely different."

Sal took a sip. "You're right. This is good."

"Yeah, it's savage," Danny added.

"Now gentlemen," Colin said, "I wish to propose something. We are in Amsterdam, residence to some of the finest looking women on earth." Danny and Sal nodded. "Amsterdam's is among the most famous red-light districts in the world. Working girls flock here from dozens of countries, and they come in all shapes and sizes. Gentlemen, there is something for everyone. I propose we partake. I've arranged a tour of the district for tomorrow evening. After, we're on our own to sample the wonders. Your thoughts?"

Sal stared at Colin dumbfounded. "You're out of your

fucking mind. I'm not interested in sleeping with a working girl. Count me out."

"Jaysus, Colin, cop on. I admit I been with a floozie er two, but never a doxie. I'm a bit choosy where I put ma flute. Bejapers, this sounds manky. But I would like ta see the place. Ya know the boys'll ask—so I'll go for a look. Ya know, Colin, I'm surprised. A high one like ya wantin' ta be out an' whorin'."

"I've been visiting here for years. I've done this many times. It's a release. I know the district and all its tricks well. I have no apologies, no shame. I'm fond of the girls, and I'm keen to get up and leave when I'm finished. I find it all quite brilliant. Perhaps when you see the area, you'll feel differently. Sal, will you join in the tour at least?"

Sal thought a moment. "Yeah, I'll take a look. Besides, you may need us to keep you from getting killed."

"It will be perfectly safe. As I said, I know all about this. I'll explain things as we walk about. You know, I believe I may know more than the tour guides. However, we'll do the tour anyway and then I'll supplement."

Sal looked at Danny, shook his head and snickered. "All right, Colin, tomorrow night we watch your obsession at work. Right now, let's have another beer. Do you know if this place has Crown Royal?"

"They do. I called ahead."

"Now we're talking. Oh, Colin, can you buy antibiotics over the counter here?"

"Why, yes I believe—"

Danny and Sal began laughing. Colin caught on and grinned.

"All right, tomorrow night we'll see who's amused," he said.

After two rounds, the visitors left the hotel and crossed a bridge to the Leidseplein. They passed through a courtyard surrounded by specialty shops. Dozens sat conversing at the large concrete game board tables strategically placed throughout the court's interior.

"That's the way to the Hard Rock Café," Colin said pointing. "Brilliant burgers and a smashing view of the canal from the bar."

Colin led through a passage and out onto the main streets. A crowd stood in a traffic circle waiting for the tram. Hawkers handed out handbills for clubs and coffee shops. Multicolored neon lights decorated tall buildings with first-floor restaurants and outside seating. A mass of people of every race and creed scampered about. Street musicians played to a casually interested audience. Sal watched a young man standing next to a police officer light a marijuana cigarette.

"We're definitely not in Kansas," Sal said.

Colin pointed to a restaurant on the far side of the square. "That's our destination, gentleman," he said.

The three carefully maneuvered through tram tracks, bicycle lanes, and a busy street to the other side and entered.

"This is a brilliant Italian place," Colin remarked. "Of course, you'll let us know if it's authentic, Salvatore."

"You bet your ass I will."

The waiter sat the guests at a window with a full view of the action outside. They ate, drank, and chatted until the sun set.

"When will we get the bill?" Sal asked.

"Only when we ask for it. They're in no hurry here."

Sal picked up the tab—despite mild protests from his friends—and they left for a club. They sat at a table near a low stage with one microphone. Soon, a comedian bounced up and began working the crowd. The audience chuckled at some of the jokes. Others fell flat. When he told a story about an Irishman, an Italian, and a Pollock, Sal stood and cracked his knuckles. The crowd laughed hysterically, and Sal bowed. His thunder stolen, the comedian wrapped up and left.

"The guy hit two out of three with that joke," Sal said.

"Three out of three," Colin said.

"Who's the Pollock?"

"You're looking at him."

"I thought your name was Oakman."

"That's the English translation."

"Well, what is it?"

"Debski."

"What ski?" Danny said.

"Debski. It means oak man. You know—like a man with the heart and strength of oak. My grandfather changed the name officially before the first war."

"So, you're a genuine Ski?" Danny asked.

"Yes." Colin paused. "Remember we're in Amsterdam and nothing said here leaves here."

"No problem, Mr. Debski," Sal said.

The new league of nations spent the rest of the evening bouncing from bar to bar and joking with each other. Colin announced he had arranged a canal ride with a local boat club for the next day, and they returned to the hotel for another round before turning in.

"Don't forget, tomorrow," Colin said as they stood to retire. "After the boat and some rest, we visit the ladies of the evening."

***

Sal sat in front of a big Dutch breakfast and a mug of coffee.

"Ah, there you are, Salvatore," Colin said walking into the dining room. His bald head glistened from a fresh shave, and his mustache was newly waxed into uniform curls. "Are you ready for the canals? Did you dress warmly?"

"I'm good. Three layers," Sal replied. "I'm from northern New York—know a little about the cold."

"Smashing; well then, what's for breakfast?"

Danny entered with a bottle in a brown paper bag.

"What's that, Danny?" Sal asked.

"Jameson—Colin said it'd be nippy."

Sal laughed, and Danny sat.

"We join our shipmates at a place on the Leidseplein," Colin said. "I ordered some sandwiches. They'll bag up anything else you want to drink."

"I'm set fer the first hour or so," Danny said.

"Yes, so I see. The boat takes up to ten. I reserved six places, so we'll have plenty of room. This is a brilliant ride. The captain knows his business, and this boat is small enough to reach places the big tubby tour barges can't. Let's proceed."

Few people strolled about in the early morning. Colin,

Danny, and Sal casually walked through minimal traffic to the club. Inside they met their shipmates.

The crew loaded up with drink and food and followed the captain to the boat. Benches with cushions stretched the length of the craft on both sides. As the captain started the engine, Danny opened his bottle and took a swig.

"Ah, praise ta ol' Ireland," he said and offered the bottle to Sal. Sal shook his head and took his flask from his coat pocket.

"Oh, Canada," Sal said and grinned.

The captain pushed the boat from the pier, and the tour began.

As the group chugged through the canals, the captain pointed about explaining the origins of landmarks and telling stories. The passengers listened and asked questions as they drank. Sal leaned over. He put his hand in the water, and watched the slight wake of the boat. He looked up at the bright blue sky and exhaled. Boats always relaxed him.

Sal was taken by a three-story statue of a fat, bald, businessman holding a briefcase at his side and the torch of freedom over his head.

"It's called the Statue of No Liberty," the captain said. "It's quite popular. Many visitors say it sums up their lives."

Sal snickered. His summary was more complicated.

The boat glided past the Rijksmuseum, an ornate red-stone castle, home to many of Holland's best paintings. A woman passenger asked Sal, "Have you visited?"

"No, but I will before I leave," Sal said. "There and the Van Gogh. They're not far from our hotel."

"It is wonderful," she said. "The Rembrandts are stunning."

The tour went slowly through the city past museums,

churches, theaters, parks, and historical landmarks. Colin pointed as they passed the Anne Frank House. Danny made a comment about "Feckin Nazis." Everyone nodded.

"Most of my family was gassed in that war," Colin said.

"You're Jewish?" Sal asked.

"I don't practice, but yeah, I'm a Jew."

"Is that why the name change?"

"My grandfather wanted our family to appear traditionally English. And he was quite wise. A simple change of name and we became instantly respected—damnedest thing."

"What do you do for a living, Salvatore?" the captain asked.

"Real estate," Sal answered.

"And you, Colin?"

"Stocks and bonds."

"Two very tough businesses right now, are they not?"

Sal shrugged, and Colin lifted his eyebrows.

"And you, Danny, what do you do?"

"Construction. I own the grandest company in all a Dublin. We build it all. Got better than fifty men in my employ."

"You never told me this," Sal said.

"Ye never asked."

"I think you will have a black man for your president soon," the captain said.

"Yes, this election of yours is quite interesting to watch from this side of the pond," Colin said looking at Sal.

"I don't know what will happen," Sal said.

"Who will you vote for?" the captain asked.

Sal paused. He was reluctant to reveal that he hadn't voted for decades—it always raised eyebrows. He seldom saw differences between the candidates—never any that would affect him. "I haven't decided," he said.

The sightseers chatted for over two hours. The boat steered toward the dock.

The passengers jerked forward as the captain butted the boat against its pier. He thanked them all and explained the boat club's mission before politely asking for donations.

"And tips to me will make you an honorary deck hand for life," the captain announced.

Sal slipped his hand into his pocket and felt a sharp prick. The brooch had bitten again, just to remind Sal it was along for the ride. He licked a drop of blood from his finger and peeled a bill from his money clip.

Sal looked at the captain and smiled. "Thank you."

Sal gave the captain a fifty-euro note. "This might be the best 'lifetime' offer I've ever had," he joked as he jumped out of the boat.

***

Sal always liked the vintage instruments and music memorabilia at the London Hard Rock Café. The Amsterdam Hard Rock was far smaller with less on the walls. But the bar looked onto a canal, and the beer tasted superb.

"We've got a couple of hours before we leave for the tour," Colin said. "We meet the guide near Central Station."

Sal sat with his back to the bar, gazing at the canal and barely listening. He watched a glass-covered tour boat glide by. Inside, passengers sat and yawned. The boat's wake raised and lowered a family of ducks. He wondered how deep the water was. It couldn't be much. He envisioned the Hudson with tour boats fighting the rapids and snickered. His mind wandered to his mother. She used to sit by the window and watch the river, like he did. How proud she and Pop were of that house. They were petrified that it would leave the family if anything happened to either of them. But Sal assured them he'd move in. When he did, Johnny was pissed. He wanted the place sold and gone. But he was in the Dannemora prison, where he belonged. How he'd fucked up his life—and Sal's. Sal looked at the tiny prick mark on his finger, reached into his pocket and held his brooch. "And you won't let me forget that, will you?" he whispered.

"Ya OK, Sal? Yer off in a dream?" Danny asked.

"Just fine. Danny, when are you going back to Dublin?"

"Next week. My sons are comin' ta fetch me. They run the outfit when I'm away."

"We'll have to go back to that bar in White Chapel before you go."

"Feckin' yes, we will. I could use a good row. Can't do much of it back home. Yeah, fightin's bad fer business. Have ta look the part, ya know—respectable." Danny laughed. "*You* been feckin' calm lately."

"With me, it comes and goes. Used to be a lot worse."

"What ya figer yer mad at? I mean with me I just like ta blow out the cobwebs—and ta meet new friends a course." Danny laughed again. "But yer feckin' *mad* at somethin'."

"Just some old shit I carry around."

"The best thing ta do with shite is ta flush it."

Sal smiled, "Good advice."

"And you, Salvatore, when will you return to the States?" Colin asked.

"October, when the leaves have changed—everything is different in October."

The gabbing continued for over an hour. Colin looked at his watch.

"OK, Gents, time for our tour."

A light drizzle began. Colin and Sal put on fedoras. Danny slapped on a Notre Dame ball cap.

"Notre Dame?" Sal said.

"Yeah, ya gotta love a little green fella preparin' fer a ruckus," Danny laughed.

The adventurers hopped a tram to the Central Station. Danny's and Sal's skepticism showed on their faces. Colin looked like a school kid on the way to the circus.

"Remember, when the tour is finished, I'll expand upon it as we shop around."

Sal looked at Danny and smirked. The tram reached Central Station. The troupe jumped off and found the meeting point in front of a hotel across the street.

"Greetings, Gentlemen," the tour guide said. "Please remember the tour includes one free drink. Now let's all cross over there. Then we'll take a short walk and begin."

Sal looked at a husband and wife with their two kids strolling along with the group.

"That's not unusual," Colin said. "The tour will include

plenty of history as well as local legends. In fact, many families live in the district."

Other tourists included a pair in their seventies holding hands and grinning, and two young couples. The guide led the pack up and down streets pointing out details.

"That's the flat where Tarintino wrote *Pulp Fiction*," Colin said pointing. "The guide really should have pointed that out."

The guide explained the district's organization. "There are about 400 small rooms each with floor-to-ceiling windows and doors—and, of course, red fluorescent lighting. The landlords rent them to the prostitutes. Some reports say that most of the women are from the European Union because working permits for prostitution are limited to E.U. citizens. Others claim most come from Eastern Europe, Africa, and Asia through less than legal channels."

The guide explained the Red Thread, an informal labor union for sex workers. "Prostitutes pay taxes and have health insurance," he added. "And—while there are certainly girls who work from desperation—many report they prefer their profession. Our new mayor is talking about closing up to one-half of the rooms because of excessive pimping. De Rode Draad, the prostitute's rights group, is fighting the plan. They say fewer rooms will just mean higher rent and less business and won't change anything else."

The tour continued for ninety minutes. The group passed scores of women of all nationalities and races, shapes and sizes. They presented themselves standing in lingerie bathing in rufescent light behind glass doors or windows. Colin surveyed, eyes wide. At the end, all piled into a pub and sipped Heineken.

"OK, Gents, drink up and we're on our way," Colin said. Danny and Sal reluctantly finished their beer and followed Colin onto the streets.

"Colin's not the full shillin' at present; I have ta say," Danny commented. "These girls have him bein' thick."

"Yeah, I've seen brighter moves," Sal said and grinned.

As they walked over a bridge, a man approached Sal and offered cocaine. Sal gestured with his fist and told the pusher he had one minute to get out of his sight or he'd be swimming in the canal. The man scampered away. Colin's eyes widened. He'd heard of Sal's aggressive side but had never seen it.

"Best be careful with any action looking violent," he said. "I know it appears to be unpatrolled here, but there are many plain-closed police who are quick to act."

Sal nodded. "Just a little threat, Colin. Nothing to worry about."

They walked on to "The Old Church." The setting sun shone through a crack in the clouds making the stained-glass windows glisten.

"This is one of the oldest churches in Holland," Colin said. "There's been a church on this site since the thirteenth century. This one was built in the fourteenth."

"I'm thinkin' I seen more churches round here than women," Danny said and chuckled. "Quite the mix."

"Look over here," Colin said and pointed.

On the plaza in front of the church stood a bronze statue of a working girl proudly offering her services. "That's *Belle*. The inscription says, 'Respect sex workers throughout the world.'"

"Jaysus," Danny said and shook his head. "Yep, it's quite the mix."

Colin led Sal and Danny to a side street. "I've never been down this one. I like to try something new whenever possible." They walked along as Colin assessed each option. A tall, slim woman with light brown skin caught his eye. "Oh yes, this is the one."

"OK, you do your thing, and we'll wait for you on that bridge," Sal said pointing.

"Are you certain you do not want to partake?" Colin said. "There are many fine ladies on this street."

"We've been through that," Sal said.

"Sal's right, I'll keep me flute where it 'tis," Danny added. "How long you reckon you'll be?" Danny looked at Sal, and they chuckled.

"Yes, yes, very funny. I'll be about a half-hour or so. I'll meet you on the bridge."

"Say, Colin, what's that *quare* shape on that door?" Danny asked pointing.

"That usually is a personal thing," Colin answered. "You know, lets the other girls know where you're from or something the like."

Colin approached the door. The prostitute opened it part-way until a deal was reached and Colin was invited in. The shades were pulled down. Sal and Danny headed for the bridge.

Sal looked down at the canal. Danny watched a plain-clothed officer confront two loud drunks and politely escort them beyond the perimeter of the district. A young man in clean but worn clothes approached Sal.

"Sir, do you have any spare money? I need to eat. It's been almost two days."

Sal turned his stern face to the young man, relaxed his stare, and nodded. "OK, you look pretty hungry to me."

Before Sal could peel a note from his money clip, Colin came tearing around from the back street. He paused to find Sal and Danny and ran to join them.

"Jaysus, yer lookin' scarlet," Danny said.

"What the fuck happened?" Sal asked. "You've only been in there ten minutes."

"Son-of-a-bitch, well I went in, you know? And she undressed me." Colin panted as he spoke. "Then she took my willy and worked it up, you know—"

"We don't need a play-by-play—"

"I'm getting to it!" Colin interrupted, yelling. "Well, she took it and tried to put me up her ... up her bum, you know? I told her I didn't fancy that. She kept smiling and saying—she spoke sweetly, you know?" Colin stopped to catch his breath. "She kept repeating, 'You'll love it, you'll love it.' I said no, please turn over, and she kept saying, 'You'll love it you'll love it.' Well, I turned her over myself and," Colin paused.

"And what?" Sal insisted.

"And her fucking package fell out. She had it packed away somehow, and it fell out—the whole stick and berries, the whole fucking package. SHE WAS A HE!"

Sal looked at Danny, and they exploded into hysterical laughter.

"I know everything about the red-light district, gentlemen," Sal said bent over giggling. "I might know more than the tour guides." Sal slapped his knee and laughed. "I'll supplement what the tour doesn't include." Sal looked at Danny, and they broke out again.

"Excuse me, sir," the young man said. "Did your friend come from that back street?" The young man pointed and Sal—still chuckling—nodded. "Sir, that street has many pre-op transsexuals. There's usually a symbol on the door like this." The young man drew a figure in the dew on the rail.

"That's the *quare* thing I asked ya 'bout," Danny said. He looked at Sal, and they cracked up again.

"I know everything ... the guide really should have pointed that out." Sal continued to tease and laugh.

Colin was fuming until the contagious laughter infected him too. He started to grin and then chuckled. Finally, he broke into laughter with the others. They stood on the bridge and roared, occasionally stopping until someone echoed one of Colin's bragging's and they all cracked up again. Even Colin put in a jab or two at himself. Finally, the patient young man spoke. "Sir, I am really hungry."

"Yeah, Kiddo, sorry to keep you waiting," Sal said as he handed him a fifty Euro note.

"Sir, this is a lot of money. Did you mean to give me that much?"

Sal took back the note and gave the young man one hundred. "Now get something to eat," he said, still chuckling. The young man thanked Sal three times and trotted off toward a restaurant. The three cheerful companions made their way to the tram.

***

The crowd in the hotel lobby chattered and bustled as the three found a vacant area. They settled into overstuffed chairs arranged around a coffee table. A waiter took their order and soon delivered three frosted mugs of Heineken.

"I haven't laughed like that in years," Colin said. "I needed it."

"Yeah, was a gasser," Danny added. "We all musta looked ta be a pack a feckin' eejits. Funny, ya'd think this wouldn't be a time fer it, but I miss my wife."

"Where is she?" Sal asked

"Oh, long with the Lord. But she'd a loved watchin' us loopers laughin' like we were."

"I do not miss mine," Colin said.

"Was she that brutal?" Danny asked.

"Worse," Colin said. "She exploited everyone she ever met, especially me. I don't miss that bloody tart one farthing's worth."

"I've never heard you speak of her," Sal said. "Didn't even know you'd been married."

"Oh yes, six long years." Colin snickered and paused. "Ever been to New York, Danny?" Danny shook no. "Salvatore will know what I'm talking about. I was in Central Park one trip. I remember watching a female blue jay—the first time

I'd ever seen one. She flew about, wings stretched to their limit, searching for the strongest, loudest, 'best dressed' male, chasing all the other females away with her screeching—like a banshee. Once in a while she'd land and peck at something until it was thoroughly worked-over, and then, back to the sky where the real action was. But, God that mean, heinous bird was beautiful—stunning in fact. Her colors were so vivid but still soft, and she flew with such grace—it easily fooled you into thinking it must somehow be angelic. That's my ex."

"Jaysus."

"Her name was Cynthia. She came from an upper-middle-class family, mostly nice people. But she had an evil drive. All she wanted out of life was *more*—it didn't matter much what of, as long as there was bloody *more*."

Colin twisted the curl in his mustache. "I didn't know all of it up front—one never does. I fell for her, head over heels. She knew I was completely beguiled. We married, and as soon as the ring was on, she showed her true self. She'd humiliate me for fun. She'd taunt that I didn't make enough money, I was stupid, my penis was too small—anything she could say to peck away—often in public." Colin paused to wipe his bald crown and take a sip from his mug.

"She slept around with whomever she pleased and told me about the sex—every detail. She loved to see me suffer. I didn't know what to do. I saw no way out. In a sordid way, I didn't want out. So, it went on for six years. She just kept looking for more—the better male—the brighter blue feathers; the stronger and richer."

Colin paused and looked out the window at a light on the street.

"But you divorced," Sal said.

"Yes. I was involved in a rather risky venture. It failed—quite miserably I might add. I was ruined. After barrages of insults and threats, she moved in with one of her regular paramours and soon filed for divorce. It was granted quickly. She grabbed what little was left as hastily as she could. She couldn't wait to move on."

Colin chuckled and smiled. "In two years, I'd recovered—actually I was far wealthier than before and much richer than her new husband—and she began making overtures. She sent letters—you know, with regrets and longing for her past life, but never accepting any responsibility and tacitly saying I was not to forget I was the one at fault."

"What did you do?" Sal asked.

"I sent the letters to her new husband. He wasn't as smitten as I'd been and quickly cut loose. I never heard from her again. But I bought a watercolor of a blue jay and often gaze at it. It keeps me alert—if you follow my meaning. She's a person I can say I hate. Not ambivalence mind you. Not an I-don't-care-if-she-lives-or-dies thing. I wish her dead."

"That's a hard one," Danny said. "I don't figure hatin' ever did nobody no good. Fightin' maybe—sure helps me." Danny grinned. "Hatin' though—that's a curse. The only one feelin' that burn 'tis the one on fire. That flame never touches who ya hate. Na, hatin's no blight I'd care ta bear."

"Oh, it's not so bad," Colin said and chuckled. "Some days it gives you a reason to get up in the morning. But do you see my attraction to working girls? You can't hate a woman who follows through with an honest arrangement."

Sal sat back and sipped from a glass of Crown. "That's why the prostitutes."

"Yes. A good honest understanding. Each party knows exactly what they're getting—well usually." The group broke back into laughter. "All right, all right, you know what I'm saying. None of the bloody 'I love you, I love you' bullshit. Your wants are satisfied at an agreed price, and you're on your way. No talking things over in the morning, no jealousy, no fine print, no mind games, no divorce, no payments to someone you hate. Just one good honest deal."

The conversation paused. They all sipped.

"And you, Danny," Colin asked. "What was your wife like?"

"Not a bit like yours. My wife was glorious. Never give me scuff over bein' on de tear or hanging with pals. Gave me three big strappin' sons. She was firm on only a few things—that we all be at the table fer supper, and we be reverent ta Jaysus. She was a fierce cook and a real looker. Naw, she never got up my cacks. She was a churchgoer. But she didn't squawk ta me when I quit it—the boys were brought along Catholic, but they broke off too, with no bitchin'. She'd do anythin' for us. And there was no foolin' about. Neither of us drifted. I miss 'er somethin' fierce."

"How did she pass?" Colin asked.

"Cancer," Danny said. "The pancreatic. Had a terrible dose en passed soon after. Been gone donkey's years. I never fancied ta redo, ya know. Had a few mots, but never wanted the deal again. Guess I miss Colleen too much."

"Colleen?" Sal said.

"Yas Colleen O' Rourke. Jaysus I miss her."

"And your sons?" Colin asked.

"Ah, Matthew, Mark, and Luke. All of em work with me in the business. Truth be, the boys run it now. All in their thirties and all deadly hardchaws. No better boys ta have in a real knock-down." Danny gulped down his beer and signaled for another. "Ya know, speakin' 'bout New York, I been thinkin' of a trip with the boys. We're all savage wantin' ta see The City. So be on your guard, Sal, we might be bustin' in on ya when ya least expect us."

Sal smiled, "You're all welcome anytime. I'm a bit north of The City, but we'll go down on the train, and I'll show you around."

"Cheers ta that," Danny said and clicked his mug with Sal's glass. "I'll be holdin' ya to it."

"And what about you, Sal?" Colin said. "let's go full circle. What about your wife?"

"You mean wives," Sal said. Colin's and Danny's eyebrows rose. "Just two, you can relax." Sal chuckled. "Well, my first was a little like yours, Colin. And my second was more like yours," Sal nodded to Danny. "Number one wasn't as bad as you've described but still a spoiled bitch. I could never do enough for her. It was always going to be the next thing that would make her happy. I gave her the house, cars, clothes, jewelry … then she wanted kids. I made sure that didn't happen. The marriage was a train-wreck waiting to occur. I wasn't bringing kids into it. She left me and hooked up with another sucker. They had a couple of girls and then divorced. You know the story."

"Yeah, I seen it," Danny said. "And number two?"

"She was no saint, but she cared about me and the marriage. She tried hard to get close, maybe too hard. But I learned a lot about myself. I doubt that living with Sal Esposito would be a good time for any woman. Well anyway, we split as friends. She's remarried to a good guy. They have a daughter. It's all good. And she deserves it. So, I didn't get the demon Colin had or the saint you got, Danny."

"Yeah, I figure women come in all sorts," Danny said.

"Just like men," Sal added.

The three drank silently. Danny nodded to a priest walking by.

"Were ya ever holy, Sal?" Danny asked.

"I was brought up Catholic. My pop—he was an Italian tailor—he went to mass. But he didn't buy it all. Ma didn't go to church, but she was ... spiritual. Said she saw the divine all around her and didn't need a system. She had an," Sal paused, "'unfettered' way, wanted nothing to do with any dogma. I dumped it all sometime in high school. Too many unanswered questions, I guess. Never missed it."

"And you, Colin?"

"I was brought up to be a real Jew. Went through all the rituals and initiations and the like. As Salvatore put it, I dumped it all too. It's complete nonsense. There is no God. If there were, there would have been no Holocaust. Think of all the pure shit in the world. All the wars and constant epidemics and starvation in the Third World. Where is God? He's just happy mythology to help children sleep."

"I think yer probably wrong on that. I know my Colleen believed. And when I started up my comp'ny, I felt I was gettin' help from somewhere. I'm thinkin' there's reasons for things. Even the bad times we can't reckon with."

"Did God help Colleen with her cancer?" Colin asked and smiled.

"Maybe … in a way. She was quite peaceful through the whole of it—never complained, smiled a lot. Said it was all natural … just her time. Maybe God put her like that."

"Well, perhaps we agree on one thing," Colin said.

"Yeah, what?" Danny asked.

"It *was* her time. Have you ever read Marcus Aurelius, Danny?"

"Can't say that I have. Wait a sec. Is he the one who made that manky movie 'bout the Roman boyo feckin' all them bettys and the like? I seen a bit a that when I was a boyo, left me scarlet."

Sal laughed. "No, Danny, that was Bob Guccione."

"How'd ya know that, Sal?"

"It's an Italian thing." They all laughed.

"Marcus Aurelius was a Stoic," Colin continued, "a Roman emperor, and a philosopher. His point was when it is time, it is time. And if life is completely awry and you've had enough, the proper and noble thing is to take yourself out."

"I don't know 'bout offin' yerself. Naw, sounds like a coward's way."

"Nothing cowardly about it; it's perfectly reasonable and

practical. There is no God, Danny, and if life becomes nothing but pain, the only logical thing is to end it. What do you think, Sal?"

"I think I liked the discussion about Guccione better." The three chuckled.

"Naw, really Sal, you got anythin' ta put inta this?"

"I don't know, Danny. I guess—once again—my experience is somewhere between you two. I just don't know."

"Well here's ta not knowin'. Maybe we're all full a shite." Danny raised his mug, and the friends toasted.

A woman in an evening dress strolled close behind the three accidently touching Colin's shoulder. "Excuse me," she said. Colin nodded, and she continued to the concierge.

"Probably an escort," Colin said.

"She's quite a looker, but not my kind," Danny said. Sal nodded.

"I wonder what that's all about," Colin said. "I mean, why are we attracted to some and not to others?"

Sal recalled a conversation with Jimmy Eagleson years before. "A friend once told me it was smell."

"Well, she walked by within inches of us, if we could all smell her, why don't we all find her attractive?" Colin asked.

"Maybe there's something to the pheromone concept. If so, the slightest scent could affect someone who's naturally enticed by it and do nothing to someone who isn't."

"Do you think that's true? You're the doctor," Colin said.

Sal's eyes narrowed. "Who told you that?" he said.

"Your man Angelo."

"Sufferin' Jaysus you're a doc?" Danny said.

"Technically. I never practiced." Sal turned back to Colin. "What else did he tell you?"

"He said you were the only one he ever met who's both a doctor and a lawyer."

"Shite. Didn't know I was gabbin' with a feckin' genius," Danny said.

"Angelo is proud of you. I asked him exactly what you do, and he said you could have done anything you wanted and told me about your degrees. But he wouldn't budge on any details of your business. He said it wasn't his place."

Sal relaxed.

"So, how'd ya do all that schoolin' and come out so feckin normal?" Danny said and laughed.

"Just good with books. No big deal."

"Gentlemen," Colin said, "it's only around ten o'clock. Our flight's not until tomorrow afternoon. Let's walk over to the Leidseplein and have some dinner."

"Sounds good," Danny said.

"Yeah," Sal added. He'd be up early anyway, but tonight was still young and the conversation therapeutic. Not as good as a fight, but still a bit like confession.

***

The morning sun was low. As Sal walked out to the street, a couple on a bicycle zoomed past. The woman wore a skirt and sat side-saddle on the back-rack with her legs crossed as her boyfriend feverishly peddled. Holding an open compact, she carefully applied her makeup, unaffected by the bumps and swerves. Sal was impressed.

Sal walked along the canal toward the Rijksmuseum, careful not to step in another dog deposit. The boats were just starting their tours. Hundreds of birds flew and chirped. Sal thought of Colin's blue jay. His tough-skinned friend had come through some real shit. At least he never had to deal with an asshole like Johnny. He thought of Danny's warning about hate. Maybe Danny was right, but for Sal the infection was chronic, and Johnny was the source.

The museum was being renovated, but the Rembrandts were still on display. Sal walked through the temporary maze to a large room and sat on an oak bench in front of *The Night Watch*. He was stunned by the size and reality of the characters. The three-dimensionality was particularly vivid with the center guard's hand reaching out as he spoke to his companion. Sal wondered what he was saying. The companion clenched a spear. Its blade thrust into the room threatening to cut anyone too close. Others prepared muskets. Sal thought of his stick and Jimmy Eagleson. Thoughts of Johnny returned, and he knew where the guns should be aimed.

Sal sat gazing for a half-hour until a group of noisy grade-schoolers arrived. He stepped outside the museum and saw an empty wallet on the lawn. A day gone bad for someone. Sal found street-thieves contemptible. There were honest ways to fuck someone out of their money. Reaching into a pocket wasn't one of them. He stopped for coffee at a stand behind the museum and watched an elderly woman playing with her dog. The ten-pound Jack Russell leaped five feet into the sky, grabbed its ball, and returned it for another throw. Sal thought of his buddy Boozer. He looked forward to spending time with him—throwing his stick and hanging out on the porch. Sal had a vision of Kate driving along in her microbus with Boozer riding shotgun, hanging his head out the window panting.

At the Van Gogh Museum, Sal stared at several of the dream-like pictures—far different from Rembrandt. He was taken by the soft colors and blurry feel. He wondered what Vincent thought as he painted. Did he have dreams like Sal's? He snickered. Vincent had followed Colin's philosophy and "offed" himself. He wondered if that would be the way out for Colin. He went floor-to-floor, twice returning to gaze at the sunflowers. When another band of grade-school rug-rats scurried in, he left.

Sal stood by the canal watching an old boat maneuver into its pier when his phone rang.

"Sal, it's Ange. Just wanted to give you a quick update and I figured you might be out for a morning walk and away from the guys."

"Yeah, Ange. What's up?"

"I met with Roger. He's prepared a new report for you. I think it looks good. Roger is still convinced that long-run investments are safe. The new regulations hit the day guys hard. But that's good for us."

"I'll be back in London tonight. Fax me everything."

"Will do."

"How are things at the club?"

"Good, the new chef is great. Mindy loves his cacciatore."

"Who is Mindy?"

"You met her—you know—Frankie's ex." Ange sounded nervous.

"Jesus Christ!"

"Sal, it's all OK. Frankie dumped her again. This time for good. He's in Vegas with another woman. I mean, it looks like he's gone from New York completely. And she'd told him about us already. He didn't do anything then. I just don't see why he'd give a shit now. And, Sal, if I'm already on his list, being with her again won't matter anyway.

"Oh yeah, you've got this all figured out. You're out of your fucking head! What is it about her? You've got other options."

"I don't know. We just click, you know?"

"No, I don't fucking know! You'd better watch your ass. With a crazy fuck like Frankie, you'll never know what's coming or when. And Ange, don't expect him to just let it go."

"OK, Sal, I'll be careful. But I think this is going to be OK."

"OK my ass. But you're right about one thing. The damage is done. All right, just fax me the report and keep me informed. And Ange, be careful. You're fucking around with a lunatic." Sal flipped his phone closed.

On the way to the hotel, Sal watched a man bend his head back and swallow a salted herring in one gulp. What the fuck are people thinking? he thought. He shook his head and got a cramp in his gut—usually a bad omen. His intuition told him something big was coming.

CHAPTER VI

Something Big

Hanuman stared into the room, his club ready to strike. "I hope you've had a pleasant few days," Sal said to his ape-like friend. "I'll place this back here for your keeping."

Sal took the brooch from his pocket and laid it on the mantel. He settled into in a wing-back chair looking down onto the courtyard. What a trip, he thought. He'd learned much about his friends. Maybe his first marriage wasn't so bad—maybe worse. Danny seemed content for a street-smart scrapper. And Colin, the rich one, was so bitter and unhappy. Maybe Danny was right about Sal's anger. But Danny didn't know where it came from and couldn't possibly understand. Sal looked up at Hanuman. "You do, don't you, big guy?" he whispered.

Time for a few days alone to clear the head. It seemed he was always clearing his head—taking a few days and then realizing it was still fucked up. But the intention gave him hope for a little while. He chuckled. What a fucking game.

The hotel bar was too crowded and noisy. Sal took a cab to

an Italian place the bartender recommended. He walked down the narrow stairs to the cellar dining room.

"Welcome, sir. How many tonight?" a young hostess asked.

"Three," Sal replied. He knew not to ask for a table for one and expect to be seated anytime soon. "The others will be along, but I'd like to sit as soon as possible."

"Certainly, sir. But it will be a bit; we are very busy tonight. Perhaps 15 minutes?"

"I'll wait in the bar."

"Brilliant. We'll be back for you soon." The hostess smiled and pointed to the bar.

Sal weaved his way through a long, jam-packed dining area. The room bustled with chatter and clanging dishes. The wait staff moved carefully through cramped lanes between overfilled tables. The aroma of fresh marinara filled the air.

At the doorway, Sal pushed aside the hanging beads and walked into a silent, almost vacant bar area. He sat on an acrylic stool and saw his knees through the Plexiglas bar. Colored lights, mirrors, and framed posters of 70's disco stars covered the walls. What the fuck was this doing in an Italian restaurant? An extra-tall, scrawny man with an enormous head turned and smiled. His gapped, stained teeth and overbite made his head look even bigger. Sal wondered how his narrow shoulders could support it. Like a seventies throw-back, he wore tight jeans and bright floral shirt with a paisley bandanna wrapped around his neck. His hair was died black. But his gray roots, wrinkled face, and faded blue eyes gave his age away.

"Hi Mate," he said in a loud bass voice. Sal nodded.

"You came to a bloody good restaurant, I can tell you," he continued in a pronounced Australian accent. "Nope, none better than this one anywhere in London. And I been to em all. Know this town like the back of my hand. Jesse is the name, Jesse Adderley. Didn't get yours."

Sal looked back reluctantly. "Salvatore."

"Ah, then you'll know."

"Know what?"

"How good this restaurant is. A real Italian always knows."

The Aussie drank the rest of his beer and signaled for another. "Watch my seat, Mate. I'm going to skip to the loo." He laughed like a fog horn.

Sal looked at the bartender. "Is there a story here?" he asked.

The bartender smiled and nodded. "He's been around for a year or so. Comes in most nights. He's our local celebrity. The owner likes him. Has to do with the Bee Gees."

Sal smiled. "Is that why the decor?"

"Yes. The owner loved the disco era. When this fellow came in, he reminded him of Andy Gibb. I don't understand it myself—an off-the-boat Italian so fond of disco—but the bar is doing well, and the owner thinks Jesse is a big reason."

"There's no one here," Sal said.

"They come in around ten o'clock. Stay until one or so. Three hours of pandemonium. There'll be two more bartenders in at nine. Makes no sense to me, but it works. I'll tell you one thing, though. If they don't get that 'Disco Duck' song off the music machine, I'm going to go out of my bloody skull."

Jesse returned with a wet spot near his fly. "OK, Mate,

where were we? Oh yes, Salvatore. Comes from the Latin for salvation. It's a fine name. May I ask your last?"

Sal was surprised at Jesse's apparent knowledge. "Esposito."

"Esposito, another classic. Means one who's put out of the family or group. 'Cast out' might be more accurate. Sometimes refers to a tot who's saved after being left behind by its folk. An interesting combination, Salvatore Esposito. Yes, a fine name."

Sal's skepticism was fading.

"I'm here from Sydney. Had a boat in the harbor there, ya know. Big guy, the boat was. Had a dance club for many years. Hoppin' place. Eventually, it burnt out—they all do, you know. In'' place though, in her prime. Now I'm here. Been in London maybe a decade or so. It's a good town—not Sydney, mind ya—but a good town. And you, Salvatore, where are you from, Mate?"

"New York."

"Upstate I reckon. You don't sound like a city man. Maybe more like the mountain area. Let's see, the Adirondacks they call em, is that right?"

Sal was impressed. "Yeah," he said. "How could you tell that?"

"Oh, I been around. I liked those hills when I visited. Drove south from Montreal. Spent a week floating about. Particularly liked that Lake Placid. Fine place, fine place. Are you near there?"

"Yeah, Plattsburgh and Saratoga."

"Been to both—fine places both of em, fine places. If you don't mind my saying, you look a bit troubled. Maybe you've come here to clear the head and such. Interesting that you'd leave those lakes and rivers for head cleaning—if I'm right I mean. I found that part of the world some of the best thinking territory I ever looked in on. The water—that clear water. I watched the Saranac River once for near a day. Then popped by your Lake Champlain near that Valcore Island. Cleanest, most telling water I ever saw. They tell me there's a monster in that lake. That true?"

Sal shrugged. "Don't know."

"I hope so. I like tales like that when they prove true. Some claim to have seen it, haven't they?"

"Yeah, but not many believe them."

"Funny thing how a guy can see somethin' and others think he's bonkers. You know? Like when you see a serpent and some scientist who wasn't even there says it was a big fish or a log or some other thing. You couldn't possibly have seen what you saw; such things aren't possible. But you know you did—you saw it, you experienced it, it's true as day and night. So you're left to know it on your own—or maybe with the other bonkers folks who've seen the same. And you wonder why more haven't seen it. Happens a lot, I reckon. Funny thing what people do and don't see—funny thing."

"I suppose."

"And your home's always the last place you see clear—can't see your own back yard and the like. Sometimes you can't see what you're looking at 'till it's out of sight."

Who is this fucking guy? Sal thought.

"But an upscale hotel with a fine bar might be a good place too—for a while—for one whose been cast out." The Aussie laughed in his bellowing voice and winked. "Hey, watch this," he said. The Aussie walked to the jukebox pushed some buttons and scrambled back before the bartender could see. "Disco Duck" began.

"Fuck off, Jesse," the bartender said. He reached under a shelf, pressed the eject button. He turned and smirked.

"I don't know if you can feel it," Jesse said to Sal. "I sense you can. I think somethin's commin'. There's change in the air, Mate. I hope you come out of it well—reckon you will. Some won't though, if it's as big as it feels. And the other things that haunt you … I reckon they'll be fixed up too—sooner or later that is. But then I'm noted for being full a shit. Always changing my tale to suit the conversation, you know? Always a different skin covering this old snake."

Jesse's low-pitched laugh filled the room again.

Sal's eyes widened, and his lips tightened. What the fuck is happening here? He hadn't said ten words and this guy knew his life story. Who the fuck is he?

"Mr. Esposito, your table is ready," the hostess said.

Sal stood. "Good to meet you both," he said, still stunned. "Maybe you'll still be here when I finish."

"Maybe," Jesse said and smiled. "But if not, I hope you get it all put to bed—tucked in snug as a hedgehog. I reckon you will—sooner or later."

Again, Jesse laughed.

"Yeah, a full-a-shit old snake, that's Jesse."

Sal smiled, ordered a drink for Jesse, and followed the hostess to a table set for three. He still wondered what had just happened. The guy couldn't really *know* anything. No, it was just Barnum effect—say a lot of general shit that could apply to anyone and most people will believe you're psychic. Yeah, a sucker born every minute. But how did he tune in on the Adirondacks? And the hotel bar?"

"Sir ... sir," Sal's brain snapped back, and he looked at the waiter. "Should I serve you now or do you prefer to wait?"

"I'm sorry, the rest of the party has just called and canceled. I'll be alone."

The waiter looked disappointed; he just lost two-thirds of his table. "Have you had a chance to look at the menu or should I come back?"

Sal paused. He'd come for veal, but for some reason now the thought repulsed him. "Do you have chicken parmesan?"

"Yes, certainly, and could I get you another drink?"

"Yeah, another beer please."

"We have some very good white wines if—"

"Just a beer. I know the proper complement, but just a beer will be fine."

The waiter's eyebrows raised. He nodded and left for the kitchen. Sal's mind returned to Jesse. Jesse was convinced that something was coming. Sal considered asking the waiter to serve him in the bar. But, before he knew it the waiter placed a large, colorful salad among the silverware. Sal's stomach told him to eat, and he dove in while the waiter cleared the other place settings.

As he crunched on a piece of carrot, he stood to make room for a woman and her adolescent daughter as they squeezed into their seats at the next table. Without acknowledging Sal's politeness, they pushed the table and wriggled until they were satisfied.

"There's barely room for a mouse," the mother said.

"Mummy, you haven't been listening to a word I've said," the daughter whined. "He's completely icky, I mean it, Mummy, ICKY! And I have to sit by him every single, solitary day. Mummy, are you listening? Every single, solitary day! The others think it's all amusing. That Olivia Crabtree makes fun about it. Every single, solitary day I have to listen to her make fun about it. Every single, solitary day. Mummy, are you listening?"

The waiter brought Sal's beer, and Sal took a large gulp. He looked at the girl and snickered. He was about the same age when Johnny "made him a man." No fucking schoolyard silliness then. If a kid became a bother, Sal smacked him, and it stopped. Maybe that's why he didn't want kids. He didn't do well with the chicken-shit bellyaching. And yet, with his second wife it might have been different. He remembered how bitter he was when they divorced—mostly about the settlement. But now that was gone. He was happy for her. And she had a daughter. He didn't see much of them. He wondered if she'd whine about boys when she was older—every single, solitary day.

He watched a couple across the room. The man was angry. Sal wondered what about. Maybe an infidelity or something she bought with his credit card? The man's stern face looked away from her as he sipped wine. She smiled and brought her face in front of him forcing him to look. Her smile broadened as he stared at her. She ran her fingers through his hair. He didn't respond. She tried to put a breadstick in his mouth. He kept his lips tight. She drew his head to hers and kissed him on his closed lips. Still, he didn't respond. Rejected, she looked away and sighed. She sipped her wine. His eyes went to her. He held her head and kissed her. She smiled. He raised his hand and pointed his finger. She gently grasped it and put it back on the table. She kissed him again. He looked at her and smiled. Fucking fool, Sal thought. Pulled right into the web, despite a good fight. Now he's hers to devour at her will.

Finished with dinner, Sal squirmed from his seat and returned to the bar. A slight, female bartender turned to him and smiled. "Would you like a cocktail, sir?"

"Just a beer. Where are Jesse and the other bartender?"

"I don't know, sir. I've been here near a half-hour alone."

Sal smiled. "So the mystery grows," he whispered. He sipped a moment and looked around for any signs of his first visit to the "Bee Gees memorial." He walked to the jukebox and scanned the selection. There it was, "Disco Duck." He smiled. He'd suggest to management that they take that fucking song off before he left.

***

Sal's fists hammered the bag. Rapid thuds filled the room. Gut, gut, gut, head, he huffed as he struck. Head, head, gut, gut, head. Breathing hard, he stopped and looked at the clock. Half-an-hour, he thought. Good, time for leg lifts. He loaded the machine with two hundred pounds and began. His leg muscles constricted, and he grunted as he hoisted the mass. He counted to fifty, and the load dropped with an ear-splitting clang. He moved from station to station until he'd worked every body part. Finished, he breathed deeply and wiped the sweat from his saturated forehead. He smiled and sat. In a moment, he slammed his fist into his palm and hopped up. This was a good one.

Showered and changed, Sal gathered his money clip, wallet, and brooch from under Hanuman. He looked up. "How are you this morning?" he said. "I had an interesting evening. Maybe you already know."

Sal chuckled and sipped his coffee. He looked down into the courtyard. A few guests in sweaters and jackets sat reading the paper and sipping tea. The cool weather reminded Sal of the North Country in fall. He wondered how Kate and Boozer were. He glanced at a calendar, September 25, 2008. Soon it would be too cold for Boozer to swim. He thought of his buddy bounding through the snow to retrieve his stick. Sal would be there for that, his first North Country winter in years. He looked forward to the peace and quiet.

A limo seemed overkill, so Sal requested a cab. "Where to, sir?" the driver asked.

"How about the Tower?" Sal said.

"Fine with me, Sir, if that's your pleasure. Good day for it—being a Thursday and all. Shouldn't be much of a crowd."

"Then it's decided. On to the Tower."

Sal knew the Tower well. He didn't like the tourist places, but the Tower was different—as long as it wasn't infested with school kids. The cabbie dropped Sal as close to the walk as he could. "Thanks much," Sal said.

The sun came out as Sal strolled alongside the now dry moat. He'd heard stories about the smell when it was filled in centuries past. A water supply and open sewer all wrapped into one—how convenient. No wonder the Brits were always sick back then.

A Beefeater greeted Sal at the gate. Sal nodded and walked on; he didn't need a guide. He walked along the ramparts and through the chambers, placing himself back in time. He stopped at the White Tower at the spot where the murdered princes had been found. He watched the Royal Ravens, remembering the myth—if the ravens ever left the Tower the Empire would fall. He saw a keeper approach one bird, grab him and clip his wings. He smirked—Medieval insurance.

Sal walked through and examined the weapons and armor. He gazed at Henry the Eight's suite. What a fat fuck. How the hell did he get on a horse? He strolled through other exhibits, skipping the crown jewels, and stopped to rest on a bench. He watched three ravens hop onto a trash can with a royal insignia, pecking and squawking as they fought for position. Triumphant, one pulled a bright green Harrods bag from the bottom and tore it to pieces. Finding nothing inside but garbage, it tilted its head, reexamined the spoils, and hopped back to join his companions. As the birds scurried around harassing the tourists, a young girl in a stroller tossed one a piece of her cookie. All three descended on her. One jumped on her tray. As she screamed and cried, a boy wearing a silver Styrofoam helmet came to her rescue and whacked the bird with his plastic toy sword. Finally, a keeper came and scolded the naughty birds back to the lawn. Just another day at the office.

Sal stopped at the Tower restaurant. He grabbed a tray, coffee, tomato soup, and a piece of fresh bread. He found a seat near a man and his young son. The boy was playing with bits of his tuna and cucumber sandwich. His father quietly asked him to stop. The boy raised his voice. "No, I won't!" His father calmly reasoned with his son, but the boy covered his ears and babbled back in gibberish. The father put his finger to his lips and said, "Shoosh." The boy mimicked his father, saying, "Don't you shoosh me, Daddy. I'll shoosh you." The boy kept on shooshing, moving his face closer and closer until he was an inch from his father's nose. "Shoosh, shoosh, shoosh," he taunted. The father remained calm until the boy took hold of his dad's nose and twisted. Sal's eyes opened wide. The father gently took the boy's hand and laid it on the table. The boy screamed. People from tables all around stared and shook their heads. "What an awful parent," a woman said. "What a fucked-up kid," Sal whispered, blood boiling. He dumped his trash and left. His attempt to decompress by himself hadn't been a total loss, but it was finished. Time to call Colin and Danny.

***

For Friday night, Colin chose a Moroccan restaurant. The lamb melted off forks. The belly dancers spun and jiggled for nearly an hour. Sal remarked on the posh men's room. Outside, Colin, Danny, and Sal smoked a hookah. The waiter suggested a vanilla blend. Sal drew the mild smoke deep into his lungs and exhaled a white cloud. This was better than listening to spoiled children, he thought.

On Saturday, Danny chose an Irish place. Sal had never cared for corn beef until then. He ate three helpings, commenting on its rich taste and soft texture. "I think all this cabbage might keep Hanuman awake tonight," he joked. Danny and Colin laughed though neither quite knew what Sal was talking about.

The bartender slowly drew Guinness over a spoon into pint glasses, finishing each with a drawn shamrock. Sal smiled, his Saratoga barkeep had learned the technique well. Freckled Irish girls in Renaissance costumes delivered the brew and performed traditional Irish step dances beside the tables. After dinner and several rounds, it was off to the terrace for cigars. Sal took a puff and thought of similar times with his friend, Jimmy Eagleson. Danny danced, told tales that filled the room with laughter, and bought several rounds for the bar. "You'd think it was his last night on earth," Colin said to Sal. "One never knows," Sal replied.

Colin was busy on Sunday evening. Danny called Sal at seven.

"It's been a stretch since we interrupted affairs in White Chapel," Danny said.

"I'm in. I'll meet you there," Sal replied.

"Savage," Danny said and hung up.

Sal ordered a limo. Like before, the driver would deliver, but speed off. “Fucking wimp,” Sal mumbled.

Danny stood at the bar in the spot where he and Sal first met. “Ah, there ya are,” he said.

“Finn, a pint for Sal.” Finn poured a fresh beer and slid it in front of Sal. “Been a while,” Finn said and smiled.

“Too long,” Sal said. Several of the regulars yelled their regards to Sal as they drank and threw darts. Sal played a few matches and almost won the second. After the fifth game, he returned to a stool next to Danny. Danny raised his glass. “Cheers,” he said with a smile.

The boys became quiet as a slight man in a vested suit and bowler hat strolled to the bar. Five-foot-seven with a pleasant smile, he quietly took his place at the corner. Finn set a shot of Jameson and a beer in front of him.

“How’ve ya been, Seamus?” Finn asked.

“Fine, Finn, just fine. And ye?” Seamus replied.

One by one, the boys walked over and paid their respects.

“Be right back,” Danny said as he left to participate in the ritual. After one round the man tipped his hat politely and walked out.

“Who was that?” Sal asked.

“That’s Seamus Clancy,” Danny said.

“Why the ordeal?”

“That man is the toughest brawler in all a Dublin.”

“That little guy?”

Danny laughed. “Don’t let the size fool ya. When ya been in a bout with Seamus Clancy, ya been whipped by a tornado. Never seen anything like it. Lightning fast with blows like a jackhammer—and he shuffles about like a ghost, always movin' ta where ya can't see 'im and then sneakin' in ta take ya apart." Danny chuckled. "I seen him take down a half-dozen boyos a yer size. Yeah, there's none even close ta Seamus Clancy."

Sal nodded. "I see he's well respected."

"Nicest fella ya ever met. Never gets mad, even when he's thrashin'—never seen anythin' like it."

Sal smiled. Never gets mad, he thought. That's his edge—one Sal didn't have.

The chatter and drinking went past midnight. The bar had thinned to a few regulars, most on their last pint. While Sal was visiting the loo, Danny noticed Finn staring toward the door. A skinhead in a sleeveless Union Jack t-shirt was marching in. At the bar, the intruder demanded a beer. He stood at six-foot-two with a scarred face, muscular, and a swastika tattoo on the back of his neck. Through the belt loops of his baggy military pants hung a bicycle chain. The man pulled his dentures from his mouth, waved them at Finn, and clicked out a second demand. "Maybe you didn't hear me. I heard you Irish have trouble with your ears. Can't hear through the dried turd keeping the shit from dribbling out of your head. I said beer, NOW!"

"Find another place for trouble," Finn said with a smirk. "Your kind ain't welcome. You'll not be served here."

The skinhead put his teeth in his pocket, took a beer from a small man standing at the bar and guzzled it down. "ANOTHER!" he yelled.

"Listen, ya moran," Danny said. "Don't be acting a maggot here. Ya heard the barkeep. Now move on."

The skinhead snickered and then slammed down the glass, and moved toward the door as if leaving. As Danny turned back to his beer, the skinhead swung around, lunged, and cold-cocked Danny on the side of his head. Danny staggered and then landed a blow to the skinhead's face. The skinhead wiped the blood from his bleeding nose and laughed. He looked at two other men preparing to jump in and again pretended to leave. Then he whipped around, pulled a flat leather club from his pocket, and bashed Danny on the back of his skull.

Walking back from the loo, Sal saw. His eyes flashed to red. He flew at the skinhead and landed three blows to his stomach. As the skinhead buckled over and held his belly, Sal—looking like a wild man—picked up the club. Sal breathed hard. He stared at the bald head below, and grit his teeth as he raised the club.

"Don't, Sal, you'll kill him," Danny said grabbing Sal's arm.

Sal struggled to get loose but saw Danny's face and calmed. He shook his head. His eyes cleared and he dropped the club.

"Not worth a murder, for this eegit," Danny said.

Two of the boys threw the skinhead onto a pile of garbage in the street.

Sal's face turned lurid. He ran back to the and hurled vomit several times. He saw himself in the mirror. In horror, he washed his face.

"Ya looked like a demon possessed ya," Danny said from the door.

"Yeah," Sal said. "I'll be OK."

"Never seen a man so unhinged."

"I'm glad you were there to stop it. No one was in Montreal—"

Sal went silent.

"Montreal?"

"Nothing, Danny … nothing."

Sal and Danny returned. Finn poured two fresh glasses.

"Here," Finn said, tossing the club to Sal. "A keepsake of a fight well ended."

Sal looked at the club. "I won't want to remember," he mumbled.

"Sure ya will," Danny said. "You'll remember that ya stopped."

Still staring at the club, Sal nodded.

"It's an interesting little slapper," Danny commented.

"We call them blackjacks," Sal said.

"Ah, I see ya know a bit about em."

"A bit too much." Sal pocketed the club.

Sal wound down as he chatted with Danny. Suddenly Sal's eyes narrowed.

"Danny, look directly ahead," Sal said. "Finn, do you have a flashlight?" Finn handed Sal a small flashlight from behind the bar.

"Now follow my finger," Sal told Danny. "Look straight ahead into my eyes."

Sal shook his head. Danny was beginning to look faint.

"Danny, don't let yourself fade. Keep awake and listen to me. Finn, call an ambulance. Stay awake and listen to me, Danny."

"It'll take hours for an ambulance ta be bothering with White Chapel at this hour on a Sunday," Finn said.

"Fuck it," Sal said. "Keep talking to him and don't let him dose off regardless of how much he tries. Keep him awake. You hear me!?"

Sal called the limo. The driver said it would be at least an hour. Sal told him there were two hundred pounds for him. Sal went to the street to look for a cab.

One of the boys chuckled. "Won't be no cabs over this way either, Sal," he said.

Finn kept Danny alert as Sal called the limo again.

"Five hundred pounds," Sal said.

"Five minutes," the driver said.

"Put cold water on his cheeks and keep him talking," Sal barked to Finn.

"First time I ever had ta work at getting Danny ta blabber," Finn joked. "Take it easy, Sal. Ya can't change fate. The car'll get here."

The limo pulled up. Sal and two of the boys put Danny in the back and climbed in with him. Finn gave the driver directions to the nearest medical center.

"I can't go there," the driver said. "The company will fire me."

"A thousand pounds!" Sal yelled. "This man is dying!"

The driver put his head down, looked up, and said, "Let's go."

The ten-minute drive seemed an hour. Sal and the boys helped Danny out of the limo. "I need to get out of here, sir," the driver said. "And I can't come back."

"I'll catch up with you tomorrow," Sal said. "You did a good thing. I won't forget,"

"Come on, Sal," one of the boys hollered. "We don't know what ta tell these feckin' gobdaws."

Sal ran through the filthy ramshackle waiting area half-filled with bleeding drunks.

"This man has a severe concussion," Sal told the nurse at the dilapidated receiving desk.

"You'll have to wait, Sir. I can't admit him until he's been seen by a doctor and we're very busy."

"I'M A FUCKING DOCTOR and I'm telling you to get him in now, or my lawyer, the press, and the fucking prime minister himself will know why!"

The nurse shook her head and on the intercom called for the physician on duty. A young Asian surgeon walked through the back doors. His bloodshot eyes reminded Sal of his own internship. Seeing an enormous, aggressive American storm forward alarmed the doctor. But Sal's rapid, detailed diagnosis impressed him, and he immediately examined Danny.

"Get him in here STAT!" the doctor ordered. In seconds, a gurney arrived and Danny was rushed inside. "Would you like to observe, Doctor?" the physician asked Sal as he turned to follow.

Sal smiled. "I'll wait; I know what it's like having someone look over your shoulder. I trust you."

"Thank you. It's a good thing you got him here; he had only minutes. The surgeon hurried through the swinging doors.

***

Sal slept three hours and woke at nine o'clock in the morning. He sat in his shorts and watched the courtyard below. Two children played tag while their parents looked over a tourist brochure. How exciting their day will be, Sal thought and snickered. He'd spent the night worrying in waiting rooms drinking instant coffee from a machine. Danny had been quickly moved to a hospital. His condition was iffy. Sal knew about head injuries. The doctor said he was stable, but who knew how much of Danny would be left. Sal would visit that afternoon.

Sal looked up at Hanuman.

"Still holding that fucking club," he said. "For eternity you get to hold that club … and your mountain too, of course. Wait here; I have something to show you."

In the bedroom, Sal retrieved the blackjack from his pant pocket. He felt nauseous and sat on the corner of the bed. He wondered why he didn't kill the skinhead. Was it Danny? Sal could have easily tossed Danny aside. Why didn't he? The worthless scum skinhead had it coming. He'd just keep fucking people up until *someone* took him out.

And that swastika. Those were the assholes that gassed Colin's family. Maybe he should have slammed the club into that cocksucker's head. If the skinhead had been Johnny, he would have killed him. But he didn't smash *this* asshole. Why? That Aussie, Jesse, was right, something big did happen.

Salvatore Esposito stood down. But was this all—the whole "big thing"?

Nothing felt settled. Sal still sensed another shoe waiting to fall. What the fuck will be next?

"Here," he said in the living room placing the blackjack on the mantel next to his brooch. "Keep an eye on this too, if you don't mind." Hanuman didn't object.

The heavy bag took a hard beating. As he struck, Sal saw the faces of everyone he'd ever hated—mostly the skinhead—and Johnny. At breakfast, he barely ate. Obsessed, he kept asking himself, why? He'd planned to meet Colin for dinner. Maybe some chit-chat would help. Maybe not.

***

Colin's eyes opened wide as Sal told him. "That part of London is exceptionally dangerous, Salvatore. Why do you go there?"

"I've got my reasons."

Colin grimaced and exhaled. "How is Danny?"

"They don't know for sure. A head injury like this is tricky. But he was hit in a favorable spot—if there is one. There's a high percentage of recovery in that part of the brain. They stopped the bleeding, relieved the pressure and stabilized him. He's groggy—not speaking yet, but they think he'll be coherent in a couple of days. I'll tell you one thing for certain; his fighting days are over. He'll probably have to wear some protective head gear. Even a slight knock could kill him."

"And the Nazi?"

"He just disappeared. Must have pulled himself out of the garbage and run off."

Colin shook his head. "Well, I wish I could help more. But I'll be smothered with work for a while. Last days of September—usually a good time to be in London. But your Congress is making life miserable. They rejected the financial bailout today. Everyone thought it would pass. They're talking about another plan, but the market didn't wait. One point two trillion dollars in wealth, up in smoke. The Dow's down 777 points. Convenient number—easy to remember. Biggest one-day drop in history. A few more days like this and I'll be finished off. This has been one bloody bad Monday."

Sal's face became serious. He hadn't talked to Ange yet, and his day had kept him from any news.

"Oh well," Colin continued, "seems like life is flying by anyway. And none of this will matter when we're dead, right?"

Colin took a sip of wine and looked at his watch. "Look at this." He held up his Rolex. "Wednesday is October first, two thousand and eight."

***

"How are ya, Sal?" Danny whispered as Sal entered Danny's E.R. cubicle.

"Fine, Danny," Sal looked around. The pumping sounds of life support machines brought back memories.

"I got a thank ya for savin' my life. I'm thinkin' Colleen was right. How is it Danny'd be chummin' with a feckin' doctor if it wasn't Jaysus who sent 'im?" Danny chuckled.

"No thanks necessary, my friend."

"Well, maybe someday I'll be returnin' the favor." Danny smiled. "Say, Sal, what day is it?"

"It's Thursday, Danny—October second."

"Shite, lost most a week. Well, the docs say I'll be out soon enough. They're makin' a feckin' contraption fer my head. Sal, I have ta wear it day and night. Can only take it off ta wash and the like. Guess Danny 'll have ta behave. Maybe that's Colleen's doin' too." Danny chuckled again.

"We'll find plenty to do."

"Well, I'll be goin' back ta Dublin' soon. My son Matthew is comin' tamorra'. He'll stay till I can travel, then back ta the Emerald Isle."

"We'll do something before you go."

"Now yer suckin' diesel."

"Sir, it's time to go," a nurse said. "Mr. Flanagan needs to rest."

"I'll see you tomorrow, Danny," Sal said as he touched his hand. Danny nodded. Sal left for the hotel bar.

***

Sal looked around the barroom. For the first time noticed American football helmets hanging on a wall.

What an odd collection. "Where did these come from?" he asked.

"All over," the bartender said. "Guests send them from time to time."

"Nothing from Miami?"

"Not unless someone sent one, sir."

"I'll have to do that—and maybe one from Notre Dame, for my friend."

"If you send them, we'll put them up."

Sal's phone rang. "Yeah, Ange."

"How's Danny?"

"He's recovering. His head's sore, and he'll have to wear a helmet for the rest of his life. But It beats the alternative, I suppose. I saw the stock market. Down 348 and change?"

"Yeah."

"What does Roger say?"

"Same as always, hang in there. The guys who are bailing out are the problem. They're pulling everything down. But Congress is voting on another bailout, probably tomorrow. If it passes, things might calm down."

"We took a big fucking hit this week, Ange."

"I know."

"Well, we're in it now, and we'll follow Roger's lead."

"Sal—if it means anything—Roger says he's never seen anything like this, but he thinks—and I quote—'your ship is as sound as possible for a storm of this kind.'"

"Yeah, the best-built rowboat in the fucking hurricane. Jesus, Ange, how the hell do trillions of dollars just evaporate? I understand real estate. You buy property, and it has some value. If you want, you can go over and look at it, touch it, tear it down, whatever the fuck you want. It's real. This stock game is nuts."

"Sal, should we call Stosh and see how *he's* fairing?"

"No. Leave him alone. I gave him my word I wouldn't second guess him, and he doesn't know about our little stock adventure anyway. He'll fill us in on his end when he needs to."

"I hear you. I'll call you tomorrow night, same time."

"Yeah, I'll talk to you then."

Sal hung up and shook his head. "Where the fuck did all this wealth go?" he mumbled. He looked back at the football helmets. Now there's something I understand, he thought. Solid, tangible, helps you from getting your fucking head smashed. I get it. He took a sip from his beer. Yeah, I'll send one from Notre Dame, for Danny.

***

Colin's voice made plain his panic. "The Dow's down over 1,400 points since Wednesday. That's 1,400 points in one week. If it doesn't recover quickly, I'm bloody broke. It's that simple."

"Wait and see where it goes tomorrow," Sal said. "From what I know, the market is very fickle right now."

"Fickle," Colin snapped. "That's a bloody kind way of describing it. I'll talk to you tonight."

As soon as Colin hung up, the phone rang. "Yeah Ange," Sal said.

"You've seen the numbers," Ange said. We're out millions if this fucking thing doesn't turn around."

"Yeah, I just talked to Colin."

"Roger says—"

"Fuck what Roger says. At this point, he doesn't know any more than the rest of us."

"Sal, ... do you think we should find out what Stosh is up to? We need some idea of where all assets are now."

Sal hesitated. "I'll call him. It will be good to talk to him anyway. He always knew enough to stay out of this kind of shit."

"How's Danny?"

"Better day by day. They're releasing him tomorrow or Saturday. He said to say hello."

"At least there's some good news."

"OK, we'll talk tonight."

Sal hung up. He paused and tapped in Stosh's number. The phone rang ten times. No voice mail picked up. Sal let it ring on—12, 13, 14. Where is he? Sal thought. He's never anywhere without that phone. Sal tried again an hour later with the same result. He decided to try Stosh's son, Cory. The number was buried in his address book. He hadn't talked to Cory in years, but if anyone could pin down Big Stosh, it was his oldest son.

The phone rang twice. "Yeah," Cory said.

"Cory, this is Sal Esposito."

"Mr. Esposito," Cory said surprised. "How are you?"

"I'm fine. Listen, Cory, I've been trying to get hold of your father. Is he around? He's not picking up on his cell."

"That's strange. The old man has always got that thing on him. Especially this time of the morning."

"Yeah, I'm sorry to call so early. It's noon here."

"Na, na, seven is the best time for us. Listen, Mr. Esposito; I'll give him a call and tell him you need to talk. He might be puttering around on the boat or something. You know how early he gets up. Maybe he turned the phone off to keep Mom from getting pissed. You know, I'm heading over that way in a few minutes. If he doesn't answer, I'll stop by the boat."

"Thanks, Cory. Tell him not to worry; I just need to check in."

"Will do. Have a good one, Mr. Esposito."

The lunch at the bar was predictable. A British attempt at an American club sandwich. But Sal'd had worse, and he knew his impatience made him more critical. By 1:30, Cory still hadn't called. Sal wondered if he should try to call again when the phone rang.

"Yes," Sal said.

"Mr. Esposito, it's Cory. I don't know what's going on. I went to the marina, and the boat is gone. I tried to call Dad's cell several times, but no answer. You know, I didn't think about it—I've been busy—but I haven't talked to Dad in a couple of weeks. That's odd too. I'm going to drive over to the house. Just thought I'd give you a heads-up."

"Thanks, Cory, I'll be with the phone all day."

Cory called back 45 minutes later. The house was locked up, and his folks were gone. He had no ideas. This is fucking bizarre, Sal thought. Where the hell could the boat be? And Sal without his cell? Something was wrong. In his room, he turned on his laptop. He reached a website and punched in some numbers. He sat back waiting. Then his eyes grew wide, and he exhaled. "What the fuck," he whispered. He picked up his cell and called Ange.

"Yeah," Ange said.

"It's Sal. Something is wrong."

"You're telling me? Have you seen where the market's going today? If—"

"I'm not talking about the fucking market. I can't find Stosh, and his boat is gone. Is there something going on up there you haven't told me about, maybe something more with your 'love' life?"

"No, Sal. I mean Frankie sent some threats my way, but he's been doing that for a while. I figure it's just wind from his ass."

"Frankie's back?"

"No, he's in Vegas. Just some guys who gesture and shit when they see me, you know make fists and shit like that."

"Why the fuck didn't you tell me?"

"It's just chickenshit. I can take it."

"This wouldn't be Frankie anyway. It's too complicated."

"So, Stosh is missing, how complicated is that? Probably out for a sail where his phone doesn't work."

"Ange, the Florida account?"

"Yeah."

"It was closed out over three weeks ago."

"What?"

"Yeah, right now the market's the least of our worries."

"You don't think Stosh—"

"No, I don't think Stosh ran off with the money if that's your question. Shit Ange, he gave away millions and still has more than he wants. But he's gone, the boat's gone, and the money's gone. Something is fucked up. Big time."

***

Sal looked at the clock behind the bar. Nine fifteen October 10. In eight trading days, the market had lost 2,400 points. And he'd spent a day-and-a-half trying to find Stosh. Darren, Stosh's other son, confirmed Cory's story. No one had seen their parents in nearly three weeks. Stosh and Deb had vanished. The bank told them Stosh had come in aggravated, demanding a lot of cash. They explained it would be at least 48 hours. Two days later he came back looking stressed with two men. He insisted they produce the money then and there. The bank cut a cashier check for two-and-a-half million dollars. Stosh turned it over to one of the men as they left. Three days later the rest of the money was transferred to another account. Cory and Darren verified it was their father's and told Sal that after a few days that money was gone too.

Sal feared the worse. That kind of money could easily invite murder.

Who the fuck were the other guys? Sal wondered. Down there it would be easy to get rid of bodies. A pro would use the swamps. They'd never be found. Maybe Frankie was involved. No, it was too big. But maybe. Frankie had been in Vegas for a while. Maybe he'd learned something. Maybe he was just a stooge, and an expert had been sent with him. But how would he know anything about the money? Only Sal and Ange knew.

Ah, fuck. The girl could know, Frankie's wife. Ange must have said something. No, Ange wouldn't. But he might. If he's into this woman enough, he could. But even if they'd been killed, why was the boat gone? What fucking reason would there be for that? Sinking dead bodies on a boat with the other options? No, that didn't make sense. Unless they killed them on the boat, then they'd need to get rid of evidence. Maybe that was it; they killed them on the boat. "What the fuck did I get them into?" Sal whispered. "My best friends."

Sal thought of his premonition and the Aussie. Something big? Yeah, something real fucking big. But this can't be it. There must be some answer. Or was this it? Had Sal fucked up and gotten Stosh and Deb killed?

Sal sipped Crown and thought of old times with Stosh and Jimmy. He remembered the fort and the few times Stosh slept over. All the guy did was work. He had three jobs before he was sixteen. He recalled road trips to the Keys. Stosh was always restless, needing something to do. Jimmy and Sal made fun of him, but he didn't mind. And now, maybe they were both gone, Jimmy and Stosh. Maybe he was the only one left. He felt lonely and abandoned. There were no other friends like these. Never would be again.

***

Sal had been in the bar for hours drinking and grinding Stosh's disappearance over and over. His head floated in a fog, and it hurt. The bartender had tapped him twice to keep him from nodding off. He flinched as a monstrous hand clamped on his shoulder. Dazed, he flashed to a vision of Hanuman.

"Hey, ya frickin' son of a loon," a very familiar voice said. "Thought I'd find ya here." He turned, and two of the most unlikely voices yelled "SURPRISE!"

Stosh and Deb stood behind him grinning ear-to-ear.

Sal sat silent and stunned. Then he grinned and nodded, "Yeah, you got me all right. Where the fuck—sorry Deb—"

"No problem, Sallie," Deb said chuckling. "We've been in Spain." Sal's expression made her pause. "Stosh didn't tell you?"

"When would I have told him?" Stosh asked Deb.

"On the boat, remember?"

"I thought you were gonna tell him."

Deb shook her head. "Well, did you ever tell the boys? It was going to be your surprise, remember? The trip they always wanted us to take. 'You guys need to get away. Go to Europe. Mom would love Spain,' ya-de-ya-de-ya-de."

"I think I did; heck they only call 'bout once a month anymore. If I forgot, it'll be an even bigger surprise when we get back to the States."

"It's going to be a *big fucking surprise*; I can guarantee that," Sal said.

"OK gentlemen," Deb announce, "I'm exhausted. I'm going to our room. We are just down the hall, Sallie. It's so good to see you and to surprise you for a change." Deb hugged Sal. "You look beat, Sallie. I hope you're not working too hard. OK, I'll leave you two to talk. See you in the morning." Deb strolled out.

Stosh ordered a beer and gulped it down. He signaled for another and sat next to Sal.

"That flight was choppy, Sallie. They shut off the drinks. Can you imagine that? They cut off the frickin' drinks? I'm parched."

"Stosh, listen. We've been looking all over for you for the last two days. I thought something bad had gone down with you."

Stosh shrugged. "I'm good."

Sal exhaled. "You've seen the market?"

"Heard it's tankin' bad. Glad I stayed away from that crap. It's just like you always said, Sallie: never get into somethin' ya don't understand."

Sal smirked. "Yeah, you've got that right. Listen, I needed to check in with you, you know, see if you've had any luck. No second guessing, just that we haven't talked in over a month."

"Yeah sure, Sallie."

"I couldn't reach you on your cell—"

"Yeah, that frickin' thing crapped the bed just as I was leavin'. No time to get a new one. And shoot, Sallie, you seen the prices a crap like that over here, I'll tell ya—"

"OK, I understand, but I called Cory, and he couldn't find you. Said the boat was gone and you weren't at home. I thought the worse, so I checked the bank account—"

"Yeah, I probably shoulda called ya on that one—"

"Stosh, listen, I thought you were dead. I thought someone went after the money and killed you. I've had crazy scenarios going through my head all day."

Stosh roared with laughter. "Now that's frickin' funny."

Stosh saw Sal was serious.

"Hey, I'm sorry to put ya through somethin' like that. If it was me, I'd be goin' nuts. I mean you're the only one left. Thanks for carin' so much, buddy."

Sal and Stosh bear hugged and patted each others' backs.

"OK," Sal said. "Fill in the pieces for me."

"Well, that bonehead Cory shoulda known the boat would be in dry dock. That hull's needed scrapin' for a year and the perfect time would be when we're gone."

"Stosh, he didn't know you were gone. He doesn't know where you are right now."

"Ah Jesum Crow, Sallie. I'll call him in the mornin'. "

"Maybe tonight after you fill me in?" Sal said. Stosh nodded. "OK," Sal continued, "the boat's in dry dock. What about the bank?"

"That frickin' place was shaky. I figure it's goin' under soon. I got a feelin' from watchin' em dick around with—"

"They said you were in with two men and needed two-and-a-half million in cash."

"Yeah, got a good deal on a new condo complex. Nice manageable size. Guys who built it ran out of money and had to bail fast. Cash deal, lower price. I looked at a lot of properties, Sallie. This one is good; I mean real well put together. You can always tell from the plumbin'—"

"OK, you bought a condo complex. Anything else?"

"Well, ya see, that's what I probably shoulda talked to ya about. But ya said no second guessin' and I had to move real fast."

"Stosh, buddy, please, what did you do?"

"Well, ya said to use my instincts. And ya said no interference," Stosh looked into Sal's eyes and Sal nodded. "I did with your money what I did with mine. That frickin' stock market's been goin' down like it was torpedoed. And banks are foldin' right and left. Not much good havin' cash around, no interest, and with all the other crap we might be seein' some real inflation. So, I looked at commodities."

"Please tell me you didn't buy pork bellies."

"Na. look, I saw an opportunity. I remembered what you said, and my pop, and Jimmy's Old Man. Ya know? Ya gotta move when it's time? So, I moved."

Stosh finished his beer and ordered another. He sat back and smiled. "So there ya have it."

"Have what? What the fuck did you buy?"

"I just told ya."

"No, you didn't, you just said you bought commodities."

"Aw heck, I'm sorry Sallie, I'm really whipped, and I never got over the jet-lag thing. Do you get that? My frickin' head's been—"

"Stosh," Sal said calmly. "What did you buy?"

"Gold."

Sal paused. "How much?"

"Seventy million, five—"

"You bought seventy million worth of gold?"

"Yeah, seventy million five-hundred-thousand and—"

"When?"

"Three weeks ago."

"Before the crash?"

"Yeah, now don't get mad, Sallie. Ya said to use my instincts, and ya said no second guessing—"

"Stosh, I'm not mad." Sal sat back, exhaled, and grinned. "You're a fucking genius. Days before the whole financial world shits the bed, you put seventy million in the only safe place left. Oh, believe me, I'm not mad." Sal thought a moment. "Where is it?"

"I've got it."

"You've got it where?"

"At my house."

"AT YOUR HOUSE?"

"It's OK, Sallie, calm down. It's in the bomb shelter. No one knows about it. It's in tubs marked as survival foods and such. I rented vault space, but I just put crap in it, ya know to make it look like somethins there? The way the banks are now, we coulda got caught up in a foreclosure. I'll tell ya, that frickin' gold's heavy. There's around 7 tons of it. The one guy who saw me load it in thinks I'm gettin' ready for Armageddon. He helped me for a while, till his back gave out. He thinks I'm nuts. But he'd be the first one over if a missile got launched. Anyway, it's safe."

Sal looked dumbfounded. "It's in your backyard?"

"Well, technically it's under the back yard. Sallie, ya said no second guessing."

Sal nodded, so far, every move Stosh made had been right. "Yeah, no second guessing."

Sal handed Stosh his phone. "Here, call the boys."

***

Sal struck the heavy bag with quick, agile taps as he worked on style rather than power. Gold, he thought. Stosh was brilliant. And Danny would be out today. Later, Sal would introduce him to Stosh and Deb. Saturday at Covent Garden—always an occasion. Sal finished on the universal machine. He moved to a bench and wiped his brow. He worried about Colin. The market fell more on Friday, and unlike Sal, Colin didn't have a private reserve of precious metal. Sal offered to back a new venture for his friend, but Colin refused—said he'd bounce back. Colin had no idea of Sal's wealth, Sal calculated. Colin probably thought he'd be tapping him out if he borrowed a couple million. Sal knew the odds were against Wall Street bouncing back anytime soon, and Colin had probably put *all* his chips there. If things worsened, he would offer again.

Sal walked into a bustling breakfast room. "Finally, someone who piles it on like me," he said as he pulled out a chair across from Stosh.

"I like the bacon," Stosh said. "And the eggs aren't bad. But this fried toast. Who thought up this crap?" Stosh held up a piece of burned bread dripping with oil.

"Did you talk to the boys last night?"

"Yeah, they're fine. I guess I forgot to fill em in. But if the boneheads called once in a while they'd know. Ya know what I mean?"

"Nope, no kids. Never had that problem."

"How are you two this fine morning?" Deb said as she sat.

"It's too bad you didn't have kids, Sallie. You would have been a good father."

"I'm not so sure. I don't like kids much. Can't understand them. The chicken shit they think is important makes me crazy. Anyway, it's a moot point."

"Well, I think if you had your own it would be different. But you're right; it's all hypothetical now. Say, did Stosh tell you about the bomb shelter?"

Sal froze. "What about it?"

"Big Stosh has decided to be one of those survival nuts like you see on TV? He's got that damned thing provisioned for the end of the world. You should have seen him loading that stupid hole in the ground. I swear he must have bought over a million dollars' worth of spam." Deb chuckled; Sal and Stosh glanced at each other and fought off laughter.

"Now Deb," Stosh said with a wide grin, "don't exaggerate. There's not that much."

"Well, maybe a half-million," Deb said, and they all laughed. "Listen, Sallie, this afternoon you give me the quick tour of Covent Garden. Then I shop. OK?"

"No problem, Deb. There'll be plenty for you there."

"Then, tomorrow night Stosh and I are off on our own. I wish we had more time, but since we're going back on Monday, we need at least one night on the town together."

"Wonderful, Deb. I'll give you some suggestions if you like." Deb nodded.

"Excuse me," Stosh said. "Nature calls." Stosh stood, stretched and made his way to the men's room.

"I have to tell you, Sallie." Deb said, "I don't know what

you guys are up to, but Stosh is happier than any time since he retired. He's got more energy and interest too. Oh, he's still forgetful—as you well know—but I have to thank you for what you've done for him."

Sal shook his head, and Deb put her hand on his. "Now listen to me, just take the thanks, OK? You've brought him back to life." Sal looked down and smiled. "And, Sallie, you don't mind us abandoning you tomorrow night, do you? I want to get him alone in London just once. Who knows if we'll get back."

"No problem. I'm flying back on Monday too, and there's a little place I need to revisit myself."

***

Covent Garden bustled. Grinning, Stosh stood and watched the street performers as the crowd bumped and pushed by him. Sal smiled watching his friend absorb the ambiance. Once inside the buildings, Sal gave Deb a quick tour while Stosh waited in the upstairs pub. They walked by dozens of crafters selling jewelry, scarves, hats, paintings, and scores of other goods. Deb grinned and clapped her hands in front of a silversmith. Happy and comfortably orientated, Deb cut herself loose. Sal chuckled watching her worm her way through the mass of shoppers, to begin her mission. Sal joined Stosh.

"Look at that guy, must a taken quite the beatin'," Stosh said and pointed at Danny standing on the balcony.

"Yeah," Sal said. "Come on over. I'll introduce you." Stosh looked curious and followed.

"Ah, Sal. It's good ta see ya," Danny said. "And who is the giant fella here?"

"Danny Flanagan, meet Yashu Stanislaus Stoshowicz." Danny's eyebrows raised. "We call him Stosh."

Danny relaxed. "Please ta have yer acquaintance, Stosh." Danny and Stosh shook hands.

"Sal's told me about you, Danny. Heard ya took quite the hit in the head."

"Yeah," Danny patted his headpiece. "Supposed to wear this feckin' thing from now on. My fightin' days are done, that's fer sure." Danny tapped his knuckles on the metal headdress. "Hear that? I sound like that tin man fella." Danny laughed, Sal and Stosh smiled. "But I found somethin's gonna make it a smart lookin' cap—an old-style American football helmet, ya know the leather type. Fits right over this feckin' ugly thing. Havin' it painted up. I'll surprise ya when I get it back."

"We're leaving on Monday, Sal said."

"Oh, that's right. Well, it'll have ta wait till next time I see ya."

"I'm not sure when that will be."

"I figure it'll be sooner than later. You won't be getting' rid a old Danny Flanagan that easy. Say, I want ya ta meet some boyos." Danny pointed to the back side of two stout redheaded men and whistled. He shook his head. "That smarts now, but I'll get used ta it."

The men turned and began walking over. "Twins?" Sal asked.

"Nope," Danny said.

"Jesum Crow they look identical," Stosh said.

"They are—just ain't twins."

From behind, a third man took his place next to Danny. "Gentlemen, may I introduce three of the finest sons a man could ask fer, Matthew, Mark, and Luke. My Colleen use ta call um the synoptic brothers, whatever the feck that means. Ta me they're Dublin's savage gingernuts."

"Gingernuts?" Stosh asked.

"Yeah, yer not used ta the Dublin slang yet. Means redheads."

Stosh smiled and shook his head as introductions were made. "Frickin' triplets, fantastic," he mumbled.

"Dr. Esposito, I want ta thank ye fer what ye done fer our da," Mark said.

"He did more for me. Kept me from killing a man. And *doctor* isn't necessary."

"From what we hear, wasn't much a man. But we're in yer debt, sir, and Flanagans don't ferget."

Sal smiled and nodded. "Neither do Espositos."

The group chatted through two rounds. Stosh was amazed by how the triplets filled in parts of each other's sentences. "Heck, they're better than most actors," he remarked to Danny.

"Ye don't know the half of it. Keepin' 'em apart's a chore. No problem when I can see all three, but if not—sufferin' Jaysus it's confusin'."

"All right, Da," Mark said as the brothers left to wander around. "Don't get inta no trouble; we'll be back in a spell."

"Yeah, I'll be behaving," Danny said and tapped the metal of his helmet.

The comrades gabbed through two more rounds. Then Danny squinted, and he became quiet.

"Jaysus, I think that's Seamus Clancy," he said.

In the corner of the balcony was the slight, short man Sal had seen in Finn's. He stood next to a petite, fair skinned woman, dressed in a long skirt and traditional Irish peasant blouse. Just as the night Sal met him, he wore a vested suit and bowler hat. Seamus spotted Danny. He took the lady's hand and led her over.

"I heard what happened at Finn's. I'd like ta find the swine and—well ya know what I'd like ta do. Is this the fella was with ya?" Seamus asked and pointed to Sal.

"Yup. Seamus Clancy meet Salvatore Esposito."

"Nice to meet you, Seamus," Sal said. "Your reputation precedes you,"

"Thank ya, but don't believe all ya hear. I remember ya now, from the other night."

"I'm flattered."

"A man yer size is hard ta miss. And who's the giant fella standin' beside ya?" Sal introduced Stosh.

"What the hell do they feed ya in the States? The two a you could move a mountain."

Everyone laughed. Seamus introduced his wife, Mary, and the group jabbered a few minutes.

"Well, gentlemen, time ta go," Seamus said. "Mary and me are on our way ta Liverpool this aft ta take the ferry back ta Dublin,"

"See ya there next week, if our ways cross," Danny said and shook Seamus's hand.

"Salvatore," Seamus said, "thanks for what ya done. Finn give me the whole skuttle. If ya ever need an extra hand in a fix, I'd be pleased ta partake with ya."

"From what I've heard you wouldn't need help from me, or anyone else."

"Ah … just stories—ya know how that goes." Seamus tipped his hat, took Mary's hand and strolled out.

Well, didn't expect ta see *him*," Danny said. "Say, what ya hear from Colin?"

"He was hit hard by the market crash. I asked him to join us, but he said he wouldn't be good company."

"None a my business, but how hard?"

"Hard. Says he's wiped out. He's having breakfast with us tomorrow."

"Well, give 'im my best. I enjoyed the talkin' we did in Amsterdam."

"See, that's what I been sayin' for years," Stosh said. "It's just like you always said, Sallie, don't get inta somethin' you don't know, and I don't see how anybody can know much about that stock market racket. You got no control. It's like frickin' gambling."

Sal smiled and nodded. "Well said, Stosh."

"I got nothin' in that show," Danny added. "But it might bludgeon the buildin' business in my parts. Just have ta see."

Sal finished his beer, "OK, Gents, let's go below and hit another pub."

"Now you're suckin' diesel," Danny said. "Let's go about and join the ruckus."

"Ah, I almost forgot," Sal said. "Here, a memento of our adventures." Sal reached into his jacket pocket and handed Danny the skinhead's blackjack.

"Japers me noggin'll never let me ferget this feckin' thing." Danny slowly shook his head as he examined the club. "I'll find a spot fer it where'll see it every day. It'll keep me honest. Colleen'll like that. Now let's go."

Stosh felt a hand on his back as he stood by the railing and watched the quintet performing in the lower court. He turned to see Deb smiling and humming along. He introduced her to Danny.

"They sure are fine," Danny said.

"Yes, excellent," Deb replied.

Danny waved across the way. "There's me boyos."

As they all stood together, the performers' friend appeared asking for donations. He recognized Sal and said hello. Sal thought a moment and took him aside. The man shrugged his shoulders. Sal showed him two one-hundred pound bills. The man nodded and lipped, "I'll ask."

Below he approached the cellist from the side and whispered in his ear. The cellist nodded. When the song ended, and the violinist approached the crowd to announce the next selection, the cellist politely interrupted and called her over. She bounced to him as if part of the act, listened and smiled, then spoke a second to each of the others and popped back in front.

"We have a very special dedication," she announced. "This is for Danny, a fine one indeed, I'm told."

The cellist laid down the opening, and the three women began singing "Danny Boy." Enhanced by Irish accents, their harmonies were perfect. Danny's eyes began to well as his boys joined in.

"I don't know who this guy is, but he must be something," Deb said.

"Darn straight on that," Stosh replied.

Sal grinned as he watched Danny in his metal cap standing proud and teary-eyed. Strange how friends come together, he thought. And this is one I will miss.

***

Drenched in sweat, Sal stepped into his sitting room. He looked at Hanuman. "What are you chuckling about," he whispered. "Well, my friend, tomorrow I'm on my way back to the west side of the water. I'd invite you to come, but others of your kind already fuck with my head there."

Sal showered and looked at the brooch on the mantel. He remembered why he carried it and thoughts of the dreams began to invade him. He shook it off; they'd be back soon enough. He dressed and poured a cup of coffee.

Sal was up early. The others wouldn't be at breakfast for an hour. He thought of Danny and the fitting sendoff the day before. His face soured as he remembered the skinhead and Johnny. Why are there such shit people? And Colin, what now for him?

Sal sat and looked down into the courtyard. A lone guest

in a cardigan sipped tea and read *The Times*. Fall is in the air, even here. It's a good time to go back. He looked forward to the red and yellow leaves. He thought of Kate and Boozer—he'd see them both tomorrow night. And Ma—he'd have to visit in a few days.

Thoughts of Johnny returned. He couldn't last much longer. Lung cancer is nasty. Good, Sal thought. Ange would be all nerves. He didn't know Stosh had saved the day. Sal chuckled—he'd call later and calm the little guy down. And tonight—the last of the trip—he'd visit the Italian place again while Deb and Stosh were on the town. Maybe the Aussie would be there.

A few scattered people sat and chatted as Sal entered the dining room.

"Over here," Stosh called out.

"Good morning," Sal said. "I hope you slept well."

"You're in a good mood," Deb said.

"Yeah, I'm glad for Danny; he's in such high spirits." Sal looked toward the entrance. "Here's Colin."

Colin strolled over, his bald head shining and mustache perfectly twirled. Sal made introductions as he and Colin sat.

"The bacon here's great, but watch out for the frickin' toast," Stosh said.

"You know they will make it for you any way you like," Colin said calling a waiter over and asking for regular toast. "You know that, Sal, don't you?"

"Yes, but I've enjoyed watching him fight with the soggy deep-fried shit too much to tell him."

The group gabbed for an hour. Then Deb and Stosh excused themselves.

"We're off to the Tower," Deb said. "See you for drinks before dinner. Nice to meet you, Colin. I hope we see you again."

Colin nodded. "One never knows."

Deb took Stosh's hand and led him toward the lobby. "Colin, listen," Sal said. "You told me about an idea you have. You know I'd be happy to back you, just to get you started. I can swing it; I've got the money."

"Thank you, Salvatore, but I must graciously decline. I got myself into this, and I must get myself out. I'm not sure exactly how yet, but friends don't make good partners, in my experience. And I don't like to pass my problems around. But again, thank you."

"I'm not going to harp on it, but it's not a problem for me, and Stosh and I are partners without problems. In fact, *he's* bailed *my* ass out."

"Again thanks, but no."

Sal knew the discussion was over and nodded.

Colin stood. "Well, my friend, It's always wonderful to see you. My best to you. And now I'm off to face my destiny." Colin grinned.

Sal stood, shook Colin's hand, and watched him stroll out. "Yeah, I'm off to face mine, too," he whispered to himself.

***

Sal strolled into the Italian restaurant and made his way to the back bar. A sign said, CLOSED FOR RENOVATION. He asked a waiter what was up.

"A new look for a new owner," the waiter said.

"Have you seen the Australian Guy, Jesse," Sal asked.

"I'm not sure who you mean, sir."

"He's very tall and thin."

"I don't know, sir."

"Real big head, too big for his body. And a voice that will blow you out of the room."

"Oh, yes, yes, that gentleman. I noticed him entering Prévoyance, the new French place on Cromwell Road. He's not Australian, you know."

"The guy I'm looking for is. He has a strong accent and a boat in Sydney Harbor."

"Yes, that was his persona *here*. He changes to fit his environment. Quite odd. Frank, our former bar manager, bumped into him at an Indian restaurant. That night he dressed in a kurta shirt and spoke in a perfect Delhi accent."

Sal stood silent. Who the fuck was this guy, the guy who knew all about him? If this was a carnival act, it was a damned good one.

"Will you be staying for dinner, sir? The menu is the same, and the chef has been retained."

Sal shook his head and asked for directions to the French place.

Now I've really got to find this guy; Sal thought as he began his march to Prévoyance. He rounded the corner onto Cromwell, hiked three blocks, and saw a bright new sign in art deco reading: "Prévoyance Fine French Cuisine and Piano Bar." Sal opened the heavy glass door and looked for the bar.

"Sir, could I help you?" a greeter said.

"I'm looking for him," Sal said and pointed to Jesse, sitting on the corner stool.

Wearing black pants, a black turtleneck, and a black beret, Jesse looked like a French boa constrictor. Now cut short, his pure white hair accentuated the look. Jesse turned, lowered his wire-rimmed glasses and—in a French accent—bellowed out, "Salvatore! I wondered when I would see you again. Join me, *mon ami*."

Sal took the stool next to him.

"So, you will be leaving us, *oui*?" Jesse said.

"Yes," Sal said. "How did you know?"

Jesse smiled. "This is a beautiful time back in your mountains. I hope your time here was most fecund and events kind to you."

"Jesse, what's the story? First an Aussie, now the French thing?"

"Ah, I find one needs to evolve, do you not agree? We all are many different things. I like to become them, rather than hide them. And Salvatore, I told you I'm full of shit."

Jesse laughed in his low, booming voice.

"And now you are off on a new adventure. I think this one will help release your demons. Perhaps the one you hate so much will surprise you. Perhaps you will see things you have been fighting to avoid. And remember the old cliché: not all that glitters is gold. No matter how much you have."

Sal's eyes widened. "What are you talking about?"

"Ah, I know I speak in metaphors. It is the French way. And, as you know well, all I just said can be found in fortune cookies, can it not?" Jessie laughed again.

Sal nodded, "It's just ... too many coincidences. It seems you know something."

Jesse grinned. "Salvatore, I have told you—"

"Yeah, I know, you're full of shit."

Jesse and Sal chatted. Sal grew comfortable with Jesse's act. He's damn good at it, but it's pure Barnum, Sal thought.

Jesse finished his wine and announced, "I must go. Have a productive journey, *mon ami.* I think it will take you much farther than you know."

Jesse stood and stretched. Then he strolled to the piano player and whispered in his ear. The pianist nodded.

"*Au revoir*, Salvatore," Jesse said, "the request is for you this time. And don't drink the water where you're going; it will make you very sick." Jesse laughed as he walked through the door.

Sal shook his head and ordered another beer. Yeah, one thing Jesse said is right; it's all clichés, all fortune cookie shit. Sal took a sip. Then his eyes widened, and he listened in wonder as the pianist played "Moon River."

"Who the fuck is this guy?" Sal whispered.

CHAPTER VII

Boozer

Boozer bounded out the door, leaping over the hedge, scampering to Sal. He bounced up, slapped Sal's lowered shoulders with his paws, licked Sal's face, plopped down, circled twice, and sat. Panting, tail wagging furiously in the grass, he managed a "welcome home" bark.

"How are you, Buddy?" Sal rubbed behind Boozer's ears.

"Welcome home!" Kate yelled from her porch. "Your friend has missed you."

"Yeah, I've missed him too. And you also, of course."

Kate walked across the lawn while Sal rubbed Boozer's belly. "Are you here for a while?" she said.

"Yeah. I've got to go down to check the club and to see Ma from time to time. But this is home base now."

"Good. Well, I'll let you two hang out. I've got pies in the oven. We've got the fresh apples now. You remember those apple pies we got on Clinton Street from that wonderful Italian lady when we were kids? I'm trying to come close. I'll be finished in the kitchen soon. Then you have to tell me all about London."

"Deal," Sal said.

Sal and Boozer headed to the camp's north woods. Boozer dashed back to Kate's lawn. He hunted and then pranced back to Sal, his stick in his mouth.

"I was wondering where that was."

Scattered among the evergreens, maples sparkled in red and yellow. Sal deeply inhaled the clean, brisk air as Boozer sniffed a late blooming rose. They hiked along the path through the three acres. Sal stopped at a clearing near the lake.

"Look at this, Boozer. The trees block out everything but Champlain. This would have been a perfect spot for a fort. I mean in the day, you know." Boozer woofed.

Sal sat on a boulder and gazed at the Green Mountains. The bright, blue afternoon sky highlighted the Vermont side of the lake. He thought of Danny and Colin. It had been one hell of a month. He'd need to call Stosh that night just to check in. He watched the waves lap over the rocks. Jesse popped into his mind. He was right; this part of the world was made for thinking.

Boozer chased a squirrel. It scampered up a tree, and Boozer sat to watch it vault from branch to branch. Sal slapped a fly on his neck. "OK, Buddy, let's sit on the porch."

The hydraulic door closer hissed as the porch door thwacked shut. Just as Sal sat, the phone rang.

"Yeah, Ange," Sal said.

"Good flight?"

"OK. I slept some of the way. What do you hear from Roger?"

"The market's still falling. The downturn's slower, but there's no sign of recovery. Roger thinks it's going to be a while. The major sell-offs seem to have lessened—those guys are losing their shirts. But Roger feels Wall Street will be back in time. The smartest move is to wait it out. Could be years, but it's the best bet. And it's looking more and more like the Democrats will take the presidency. And maybe both houses. There'll probably be new regulations and stimulus and all that shit."

"So, we stay put?"

"It's up to you, but yeah."

"I think we can ride it out."

"Real estate tanked too. Property values are in the shitter and banks are holding onto their money. It's good you got out of the Arizona holdings. How did Stosh do?"

"He did fine; I'll explain later. Are you coming up?"

"Yeah, how's tomorrow?"

"Good. I'll see you then. Oh listen, there's a box of piano rolls in my garage. Bring them up if you can."

"Will do. See you tomorrow."

Boozer sat across from Sal open-eyed as if waiting to be filled in. "Well, Buddy, here's how it went," Sal said as he began to recount the month's business.

"You think the market was a bad move, Boozer?" Boozer barked twice. "Stosh bought gold; was that good?" Boozer woofed once. Sal chuckled. "Are you answering me?"

Boozer sat silent.

"I'm going to get a beer. You want a little?" Boozer woofed. Sal laughed and got up. Boozer grunted and then plopped down and rested his head on his paws.

"Got another one of those?" Kate asked from the porch door.

"You bet," Sal said.

"Don't give Boozer more than a splash. The vet says a little is OK, but not to overdo it. Funny, a dog that likes beer that much. Oh, wait a minute, Sallie, I'll be right back."

Kate popped out and returned in thirty seconds holding a dog dish. "Look at this. I took Boozer to a pet store last month. While I looked for a book there, he wandered around and came back with this in his mouth. Of all the things in that store, he found this." Kate held a dog bowl with the image of a hunting Labrador Retriever etched on the side. "Look at what it says."

Sal chuckled, "A Labrador is your best friend."

"Isn't that perfect? I give him a little beer in it sometimes." Kate rubbed Boozer's ears.

"So, what book did you buy?" Sal asked

"Book?" Kate said.

"At the pet store."

"Oh, I tried to cook him some special dog treats. He doesn't like the packaged things. All he wants is Nutter Butters."

"How did that go?"

"Not well, Nabisco won. So, Nutter Butters it is. But he doesn't get sick, and he's not fat."

"How did he get started on Nutter Butters?"

"I found a couple of bags in the pantry here when I was moving. I don't know why I took them. I found them again when Boozer was a little guy and gave him one. Sallie, he rolled onto his back and wiggled from side to side. Then he pumped his little legs into the air like he was in heaven."

"Yeah, he still does that sometimes. OK, Kate, you're the shrink. Let me ask you a question."

"Sure, Sallie. What's up?"

"If I didn't know better, I'd think that sometimes Boozer is actually answering me. He seems to communicate—you know—as if he understands what I'm saying."

Kate chuckled. "Yeah, he started doing that when he was about six months old. But don't over-think it. There are good empirical explanations for his behavior in animal psychology journals. Some dogs—not all and it is apparently rare—but some do respond to conversation. There's debate about whether they sense how to respond from the tone of your voice, or react to the length of your speech. And there are other possibilities. There's no real evidence that they comprehend what's said. You've probably seen dogs do this before in circus acts and shows like that. I think Boozer is most likely one of these gifted dogs." Kate laughed. "Although, there have been times when I've wondered too, and there are some highly credentialed professionals who argue that we have yet to discover the real intelligence levels of dogs."

Kate paused. "You know, Sallie, in the Eastern World, many argue that reincarnated friends and family *are* around us, communicating with us, and supporting us in our lives. And those who are convinced they've found a reincarnated loved one seem very sure and very contented. But, as I said, there's no factual evidence of any of that. It's most likely just projected perception driven by wishful thinking. It's not verifiable, just belief." Kate paused and chuckled. "Did I say *just* belief?'" We're finding on a regular basis what we thought was fact, to be wrong. *Maybe* belief is better, sometimes."

Sal nodded. "Either way, he's one smart fucking guy."

Without opening his eyes, Boozer turned his head and grunted.

Kate, Sal, and Boozer relaxed on the porch for over an hour. Sal filled Kate in on the London trip, describing his friends and the excursion to Amsterdam.

"Well," Kate said, "it's almost seven o'clock. I'll change and then let's go for Michigans. The stand will be closing soon for the season."

Michigan hot dogs, a fresh frank covered with spicy meat sauce and smothered with raw onions, was a North Country specialty Sal loved.

"Fantastic," Sal said.

"We'll take my microbus. The back seat's all set up for Boozer."

"As Kate left, Sal looked at Boozer. "A little more beer, Buddy?" Boozer woofed.

***

Kate started the microbus as Boozer and Sal piled in.

"That's one hell of a smooth sound for a VW," Sal said.

"I just had a Porsche engine put in. Helps me keep up on the interstate," Kate laughed.

"You *are* a rich hippie," Sal chuckled.

The hot dog stand looked like it was blown sideways in a hurricane. It had been that way for decades and hadn't collapsed yet. A carhop popped out and trotted to the microbus.

"What can I get for you?"

Kate ordered two Michigans with onions for herself and one without for Boozer. "The onions give him gas," she explained to Sal.

Sal went for three with and fries. The order came quickly on a tray the carhop attached to Kate's window. Kate found a plastic knife in her glove box and cut Boozer's Michigan into bite-sized pieces. She reached back and placed one in his mouth. He took it gently, chewed a few times, swallowed, and burped. After taking a bite of her own, Kate gave Boozer another piece.

"I've never seen a dog eat so politely," Sal remarked.

"Yup, he's a good boy. Aren't you a good boy?"

Sal savored the taste. He found English food bland, and there was only so much ethnic he could take. Michigans hit the spot. Once they finished, the carhop quickly cleared and they sped off.

Kate drove through Plattsburgh and pointed out some new restaurants and businesses.

"There's an Indian place here now. I tried it. It's really good."

Sal grimaced. "There's something about curry that gets me. It's more than the smell. Makes me sick. Reminds me of a bad time in my life."

"Really? You never told me about this."

"Someday." Sal looked out the window.

"Well, Boozer loves the Basmati rice. I mixed it with

hamburger when he had a bellyache. Now I make it for him often. It's amazing what he can eat and still stay so fit."

"Is he swimming much?"

"A little, but the lake is cold now. He prefers to play on the lawn." Kate patted Boozer's head.

They drove by a music store. "Oh, that reminds me, the piano guy came. He tuned and adjusted your player. He wanted me to be sure to tell you to go easy on it; the bellows are old, and he can't find replacements anymore. He said he'd keep looking but not to hope for a miracle. He said several times to tell you to be gentle."

"Just like Pop," Sal said and smiled.

"Your dad?"

"Yeah, he must have said the same thing a hundred times when I was a kid. 'Go easy on those old bellows, Sal; don't pump the damned thing so hard, they'll blow out.'" Sal chuckled.

"Oh, there's one other thing. You have a letter from the prison. It's on the bar. I didn't open it, but I can guess."

Sal nodded. "I'll look it over later." Fucking Johnny, he thought, there's always fucking Johnny.

Kate pulled down the driveway; Boozer hopped out and found his stick. Sal squinted into the setting sun. Covering his eyes, he tossed Boozer's stick to the corner of the west lawn. Boozer quickly retrieved it and sat next to Kate with his prize in his mouth.

"He's had enough for today," Kate said. "And you must be exhausted, Sallie."

"Yeah, it's past one-thirty in London."

"OK, I'll call in the morning and make breakfast when you're ready."

"Thanks, Kate, but we could go out."

"Nonsense, Sallie. It's our pleasure; right Boozer?" Boozer panted and woofed. Sal smiled and walked through the garage into Camp.

Sal popped a beer and took a rocker near the picture window. He yawned and struggled to focus on a sailboat anchoring in the bay. Stosh, he thought. I need to call Stosh. He grabbed his cell from his pocket, but then placed it on the end table. Not tonight, I'll call him tomorrow. He lumbered to the kitchen, poured the rest of his beer down the sink. In the bedroom, he looked in the mirror. As he emptied his pockets, he saw the reflection of the brooch. He remembered why the smell of curry repulsed him.

He flopped on the bed and adjusted his pillow. Within seconds the dream came.

Sitting in the back, Sal rode with Kate and Boozer in her microbus down a dirt road. They passed dozens of homemade tents and shacks. People cooked outside. The smell of curry filled the VW. Boozer hung his head outside the window and panted. Kate chatted about how pleasant the scent was. Kate and Boozer disappeared, the windows and windshield vanished, and Sal rode in a dark, empty van. The vehicle filled with water. Sal sat submerged but able to breathe. A water snake circled Sal's chest and bolted to Sal's face. The snake's head morphed into Jesse's. Jesse smiled, opened his mouth, and bared venomous teeth.

The water began to boil. "Stew in it a while," Jesse said as he slithered about. Jesse stopped, darted back to Sal's face, and laughed in a thunderous voice that blew Sal from the bus into a mining shaft. Sal lay face down on a flatbed cart. The cart began to roll on tracks to a deep pit roaring with heat and sparks from a furnace below.

Sal felt a tug. He saw Boozer digging in with all four legs, pulling back on the cart's rope. Boozer growled as he struggled to hold on, but the rope pulled free, and the cart accelerated. Boozer barked twice. The cart jolted to a halt, throwing Sal into the pit. Sal grabbed the pit's edge and hung above a vat of molten gold. The gold transformed into lentil soup and boiled over. The smell of curry made Sal sick. He reached for his stomach and held on with one hand. The pit's edge turned to wet clay, and his fingers slipped through. He heard Boozer yowling as he went into free fall.

Sal sprung up awake and drenched, as always. He performed the standard ritual—cleansing, then pouring a Crown Royal and sinking into the chair by the picture window. He began to analyze the dream. New players—same scenario, he thought. He looked out onto Lake Champlain. The moon shone from the Vermont side creating a long road of light. He smiled. He wouldn't be bothered again for a while. He thought of Jesse's prophecy that Sal would find peace from it all. He hoped the old snake was right—even if he was full of shit. Sal chuckled.

Less than twenty-four hours since he was in London. That all seemed so long ago. "Well, one thing's for sure," he whispered. "I'm back." Sal looked up at the clock and picked up the phone. Still time to call Stosh.

***

Ange did well; Sal thought as he slammed the heavy bag in the garage. The new gym was almost identical to the one at the river house. Everything an angry man needed to beat up the world—or at least to pulverize Johnny. Sal cleaned up, grabbed a cup of coffee, and sat at the bar. He picked up the letter from the prison. He paused and thought about throwing it out. Then he smirked and ripped it open. So, Johnny's sick and near the end. What's new? And the prison system wants to know if I have plans for his remains. The Clinton County dump sounds fine to me. Sal's eyes narrowed, and he took a sip—and now the fucking asshole is asking to see me. Sal laughed. Wants to get in his last jabs, something more for me to grind on. Fuck that. Sal held the letter up. "You've fucked up my life since I was twelve, Big Brother. Just die and go away."

Sal's phone rang.

"Good morning, Sallie," Kate said. "Are you ready for breakfast? I thought I'd bring it over."

"Sure, Kate, I'm just going through some old mail. See you in a few minutes?"

"Yup." Kate hung up.

Sal tossed the letter on the bar and refilled his coffee. He looked through the window onto Lake Champlain. The rhythmic waves soothed him. He shook his head. Maybe

Danny was right about hate. Was Salvatore Esposito just being an asshole? Johnny would be dead soon. If he wanted to see his little brother one more time—what the hell? What could he say that would be any worse than what he'd done and said before? And—as Jesse said—these were times of big change.

The visit wouldn't be for Johnny anyway. If the bastard got under Sal's skin again, Sal would know he'd been right. If not—then even a better ending. Either way, seeing the asshole would be more for the little brother than the big.

Sal smacked the side of his head. What the fuck am I thinking? Johnny has been nothing but a curse my entire life, and now I'm going soft on him? I just had another fucking dream, a fucking nightmare *he* caused, just like hundreds of others. Fuck Johnny Esposito.

Kate opened the door, and Boozer strolled in with a "good morning" woof.

"I hope you don't mind this," Kate said. "I haven't cooked in this kitchen for a long time, and I'm looking forward to it."

"It will be great. Nothing like the smell of breakfast in the fall."

Kate set down a large bag of groceries and went to work. As she prepped, she noticed the open letter on the bar.

"You read the letter from the prison?"

"Yeah."

"OK, I'll leave it alone."

Sal took a deep breath. "It says he's near the end, and he wants to see me. He's been dying of the same *cold* for three years. Now he wants to see me."

"And?"

"I'm busy."

"How many eggs?"

Sal chuckled. "Three, please. Ange is coming this afternoon. He'll be here a day or two. Let's get ahold of Ray and have dinner tomorrow night. I'll get some steaks. Is there a grill here?"

"There's the big built-in grill in this kitchen. Nothing for outside, I don't think."

"I'll pick one up; somehow I feel like charcoal. OK with you?"

"Yes, lovely. I haven't had a charcoal cooked steak in forever."

Sal and Kate chatted and ate. Kate gave Boozer some lean Canadian bacon and one scrambled egg. Sal watched in amazement as Boozer politely consumed his meal. While Kate cleared, Sal played a few chords on the piano.

"This sounds good," he said. "Ange is bringing a box of old rolls. We can try them out tonight."

***

Angelo carried in three bottles of Crown Royal XR. "The other booze is in the trunk. I thought we'd find a place for these first. This is one hell of a bar, Sal. There still must be a hundred unopened bottles. How long have they been here?"

"A long time. I asked my friend Ray to fire up the taps. He said he'd have it done by tomorrow night. We're having a little party."

"Great," Ange said. "And this kitchen, I didn't get a chance to look it over when we moved you in; it's perfect and right off the bar. Your friend knew how to live."

Ange made several trips, covering the counter with bottles. "OK, that's it for booze. Where do you want the piano rolls?"

Sal pointed to a spot near the piano. "How do they look?" Sal asked.

"Old," Ange said.

Sal and Ange puttered for an hour getting things in order and putting the new grill together. Sal opened the fridge and showed Ange the steaks.

"Fantastic," Ange said scanning the meat, vegetables, shrimp, cheeses, and other food Sal had stocked. "I guess you have moved in. This is better than the club—which is something we need to talk about."

Sal frowned and grabbed two beers. He handed a beer to Ange. They filled mugs and moved on the porch.

"Go on," Sal said as they sat.

"Well, you know the bar business—everyone who works for you considers themselves a partner and cuts themselves in for a percentage."

"Ange, are you saying someone is skimming."

"Yeah, the place is packed, but the bar is down."

"How much?"

"Almost twenty-five percent—no reason for it other than—"

"Theft."

"Yeah."

"Who?"

"I don't know exactly. It's too much for one guy. Probably

a kind of virus, you know? Sal, you need to be around more. This doesn't happen when you're there."

"Is Robert still managing?"

"Yeah."

"What do the others say, you know, my 'hard-working' partners?"

"I haven't talked to them. Thought you'd want to know first."

"You thought right—I thought Robert was smarter. Ten percent with a good bar staff and you look the other way. But twenty-five and you're insulted. This isn't casual. It can't happen without a system. Just how fucking stupid do they think we are? Booze comes in; booze goes out. The numbers change, and you find the reason. That's second-grade shit."

"With you away, they probably think no one's watching. I'm there almost every day, but they don't see me like they see you."

Sal nodded. "And what about the other thing?"

"What thing?"

"Don't fuck with me, Ange. If the staff sees guys showing up just to dick with your head, they won't take you seriously. You know that. Where's Frankie's wife?"

"In Vegas, I think."

"You think."

"Yeah, I haven't gone near her since those guys started coming around. Like you said. I thought they'd go once I backed off. But now she's calling and trying to see me, and she's getting pissed too. Who knows what bullshit she's telling Frankie. I really fucked up, Sal. I'm sorry."

"You're lucky you're not crippled or dead. But if that were the plan they'd just do it." Sal paused. "OK, one day back and right in the thick of it. I'll go down with you on Thursday. Don't tell anyone I'm coming, even Roger. No one, got it?"

Ange nodded and smiled, "With you there, it'll go away."

"And it will stay away when I'm not. It's time for some changes. In this business, you've got to fire someone every once in a while, anyway. Keeps the others on their toes. And maybe we can ease you out of your little love thing."

"I don't think Frankie's going to forget."

"You're finally learning, Ange. But if he's left town, and the game is different, he might get tired of it."

Sal stood and looked at the shoreline. Boozer was lying on Turtle Rock watching the waves. What a life, Sal thought. "Hey, Buddy," Sal yelled, "want to join us?" Boozer snapped his head around, sprang to his feet, bolted uphill over the steps to the lawn, grabbed his stick, and trotted to the porch door.

"Remember Boozer, Ange?" Sal said.

"Nobody could forget Boozer," Ange said and rubbed Boozer's ears. How are you, Boozer? How are ya, big boy?"

"Any room for a woman among all that testosterone?" Kate yelled from the lawn as she joined the group. She welcomed Ange with a hug and took a seat. Sal handed her a beer.

"This is good!" she said as she sipped. "Sallie, I have a favor to ask. I've been invited to a retreat this weekend and was hoping Boozer could stay with you. I'll be back on Tuesday."

Sal looked at Ange and back at Kate. "I have to go down to the club on Thursday. Seems to be a problem there. How would you feel about Boozer joining me? I'll take good care of him–or maybe the other way around. Right, Buddy? We'll meet you back here on Tuesday. What do you think?"

Boozer barked, circled twice, and sat back down, his tail sweeping the floor.

"Looks like the decision has been made," Kate said and laughed. "But, Sallie, don't give him too much beer. Remember what the vet said—just a splash once in a while."

Sal nodded and smiled. "OK, Boozer, road trip." Boozer barked again.

Ray knocked at the back entrance to the great room and looked through the window. "Could someone get the door please!" he hollered. Ange hurried over and opened the door. Ray hoisted in a quarter keg of Molson beer. "There's one more barrel—the ale you asked for, Sal—it's in the trunk. Let's get these taps back online."

Kate greeted Ray and said, "While you gents work on that, I've got pies baking for tonight. See you soon."

Now on a mission, the men moved both kegs in place. Ray reached into his pocket for his glasses and examined the refrigerator temperature and CO2 pressure before twisting the tap fitting into place. "OK," he said. Sal pulled the handles until clear beer flowed.

"There's a lot of foam on the drain covers," Sal said.

"That's OK," Ray answered. "These kegs jiggled around a lot; the foam is natural."

Ange brought three frosted mugs from the freezer. Boozer ran to the porch and fetched his bowl. Sal splashed a little beer into Boozer's dish, then scooped up some foam and plopped it on top. "There you go, Buddy," he said. Boozer took a casual lick. Then he looked up at Sal and smiled.

One by one the companions pulled the tap and tilted their

mugs, letting the beer flow against the side. Then they quickly leveled their mugs to capture a half-inch head. Once they all had a fresh brew in hand, Sal raised his beer.

"Chins up," he toasted.

"Chins up," Ray and Ange repeated.

Boozer woofed.

The first round went down quickly. As Sal and Ange refilled, Ray popped out to his truck and returned with three books.

"Sal, these are yours. I borrowed them from Jimmy. They're from his library."

"You don't need to return stuff like that, Ray. Jimmy would want you to have them. You just keep them."

"Thanks, but they belong here."

"OK. What are they about?"

"Philosophy and mythology. Jimmy knew a lot about both."

Sal smiled. "Say, Ray, did you come across any snakes in those?"

"Yeah sure. Snakes and serpents are a big thing. Snakes usually represent flux in life, change, transformation, all that. Lots of snake-like gods in many different cultures."

"Good or bad gods?"

"Both, usually good in the East. In the West, serpents are usually bad, sneaky, betrayers—you know, like in the Garden of Eden. Dragons and serpents are similar, wicked hoarders blowing fire on everything, stealing gold, and kidnapping virgins they have no use for. But in the East, dragons are usually full of life and fun, and snakes symbolize rejuvenation, probably because they shed their skins. Think of that, they wriggle their way out of one life into a new one and start over. Wish I could do shit like that."

"Me too," Sal and Ange said in sync.

"Jimmy has a broad collection of books on that stuff—other philosophy too. He was really into it. He thought about going back for a Ph. D. But—"

"He told me that." Sal paused. "Ever hear of a snake with an enormous head?"

"Yeah, a couple. I don't remember specifics, but they're usually interveners, you know, show up from time to time to set things straight. Usually, they're men who transform back and forth. The old Hindu stories have a lot of that going on. There's probably some stuff on that in the study."

"Do any drink beer?"

"I don't know, but I can't imagine not," Ray chuckled.

Sal refilled and sat back. He swiveled his stool and looked at the lake as Ange and Ray talked about the Adirondacks. Boozer strolled over and sat by his side. The clear fall air made Vermont seem near. Sal watched a sailboat in the center of Champlain and thought of Stosh.

Holding two pies, Kate worked the porch door open and pushed it shut with her rear. She put the pies on the counter and grabbed a frosted mug.

"I would have opened that for you," Sal said.

"No need, just a door. A few things on my hands won't keep me from getting through."

Sal smiled, and Kate drew a fresh beer.

After two hours partying, Sal and Boozer went to the north

lawn and fired up the new grill. Sal stood back and savored the smell of burning hickory. Flames fed the red tipped charcoal.

"The coals should be ready in about fifteen minutes," Sal said to Boozer. "Four rare and one well done— Ange has fucked up tastes. The guy doesn't even like sausage. But if he wants his steak like his boot soles, so be it."

"How's it coming?" Kate said from the porch door.

"Just fine," Sal said. "What are the guys up to?"

"Angelo is on the phone, and Ray is looking for something in Jimmy's study—I mean in your study."

"Jimmy's study sounds better. Let's keep it that."

"Yup. I've got the salad ready. Did you talk to Stosh last night?"

"Yeah, he's got an idea for a business venture. Actually, he called it an 'adventure.' He didn't explain but wants to meet. The plan seems to revolve around a woman he and Deb know. I suggested they all come for Thanksgiving. As I said, he wasn't specific about any of it, but it will be good to have friends for the holidays."

"That's great," Kate said and left for the kitchen.

A strong wind blowing through the trees released hundreds of leaves.

"It won't be long now," Sal said to Boozer. "November is just around the corner. I wonder what Stosh has in mind. It's not like him to hold back on an idea. Whatever it is, it will be good to see him. Shit, I hope Deb isn't trying to set me up. She did that once before. A fucking disaster. No, she wouldn't try that again. I hope. Well, there's plenty of room here, the bar is open again, and Thanksgiving is the best of all holidays in my book. It will be one hell of a good time. OK, let's get the steaks in, Buddy."

Boozer stood and followed Sal into Camp.

Ange sawed away at his meat finally cutting a piece loose. "Perfect," he said.

Sal shook his head. Kate placed a bowl of jasmine rice on the table next to a garden salad mixed with fresh vegetables.

"What a meal," Ray said. "Thanks, you guys. Say, Sal; I found a book about serpents and mythology for you. Look at the chapter on nagas."

"Nagas?" Sal said.

"Yeah, they're all over the East. Half-human half-snake, usually associated with water—you know, rivers and lakes and the like. They guard treasure. Sometimes they show up as hooded cobras, real big heads, and pronounced fangs. You know, the whole serpent thing is ancient. Lots of snakes attached to spines or staffs. The Hindus and Buddhists still focus on the Kundalini."

"Yup, now you're in my world," Kate said. "My meditations are based on the path of the Kundalini. The serpent flows up the spine marking the seven energy centers, the chakras."

"And, Sal," Ray continued, "the symbol of medicine is the staff of Asclepius with the snake entwined around it—interesting eh, Doctor? Lots of good stuff in that book."

"My father had a recliner made of Naugahyde, any relation?" Ange said.

Sal smirked. "Eat your shoe, Ange."

Sal reached for the book. "I'll have to look this over. Thanks, Ray." Ray nodded smiling. "Tomorrow afternoon Ange and I leave for Saratoga. I didn't plan on this when I asked you to bring the taps back online, but we'll only be a few days."

"The beer will stay fresh," Ray said.

"Boozer's going with them, his first trip away from home," Kate said. "Now Sallie, remember what we agreed—about the beer."

"Yeah, no problem, Kate."

"And I'll see you on Tuesday?"

"Yes, what we have to do won't take long."

"Will you see your mom?"

"Yeah, I'll stop for a while. She won't know me, but that doesn't matter at this point. That reminds me, I'll need Boozer's vaccination records. They allow pets but only with the paperwork. The fucking place smells so bad you wonder why they give a shit."

"I'll bring it over in the morning."

Soon Sal was sorting through the piano rolls and smiling. He reached under the player piano's keyboard, pulled a strap, and the pedals smacked down on the floor. He fitted the roll in the upper cradle, connected it, set the tempo lever and began to pump. Kate smiled and hummed as the piano played "Moon River."

CHAPTER VIII

Monkey Business

Boozer stepped through the door to Sal's river house and strolled around as if on familiar turf. He stopped and looked out onto the Hudson.

"See something you like, Buddy?" Sal said. "We should get some sleep. We won't go to the club until around 2:30 when it's closed and the staff has left. I had surveillance put in a couple of years ago. We only used it for a few months until the whole idea seemed unnecessary. Tonight, we'll hook it back up. Tomorrow night we watch from my office. No one will know we're even in the building.

"I'm guessing the bartenders are too smart to pocket cash. If my hunch is right, it's a system. Ring up almost everything as lower cost drinks. At the end of the night, the cash till is way over. You just take the extra and everything balances. Most everyone would be in.

"Robert's the kingpin. When we first opened, I said it was a mistake for the manager to also be the head bartender. When the same guy who's feeding the till cashes out, there's no scrutiny, and this kind of shit will happen. Everyone gets a cut, everyone looks clean, and no one's the wiser. Except for the accountant who sees discrepancies between the booze bills and the cash flow.

"You see, Buddy, they've probably been doing this for a while. But they got greedy. You can't hide big losses. Little ones are expected, but big ones—.

"I was supposed to be a minor player in the joint, though I own most of it. But my partners—the guys who were going to stay on top of things—turned out to be lazy fucking boneheads. I can hear them now—'Don't worry, Sal, we'll take care of everything. All you'll have to do is be around once in a while to schmooze and bring in the customers.' Yeah, what a crock of shit.

"So, Ange is right; the staff needs to know I'm watching. Tomorrow night they'll find out for fucking sure."

Boozer jumped onto the couch and plopped his head on a pillow. Sal pushed his recliner back and folded his hands on his stomach. They were soon asleep.

Sal awoke at two o'clock and patted Boozer's head. "Come on, Bud, time to get up."

Boozer stood, shook his head, and drank some water. Sal gulped black coffee. "The club closes at midnight on Thursdays, so everyone's gone by now. We'll get something to eat on the road after we're done."

Sal and Boozer hopped into Sal's Mercedes and sped down the deserted streets to the club. They entered the back door to the private office, off limits to all staff.

"There you are," Ange said standing on a step ladder holding a bundle of wires. "Everything looks good."

Ange stuffed the wiring back in place and refitted the ceiling panel. Sal walked to a counter near a large desk and threw a switch. Nine television monitors lit up showing all parts of the club.

"You're sure nobody's here?" Sal asked. Ange nodded, and Sal opened the door to the club. He carried the ladder to cameras hidden above the cash registers and focused them on each register's large red display. He pushed keys, and a number appeared. "How's that, Ange?"

"The figures are clear as a bell," Ange yelled from the back.

One by one Sal adjusted the remaining cameras. Boozer sniffed about.

"OK, we're ready for tonight," Sal said. He poured a Crown XR and a white wine, and a splash of beer in a bowl.

After their drinks, the three drove to an all-night greasy spoon miles away where Sal guessed none of the staff would go. Sal told the waitress Boozer was a service dog for Ange's diabetes. She made Boozer a plate, placed it on the floor, and rubbed his ears.

"We should know what's going on soon," Ange said.

"Yeah, and then what?"

"What do you mean, Sal?"

"We can't fire the whole staff, and the reason we kept Robert in the first place was his draw—particularly with the ladies. I think we're limited to some selective pruning. Besides, Ange, a guy who's been caught in the act might be the least likely to fuck up a second time. And I don't want to be living at this joint while we try to rebuild the whole staff. Ange—I think we need to get things back on track with the least disruption. Then I'm getting out."

Ange's eyes popped. "Sal, without you —"

"Without me what? The others will have to do some fucking work? This was supposed to be a breeze, and it's been nothing but an albatross. If the place isn't watched night and day, this shit happens. And, Ange, I don't know this business well enough. I broke my own rule, just like with the stock market—if you don't know it, stay out.

"But you do, Ange, you know this game. And you've done most of the management anyway. Think about it, Ange. In the spring, if you want the place, I'll buy out the others and sell to you at a price you'll like. You'll have an unlimited source of wandering women and a place to set up as you like."

"Sal, are you serious?"

"Yeah, damn straight I am."

"I don't know, Sal, I'm a management guy—I never owned anything. I don't know."

"Just think about it."

***

Sal parked at a strip mall and walked with Boozer to the club. Parked in his private space sat a new Lexus SUV. He quietly opened the club's back door. Inside, Ange paced from monitor to monitor taking notes.

"Whose Lexus?" Sal asked.

"Robert's," Ange said.

"Isn't that a red flag?"

"He said an aunt died—left him money. Probably bullshit. He bought it a month ago."

Sal smirked. "Almost definitely bullshit."

Boozer hopped onto a small couch and watched the door while Sal and Ange stared at the monitors.

"Yeah, it's what I thought," Sal said. "You see every second or third time they're pouring top shelf and ringing up the cheap stuff in the well. And import bottled beer is going down as draught. The customers can't see the display so they don't know what their change should be. We only run tabs for credit cards we hold behind the bar—and, shit, at our club that's only about thirty percent of the night till. So, only cash customers are scammed, and there are *plenty* of them. I doubt this is going on during the day. And, Ange, I've noticed Robert's clean—smart. Only his stooges are cheating. Say, Ange, who are the new ones? There are two girls and a guy I've never seen."

"Came in last month. Robert hired them."

"And the new bouncers? Robert again?"

"Yeah."

"You know, one looks familiar. Yeah, the one in the red shirt, that guy's one of Frankie's boys. No wonder you've had trouble. One of the dickheads is in the house." Ange's face went blank.

"Say, who's this guy?" Sal pointed to a monitor as an older, medium height man with a full head of bright white hair strolled in wearing a Yankees jacket. The bouncers respectfully nodded, and the man made his way to the bar.

"I don't know. He comes in occasionally—though this is the first time I've seen him this late. He usually has one or two Budweisers and leaves. He seems to look around a lot, but he's polite and the bartenders like him. They say he speaks well, probably a retired teacher or something. He's never caused any trouble that I know of. I don't think anyone knows his name. Why?"

"Nothing, he just seems to carry some weight. Maybe not. I'm just curious."

At two o'clock Robert cleared the few remaining customers and closed. Ange prepared to enter the bar and confront the staff.

"Hold on," Sal said. "Let's watch a little longer. There's some skimming going on, but it doesn't look to me like it's enough to match the losses. After-hours could be interesting."

Sal, Ange, and Boozer watched the bar staff shut down the registers and join the bouncers for a drink. Robert locked the cash drawers in a small room, checked his watch and unlocked a side door. In minutes, a group of young partiers tiptoed in and joined the staff. Robert counted and relocked the door. With the outside lights off and the blinds closed, Robert turned on the music and the drinks began to flow.

After several quick martinis, one of the women climbed onto the bar and slowly stripped while the others clapped and whistled. A couple moved to a corner and started making out passionately. The man lowered his date's top and began fondling her breasts. She unzipped his jeans. He lifted her onto a table, raised her skirt, and they began having sex. Others watched and grinned as they prepared to follow suit.

"Well, I think we have our answer," Sal said and chuckled. "You've got to give it to them for their balls—oh, and other anatomic features as well." Sal and Ange laughed, Boozer woofed.

Sal spotted a baseball bat leaning against the desk. He grabbed the handle and pretended to swing. Take that, Johnny, he thought, grinning. "We put this thing in here for just such an occasion," he said.

Boozer barked twice, Sal looked at his buddy's brown eyes and thought of Danny. He saw himself holding the blackjack high over his head ready to strike the skinhead. He felt nauseous. He put the bat down, took a deep breath, and exhaled.

"You're right, Boozer, no need to ramp up the situation." Sal cracked his knuckles and surveyed his fists. "I'll use *these* if I have to. OK, let's go."

Boozer pranced through the door and headed toward the bar.

"Who let that fucking mutt in here?" Robert yelled.

"I did," Sal said standing by a back table. The bouncers looked over, surprised, and then began to move toward Sal and Ange. "Are you sure you want to do that, boys? I'm Salvatore Esposito, and I own this joint. Now don't get me wrong; I love a good fight. But my buddy has suggested we do this peacefully. Your choice."

The bouncer in the red shirt put his hand on his partner's shoulder and shook his head.

"Everyone who doesn't work here, get your clothes on and get out," Sal said. "We're open six nights a week. The kitchen serves until ten, and the bar closes at two o'clock. You're all welcome then. Proper attire is required; stripping and fucking are prohibited on the premises. Robert, open the side door. All other staff assemble at the bar and wait. No drinks."

The male lover from the corner stood and chuckled. Sal bolted toward him.

"You find me funny?" Sal said. "Put your little prick back in your pants while you still have it and get your fucking ass out of here."

The couple quickly dressed and ran to the door. The other partiers scooted out behind, and Robert locked up.

"Robert, in my office NOW!" Sal ordered.

Once in the office, Sal said, "You stand," and sat behind his desk. "How long has this shit been going on? And Robert, don't fuck with me; give it up straight the first time. I'm not Judge Judy."

Robert paused and took a deep breath. "We started in the spring—April maybe. First, it was once every few weeks with six or seven of us." Robert rubbed his hands on his thighs. "Then it grew and happened almost every Friday."

"And you figured the booze would just go unnoticed?"

"I tried to hide it. I knew I was pushing it." Robert began to pace. "I know I fucked up, Sal. Just fire me. You don't need to do the lecture."

"Where did you pick up the bouncer in the red?"

"He came in one day. Said he was a friend of one of your partners. He hung around awhile, and then I put him to work."

"How much did Frankie Napoli have to do with it?" Robert looked perplexed. "You know about the shit Mr. Costello has been going through?" Robert was silent. "I asked you a fucking question."

"Yeah, I know."

"And you know this guy is—how should we put it—an acquaintance of Frankie's?"

Robert raised his head, eyes wide open. "Fuck no, Mr. Esposito. I didn't. The son-of-a-bitch."

"There are three bartenders I've never seen?"

"Yeah, they're new."

"And the others, the ones they replaced?"

"I fired them."

"Why?"

"I thought they were skimming."

Sal broke into laughter. "I've been watching the tills all night."

Robert looked at the monitors, swallowed hard, and nodded.

"No, you fired them to make room for your people." Robert hesitated and nodded.

There was a knock on the door. "Come in Ange." The door opened, and Boozer trotted in closely followed by Ange. "Robert and I are just coming to an understanding. OK, here's what we're going to do. Robert, you will remain in our employment."

Robert shook his head.

"No, no, you just listen," Sal continued. "Quitting isn't an option. Do you understand me?"

Robert nodded.

"You'll be here for six months. After that, we'll reassess. Choose two of the new bartenders and fire them."

Robert's face went blank.

"That's right, *you* choose, *you* fire them, and *you* stay. You won't be making any friends tonight. Now, you can keep one of the new bouncers for a while as long as he bar-backs and does other grunt work. Immediately bring back the old bartenders you fired. The shithead in red goes. If the other guy decides he wants to quit, make sure he knows he'll have to leave the area if he expects to find work, just like you—if you had that option. And Robert, when you tell them, take responsibility for a change. You could pass on the blame like a fucking pussy, but then you'd *be* that fucking pussy, wouldn't you? I'll deal with the red-shirted turd; you take care of the rest. Do we have an understanding?"

Still looking down, Robert nodded.

"And one more thing. If you ever call my friend a mutt again, you and I will be going a few rounds. From here on you'll refer to him as Mr. Boozer, got it?"

Robert nodded and stepped over to Boozer. "Sorry Mr. Boozer," he said and patted Boozer's head.

Boozer snarled. Sal smiled. "He's got a low tolerance for insincerity. Just the apology was sufficient."

Robert's hands swayed palms up as he explained the situation to the staff. One female bartender's mouth opened wide as she stood firm and yelled back. The other just retrieved her purse from the back of the bar and walked out. The male bartender nodded. With Boozer by his side, Sal strolled over to the bouncer in the red shirt. "Your services will no longer be required," Sal said.

The bouncer nodded. "No problem Mr. Esposito," he said.

"Oh," Sal continued, "And tell Frankie hello."

“Will do,” he said smirking. He winked at Ange and swaggered out.

“You join us over here,” Sal said to the other bouncer. Sal moved to the now screaming female bartender behind the bar and pointed to the door. She frantically gathered her things and stormed out yelling profane insults.

Robert took the bouncer aside. As Robert explained the new terms of his employment, the bouncer shook his head and clenched his fists. Sal stepped over and intervened.

“You know this job is the only one available to you within fifty miles. Think about it carefully.”

“Fuck you,” the bouncer said.

Sal laughed. “Is that your decision?”

The bouncer turned and moved back. “Come on, you fucking sleazy Guinea.”

Sal faced him with a grin. “OK, make your move. I was hoping for a reason to slam somebody tonight.”

The bouncer punched Sal in the chest. Sal stepped back.

“It’s always best to go for the head with the first swing. You never know if you’re going to get another,”

Sal slammed his fist into the bouncer’s nose. Blood flowed as he bent over and grabbed his face.

“And the nose is best. If you hit it correctly, the bleeding alone incapacitates the opponent. More?”

The bouncer shook his head. Robert handed him a bar rag wrapped over ice.

“Now, one more time, are you still with us?” Sal asked.

The bouncer looked stunned. Sal extended his hand, and the bartender shook it. “Fuck yes,” he said.

"Good," Sal said. "And one more thing, are you Italian?" The bouncer shook his head. "Understand something; the term Guinea is reserved for the use of Italians only. Don't use it again."

The corner of the bouncer's swelling face curled into a half smile. "Sorry, Mr. Esposito," he said.

Sal nodded. "OK, Robert, first thing in the morning see if you can get two of the old bar staff back. Give them raises if you have to. I don't need to spell out what to expect if this shit happens again. You guys get this place cleaned up and get some sleep. Tomorrow we start fresh."

In the office, Ange shut down the surveillance and sat on the couch. Sal plopped into his desk chair. "Sal, I'm not second guessing but—"

"Ange, I told you, we can't fire everyone without shutting down, and I want Robert right here where I can keep an eye on him. And, for the regulars, we need some continuity. It needs to look like there was never a problem. You know, I knew he'd fire the women. It's the men who'll be loyal to him. And to us, once the old bartenders are back. But I am concerned about one thing."

"What?"

"This was far too easy. Frankie's boy just gave in and trotted off. He's the one I expected to fight. There was no risk for him. Win or lose; he'd go to Frankie looking like a tough hero. Nope, this was much too easy—I can't see a reason."

Sal heard a knock on the door. "Ange, will you and Boozer meet me at the bar, please? I have one more thing to work out with Robert."

Robert entered and held the door as Ange and Boozer left.

"Close it," Sal said as he fumbled in his desk drawer. "Ah, there they are, good. Robert, show me your shiny new Lexus." Robert's brows raised and he rubbed his hands against his pants as he followed Sal outside. Sal gave him three children's marbles. "Open your gas cap," Sal said. Robert looked puzzled but complied. "Now put those in your gas tank."

"Sal—"

"I said, put them in."

One by one Robert pushed the marbles past the metal flap and into the tank.

"Now, when you stop or accelerate those will roll around and clink. Maybe, once in a while, they'll make you stall. When you hear them, remember, I'm watching you. You'll leave them there until I say otherwise."

Robert's eyes narrowed, and he exhaled.

"You're one lucky man, Robert. Don't fuck with me again. Now get out of here; I'll see you tomorrow."

Sal joined Angelo and Boozer at the bar. He paused and then walked behind the bar. He poured a Crown XR and white wine and pulled a splash of beer into a bowl from the Molson tap. Boozer circled and sat.

"OK, I think we're back on track," Sal announced. Ange nodded.

Boozer plopped down, rolled onto his back, and pumped his legs into the air as he grunted and wiggled from left to right. Sal smiled.

***

"OK Ange, thanks for the call," Sal said and hung up.

"Well, Boozer, things went well last night. Ange says it was one of the best Saturdays we've had. The old bartenders are back, and things appear to be smooth for the time being. Tomorrow we're homeward bound—after we visit Ma."

Sal looked out onto the river and sipped his Crown Royal. Boozer curled up in an oversized chair. With his head on his paws and looking at Sal, he listened.

"You're a good sounding board, Buddy. Ma's in the dog house—sorry, bad analogy. She's starting to hallucinate and becoming paranoid. And she's become aggressive. Apparently, she went after another patient last week. If they have to relocate her, she'll lose her suite. That will do her in." Sal sipped from a glass of Crown. "Alzheimer's is a shit thing."

Sal took another sip and looked around the room. "You know my pop loved this place. He planned it for years before he even knew where he would build it—every detail was thought out. He saved up, put the money aside, and sacrificed. Can you imagine—a tailor saving for a place like this? How many suits and dresses did he have to stitch? That's probably why I didn't see him much—he was always working.

"We had a nice place in Plattsburgh near the shop. I liked that house. It was big enough, and people were always coming and going. Yeah, I was happy there when I was a kid. When we moved, they tore it down to make way for an office building—or some shit. Now the only place up there that means anything to me is Camp. I'm glad I bought it from Kate. Too big for her, and it feels like home."

Sal paused and smiled. "You know? Come to think of it there is one other place, that spot where Jimmy and I had our fort. We'll have to go by there sometime and see if the fucking pole barn they cleared it for is still there. I was happy there too—at our fort I mean. I think about it when I need to calm down—you know, it's my mental happy place. Maybe I should buy that property and put it back the way it was."

Sal smirked. "No—it couldn't be the same."

Sal drank his glass empty and poured another. He looked around again. "Ma was around a lot when I was a kid. She used to tell me I was a good boy; nothing meant more to me. And she read me all sorts of books. Let me show you something."

Sal shuffled to a bookcase in the dining room and returned thumbing through a copy of *The Ramayana*. "This was one of her favorites."

He smiled and opened the book wide to show Boozer a picture of Hanuman. "Look at this guy. He's been driving me nuts lately. I went to London to get away from him and his friends. And there he was, staying in the same fucking room." Sal laughed. "But I've sort of connected with him. He reminds me a little of—well, me."

Sal took another long sip. He put the book down and sat quietly.

Sal reached for the bottle of Crown and poured another drink. "Now Ma thinks Johnny lives here. And Ma thinks Johnny's the doctor. She doesn't know who I am, but she talks about Johnny every time I visit her. Now she says Johnny's a good boy—what she always said about me. I'll never hear that again."

Sal stood, reached into his pocket and took out the brooch. "Did I ever show you this? This is how I remember Johnny. I've been carrying it around for forty years. Every once in a while, it pricks my leg just to let me know it's there. It's ruined more pockets than I can count. But I carry the fucking thing around religiously. I did some bad shit, Buddy. Johnny got me into it—Johnny and that Buzzy Kline asshole."

Sal paused, took a gulp and sat. "But I did it, and I'll live with it. Ah fuck, it's not that bad. Some days, when I'm busy, I don't even think about it. But I did tonight. That baseball bat sparked it. I wanted to take it and bust someone's head open. You know I almost smashed a guy's head in London. But I didn't. My friend kept me from doing it." Sal chuckled. "A friend kept me from it tonight, too."

Sal smiled at Boozer and took another sip. "I used to swing at anyone who looked at me the wrong way. It's not as bad now. But the anger is still there. And the letter the prison sent about Johnny hasn't helped. I want to smash his fucking skull in. Well, he won't be around much longer anyway." Sal grinned. "Then I'll have to find something else to hate."

Sal sat glassy-eyed and silent for several minutes.

"We'll make big changes this spring, Buddy. I've been thinking about it for a while. The fucking stock market fiasco changes things a little, but I've had enough. There's no thrill in making money anymore. Time to do something else—I just wish I knew what."

Sal and Boozer relaxed awhile longer. They both began to yawn, and Sal stood.

"OK, I'm turning in. See you in the morning."

Boozer turned on his side and grunted. Sal took it to mean, "Good night."

***

Sal pulled open the back door to his Mercedes. Boozer jumped in and sat behind the front passenger seat where he could see and hear his friend. Sal lowered Boozer's window and sped down the road onto Route 87.

"We'll hit the Home early before it gets crowded. Most of the visitors are a pain in the ass, lots of complaining and weeping and other maudlin shit."

Boozer put his head out the window and panted as they cruised. The fresh fall wind made his nostrils flair, and his jowls inflate. Sal weaved from lane to lane in heavy traffic until the northbound cars became scarce. Exiting the interstate, he took a back road leading to the side lot of the nursing home. He looked at his watch and nodded. "Right on schedule, Buddy."

The nurse at the front desk waved her hands and scolded an orderly. Sal and Boozer waited until she calmed down. "Do you have papers for the dog?" she said. Sal handed her Boozer's information. She glanced at them and handed them back. "The supervising nurse needs to speak with you immediately, Mr. Esposito," she snapped. Sal's patience evaporated.

"It's Dr. Esposito," Sal barked, "and the nurse can find me in my mother's room."

The attendant smirked. "Whatever," she said.

Sal's eyes flared. Boozer nudged Sal's leg. Sal took a deep breath and led Boozer down the hall to his mother's suite.

Sal's mother sat staring out the window, her back to the door.

"How are you today, Ma?" Sal said.

"Is that you, Johnny?" she replied.

"It's Sal, Ma."

Sal's mother turned and stared. "Who are you?" she said, "and stop calling me Ma. You don't even know what it means, and I'm not your mother. My son is a doctor, and his name is Johnny. Is that your dog?"

"He's a friend's; his name is Boozer."

"Does he bite?"

"No."

"Too bad, there's a man down the hall I want him to bite."

Sal looked around the room. "Where's your stereo?"

"They took it."

"Who took it, Ma?"

"I said, stop calling me that. They did, the ones who are out to get me. The ones who helped him steal my songs."

The supervising nurse walked in.

"Where's my mother's stereo?" Sal said.

"Could I talk to you in the hallway please, Dr. Esposito," the nurse whispered.

"Are you a doctor?" Sal's mother said. "You must know my son Johnny. He's a doctor too. Could you get him for me? I need to talk to him."

"You want to wait here, Buddy? I'll be right back." Boozer stepped over to Sal's mother, licked her hand, and sat beside her.

"You're a good dog," Ma said. "Would you bite someone for me?"

"OK, fill me in," Sal said in the hallway.

"As you can see she's become much more aggressive. Last week she tried to kill another resident."

Sal's eyes widened. "Tried to kill?"

"Yes. He's a few doors down the hall. He has severe sleep apnea and requires a CPAP device to keep his airways open and his breathing consistent." Sal nodded. "Your mother snuck into his room and unplugged the machine. A nurse saw her as she left. She checked his room and restarted the device.

Your mother doesn't deny anything. She insists the man stole songs from her and intends to kill her so she can't expose him. Doctor, she thinks the man is Johnny Mercer, and she's convinced she wrote most of his songs. She's especially adamant about 'Moon River.'"

Sal shook his head and then began to chuckle. Soon he was laughing. The supervisor looked serious, and then cracked a smile and joined in.

"This really *is* serious now that she's acted out." the supervisor said, still snickering.

"What happened to her stereo?"

"One afternoon, before the incident, she turned it up full blast and started to scream, 'Johnny Mercer, you stole my song! Johnny Mercer, you stole my song!' Then she yelled out some gibberish calling him a 'Kuttey' and a something that sounded like 'Ka-mean-a' I think. We didn't know what she was saying or talking about, but when she wouldn't stop, we had to confiscate the stereo."

"Kuttey and Ka-mean-a? What the hell. Where would she get words like that? And you've got no idea what they mean?

"No, but nonsense expressions aren't uncommon with a condition like hers. And she could be pulling something back from childhood, from a story or expression she heard then. Something so remote she'd never remember it under normal conditions."

"OK, where do we go from here?" Sal said.

"She's had no problems with any of the other residents, so I don't think she's generally violent. And we've had incidents of incompatibility before—although never this severe. But she's so focused on this man I don't think she'll stop until he or she is gone, and I can't ask that he leave when *her* behavior is the problem."

"Could he or she be moved?"

"She knows where he is, so moving her probably wouldn't make a difference. We have no other place for him. He's in a basic room. He has no family, and some of the cost is already being deferred. The only other accommodation that's open is a suite, like your mom's, in another wing. She wouldn't see him there, but the cost is prohibitive. And I don't believe she'll leave him alone wherever he is."

"As long as he's alive."

"Yes, and we intend to keep him that way."

"Yeah, of course, but if she thinks he's dead, she'll leave him alone."

"Doctor, we can't give her any information about another

patient, especially a lie. If you're suggesting we tell her he's dead, no. And that still doesn't solve the problem of his room. She will inevitably see him if he stays where he is."

"Let's do this in stages. First the room. Move him to the suite in the other wing. I'll pay his costs. Is that acceptable?"

"Well, yes, but it is expensive. The same amount as your mother's room."

"Fine, we'll do that then. Second, there's no need to tell her *he's* dead. The problem isn't *him*; the problem is Johnny Mercer. Johnny Mercer *is* dead, and we'll simply tell her that."

The supervisor thought and nodded.

"Then," Sal continued, "once the change is made and if she calms down, give her stereo back to her. OK?"

"If it all works. But remember she's losing ground. There could come the point where we can no longer keep her, and she has to move to an advanced Alzheimer's center."

"I understand. Now I would suggest that you move him. Make sure Ma knows the room is empty. Then I'll tell her about Johnny Mercer. We'll Let her make the connection."

The supervisor smiled. "This is very generous of you."

Sal smiled back. "If you could, draw up the necessary papcrwork, I'll sign while I'm here, and we'll wrap it up. And one more thing, if you could. Your receptionist could use a personality."

"Can't help you there."

They both chuckled, and the supervisor left for her office.

Ma faced the courtyard with Boozer still sitting next to her. "Who's that?" she snapped.

"It's me, Ma." Sal's mother swiveled around. "You again?

I told you not to call me that. Do you like my dog?" Boozer licked her hand, stood, strolled over to Sal, and sat. "I think he likes you. His name is Blackie. I've had him for years."

Sal grinned and looked at Boozer. Boozer opened his mouth and panted.

The receptionist did her best with her forced apology. Sal didn't care; the problem was resolved—at least for the time being. Preoccupied with celebrating Johnny Mercer's demise, Ma didn't notice when Boozer and Sal left. But Sal regretted that she didn't sing this time. He wondered if he'd ever hear her sing again.

He vowed to visit at least weekly from now on. But right now, he and Boozer would jump in the Mercedes and head for Camp where there were two fresh kegs. And some peace.

CHAPTER IX

Sita

Salvatore's boots crunched the dry, dead leaves as he plodded down the path to the clearing near the lake. Fall had thinned the woods, stripping all but the evergreens and leaving a rich pine scent. He drew the smell through his nostrils and exhaled a small cloud from his lips. Stick in mouth, Boozer jumped and ran, making his own slapdash trail and chasing an occasional squirrel. Sal sat on his usual rock and watched Lake Champlain.

A cold November wind nipped Sal's face. Soon it would bite. Vermont rested hidden behind the mist. Frothing whitecaps covered the water. Boozer circled Sal twice and sat. Sal rubbed his buddy's ears.

"Thanksgiving is Thursday, Buddy. I'm glad everyone's coming. Stosh will be frozen though. He hasn't left Florida in the late fall for years. His blood will be as thin as his head can be thick—thick as gold, thank God. I have no idea what he has in mind, but we'll know in a few hours."

"I hope he likes the steaks. I had the butcher cut them just as I remembered. They're always a good thing for a new guest too—unless she's one of those health food nuts. Well, no one mentioned any pain-in-the-ass dietary restrictions. You know, Boozer, no one's said *anything* about her. I hope the room is OK. Jesus, I sound like a fretting housewife, don't I?" Boozer woofed; Sal laughed.

"OK, let's head back. Ray should be here with the new kegs."

Sal tossed his coat and gloves on a chair. Then he picked them up and put them in a closet. He looked for other things to neaten.

"What the fuck am I doing?" he whispered. Boozer ran to the garage door anticipating Ray's knock.

"Come in, it's open," Sal yelled. "Oh shit, just a second; let me give you a hand."

Sal hurried to the door, greeted Ray and marched to Ray's pickup. "Let me get these," he said as he effortlessly lifted a quarter keg and carried it to the bar.

"Thanks," Ray said. "Those damned things are almost too heavy for me anymore."

The taps soon flowed with fresh beer. Sal poured two mugs and a splash in Boozer's bowl. He took a long sip and slowly exhaled.

"I hope I've got the bases covered, Ray. I don't know what Stosh is up to, and I've got no idea who this woman is—shit, they haven't said anything about her. I'm used to living alone. In a place this big, friends are no problem, but a stranger in the house is new. I don't like not knowing what to expect."

"Stosh wouldn't bring anyone here you wouldn't like," Ray said. "No worries."

"Yeah, but lately he's been forgetful–told you he forgot to tell anyone he was going to Europe." Ray smiled and nodded. "But yeah, no worries."

"How are things at the club?"

"Good. The spot-checking did the trick. And the harassing with Ange has stopped—although I don't know why. The guy he was fucking around with isn't the forgiving kind. We'll just have to keep our eyes open." Sal chuckled. "Robert the bar manager seems irritated. But he's towing the line."

"Irritated?"

"Yeah, last month I made him put some marbles in his gas tank. I figured the rolling around would be a good reminder that I'm watching. We'll keep them there for a while—until the spring I think. Then I'll change out his tank if he stays on the straight."

Ray laughed. "That would drive me nuts."

"That's the point."

Ray took a long sip and refilled his mug. "And your mom?"

Sal smiled. "She's got a boyfriend—or so they tell me. You know about the guy she thought was Johnny Mercer?" Ray nodded and laughed. "Apparently, the guy who moved into his room is quite the charmer. The supervisor says Ma's sweet on him. So, she's been extra polite and cooperative. And she has her stereo back—she even sings again. Things there seem good." Sal knocked his knuckles on the oak edge of the bar.

"Hello!" Kate yelled from the porch. Boozer scampered and

escorted her to the bar. "You two look fantastic on this beautiful day. I bought a pumpkin scented candle. Let's try it."

Sal went to the fireplace for matches while Ray filled a mug for Kate. "I think we're all set for Thanksgiving, Sallie. It's only two days away—doesn't seem possible. Is Stosh's flight on time?"

"Yeah, he called before they boarded. He'll be here at Camp in about an hour. Do you know anything about our mystery guest?"

"Nope, but I'm sure she'll be wonderful; she's got Stosh's and Deb's endorsement. Don't worry Sallie. You'll feel comfortable in no time."

"The candle smells great," Ray said.

"Hey, anybody home?" Stosh yelled from the north porch door.

Sal looked at his watch. "Shit, they're early."

Boozer, Kate, Sal and Ray paraded to the porch. Stosh stood at the door grinning broadly.

"There are my favorite people," Stosh said, and one by one hugged them. "And who is this?" he asked as Boozer circled, and then jumped and planted his paws on Stosh's waist. "You'd think this fella knew me his whole life." He held Boozer's head and swayed it from side to side.

"That's Boozer," Kate said. "He's the newest member of the gang."

"Well hello, Boozer," Stosh said. Stosh turned toward his car. "Oh, here come the girls. We're a little early, and I didn't see any cars or nothin'. We didn't want to bust in with nobody here."

Deb walked across the lawn smiling and waving. A radiant East-Indian woman followed her.

"OK, everyone knows Deb—'cept Boozer here—and I'd like you all to meet our good friend, Sita Patil."

Sita bowed and placed her palms together. "Namaste," she said and smiled.

Sal's eyes showed his surprise, and he paused awkwardly. "Please, everyone come in. Ray brought new kegs, and we're testing the beer."

They all sat at the bar. Ray pulled three mugs from the freezer and poured.

"If you please, none for me," Sita said in a pronounced East-Indian accent. "I do not drink very much."

"Tea?" Kate asked.

"Oh yes, that would be very, very lovely if it is not a bother for you," Sita replied and smiled.

Sita carefully moved her waist length black hair over one shoulder and offered to help. Kate graciously accepted. Lit by a skylight in the kitchen area, her black eyes and perfect white teeth glimmered. Her light brown skin likened a carefully nurtured Mediterranean tan, and her slightly Western features and full lips made her look doll-like. She wore a bright blue kurta shirt over her jeans modestly covering her body to the knees. She stood in socks, having instinctively removed her shoes before entering the porch.

"She's stunning," Ray whispered to Stosh.

"Yup," Stosh replied, "and just as frickin' smart as she's good lookin'. What's the matter, Sallie, you look confused or somethin'."

"I just wasn't expecting, well … her," Sal said as he watched Sita comfortably chat with Kate. Sal's eyebrows rose when he noticed the bracelet on Sita's left arm. He recognized the pattern, reached into his pocket and touched his brooch.

"Patil, you said?" he asked Stosh.

"Yeah. You might a heard of some of her family—maybe second cousins or somethin' I think. Years ago, they had a jewelry store in Montreal, advertised a lot on one of the Canadian channels—remember that one with the funny puppets? But they moved back to India. Heck, Sallie, all that was when we were kids. You probably never heard nothin' about it."

Sal felt sick. He excused himself and hurried to the study. Boozer followed. Sal sat in a rocking chair, breathed slowly, and looked at his brooch.

"This is truly fucked up," Sal whispered. "Too many coincidences. This one is just whacked."

He sat for several minutes rubbing the brooch and looking at his stick.

"OK, it is what it is; the only thing to do is let it play out." He snickered. "Here we go, Buddy. Let's find out what this is all about."

Sal returned to the bar with Boozer. He sat back on his stool, finished his beer, and poured another. "Sorry, just a little indigestion, I'm OK now."

Sita sat across from Sal and smiled. "I hope my presence isn't responsible for your discomfort. I am hoping very much to get to know you so that we can work together on a very, very exciting project. I believe Mr. Stosh wishes to explain the idea this evening. He has told me that you are a medical doctor as well as an attorney. That is most impressive. May I call you Dr. Esposito, or do you wish for me to address you otherwise?"

Relaxed by Sita's mellow voice, Sal smiled. "You may call me whatever is most comfortable for you. I prefer Sal or Salvatore, but the choice is yours."

"Wonderful, if then you do not mind, I will call you Salvatore in informal surroundings and refer to you as Dr. Esposito at all other times. Your friends have all earned the privilege to call you by your short name, but I have not. Is this to your liking?"

Sal nodded and took a long sip.

"And your dog—his name is Boozer?" Sal nodded. "In the Indian culture, we do not often have such large dogs in our houses. His presence inside is different for me. But he appears to be quite well behaved, and he is very clean and friendly. I hope you will allow me time to become accustomed to him."

"What do you think, Buddy. Can you hang in while Ms. Patil gets used to us?" Boozer woofed. "He says yes."

Sita laughed. "I know of people who believe their animals are able to communicate. It is quite a charming idea. Now please, Salvatore, I wish for you to address me as Sita. It would make me much more comfortable and would please me very much." Sal nodded. "And, so there is no confusion, I am actually Mrs. Patil."

"Sallie, these steaks look fantastic," Stosh yelled from the refrigerator, "but I don't think Sita eats beef."

Sal looked at Sita. "I do not. I am Hindu. However, I am

not completely veg, and I do not want for you to cook special things to accommodate my religion. I am in your home. Without you needing to have particular concern for me, I will most thankfully take what food you offer that I can eat."

"How about chicken; do you eat chicken?"

"Yes, but please—"

"Please, you *are* in my home, and it is our pleasure to make sure you are comfortable. Hey, Stosh, look in the meat bin, there should be chicken there."

Stosh looked, held up his hand, and signaled OK.

"Good, steak and chicken it is." Sita shook her head in protest. "Please Sita, it's our pleasure, and we are happy you are here."

Sita smiled and nodded.

***

"If you're going to talk business, maybe Ray and I should leave," Kate said.

"I'd kinda like to hear your thinkin' on this if Sallie and Sita don't mind," Stosh said.

Sal opened his folded hands and nodded. "Sure," he said. "Sita, are you OK?"

"Yes, I am quite fine with everyone hearing the idea."

"OK, here it is," Stosh said. "Now Sita comes from a family of jewelers, and she knows marketing. Deb and I got to know her a couple of years ago. Shoot, Sallie; she's the gal I told ya about on the boat—the one we bought the rugs from, remember? Ya know, why don't you explain this, Sita. I'm already startin' to ramble." Deb nodded.

"As Mr. Stosh has said, my family's business specializes in gold jewelry. This has been so for very many generations. Their products are quite well known to Indian people, and Patil designs are sought by many. In Indian culture, gold jewelry is looked upon as an investment. Indian people love to wear gold, but they also buy for financial purposes like Americans buy their stock or real estate."

Sal looked down and chuckled.

"I have an MBA from the University of South Florida," Sita continued. "And have studied marketing very, very thoroughly. I have had a full business plan for an exclusive, gold jewelry business for many years, and I believe it to be very, very well designed. But for it to work, the product must be authentic, and the gold must be pure. Indian people will seek twenty-four karat yellow gold. And the craftsmanship is absolutely essential. Mr. Stosh has suggested that you might be able to provide sufficient quantities of the pure gold necessary for such a venture."

Sal stared at Stosh who gently waved an "I'll explain later."

"I believe that if we go to India and propose my plan," Sita continued, "my uncle will release one of his master artificers and allow us to use my family's name. If so, we could begin this summer and would be in full operation by next autumn. I can assure you that this plan is very, very well thought out and the product will sell very, very well. I have a comprehensive marketing plan that includes the use of many, many good contact points for potential buyers. Please be assured that I know what I am doing. I would not let you gamble with your wealth. I am very, very certain this will be a great success."

Sal took a deep breath, sat back, and was silent.

Finally, Sal spoke. "Four questions. Where's the profit? If you have a good plan, why not do this with your husband? Why would your uncle give up a piece of his action? And, why is a trip to India necessary?"

"To address question one, the return after all expenses for such items can exceed one hundred twenty percent. The markup on gold jewelry in commercial outlets is often as much as five hundred percent. We cannot expect to see that kind of return-after-expenses and still be attractive to the clientele we will target, but the gains are still very, very significant. This is much, much better than other investments I am aware of."

Sal's eyes opened wide.

"Question two and three are related to one another. My husband was much older than I and is deceased now for five years. My parents passed very young, and ours was an arranged marriage that my uncle was very involved in bringing about. He is likely to feel indebted to my husband, something he can resolve by granting the necessary help for this plan."

"And for the last question. For him to seriously consider such a matter, my uncle will require the respect of a visit to him personally. But, he will not deal directly with me. I am a woman. He will expect men to be in charge. It is most important that he see me as the intermediate *only*. And, I cannot go to India alone. He will expect a man of esteem to propose the project. A wealthy American doctor will fit that requirement very, very well."

"*Me*?" Sal said.

"Yes, Dr. Esposito."

"You want *me* to go to India?"

"Yes, Dr. Esposito."

"No fucking way! India?! *Me*?!"

Sita sat up straight and looked down.

"Sallie, calm down," Stosh said. "Sita, Sallie didn't mean to insult you. He's a tough businessman who sometimes talks before he thinks. Sallie?"

"Mrs. Patil, I apologize for my outburst and my language. You can see I speak my mind. I have reasons why I can't go to India. Why not Stosh?"

Still looking down Sita sheepishly replied, "You are a doctor. That makes much difference in my culture. But if you are to act as you just have with my uncle, this cannot work."

Sita sat shaken.

Sal exhaled, pursed his lips, and shook his head. "I sincerely apologize. You are welcome here, and I have made you uncomfortable. Please forgive me and give me time to think about your proposal. The profit margin is attractive and the concept interesting. But, there must be some way to do this without my going to India."

"I do not see another alternative. But please consider the idea more, as you suggest. And you do not need my approval to speak as you wish in your own home. I am not used to your approach or to the language you choose, but I will try to learn and accommodate." Sita raised her head and smiled. "Thank you for listening and for caring about my feelings."

Sal nodded. "Thank you for coming. We have a few days."

Boozer walked to Sita and licked her hand. She flinched and then began to laugh. “Thank you, Boozer. You are a sweet boy.”

“Now I have a proposal,” Kate said. “Tomorrow, Deb and I would like Sita to visit my house. We have many questions about India. We would also like to take her shopping. Then on Thursday, we feast. It’s Sallie’s first Thanksgiving at Camp; let’s make it a great one. Is Angelo coming?” Sal nodded. “Great, we’ll have quite the gang, just like the old days.”

***

“Look, Sallie, you said no second guessin’. I didn’t tell her nothin’ specific about the gold, just that we could get it. Heck, even Deb doesn’t know *where* it is. This is a good plan. Shoot, we don’t even know if it’ll fly. But you won’t get a hundred twenty percent anywhere else.”

Stosh gulped his beer and set the mug down. He looked at Boozer sitting on the porch beside him and shook his head.

“Why do we need one hundred twenty percent?”

Stosh sat back, blank faced. “Jesum Crow, Sallie, that’s a new twist. You come down to Florida and ask me to help ya make money. Now you don’t wanna?”

“Stosh, I’m getting tired of it all. I’m thinking of getting out.”

Stosh chuckled, picked up his mug, and stood. “Get out and do frickin’ what? You’ve been turnin’ a buck in the craziest ways your whole life. It’s in your blood. Look, if nothin’ else, this can be a real adventure for ya. And she deserves a break.

She's a good egg, Sallie, and she's been through a lot a crap. I see it as an all-around winner."

Stosh motioned toward the bar, "You ready?" Sal finished his beer and handed Stosh his mug.

As Stosh left for refills, Sal patted Boozer's head. "I don't know, Buddy. Stosh just doesn't know, and I can't tell him. I can't tell anyone. Except maybe you." He breathed in deeply through his nose and out through his lips, and sat thinking.

Stosh stepped back through the doorway, sipped the head from his mug and handed Sal a fresh beer.

"Well, we leave Sunday," Stosh said. "We all got some time to mull the thing over. I'm just asking ya to consider it carefully."

"Stosh, there are reasons I can't do this. Reasons I can't explain to you. Of all the deals that have come my way, this is the most bizarre. In fact, I can't believe this is happening. It's fucking surreal. Going to India is a nightmare for me." Sal smirked. "*Literally*," he said, under his breath,

Sal looked at the lake and shook his head. "I can't do it. If you can figure out a way to do this without me, use the gold and make it all happen. Have a fucking ball with it. But I'm not going to India."

"Sallie, I can see you're squirmin'. I never meant to make ya uncomfortable. And I can't figure why this trip is a big deal. I've seen you take on the craziest crap without battin' an eyelash. Think about it till Sunday. I'll talk to Sita; I'll let her know *your* goin' ain't likely so she can think about another way. But let's not decide till Sunday mornin'."

Still looking at the Lake, Sal nodded. "Yeah, we'll let it go until Sunday."

Boozer popped up and ran to the garage door. "Looks like the ladies are back," Stosh said.

Stosh and Sal hurried into the bar, put their beers down, and offered to unload Kate's microbus. The women sent them back as they gathered their bags. With a broad smile, Kate headed for the kitchen with groceries. Sita and Deb carried stuffed shopping bags to their rooms, giggling and chatting. Sal and Stosh sipped and watched.

"Looks like a successful trip," Stosh said. Sal cracked a smile and nodded.

"OK, you guys," Kate said, "I talked Sita into cooking for us. Sallie, I know you're not into Indian food, but I think we've thought of something you'll really like. And Deb tells me you like it all, Stosh." Stosh vigorously nodded.

Stoic and expressionless, Sal forced a smile. Sita and Deb reappeared from the wing and joined Kate. Stosh poured two beers and took them to the kitchen. To everyone's surprise, Sita asked to take a taste of Kate's. After one sip, she shook her head and grinned. "It is interesting, but I think I will make some tea if that is all right."

Deb signaled for Stosh to meet her on the porch. Looking at Lake Champlain, Stosh and Deb clicked their mugs. Stosh put his arm around Deb's waist, and she gave him a kiss.

"Well?" Deb said. Stosh shook his head. "Too bad," Deb continued, "I hope he changes his mind. This girl is wonderful. I know she can pull this off."

"We'll decide Sunday mornin'. Till then, best for us all just to let it go. The more I talk about it, the more nervous Sallie gets. I never saw him like this. We got time to let everybody get to know each other. Maybe that'll help."

"Oh look, here's Ray," Deb announced. "Oh, and smell that curry. Dinner will be delicious."

"I hear another car. Must be Angelo," Stosh said.

Ange and Ray stood on the lawn shaking hands and patting backs before a sudden freezing rain made them jog to the porch.

"Jesus, it's cold," Ange said as he pulled the door closed. "Is that curry I smell? Curry in Sal Esposito's house? Shit, that's something new."

"How are ya, Ange?" Stosh said.

"Great, Stosh. Who's cooking?"

"Come in and see. Anythin' left I could help ya bring in, Ray?"

"Nope we're good," Ray said as he pulled two books from under his coat. "Just brought these. How's the beer holding out?"

"Good, let's have some."

Ange noticed Sal's displeasure as he sat beside him at the bar. "I can see this wasn't your idea," he said and grinned. Sal looked back stern-faced and silent. Angelo's grin disappeared.

Kate strolled to the bar and greeted the arrivals. She too saw Sal's face and stepped behind him.

"Don't worry, Sallie, we've got something special for you," she whispered in his ear.

Sal forced a smile. His eyebrows raised. He jumped up and rushed to his wing, closed all doors tight, and returned to his seat. "I just don't want to smell that fucking curry all night," he said to Ange.

For the first time, Ange noticed Sita cooking in the kitchen. "Who's she? She's gorgeous," he said.

"I'll explain later," Sal said. "And reel your tongue back into your mouth. She's here on business."

Sita turned Sal's industrial exhaust hood on full. In moments, the curry smell was gone. Sal smiled, looked at Ange, and nodded. Kate set seven places and called the gang to the bar. Sita prepared six plates from a large skillet and one from a smaller saucepan. Kate mixed saffron rice with bits of unseasoned chicken in a bowl for Boozer.

"Anyone need a drink?" Stosh yelled. Hearing no takers, he filled his mug and sat beside Deb. Sita placed the carefully arranged plates in front of each guest.

"This is a special dish for you, Salvatore," Sita said as she presented Sal's plate. "Kate told me your preferences and that you do not like curry. I hope this will do. I have used a combination of ground chili, cumin, and garlic with some chopped onion. The chicken should have a flavor familiar to you. The rice is mildly seasoned with saffron. I hope that will be acceptable. And the vegetables are prepared in light oil mixed with light spices common here in the U.S." Sita smiled. "I hope you will find this enjoyable."

"Thank you, very much. You've gone to a lot of trouble." Sal took a taste and sat back. "This is fucking great." Sal exhaled and shook his head. "Sorry."

"I'm pleased you like it," Sita said and grinned.

"This tastes like Michigan chicken—it's wonderful. I think you're onto something here. Thank you."

Sita smiled and took her place next to Kate.

"Did everyone know that Sallie's mom is in love?" Kate said.

Ange, Deb, Sita, and Stosh looked up wide-eyed. Ray grinned and nodded.

"No crap?" Stosh said. "Sorry, Sita."

"There is no need to apologize. I believe I am becoming less sensitive to this use of language. We do not often use vulgar words for reasons of emphasis in my culture, but I have heard much of it here in America. My husband even began the practice near the end of his life. It was not becoming for him. Somehow it did not seem genuine. I think those he tried to impress with it found it very, very comical."

Sal chuckled, "Well, we'll try to back off," he said.

"So, what's the story with your ma?" Stosh asked.

"Last month she was convinced that Johnny Mercer was in a room down the hall and he'd stolen her songs. She was particularly pissed—sorry Sita—mostly upset about 'Moon River.' So, she snuck into the guy's room and unplugged the breathing machine for his apnea. She got into a whole lot of shi—trouble. So, we worked out a deal, they moved the guy, and she's happy again. A new guy moved into the room, and Ma has a crush on him."

"What is a crush? Sita asked. "Does that word not mean to do something physically harmful? In India, they have machines that do this to garbage."

"It means she thinks she's in love," Kate answered.

Sita smiled. "Odd," she said.

Everyone laughed. “And talk about vulgar words,” Sal added, “when Ma was mad at the first guy, she started making up her own. She kept yelling he was a *kuttey* and a *ka-mean-a*, or something like that. No one could figure out what the fuck she was saying.”

Sita turned pale. “Oh, sorry, Sita,” Sal said.

“No, Salvatore I am not upset by *your* words. You said she called this person a kuttey and a kaminé?” Sal nodded. “We have words sounding like these in Hindi. They are very, very derogatory.”

Sal looked perplexed. “What do they mean?”

“A kuttey is a filthy dog. That one is bad, but to call a person a kaminé is a very, very great insult. I do not know if there is an equivalent word in English. It means scoundrel but in the worst of all ways. You would not often hear this word and usually only from one of low caste.”

“I must have the words wrong. Where would Ma hear Hindi?”

“If she had and she was very, very angry, these would be the kind of words that would substitute for American slang such as your terms—I should not say this but—mother f-er or rooster s-er. They are very, very bad.”

Sita looked confused at the chuckling. Kate whispered in her ear. “Oh yes, ‘cock?’” Sita whispered. Then her face lit up, and she too laughed.

Sal nodded. “Maybe she got these over the years from a friend or someone, you know, as a kind of an inside thing. Yeah, I remember an Indian woman she knew. Nothing better for a social butterfly like Ma than an insulting phrase no one else understands. And maybe I got them wrong. Either way sounds like she really told that guy off."

Sita nodded, "Oh yes, very, very much so," she said and giggled.

Kate hopped from her stool. In the kitchen, she opened the oven and announced, "The pies are done. Tonight, we have the last of the fresh apple. Tomorrow we're on to the pumpkin. I hope everyone brought their appetite. We're going to make this the best Thanksgiving ever."

***

"This is the first Thanksgiving dinner I have been part of," Sita said. "I have never tasted a roasted turkey before this day. I have only known turkey in a salad or a sandwich. It is most delicious freshly cooked in this way—and thank you all for inviting me into your celebration and making me feel so very welcome. Salvatore, your home is so very exquisite. I have never seen as large a living room with such windows and beautiful scenery. And the room you have allowed me to use is so very large and comfortable. This visit has been most delightful. I am very, very grateful."

Sal smiled and nodded. "You have a few more days to get tired of us," he said. Sita looked confused. "I'm sorry, that's an American style joke. We say the opposite of what we mean."

"Oh yes, like sarcasm. I understand, I just have not heard this particular phrasing before." Sita smiled. "Yes, I have a few more days to get tired of everyone," she said and chuckled. "May I ask a question?"

"Certainly," Sal said.

"I do not mean to be annoying, but I have noticed some differences at your home from others I have visited in America. I am wondering why."

"Yeah?" Sal said.

"Yes, I think in most homes it is common to dine at a table. But with all this space you do not have one. This bar is lovely, and these high stools are most comfortable. And you have much liquor on the shelves. I have also never seen running beer in a house before. But this arrangement seems to be very nontraditional. I do not mean to offend you with my observations."

"No offense taken. My friend built this house in the early 80's. He had a big dining area at first. No one ever sat there. Everyone seemed to prefer the bar. So, he gave the table and chairs away. I guess the bar feels ... friendlier. Maybe it's because he designed the kitchen so this whole area is open. I suppose it's the cook, drink, and chat design." Sal smiled, and the others nodded.

"He was correct," Sita said. "This bar is very friendly, and I love the connection to your excellent kitchen. And your friend, where is he now?"

The others smiled. "He passed away," Sal said.

"I am very sorry; I did not mean to meddle into hurtful things."

"No problem," Stosh said. "His name was Jimmy, and he

was the best. We all miss him, but somehow it always seems to feel like he's still around."

Everyone smiled. "Perhaps he *is* still *around*. In my culture, we might say that one has passed on, not away. We do not know what life one goes to, but we cannot imagine that one simply goes away. Where would one go? We believe good people go to a better life, perhaps one they had wished for. If they were evil, they have a difficult new existence. My husband referred to Christians and Muslims as 'one trippers.' After only one life, there is a final judgment. Hindus, Jains, Buddhist, even Sikhs believe in reincarnation. In my religion, one continues to exist in many forms until the soul advances to be complete and pure and unites with the oneness of all things, Brahman. Of course, many people have left these beliefs altogether and no longer have a religion. I am sorry; I am talking too much and being quite boring and inappropriate."

"No, Sita, your thoughts are wonderful," Kate said.

"Yes," Ange added and smiled. "I've been to India. I found it peaceful, not so judgmental. I think belief in reincarnation is part of that."

"Reincarnation is part of some Western philosophy too," Ray added. "There's considerable evidence that Pythagoras, Socrates, and Plato all believed in it."

"Well," Stosh announced. "I don't know exactly where he is, but I got one thing to say: chins up to Jimmy Eagleson."

"Chins up!" the gang toasted.

"What does this expression mean?" Sita asked.

"I'll give you a full explanation later," Kate said. "But for right now it means we love Jimmy Eagleson and wish him the best wherever he is."

"I like this expression," Sita said and raised her glass of water. "Chins up to your friend Jimmy Eagleson. And chins up to all of you."

Ray and Ange started talking politics. Sita got up and went to the picture window. She smiled as she passed Boozer curled up and snoring on Jimmy's favorite couch. Through the light fog, she saw gray rippling waves on Lake Champlain. November's presence was evident. About one hundred yards out, she thought she saw a large object moving slowly.

"Look," Sita said. "Do you think that could be him? I am told there is a monster in that lake."

"It's probably a tree limb from the wind last night," Ray said. "Champy would probably be farther south this time of year." Ray walked over for a better look. "Yeah, that's just some debris. It's too small to be Champy and not the right shape."

"Is that his name, Champy?"

"Yes."

"Then you must believe he exists if you have named him and know what he looks like, and you even know where he is most likely to be."

"Wouldn't be surprised. There are all kinds of legends about mythical creatures that people dismiss out of hand. Sometimes they deny what they are staring at, something right in front of them—can't live with the thought of it being real." Ray chuckled. "Then there are those who do the opposite—see something in every little thing they see."

"Like a branch?"

Ray smiled. "Maybe."

Sita looked at the floor. "This is oak, I believe. It is beautiful, such pronounced grain and brilliant finish."

"Yes," Kate said and walked over. "I must admit I was never fond of the rugs. I did all the interior design for Jimmy. But I never found rugs that would make these floors pop."

"Oh, well, we should talk more about this," Sita said. "The company I work for imports very, very good hand-woven wool area rugs from India. That is my specialty. Oh my, I hope you do not think I am attempting to sell you anything. I am most embarrassed by that idea. I only meant that I could show you many options on the market in hopes that I could help you find something you like. I am very sorry if I am misunderstood."

Kate laughed. "Sita, you are so sensitive. I would love to see what you have and get some advice. But this is Sallie's house now." Kate paused and smiled. "Let's see what he thinks. SALLIE," she called turning toward the bar.

Sal was listening to Ange and Ray debating Obama. "Yeah?" he said turning to Kate.

"Do you think it might be time to replace the rugs in here?"

"Yeah—you choose—buy whatever you think. As I've said before, Kate, don't ask when you have a plan, just do it." He returned to the debate.

Kate and Sita looked at each other and laughed. "There, it's settled. Before you leave, you must show me some options. I love decorating, and the right design will make all the difference in this room."

Sita nodded. "But I will prepare a list for you of contacts for many sellers."

"OK, tomorrow at my house, we look at rugs."

***

Sal sat in a rocker on the porch with Boozer. Kate banged pots and pans looking for the right one for her marinara sauce.

"Did you ask Deb and Stosh to pick up some spinach pasta while they're out?" she said. "I don't know why they decided to shop today. The day after Black Friday is bad enough, but *any* Saturday in Plattsburgh—particularly after an American holiday—is insane with Canadian traffic. The stores are so packed you can barely get to the shelves."

Sal read the paper and nodded; Kate continued talking. "I hope Sita likes the sauce. She's delightful. I'm going to miss her. This holiday went by so fast. Tomorrow's already Sunday, and then they're gone. She's wise to take a long nap. It'll be a long journey."

Sal thought of the next day. The time with Sita had its effect. He'd come to like her and wondered if he could somehow suck it up and go to India. After all, the curry smell wasn't *that* terrible, he chuckled to himself. But it might be a bad idea. Going to the source of his haunting could fuck him up, badly. She'll be heartbroken when I say no. Shit, this isn't as clear cut as it was on Wednesday. He smiled. Stosh knew this would happen. He's a sly one.

Refreshed from her nap, Sita strolled into the kitchen. She

stood in front of Kate in her new thick-flannel, paisley shirt, raised her arms, twirled and asked, "What do you think?"

Kate nodded vigorously. "It's you. Wow, that deep purple is something."

"Should I tuck it in?" Sita asked.

"No, it looks charming with the tails out."

Sita smiled, twirled again, and walked to the porch door. "Oh look, it is snowing!"

Sal turned and watched the flurries dust the front lawn. "Yeah, just a little bit. A hint of what's to come."

"When I was a child my uncle told me of the snow in this area," Sita said. "He lived in Montreal for a few years."

Sal put the paper down and looked at the woods. His hand patted his knee. "Is this the uncle you want me to meet with?"

"Yes. He is the elder in the Patil businesses. My grandfather who was also with him in Montreal, died many years ago, shortly before my parents. My father was older than my uncle, but he never had the opportunity to lead the family. My grandfather was a wonderful man. He was blinded by a thief. But he remained most positive and very, very kind-hearted. Oh, I must go outside. I have never actually been in the snow. I must see what it is like."

Sita slipped on her shoes and opened the porch door. She took in a deep breath of the brisk air. As she stepped out, Boozer scampered out behind her.

Sal stared at his feet, his fingers continuing to tap his knee. He shook his head. I can't fucking believe this, he thought. The same fucking guy! This kind of shit just doesn't happen. That's it; I'm not going.

Outside Boozer began barking loudly. He circled Sita as she walked toward the bank and then stood firm, blocking her from the edge. Kate rushed to the porch. Sita stood still, confused.

"Don't worry, Sita. He gets upset when anyone nears the bank's ledge, especially when it's slippery. He's just guarding you. It's his instinct."

Sita looked at Kate. She smiled and stepped back. Boozer licked her hand.

Sal poured a whiskey at the bar. He swallowed half and refilled his glass. He stared into the kitchen trying to think of nothing. He looked through the picture window. The flurries became snowfall. Sita stood with her arms out, face to the sky, smiling, and collecting thick flakes all over her. Boozer circled and ran about, and then rolled on his back. He stopped, darted to Kate's porch, and snatched his stick. He pranced back and dropped it at Sita's feet. Sita patted his head and tossed the stick a few feet. Understanding that she didn't know the game, Boozer trotted over and casually picked it up. Covered in snow, Sita walked back to the porch door. Boozer—stick in mouth—led the way.

As Sal opened the door, Boozer jumped in, shook off the snow and hid his stick under an end table.

"The snow is magnificent," Sita proclaimed brushing herself off. "It covers everything in cool white crystals as if healing sores and removing the pain of sins. I have never felt such a thing before. It is absolutely miraculous."

Sal squatted and rubbed under Boozer's chin. "Yeah, fuck that," he whispered, "she never had to shovel the fucking shit."

"Hey, you guys!" Deb yelled from the north lawn. "I was

hoping we'd get some snow. I miss it. Not enough to live in it again, mind you, but it's beautiful today."

Stosh followed carrying three grocery bags. "Fresh salad, spinach pasta, Italian bread—" Stosh held up one bag— "and hot chicken wings for the side. What a feast. Too bad Ange and Ray couldn't stay." He took dinner to the kitchen.

Sal sat at the bar. He forced a smile as Stosh opened a large Styrofoam box and showed him the wings. "What do ya think, Sallie?" Sal looked away and nodded. "I see you're inta the rye. Maybe I'll join ya." Sal nodded again and looked out the window.

"Jesum Crow, you're in a great frickin' mood," Stosh continued. "What happened?"

Sal looked at Stosh and shrugged. Stosh poured himself a vodka. "Well, somethin's up." Sal remained silent. "OK, if you don't wanna talk about it, I'll let it be."

"I'm not going," Sal said.

Stosh took a sip and thought. "I figured that was likely on Wednesday. But I thought ya might be comin' around. Did you say anything?"

"No, tomorrow, as we planned."

"Well, I figure you got your reasons. And you weren't hot on this from the start, so it ain't like ya led anyone on. Still, she'll be disappointed."

Sal nodded and sipped. He looked around the great room and thought of Jimmy. If he were here, Sal might be able to explain. But as good a friend as Stosh was, Sal couldn't open up, not about this. He closed his eyes and saw the fort. He inhaled deeply through his nose and exhaled through his lips.

Now back in time, he smelled the hot dogs and felt the fire. He started to relax. He opened his eyes and gazed at the player-piano. He listened to Ma sing "Moon River."

Sal stood and stretched, rolling his head and loosening his neck. He sat back down, refilled his glass, and watched Boozer curling up on his favorite couch. He smiled. "We'll come up with something else, or maybe not," he said to Stosh. "What the fuck's the big deal anyway? It's not like we need more money."

"Yeah, I suppose. I was hopin' we could help Sita out. But she's a big gal. She'll be OK."

"We can still help her. My problem's not her fault. Shit, this isn't the only option out there, is it?"

"Maybe not, but to her, it's a chance to show her family her worth. Women don't get many shots like this in her world. She'll be real disappointed."

Sal peered at Stosh. "I can't go. If that ends the plan, then the plan is finished."

Stosh nodded. "Yup," he said and sipped his vodka.

Hours later, Sal and Boozer sat on the porch. Sal stared into the north woods.

"Sita and Deb are coming to my house for some good old-fashioned girl talk," Kate said. "You guys enjoy your time alone." Kate turned and yelled to the great room, "Stosh, thanks for the wings. They were delicious."

Hearing no response, she peeked in and chuckled. "Well he's out cold on a couch, Sallie, so I guess it's just you and Boozer. We won't be too long. It's already nine o'clock, and Sita and Deb have a long journey tomorrow."

The girls left, and Sal ambled to the bar. On a couch, Stosh lay on his back snoring. Sal refilled his whiskey glass and splashed Boozer's dish with beer. He tiptoed back to the porch, and quietly closed the great room door behind him. He placed Boozer's beer on the floor and put his glass on a table. He turned the ventilation system on and pulled a cigar from his pocket.

"I drank a lot today," he said to Boozer. "I must admit I'm getting drunk."

Still standing, Sal lit his cigar, sucked in, and blew out a cloud of smoke. He sat and sipped his drink.

"I'm sure you heard I'm not going. I've got a lot on my mind. You see, this whole thing is more complicated than they think. It's a real fucking problem for me. You think I made the right decision, Buddy?"

He chuckled. Boozer barked twice.

"No? So, let me get this straight, you think I should go to India? You know, I told you I did some awful shit when I was a kid. In a rather fucked up way, it's all coming back around. And I have dreams—nightmares. I can't stop them. If I go, they'll get worse.

"Shit, I've got them under control now. It's not *that* bad now. I'm feeling pretty good, and I could fuck that up. So, going is a really bad idea."

Boozer barked twice, and Sal laughed. "You still think I should go? One of those face-your-demons things?"

Sal laughed again and then puffed his cigar and paced.

"I've thought of that angle, but going there, going to India, it's too much. Shit, I've never been afraid of anything, always had balls to the ground. But when it comes to this—this one thing—I'm real short on ... courage."

Sal paused. "You know, I was almost ready to go, but it's him. Her uncle is him! No, it's a bad idea. I'm not going." Boozer was staring at him. "You're adamant about this?"

Boozer got up and licked Sal's hand. "OK, Boozer, you tell me what to do. I don't want to go. I think it will do me much more harm than good. You don't know my reasons, but you still think it's what I should do?" Boozer woofed.

Sal laughed and took a drag from his cigar. He walked to the end table, picked up his whiskey and drank it down. Boozer followed him.

"OK. Maybe I should give you my reasons. Hell, I've never told anyone, even Jimmy. OK, Buddy, here it is. I was twelve. My brother Johnny decided it was time I learned his 'trade.' He and this asshole Buzzy Kline had a plan for a major heist. Johnny didn't tell me any details. They picked me up—"

Boozer barked twice. He scratched Sal's shin, ran to the door, put his paw on the latch, and whimpered. Sal hurried over and opened the door. Boozer bolted through, sprinted to the woods, circled, sniffed a spot, squatted, and looked back at Sal, relieved.

Sal laughed hysterically. "Yeah, Buddy, it's no big deal anyway, and sometimes the most important thing is just taking a good shit."

***

Sal appeared from his wing the next morning.

Kate laughed. "I think I know someone who could use a Bloody Mary," she said.

Sal wandered to a mirror near the door and smirked at himself. "Make it a double, please."

The smell of frying Canadian bacon filled the air. Stosh and Deb chatted on the porch.

"She's going to be devastated," Deb whispered. "I could tell last night that she thinks Sal's going to agree."

Stosh nodded. "Yeah, but she'll get over it. If Sallie says he can't do it—well he's got his reasons."

Deb and Stosh moved to the bar and sat near Sal. Deb smiled and shook her head. "You look like you've got a little thumper going, Sallie."

Sal tried to smile as he sipped his Bloody Mary through a straw.

Sita entered the room glowing from a good night's sleep. "Good morning everyone. What a lovely day."

Stosh looked away and drank his coffee.

Sita strolled to the picture window. "What a beautiful blue sky and the water looks so friendly with its little waves. I hope Champy is having a nice morning, wherever he is."

Droopy-eyed, Sal looked at Stosh. "I'm glad someone's chipper," he mumbled. "Sita, we should sit and talk. We only have a few hours before you leave, and we have decisions to make."

Sita sat. Deb and Stosh stiffened, eyes on Sal. Sal focused on his Bloody Mary.

"Listen, I've given this a lot of thought. I'm afraid I can't go to India in February. It's just not possible."

Sita's face lost expression. She looked down and forced a smile. Her eyes began to glaze.

"I understand, and I thank you for giving the idea the considerable attention you have," Sita said. "I know that you did not approve of the plan from the beginning and that you have many reasons for not wanting to go to India. You have been so very, very gracious and generous, and I have totally enjoyed my stay in your home."

Sita's eyes welled, and a tear ran down her cheek. Kate handed her a tissue.

"I am sorry. I am very disappointed, but I do understand, and I respect your decision. Dr. Esposito, it was so kind of you to give the idea such thorough consideration."

Sal looked up, saw Sita weep, and shook his head.

"Just wait a minute; stick with me. My head is throbbing, and I'm not all that coherent. I can't go in February, but if we can move this to early March, I'm in."

Stosh sat up. He looked at Deb as she put her arm around Sita. Sita wiped her face.

"Then you will give the plan a chance?"

Sal nodded. "Yeah, but we need to work out some details. I have a few ideas and want to be sure we're all on the same page."

Sal slurped the last of his Bloody Mary. Kate took the glass and mixed another.

"And I want Ange to go. He's been there, and he knows how I travel. Oh, and Stosh too. He's not getting out of this either."

"Most certainly. Mr. Stosh and Mr. Costello will be most welcome and very, very helpful. We must get your visa applications in process immediately. Oh, and we must find dates that will be good for both you and my uncle. And we must make reservations with the airlines soon to insure we get the best possible price. And—"

"Whoa." Sal raised his hands and waved them downward over the bar. "But please slow down. We're not leaving tomorrow, and today my head hurts. And we'll take my plane."

Sita looked astonished, "You own an airplane?"

Sal looked at Stosh, who shrugged. "I didn't tell her. I guess it slipped my mind."

"My uncle will be very, very impressed. This is a most positive thing and a most wonderful day."

Sita approached Sal and bowed with her hands together. "You will never know how much this means to me and how grateful I am to you. And we do have many things to finalize."

"Listen," Sal said sternly. "We don't have a deal with your uncle yet. I've been in business a long time; we don't know how all of this is going to play out. Don't let your expectations get too high."

Sita grinned and nodded, and then returned to her stool. Kate put Sal's fresh drink in front of him. He slurped a long sip through his new straw.

"You should all stay a few more days if you can," Sal said. "Let's get things as finely tuned as we can while we're all together. I'll call Ange and get him here first thing tomorrow morning."

"I have a bit of vacation time available," Sita said. "But my employer will not be happy that I have given him so little notice. Still, I think you are correct to carefully reexamine the plan while we are all here."

Sal put his hand on his forehead and tried to grin. "Tell your boss that if he gives you any shit, I'll have his knees broken."

Sita sat shocked. Sal exhaled.

"Sorry Sita, that was just a bad joke from old movies. My apologies."

"I believe I understand. There are many peculiarities I am learning about. Sometimes yours initially disturb me. I will try to learn when you are not being serious."

"I don't know if we'll be able to change our flights, Sallie," Deb said. "Flying around Thanksgiving is a pain."

"No big deal. I'll fly you back. I should have brought you up in the first place."

"Everything's ready—let's eat," Kate announced.

Sita grinned, nodded, and looked out the picture window. "Yes," she whispered, "I hope Champy is having a nice morning, wherever he is."

***

Holding a bag of garbage, Sita stepped into the garage. She stopped to watch Sal, naked to the waist and covered in sweat as he slammed the heavy punching bag. He struck high, then low, then high again, springing on his feet, bobbing and weaving with every muscle taught. He attacked again and again until he saw her. She stood silent. Sal could see she was mystified.

"It's my way of relaxing," Sal said wiping his brow with a towel.

"It appears most violent and aggressive," Sita replied. "I can see it keeps you in excellent physical condition. It must be very disquieting on your mind, however."

"No, actually, I feel quite content afterward."

Sita nodded. "Kate has asked me to place this in the bin. I will hurry and leave you alone to relax more."

Sita quickly placed the bag inside a wheeled trash container and turned back to Sal. "You have many aggressive tendencies that I find very peculiar. I hope you do not suffer from inner turmoil. Forgive me for saying, but I heard you in the large room very late last evening. I feared that you experienced an unpleasant dream. This is not my business, but something troublesome shows on your face. Perhaps beating on your bag helps this to go away?"

Sal nodded and slammed the bag in the gut zone. "Yup," he said.

"You are a very tall and muscular man, Salvatore. In India, you will stand out. Very, very few men there are your size. Many people will stare. I hope you will not be offended; they will just be curious and will mean no disrespect."

"Don't worry. I won't punch them."

"I did not think you would," Sita said. She smiled and left the garage.

Sal sat on his weight bench. How the hell did she know there was a dream? He remembered some parts well; the curry smell and the heat from the gold were particularly powerful this time. He knew it would come last night after yesterday's conversation. He wondered why she was up at that late hour.

Sal's thoughts wandered to the trip. He felt anxious. One week ago, even the idea would have been impossible. But by tomorrow, the dates would be set and the plan fine-tuned. How did things change so fast? He hoped he was doing the right thing—the right thing for him.

CHAPTER X

Welcome home

Ange pressed Sita's back as she climbed the slippery stairs up to Sal's jet. Sal glared. Ange removed his hand. A gust of March wind blew through her hair. Familiar with the plane from her flight to Florida, Sita stowed her carry-on, a garment bag, and packages.

"Sit up here next to me," Sal said. "We have a lot to talk about."

Sita nodded and took the window seat in the front row.

"It is amazing to be on an airplane with so much room and such a large washroom, even with showering facilities," Sita said. "It will be a very, very long journey, and we will need to freshen up before we land. If my uncle is to meet us at the airport, I will need to change into a sari. He will not receive me in Western clothing without having much criticism."

Sal nodded. "We have plenty of time. the pilot says the flight plan is seventeen hours with one stop for fuel."

Sita arranged her seat with a blanket and pillows and stuffed organic snacks in the side pouches. Ange sat behind Sal where he could lean forward and hear the conversation. He removed his laptop and tossed the case on the seat beside him.

"Drink anyone?" Ange asked. Sal ordered his usual; Sita asked for water. "And I'll have white wine," Ange said to himself. Drinks in hand, the three stood and toasted to a successful trip.

"It is most unfortunate that Mr. Stosh has had such a terrible accident," Sita said. "He will be missed. My uncle would have been most impressed to meet *two* men of your stature, Salvatore."

"He's supposed to leave the hospital today," Sal said. "You know, Deb had worried he might fall down the stairs to that stupid bomb shelter. Now he must be out of his mind with boredom—the rehab for his broken hip took weeks, and he hates hospitals. But, at home he'll soon be out of his wheelchair and hobbling around on crutches, Deb said."

Sal handed Sita a list of movies from the plane's entertainment center. After a quick review, she was unsure, so Sal suggested music until they are in the air and settled in. Sal excused himself and joined Ange.

"Roger thinks the market has bottomed out and things will begin to improve," Ange said. "This morning, gold was near one thousand. That's almost three hundred percent above where Stosh bought, and Roger doesn't think it's anywhere near peaking,"

"I know the club is chicken shit financially, but how's it going?"

"It's good. Things are stable; revenues are where they should be. Robert's doing a good job. He said to thank you for changing his gas tank. Even with you gone most of the time now, no one is dicking around."

"Remember what I said last fall. When we get back, we'll get it into your hands."

"Sal—"

"Just do what I ask." Ange nodded. "You know," Sal said, "even with the shit in the market, we sold the Arizona property at the right time. Its value tanked too, and at least the stocks have long-range potential. With the gold and other cash I socked away, overall things look good. Let's see how this India thing goes. After that, I think Salvatore Esposito is looking at retirement. Any more shit with Frankie?"

"Nope. It's been quiet for months." Ange grinned. "That older guy—remember the one with the Yankees jacket?—he still comes in from time to time. Always the same, one or two bottles of Budweiser. Seems like a nice fella, the bartenders like him. But somehow, he's out of place, you know?"

The pilot announced takeoff. Sal patted Ange on the shoulder. "We'll talk more," he said and returned to his seat. Sita clinched Sal's arm as the plane thrust into the air and held tight until it leveled off.

"I'm afraid I am a very nervous flyer," Sita said.

Sal nodded. "OK, Sita, fill me in on what I need to know." Ange leaned forward to listen in.

"You have seen the business plan and have made many good changes to it. I think you already know very much. I don't know what more I can add."

"Not that, cultural things. I need to know what I'm stepping into. How people think. How they act. Things I'll encounter.

Last fall you told me to expect to be stared at." Sita nodded. "That's the kind of stuff. Don't hold back—you tend to be very polite and reserved. Let that go and be brutally honest."

"Brutally?"

"Yeah, not literally, it means—"

"Yes, I know what you mean. Let's start there. In India, people will be very literal. You should phrase your sentences carefully without the colorful adjectives you like to use. Be very precise. And you must make a very, very great effort not to use profanity."

"Back off on the F-word."

"Most definitely. It is also important to never touch a woman. Public affection such as kissing is illegal in most of India. Any physical contact, even that seen as casual in the west, suggests an impropriety."

"Hear that, Ange?" Sal said.

"Got it," Ange answered from behind.

"It is also very, very important to eat only with your right hand. The left hand is considered dirty. It is used for personal cleansing. In many lavatories, you will still find no soap and see only a container for water next to the toilet. Even the finest restaurants may not have tissue paper or be as clean as you are used to. And, you may be required to eat with your fingers. Knives and forks are usually available, but Indian people seldom use them. After we arrive, I will show you how to break naan and meat with just your right hand.

"OK, this is most necessary to know. You have often seen me bow with my hands in a prayer position and say *namaste.* This is not just a greeting like a hello or good evening. Many

Indians overlook it when foreigners use the salutation casually. However, *Namaste* and *Namaskār* express one's respect for another's soul. Both words mean that you recognize the divinity within others, that you see their eternal worth. It also may mean that you understand who they *really* are, not only in their present form but in other incarnations. It is important that you understand this. Use these actions only when you are sincere."

Sal nodded. "What if I'm holding something?"

"Put one hand on your heart."

"Good, Sita, this is exactly the kind of information I need."

"There are a few more things. You will see much begging, particularly children. Avoid acknowledging them. Telling them to go away or saying no, tells them they are having an effect and will make them more aggressive. Then they will pester until you give them something."

Sita paused and sipped. "From time to time," she continued, "you will need to pay a tip to get someone to do their job."

"A tip or a bribe?"

"Your term is more accurate but less polite. I will try to help you anticipate this. There is much poverty in India, and people will find ways to get even a few extra rupees. A person is only considered poor if they earn less than seventy-five rupees a day. About one dollar and twenty-five cents."

"So, five hundred a year puts you over the poverty line?"

"That is correct. But there is a growing middle class that earns much more and is now larger than the population of the United States. However, most people are very, very poor."

"Because of the caste system?"

"Partially. But economics and caste are less related to one another than most westerners realize. It is not unusual to see one of low caste who is wealthy and one of high who is not."

"Four Levels?"

"That is the *Varna*. The *Brahmins* are the highest. Their work was to be our priest and teachers. But they are found in many professional vocations today.

"Second, but still very high, are those who are *Kshatriya*. They were our leaders and warriors. Third are the *Vaishya*. They are merchants, business people, civil servants, and others of similar responsibility. My family is of the *Vaishya* caste.

"The lowest class is the *Shudras*. They are manual laborers and considered only as partial members of the society. They are sometimes called *once born* and only allowed to participate in a few religious activities.

"Below the Shudras are those who are not of caste. You have heard them called *untouchables*. They are now most often referred to as *Dalits*—which means oppressed ones. They have only the dirty jobs, and few people of the castes associate with them. Gandhi was responsible for laws that require them to be recognized as Shudras. But not all people pay attention to these regulations. For many, the Dalits are still considered to be *untouchable*."

"Why do people put up with this? In America, this would never be accepted."

"America has a different past. A very, very young one compared to India. Our traditions have developed over many thousands of years, and the belief in reincarnation means your present life is only one of many you will experience. I know you are familiar with our commitment to karma. Each of us has been born into our present life because of our actions in previous ones. You will have perhaps countless chances for other lives, and if you perform well in yours now—fulfill your *Dharma,* your duty—your next one will be better. In Western belief, after one try you might go to an eternal hell. In ours, hell comes and goes in different ways and in the end all are at peace.

"But, you provide an excellent observation, and many Hindus *have* rejected the system and have become members of other religions. And, Salvatore, America has its own caste system that few choose to see. Yours is based almost solely on wealth. There is much opportunity in America, but there is also much separation of classes depending upon how much money a person acquires."

Sal nodded. "Yup. I assume you were married in caste?"

"Yes, my husband was a merchant of hand-woven woolen carpets. As I have I told you, my uncle arranged the marriage when I was quite young. My husband was much older and a distant relative. His name was also Patil. He chose for us to move to America in the later part of his life—after waiting for several years for permission from your government. We lived in an Indian community and had few friends outside of our ways.

"I was permitted to attend a university where I learned much about business and much about your culture. But my classes and time in libraries were my only outside contact before my husband's death five years ago. I still live in the community, but I have been able to learn much about American life since then. His partner employs me in the carpet business they had built. There I have come to know many Americans including Mr. Stosh and Deborah. On several occasions, I was invited to visit their most lovely home and their very, very excellent boat. They are very, very wonderful people."

"Yes," Sal said.

"I must say two very important things," Sita continued. "I do not mean to offend. It will be most important that there is no misinterpretation of my relationship to you or Mr. Costello. From the moment we arrive, you will be Dr. Esposito *only*. Never will I use your first name. And you must call me Mrs. Patil. If we are seen to be connected in any way other than professionally, an agreement will be impossible. And it is necessary that my uncle believes that the business plan comes *only* from you and that I am here *only* to make your introduction. Our respective positions must be clear.

"At the hotel, you will have a deluxe suite. We will have basic rooms. At meetings, greetings will be friendly. But when discussing business, if my uncle has a subordinate speak, Mr. Costello must respond. You should address my uncle *only*, unless *he* asks you to explain something to another person. You must *never* refer a question to me. You must be clearly seen as the person with *all* of the authority."

Sita exhaled and smiled. "I believe it is very, very difficult to explain India to one who has not lived there. But please try to look at our country with an open mind. You will find it a place of much contrast and inconsistency. Some Westerners have told me they felt they had stepped back in time the minute they arrived, and I think this is true—our traditions are ancient. Some have also said they find that the pace in India is much like a sine wave. The 'quickness' you are used to is even greater at times, but with a placid rhythm intermixed.

"However, Salvatore, what is *most* important is that beneath our ways is something very deep and often rich in meaning. Please try to let yourself see this."

Sal nodded as the plane began to bump from turbulence. Sita grabbed his arm and held tight until the jet settled down.

"May I have a small amount of Mr. Costello's wine if it is not too much trouble?" Sita asked.

Sal unbuckled, refilled his whiskey at the beverage cabinet and poured half a glass of wine. He saw Ange sound asleep, took Ange's empty glass back to a storage bin, and returned to his seat.

Sita took her drink and smiled. "I do not often have alcohol, but I find it helps me much when I am flying. When I finish, I will go to a seat in the back where I will sleep. I don't mean to be impolite, but it would not be appropriate for me to be next to a man while I am horizontal."

Sal chuckled and nodded.

Sita looked at the clouds and shook her head. "I cannot help but wonder how Mr. Stosh is doing at this moment. It is truly regrettable that he was not able to join us on this wonderful journey."

Sal glanced at his Rolex. "It's early afternoon in Florida. He's probably getting to his place as we speak."

"I hope his homecoming is most relaxing and comfortable." Sita smiled. "This wine tastes very, very good."

***

"Where did that frickin' ramp come from," Stosh asked as Deb drove him into the driveway.

"It's only temporary. You're not supposed to walk for a few more weeks. Remember what the doctor said—just a few minutes a day on the crutches and only when someone else is around."

"Yeah, I heard him."

Deb helped Stosh from the front seat and into his wheelchair. She rolled him through the door into the living room of their large ranch house.

"Would ya get me a vodka on the rocks, Deb?"

"Just one, remember. That's what caused your accident in the first place."

Deb left for the kitchen. Stosh gripped the round bars on his chair and rolled himself to the Florida room. He smiled as he picked up the remote and flicked on his own television for the first time in six weeks. The air conditioning was at the perfect temperature and the curtains closed to block the afternoon glare. Stosh took a deep breath; it was good to be home. Deb returned with his drink and sat.

"I need a few things at the store," Deb said. "will you be all right by yourself for a half-hour or so?"

"Yeah, of course."

"OK, I'll get the chips you like; anything else?"

"I'll call if somethin' comes to mind."

Stosh heard Deb drive off. He flipped through the channels

and found nothing interesting. He turned off the TV, rolled himself to the windows, pulled the cord, and drew open the curtains.

"WHAT IN THE FRICKIN' WORLD!" he yelled. He stared in disbelief at the freshly graded back lawn. He flipped his cell to call Deb. He peered at the phone's blank screen and threw it on the counter. "The frickin' thing's dead."

Stosh frantically rolled to the front door, down the ramp to the driveway and struggled to push across the grass to the flat, fresh dirt.

"SHE FRICKIN' DID IT!" he screamed. "SHE FILLED IN THE FRICKIN' BOMB SHELTER!"

Stosh saw a tarp covering something at the back corner of the garage and worked his way over. He lifted the canvas and slapped it back down. "Frickin' patio blocks!"

Stosh pushed on to another tarp and lifted it—more of the same. Nine other tarps covered materials across the entire back area of the three-car garage. He checked one after another and then stopped. He understood.

Stosh sat nauseated and shocked. Maybe she'd had everything stored. Yeah, Deb would never just get rid of his stuff without asking. Or would she? She filled in the frickin' bomb shelter without sayin' nothin'. Now what? He sat dumbfounded wondering in panic for what seemed like hours. Then Deb pulled back into the driveway.

"What are you doing back here?" Deb said walking over to him. "Do you want to end up right back in the hospital?"

With a pale blank face, Stosh stared into Deb's eyes. "What did you do?"

"Stosh, I told you in the ambulance after you fell that I was going to get rid of that damned bomb shelter. You gave me a thumb up."

Stosh struggled to remember. "I was on painkillers. I must a not known what you were sayin'. Deb, what did you do with the stuff that was in there?"

"Most went to Goodwill. The old TV and worn out couch were not coming into the house. Damn it Stosh; we talked about that too."

"And the tubs a food?"

"I told you months ago I was going to clear that out. A rescue place took it. They were happy to get it. They love the crap that's packaged to survive even Doomsday. It never spoils, so they send it overseas. That went the first week you were in the hospital. It's probably somewhere in Africa by now. Stosh, I was clear with you about everything I was planning. And what's the big deal? "All we did was get rid of all that *garbage* anyway."

Stosh stared at the dirt.

"Do you want me to roll you back into the house?"

Stosh was silent.

***

As Sita and Ange slept, Sal thought. He'd never seen Sita's uncle in person, but he was resolved—they *would* face off. The old man couldn't possibly know who Sal was. But Sal knew him. Amol Patil, very successful in his little world of

Indian jewelry, a world Sal fucked up for a while. He pulled out the brooch and stared at it. His recurrent cop-out rolled through his head—the idea that it wasn't really his fault, that Johnny and that asshole Buzzy Kline set the whole thing up. Little Sallie was just their stooge. But, he knew little Sallie was the one who did it. He wiped his face with his bare hand. This had been his obsession for far too long. Now he was on his way to India with Mr. Patil's niece for a meeting. He shook his head and smirked. Shit. What a world.

The thud from a dropped tray turned Sal's head. "Shit," Ange said. "Sorry, didn't mean to wake anyone."

"Then be quiet," Sal said.

Ange looked back at Sita sleeping soundly. He smiled and took the seat next to Sal. "We'll be on the ground in London for fuel in an hour," Ange whispered.

Sal nodded. "Is Sita asleep?"

"Yup."

"OK, I have a few questions for you. You've been to India. You heard what Sita said. Now give me your take."

"Sita told you most of what I'd say. But there's the water. Don't drink it, brush your teeth with it, get it into your mouth when you shower, or eat anything that might be washed in it, even salad. And no ice. You'll have the shits like you never had the shits. And the food will be slow to come when you order, so be patient with the waiters. Oh, yeah, and the coffee, the coffee sucks; all you'll find is instant.

"You'll see feral dogs and garbage everywhere. But no one gives it a second thought. She already told you about the beggars. They'll know you're from the West and think you're an easy mark. And Sal, there are thousands of deities, and people who stand out physically—like you—can be taken for powerful avatars."

"Yeah, Sita said people might stare."

"Or more. With your build, someone might mistake you for a god. Then they'll try to worship you."

Sal shook his head and chuckled. "Yeah, that would be rich."

Ange stood and stretched. "You want something to drink, Sal?"

"Some black coffee if it's easy. No instant."

***

Deb rolled Stosh into the living room. "Are you all right?" she said. "You sat looking at that dirt for an hour. I'm beginning to wonder if you've had a stroke."

Sal turned and looked into her eyes. "Which one a them Goodwill places did you send the stuff to?"

"Well, he talks." Deb forced a chuckle. "I don't know, exactly. Cory took care of it for me."

"Get him on the phone."

"Yes *sir*, whatever you say, *boss*," Deb snapped back.

"My phone's dead. Please get him on yours. It's very important."

Deb fumbled in her purse and pulled out her cell. Her head bobbled as she listened to the message. "Cory, it's Mom," she said. "Dad is home and very upset about the bomb shelter. He needs to talk to you right away. Please call back as soon as you get this. Love you."

Deb snapped the phone shut. "I got his voice—"

"I heard … please get me a vodka and tonic."

"Stosh—"

"Please Deb, I really need a drink."

"Weren't you going to contact Sallie?"

Stosh went pale. "I got nothin' to say to him right now. Please, Deb, get the drink."

Deb tried to smile and left for the kitchen.

Stosh's mind whirled. "Sallie is going to be insane about this," he whispered. "He'll never talk to me again—if he doesn't kill me. Maybe we'll find it. Yeah, fat frickin' chance, find gold that's been shipped off to Africa. But the guys who moved the tubs must a felt how heavy they were. They must a looked. If they got it, we'll get it back. Come on, Cory, check your frickin' phone."

***

Sal stepped onto the steaming tarmac and breathed deeply. His nostrils filled with thick, musty air. He breathed deeply, smelling an unfamiliarly sweet scent sporadically fouled by whiffs of baking garbage. The sun parched like a heat lamp. Sal began to sweat.

Six men in green work clothes took their time loading four suitcases onto a motor-cart while four others watched. The work crew chatted in rapid-fire Hindi and pointed to details of the plane.

Three skinny dogs with long snouts and bent ears roamed the area. Sal watched one lift his leg and squirt Ange's bag. A worker chased the dogs off and turned the bag to hide the wet spot before placing it on the cart. Ange joined Sal and Sita followed, insisting she be last in all exits and entrances. Sal didn't mention Ange's bag.

Sita wore a yellow and green sari and carried a multi-colored bag. Sal and Ange stood in white Western casual. One of the workers approached Sal.

"Sir," the man said. "We will take very, very good care of your luggage for you." Sita nodded, and Sal gave the man fifty rupees. Sita shook her head, and Sal knew he'd paid too much.

A second motor cart with two front seats and a back bench buzzed out toward the plane. The driver pulled over and chatted with the crew awhile. Finally, he looked at the roasting visitors. He fumbled behind the front passenger seat and held up a sign reading, "DR ESPOSITO."

"Yeah, no shit, you see another fucking plane?" Sal mumbled as he raised his hand and flagged the cart over. They piled in.

The driver thrust ahead, swerving around obstacles, carelessly hitting potholes and bumps, jolting and jarring the passengers. He slammed on the breaks at the terminal, nearly tossing his riders from their seats. He hopped out and watched the travelers wrenching and twisting out of his cart. Then he extended his hand for his tip. Sal gave him ten rupees. The driver left his hand out and looked away. Sal looked at Sita.

Sita sternly shook no. The driver crushed the money in his hand, jumped in his cart, and sped off.

Inside, Sal felt the relief of air conditioning and remarked at the airport's advanced design. After twenty minutes, the second cart arrived with the luggage and three new men. Each carried one bag. They carefully placed the suitcases in front of Sal and stood with their hands out. Astonished, Sal looked at Sita. Sita looked away chuckling. Sal fumbled through his pockets and, out of Indian money, gave them each one American dollar. They all smiled and bowed.

Sita spoke for the group through three levels of customs as Sal and Ange stepped along. The agents casually yakked with each other, briefly interrupting themselves to glance at passports and visas. One yawned as he watched bags slowly pass through the scanner. After nearly an hour they were finally beyond the last gate. Five men with pushcarts ran and struggled to shove each other out of the way as they grabbed at the bags. Sal acknowledged one, and the others resentfully backed off. As the three travelers paced to the exit, more men approached offering to sell brochures or arrange cars and tours. Sal fruitlessly tried to wave them off before stopping, standing firm and glaring at each. One by one they left to hound other travelers.

Standing outside at a modern traffic circle, they spotted another Doctor Esposito sign and worked their way into a large Toyota SUV. A man helped Sita into the back seat and Ange next to her. Sal waited as a man loaded the luggage. Sal tipped him fifty cents. The man looked at Sal disappointed and kept his hand out for more. Sal looked at Sita, who shook her head. Sal waved the man away and climbed into the left front seat.

"We drive on the left in India," Sita said. "As in Britain."

A minibus partially blocked the end of the circle. The driver zipped by, using half of the sidewalk and barely missing several vehicles, and sped out onto the road. Horns blasted from every direction. Sal's eyes widened. Cars, buses, trucks, bicycles, pedestrians, motor scooters, camel-drawn carts, and motorized and pedaled rickshaws wove in and out of any hole in the traffic.

The driver ignored a traffic light and turned left darting in front of a dilapidated bus covered with elaborate murals and overstuffed with passengers, some hanging from the sides. Sal grabbed the handle above his window. The driver slammed on the brakes as an auto-rickshaw cut them off, throwing Sal forward. The driver immediately stomped the accelerator, jerking Sal back to his seat. The rear end of a rusted truck read "HORN PLEASE"; the Toyota driver beeped four times and thrust into on-coming traffic. Miraculously, a sliver of road appeared. The driver flew through past the truck and jammed back into the proper lane.

Sal turned around and saw Sita unconcerned and Ange looking out the side window.

"We'll be there in a few minutes," Sita said smiling at Sal's alarmed face. Sal turned back to the terror in front as the driver cut across two lanes of traffic and blindly turned onto a side street.

"FUCK!" Sal yelled as the driver reeled the steering wheel, turning sideways to avoid colliding with an ornately decorated elephant plodding its passengers down the middle of the lane. The driver nodded to Sal, and while still weaving between vehicles and animals, reached into his glove box and rifled through the contents until he found a plastic bag and handed it to him. Sita broke into hysterical laughter. Mystified, Sal looked back at her.

"The driver does not speak much English," she said continuing to chuckle. "Your favorite word is pronounced much like the Hindi word *faankh*. It means to chew something, like tobacco. He believes you have asked for some." Ange joined the laughter as Sal looked at the bag and shook his head.

After ten more minutes of panic and several near collisions, they reached the hotel. The driver pulled forward to a checkpoint, and three armed guards began to search the car. They rolled a large mirror underneath and examined the trunk's contents. One walked to the car windows. Sita spoke in Hindi. The guard nodded, and the car moved forward.

Three men rushed to open the doors. Sal, Sita, and Ange stepped out.

Sal stood still. He breathed in deeply and exhaled, and then turned to Ange. "What the fuck!"

Ange snickered. "It's best not to look forward. Use the side window."

"Now you tell me!"

A porter placed their luggage on a surveillance conveyor, and one by one they stepped through the front door metal detector.

"This is a lot of security," Sal said.

"Yes," Sita explained. "Since the bombing in Mumbai, all the main hotels do this."

They strolled by the last guard who stood rigid, dressed as a traditional Sikh warrior with a long black beard, red short pants, a turban, and ceremonial dagger. Reflections from a three-story chandelier glistened throughout the voluminous marble-floored lobby. Sal looked up at the second-level restaurant complex and around at the ornate Eastern furniture and blooming plants, all highlighted by an exterior glass wall looking out upon an enclosed courtyard with a forty-meter meditation pond. Sita strolled to the mahogany reception counter and waited for one of the six greeters to acknowledge her. She signaled for Ange and Sal to join her.

"Yes, Dr. Esposito, we are very pleased to have you as our guest," the clerk said. "I have a suite on the top floor, just as requested, and two very nice rooms for your assistants on the fourth level. Now may I have your passports, please?"

Sal and Ange handed over their passports and watched the clerk review them and take them into a back area. The clerk returned empty handed.

Sal turned to Sita who said, "In India, the passport is kept in the hotel safe unless it is essential for some special purpose. It is part of our regulations. We will retrieve them if we travel outside of Delhi."

Sal's face soured, but he didn't speak. Sita handed the clerk two hundred dollars. Once again, he went to the back, this time returning with a stack of Indian currency. Sita gave the bills to Sal and Ange. "You will be needing this."

"No shit?" Sal whispered and snickered as he shoved his wad of bribe rupees into his pocket.

Porters gathered the baggage and loaded a cart. "They will deliver to the rooms only after we have gone up," Sita said as they walked to the elevator. The elevator door opened, and a man inside stared at Sal before cautiously passing around him.

Sal smiled. "That happened at the airport a few times too," he said to Sita. "I see what you mean."

Sita smiled back. "It would be good to meet in the lobby in three hours. I will make some calls and confirm our meeting. Then perhaps you will wish to eat. There is also a very good bar."

"Good," Sal said. "That will give me a chance to settle in and see if there are any messages from Stosh."

***

Deb grabbed her phone and flipped it open. "Cory, your dad is very upset. He needs to talk to you immediately."

"Sure, Mom, put him on."

"He wants you to come over, face to face."

"Give me the phone, Deb ... please," Stosh said. "Cory, where have you been? We called hours ago. Get your butt over here; we have to talk, NOW!"

"Dad, I'm in Gainesville, and it's almost midnight. I can't get there for at least a couple of hours, and I'm almost finished with a job. Can't this wait until tomorrow?"

"NO! Get in your frickin' truck and drive over here NOW!"

"Stosh," Deb said. "He's only doing his job like you taught him."

Stosh took a deep breath. "Sorry I yelled, Cory. But do as I ask. There's no time to waste on this."

"Can I at least ask what it's about?"

"JUST GET YOUR BUTT OVER HERE!" Stosh flipped the phone closed and reached for his drink.

***

Sal inspected the suite to see if Hanuman was about. Finding no sign of the monkey god, he stretched and sat at the desk. He looked at the clock, 10:30 A.M. He opened his briefcase and removed a synopsis of the business plan. He put the papers down and moved to a chair by the window. He shook his head.

Sal was sitting in one of the best hotels in India—as good a hotel as he'd *ever* stayed in. He looked out at a hodge-podge of roofs ranging from designer terracotta to rusted tin. Narrow dirt streets were laced between tightly fitted dwellings, ranging from well-kept two-story concrete houses with rooftop terraces, large windows, and new cars in the driveways; to shacks made from pieces of leftover construction junk. Small, nearly naked children ran about playing and jumping in mud puddles. Older kids walked by in jeans and trendy t-shirts. A private dump filled with loose garbage hugged the street. From its middle rose a metal pole holding a satellite TV dish.

A donkey strolled down the lane and shat. A motor-scooter buzzed around the corner and through the dung, splattering the donkey's legs and driving off into the maze. Women dressed in clean, colorful saris wandered about, chatting. Spotted throughout the neighborhood, small shrines protecting brightly painted icons stood spotless and garnished with fresh flowers. The contrasts amazed. What a bizarre fucking scene, Sal thought.

Sal opened a bottle of water and filled a mug. He placed it in the microwave and tapped his fingers. The microwave bell rang. He mixed instant coffee and tasted it. He poured it out into the sink and opened the mini-bar. Six brands of scotch, three of vodka, and several twenty-ounce bottles of beer. He read the beer label. He opened a bottle and took a sip. He smacked his lips and sipped again. "This is good," he whispered. "*Kingfisher*, I'll have to take some of this back home."

In a few hours, Sal would meet Mr. Patil. He pondered what the old man looked like. He stood and walked to the window, glanced out, paced around the room, and sat back down. He looked the walls over for the tenth time. He stood again and gulped his beer. He reread the label. He glanced at the clock, 10:40 A.M.

Sal clicked on the television and flipped through channel after channel of Hindi music videos, mostly love stories with elaborate choreography. He stopped to watch a guru on a pillow in front of a red curtain, and then flicked on through more channels. The news focused on a protest; hundreds of truckers had parked their rigs on the highway and set old tires ablaze, blocking a major road for miles. Sal flipped again. A cartoon. Sal smiled as Hanuman led a heroic army of monkey men to battle against the forces of the evil king Ravana. I knew you'd show up sooner or later; he thought and chuckled.

A loud knock on the door snatched Sal's attention, and he quickly clicked back to the news.

"Hello, hello, Dr. Esposito? Hello, I am here with your luggage." The porter and two others brought in Sal's two bags. They rolled the luggage to the bedroom and roamed about pretending to check the amenities before gathering at the door and waiting. "Can we be of more service to you, Dr. Esposito?" the spokesman asked.

"No thank you." Sal reached into his pocket, pulled out his new bills and gave each man fifty rupees. Looking disappointed, the three nodded and strolled to the door.

"Oh good, you're not sleeping," Ange said from the hall.

"No, I'm not; it's daytime, Ange. What's up?"

"I'm just wandering around bored. I saw Sita in the lobby. She has news."

"News?"

"Yeah, said she'd fill us in when we meet. She seemed pissed."

"No shit, Sita pissed? Well, come in. Have you tried this Kingfisher?"

"I'll pass; you know I'm not much on beer. Say, Sal, does your luggage stink?"

***

Stosh sat in his wheelchair staring out the front window when Cory finally arrived.

"Deb, I need to talk to Cory alone, please." Deb nodded and left.

"Sit down," Stosh said as Cory walked in.

"Jesus, Dad, I just got here. Let me get a beer."

Stosh exhaled. "Get it fast."

Cory grabbed a beer, darted back, and sat. "OK, what's going on."

"What happened to the food?"

"The food?"

"Yeah, Cory, the food. Your mother said you took care of it. What exactly did you do?"

"That stuff. I took it to that Goodwill place near the church on Vesper Road. You know, the one that sends everything overseas. You always liked that place because you said you didn't want to see your old stuff on someone's back in some grocery store. Remember? So—"

"When?"

"Three or four weeks ago. They were tickled to get it, said the packaging was perfect for the overseas missions and a shipment was going out in a couple of days. I got the receipt."

"You sure they shipped it?"

"Yeah, the guy called to thank me again. Said it was on its way, and a lot of people would be well fed for a while."

"And you took it yourself?"

"Yeah, Mom asked me to."

"You know, ya knew she was fillin' in the frickin' bomb shelter, and you knew she was getting' rid of everythin' in it, and ya never said a frickin' word to me about it?"

"She said you'd given it the OK."

Stosh took a long sip of his vodka. "Well, then that's that."

"Look, Dad, I don't know why this is such a big deal. You said yourself you had to move all that crap out of there. Hell, Mom couldn't even get her car into the garage."

Stosh shook his head, then his eyes lit. "The garage?"

"Yeah, Dad those piles of boxes filled with that vacuumed packed crap. You were going to get rid of it last fall. Remember?"

Stosh leaned forward. "What about the tubs in the shelter."

"Yeah, those frickin' things were heavy, a lot heavier coming up the stairs than going down. Why the hell did you buy all that anyway? You know—"

"What happened to them?"

"I got rid of them too." Stosh sat back and looked down. "Look, Dad. I didn't think you'd care. You've always been more than generous. I figured when the guy asked for them you'd have given them to him yourself."

Stosh raised his head and sat forward again. "A guy asked for them?"

"Yeah, one of the workers. He helped me haul them up, said his cousin—I think—has a place in the woods—a prepper sort of guy, I think. He was going to be moving in with him. Said that load of food might last them a half-year or more. So, I gave them to him."

Stosh's eyes popped. "So, they weren't sent overseas?"

"Not the tubs; the guy said their place was a little over an hour from here, I think."

"Who was the guy?"

"I'm not sure—wait—Butch, I think—or something like that, the contractor will know."

Stosh smiled for the first time in hours. "Get him on the phone."

"It's the middle of the night."

"NOW!"

***

Sita sat in the lobby reading brochures. She stood as Ange and Sal approached.

"I have spoken to my uncle," she said. "He sends his apologies, but he cannot meet with us until Friday."

"That's three days," Sal said.

"Yes, I am very, very sorry for this delay."

"Did he say why?"

"No. I stressed the importance of your time when we agreed to meet today, but I am not surprised."

"A power play to let us know he's holding the cards," Sal said.

Sita nodded. "Well," she said, "we are here for longer than the two days we had planned, and immigration will not allow us to leave India and return without waiting several months. I have been reviewing some material about places we may wish to visit, if that is what you would prefer."

"How far is the Taj?" Ange asked.

"It is a long day trip to Agra by car."

"What do you think, Sal? I haven't seen it. I'd like to go."

Sal's looked down and exhaled. "Half an hour in the room and I'm climbing walls. Let's go anywhere. The Taj it is."

"It is too late to leave today," Sita said, "but there is much to see in Delhi if you wish. We can hire a driver and guide for both days." Sal and Ange nodded.

Pointing to Ange and Sal, Sita spoke to the concierge and returned. "The concierge can have a driver and guide in half an hour. He knows a pair that American visitors have liked. Perhaps we should change and meet here at 11:30. I am very sorry for the delay."

"Your uncle's game is international," Sal said. "I've played it many times myself. Timing is everything. We need to be patient and professional. I hope I brought enough XR."

***

Stosh sat in his wheelchair listening anxiously.

Cory closed his phone. "The contractor says the guy's name *is* Butch. The bad news is he doesn't work for the company anymore. He bolted a couple of weeks ago. Told them he came into some money."

Stosh smirked. "Yeah," he whispered. "*Some* money."

"The good news is I've got his address. Looks like he's living with his cousin in Green Swamp. The contractor said the place is like an arsenal. They're both gun nuts and paranoid as all hell."

Stosh wondered if he should call Sal. "Nope, we'll go ourselves," he said under his breath. "At least we know where it is, and if we can't get it, we'll get Sallie involved. I don't want him to think I'm a total frickin' idiot—unless I have to."

Looking confused, Cory listened but couldn't decipher the mumbling.

"Tomorrow, first thing, we're going over there," Stosh said.

"Dad, is this worth it for some tubs of dried-out food? I've got work to do tomorrow."

Stosh looked sternly into Cory's eyes. "First thing tomorrow."

Cory nodded and left for the Florida room. He walked in and saw his mother sitting quietly on the couch.

"How is he, honey?" Deb asked.

"I don't know. He's crazy about the lost food. I don't get it. Did he hit his head when he fell?" Deb shook no. "I'll do what he wants tomorrow, but if this goes much further, we're going to have to have him checked out. Mom, he's sitting in there talking to himself."

***

"Dr. Esposito, I am very, very pleased that we can be of service during your time in India, I must say you are a very large and fit man."

The guide smiled and pushed back his long black bangs.

Standing at five feet nine with light skin and a cherub face, he wore jeans, cowboy boots, and an American western shirt. His thin, slightly shorter partner had much darker skin, narrow eyes, a hooked nose, and wore a faded shirt and slacks.

"We will do our very, very best to be sure you and your associates are very well attended to and that you see as much of our beautiful country as possible. This is my associate Munére; my name is Jayanta. But I am more often called by my nickname, as you call them in America. Since I was a child, I have been a very, very big fan of American western stories. So, my friends gave me the name Duke. I prefer it."

Sal shook his head and grinned. "Is this fucking guy for real?" he mumbled. "OK, Duke it is. Let's see some of India."

"Thank you, sir, I will do my best to be your very, very ace-high guide man, and when it comes to driving the trails, Munére is your huckleberry."

Sal looked at Ange and chuckled. "This is too much."

"Now, Doctor, if you are ready, Munére will bring the car, and we can begin our tour."

Munére pulled up in front of the hotel in an extended SUV with three rows of seats. Duke climbed in the front, and Ange rushed for the back, leaving Sita and Sal in the center. Munére pulled out into the drive. Encountering a stopped vehicle, he quickly reversed, spun around, and raced in the wrong direction down the one-way entrance. Sal reached for a handle. Finding just a shirt hanger, he grabbed the front of his seat.

Sal felt a tap on his shoulder. "I have low dose Xanax," Ange said. Sal shook his head and reached into his bag. He pulled out his flask and took a gulp. Munére clicked on a tinny

AM radio and turned it up. A woman with a high, nasal voice sang a pop song in Hindi. A baritone chanted back while sitärs played in the background. "What's she saying?" Sal asked Sita.

"She is singing about her wedding and the wonderful married life she will have. Her fiancée sings reassuring pledges and promises an ideal life together."

"Same bullshit everywhere," Sal whispered.

"What?" Sita said.

"Nothing."

"Most of the songs in India have this kind of romantic theme. Marriage is taken very seriously, and girls spend many years dreaming of their weddings."

"Would you like to hear something else?" Duke shouted from the front.

"No, but we'd like you to turn it down," Sita responded.

Duke's eyebrows rose. He reached over and lowered the volume. "Is that good, madam?"

"Yes, much better."

Sal caught a glimpse of Munére checking out Sita in the rear-view mirror. Munére saw Sal and quickly turned his eyes back on the road. A bump threw everyone against their seat belts. Duke glared at Munére, who flaccidly drove on. Sal took another gulp.

Duke turned around to talk to his passengers. "First, we will visit the Red Fort and the Old City. There you will see many, many interesting things."

Sal glanced at a family with a tarp tent, cooking over an open fire beneath an overpass. "Do they live there?" he asked.

"No, they are not allowed," Duke said. "Authorities will come and remove them."

"They will have no other place to put them," Sita said to Duke. "They may be there for a long time." Sita turned to Sal. "Many homeless people must make a shelter and live wherever they can, without water or bathroom facilities. It is not legal, but there is no solution. You have seen many of their blue or yellow tarps. These people suffer greatly when the monsoon comes. Everything will be drenched."

"But the government is making housing for them," Duke argued.

"Not nearly enough," Sita snapped. "The population grows faster than the projects."

Duke stared forward. "Yes, of course, madam is correct."

Paying no attention to lights or signs, Munére wove through three miles of thick traffic and a menagerie of animals. He pulled into a carpark across from the entrance to the Old City. Sal took a deep breath and then pushed open the car door and stepped out. Ange climbed out behind him. Sal looked at Ange and shook his head. "I should kiss the ground," Sal said. Ange nodded.

"I am used to the driving in India," Sita said to Duke. "But perhaps you could ask our driver to go slower. He is making my associates very, very nervous."

"Certainly, madam. Munére is your huckleberry. I would suggest that we arrange two bicycle rickshaws for our visit through the Old City. You are so well informed about India; perhaps you could ride with Dr. Esposito. I will accompany

Mr. Costello. I will ask that the rickshaws stay close together. Is this acceptable, madam?"

"Yes, that will do very well."

Duke flagged over two rickshaws, and Sita stepped into one and scooted over. Sal hopped in beside her. The driver looked worried.

"He is afraid he will not go very far with such a large person," Duke said. Duke put on his Stetson and spoke in rapid-fire Hindi to the driver. The driver took his seat and placed his feet on the pedals. Duke swaggered to his rickshaw. He whistled through his fingers, waved his arm, and yelled, "Forward ho!"

"Why does Jayanta insist on calling Munére a huckleberry?" Sita asked Sal.

"It's a line he probably got from a movie. That's all."

"I do not think I like it. And I see the way Munére looks at me. I do not like that either."

"Maybe it's a caste thing."

"He is a Muslim. He is outside of our system."

Sal looked at Sita. "I'll keep an eye on him. We won't need these guys for long anyway."

The rickshaws passed through the gate to the Old City and peddled by the markets. Hundreds of large baskets overfilled with flowers, vegetables, and spices lay in front of ancient three-story buildings painted in yellow and red and plastered with bright signs in Devanagari script. Scores of loosely bundled power lines swayed haphazardly from building to building and across the streets, some low enough to touch. Hordes of people bartering for goods flowed through the narrow lanes. Shops overflowing with books stacked four feet high in the streets stood between small temples and countless food stands. The smell of cooking onions and curry permeated Sal's nostrils as people pointed at him or just stared.

A pot-bellied man stood between a Mercedes and a water buffalo pulling a wagon piled high with textiles. He wore an orange angry birds t-shirt, smoked a cigarette, and talked frantically on a cell phone. Sal moved closer to Sita as carts, animals, and other rickshaws passed within an inch of his arms. They rode and watched for over an hour. Then they turned at an ornate mosque and passed back out the Old City gates. They returned to the SUV.

For the rest of the afternoon, Munére dashed through traffic to Delhi's famous sites as Duke—occasionally corrected by Sita—provided background. They passed dozens of temples and mosques, monuments to Indian heroes, parks with lush lawns, walks lined with palm trees, and hedges sculptured in animal shapes.

Duke proudly showed off the impeccable colonial sector with its classic British mansions and wide streets, separated by carefully landscaped medians. When they attempted to stop in front of the Indian parliament buildings, a police officer with a machine gun signaled them to move on. Duke said it was standard procedure. But Sita pointed out that the Prime Minister was in attendance. Duke nodded, conceding to her correction.

Duke had little to say as they sped through an area lined with seven-story concrete housing projects stained with black mold. A sea of tattered laundry waved from lines hung on small balconies. Below, scrawny animals and poorly fed children followed as adults led the way through a maze of abandoned junk. Munére moved to the middle of the street to avoid the piles of garbage sprawling beyond the curb. Sal took a sip of whiskey and suggested they'd seen enough for one day. Sita nodded. Munére spun the car around and raced back to the hotel.

Duke slapped on his Stetson and swaggered onto the walkway. "We'll catch ya in the mornin', pardners," he said in his best Indian-cowboy accent.

Chuckling, Sal led the others into the lobby.

"Perhaps we could meet here in two hours for our dinner," Sita said. "I would suggest that we eat at the hotel so we can begin sleeping at an early hour. The trip to the Taj will be very long, and we will be leaving very early in the morning." Sal and Ange nodded, and Sita left for her room. Ange and Sal went to the bar.

"Do you have Canadian whiskey?" Sal asked the bartender.

"Yes, sir." The bartender pointed to three bottles, all bourbons.

"Never mind. How about Kingfisher beer?"

"Yes, sir."

"OK give me a Kingfisher and a small glass with ice."

"Can the ice, Sal," Ange said. "It'll make you sicker than shit."

"No ice," Sal said to the bartender.

"And I'll have a glass of white wine," Ange added. He turned to Sal. "That Duke guy is a hoot. He told me all kinds of crazy stories in the Old City. And that cowboy accent. He sounds like Gandhi impersonating John Wayne."

"Yeah," Sal chuckled. "But Sita seems to think he's full of shit—my words, not hers."

"Munére is creepy."

"I've got my eye on him. Ange," Sal said and paused. "Ange, did you see that guy with no legs scoot through the traffic on his hands? Shit, he barely made it to the other side—six lanes. And then, he flopped himself around, looked up at the sky, and beamed. No fucking legs and the guy looked happy—I mean fucking happy!" Again, Sal paused. "And the driving—they're all crazy, cutting each other off, nearly running into anything moving or not, honking those fucking horns. But Ange, there's no road rage. They smile and wave at each other. How can a place with so much chaos and poverty be so content?"

Ange grinned. "It's a different world, Sal. When I came before, I wondered the same thing. Still do."

Sal exhaled. "Tomorrow I'll take you up on the Xanax."

The bartender brought the drinks. Sal poured whiskey from his flask into the glass, and Ange checked his messages. "Gold is up again. It just keeps growing. You know, Sal, it might be better to sit on the gold for a while even with the profit the jewelry could bring."

"I've been watching."

"Yeah, the jewelry thing might not be a good move right now."

"No shit. I can see."

Ange thought a moment. "Then, why are we here?"

"We're here to meet with Sita's uncle, Ange."

"I know. On Friday, but—"

"Ange, one more time, we're here to meet with Sita's uncle."

Ange was confused but knew from Sal's tone to let it go. He looked back at his phone.

"Things look good at the club. I texted we were delayed and would be a few more days." Ange clapped his phone shut. "The trip tomorrow should be interesting. We'll see a lot of the rural areas and villages, lots of tarp families. All right, I'm going to my room. See you at dinner." Ange took his wine and strolled to the elevator.

Sal looked up at a cricket match on the television. The bartender brought munchies and stood by.

"Look at that hit," Sal said. "Four points, right?"

"Yes sir," The bartender said bobbling his head from side to side.

"No, wait a second, it's two I think."

"Yes sir," the bartender repeated still bobbling.

"Is that player the guy from Australia?"

"Yes, sir."

Sal had an urge to hold the bartender's head still.

"Say," Sal asked.

"Yes, sir."

"Do you think the Islanders will beat the Lakers in the Super Bowl this year?"

"Yes, sir."

Sal chuckled. "How about another Kingfisher?"

"Yes sir," The bartender said and bobbled as he left for the cooler.

***

Stosh grabbed the hand-grip as Cory helped hoist him into the F-350 pickup. Cory reached for Stosh's wheelchair.

"No," Stosh said. "Just the crutches; toss em in the back."

Cory reluctantly followed orders and climbed into the driver's seat.

"Green Swamp is a crazy place, Dad. I hope this is worth it. Some of the guys who live there are complete nuts. This could be real dangerous."

"It's only an hour or two. We'll get the tubs back and be back before dinner. We'd be back by *now* if we'd left when I said."

"I did the best I could. I have a business to run, remember? You set it up, remember? Said you'd kick my ass if I didn't run it like you taught me, remember? And that always meant nose to the grindstone, remember?"

"You say *remember* one more frickin' time, and I *will* kick your ass. Now punch the address into the satellite thing and let's hit the frickin' road."

As they buzzed along the busy Tampa highway and out to the rural, single-lane road to Green Swamp, Cory continued asking why the tubs were so important. Stosh gave no answers. He thought of Sal and looked at his watch. Ten and a half hours' difference in India, he thought. Sal is fast asleep now. Cory glanced at his GPS and slowed.

"It's around here somewhere," Cory said.

"I don't see a frickin' thing."

"There," Cory said and pointed.

"How did ya see that? It's nothin' more than two tracks a dirt in all that rough grass. Heck, Cory, that path barely makes it between all them frickin' pine trees."

"Come on, Dad. We've had to find more remote houses than this. People build in the damnedest places."

"There was usually a sign or a mailbox or somethin'. These guys don't wanna be found."

Cory flipped the truck into four-wheel drive and slowly drove fifty yards into the woods. He stopped at a rusted cattle gate held up by two rotting fence posts. Just beyond he spotted a concrete block shack with an old pickup parked near the side door.

"This must be it, Dad."

"Yeah, help me out of this frickin' seat."

Cory pushed open the truck's door and started to hop out.

"JUST STAY WHERE YA ARE!" a raspy voice hollered from the shack's window. "THIS HERE IS PRIVATE PROPERTY. GET YOUR FUCKIN' ASSES OUTTA HERE!"

"WE JUST WANT TO TALK TO YOU," Cory yelled back. "BUTCH BROUGHT SOME TUBS OF FOOD OUT HERE FROM OUR PLACE, AND THERE'S BEEN A MISTAKE."

"BUTCHIE AIN'T AROUND, AND THE ONLY MISTAKE'S GONNA BE WHEN YOU PUT YOUR FOOT ON MY LAND. GET THE FUCK OUTTA HERE NOW!"

"JUST LISTEN A MINUTE," Cory stepped on the ground. A rifle blasted splintering a branch six feet from the truck.

"I AIN'T BLOWIN' SMOKE OUTTA MY ASS. GET THE FUCK OFFA MY PROPERTY!"

"JUST GIVE US A SECOND TO TALK TO—"

A bullet snapped a rock six inches from Cory's foot. "GET THE FUCK OUTTA HERE!"

"Come on, Cory. We'll have to figure another way," Stosh said. "This guy's crazy and it ain't worth gettin' killed over."

Cory hopped onto his seat, slapped the steering wheel, and backed the truck to the road.

"OK, what now, Dad?"

"Ya might as well start back home. We're not goin' to be able to do this alone."

Cory backed onto the road and sped off.

I'll have to call Sallie as soon as we get back, Stosh thought. He looked at his watch and shook his head. Crap, it's 12:30 there, way too late to call. I'll wait. Guess he gets to see how stupid I am after all. At least we know where it is and what we're up against.

Cory broke the silence. "All right, Dad. Now this is *real* serious. I've been shot at twice, and I can tell you're cooking up a plan to come back here. Dad, I'm wondering about your sanity. Shit, I could have been killed! Will you at least tell me what the fuck is going on?"

Stosh nodded. "We're comin' to that town we drove through. Stop at the coffee shop we passed."

Cory pulled in, hopped out, grabbed the crutches, and helped Stosh from the truck. Cory stepped slowly as Stosh hobbled in. They took stools at the lunch bar.

Stosh sipped his coffee and gazed off.

"OK," Cory said, "what's in the tubs. I don't think we're here for freeze dried food."

"The gold," Stosh mumbled.

"What?"

"The gold!"

Cory sat back. "No way."

"Been in them all along."

"Dad, I took the gold to the vault with you, remember?"

"We took boxes with bricks and other crap. The gold's in the tubs." Stosh paused. "Look, banks were crashing all over the frickin' place—the one where the money was went belly up just a couple a weeks after we got it out, remember? I got the vault space so people would *think* it was there. I put it in the tubs with some wadded up newspaper and spread a layer a packs a that freeze-dried crap over the top—just in case somebody snooped around and looked in one. The gold's why the frickin' things were so heavy. And that's where the crap in the garage came from." Stosh chuckled. "All this time and you never asked about that, and you think *I'm* goin' nuts."

Cory put his hand over his face and exhaled. "You should have told me. None of this would have happened if you had told me."

"I didn't want you or your mom to worry 'bout it. I only told Sallie."

Cory dropped his hand to his knee. "Shit, Mr. Esposito's going to explode."

"Well, he ain't gonna be singin' and dancin'."

"Maybe we can do it. I'll call Darren; we'll get the crews together. Shit, Dad, that's a small army."

"No, keep your brother and the others out of it. After what we just went through, I figure this is gonna take Sallie's expertise."

Corry thought and nodded. "Maybe you should call him now. Waiting will only make you crazier."

"Can't. It's the middle of the night in India. This'll have to wait."

They finished their coffee without speaking, loaded back into the truck, and drove on.

***

Sal awoke. He sat and waited for his eyes to focus on the clock, 1:30 P.M. He swung his legs over the side of the bed, stood, and stretched. Dreams of Sita's uncle had raided his sleep for hours. He'd never seen the man, but the image of a strong, handsome warrior dressed in imperial Indian regalia fighting to push Sal into the caldron of molten gold stuck in Sal's head.

He washed his face, poured a drink, and sat by the window. Groggy, his thoughts drifted. He knew Ange was right. This whole idea was crazy, and using the gold now made no sense—and here was Salvatore Esposito, preacher of the informed investment, once again getting into something he knew shit about. But, he knew he needed to face him. Once he'd decided to come, there was no turning back. Seeing Mr. Patil had become the real mission.

Wailing and yapping from the street snatched Sal's attention. He looked down. A litter of puppies struggled for position to suckle their mother as she lay on her side in the center of the deserted road. "How can they be so fucking loud through a closed window?" he whispered. He watched the rumpus and knew there would be no sleeping until it ended. He turned on the television, watched a few seconds, and turned it back off. He took a sip of whiskey, and then remembered the Kingfisher beer. He strolled to the fridge and popped open a Kingfisher. He took a gulp. He held the fridge door open looking at the light on his feet and then looked inside. A mini-bottle of vodka caught his eye. He thought of Stosh.

"Shit," Sal whispered. "I haven't talked to Stosh since we got here." He reached for his cell, scrolled through his contacts and pressed the button for Stosh. The phone rang twice. "I'm sorry sir," a woman said in a barely understandable Indian accent, "this number cannot be connected as dialed. You must use the code for the country you wish to reach. A list can be found at—"

"I know the fucking code," Sal snapped at the phone. He scrolled back to Stosh's number. Knowing he'd have to enter every digit, he wrote the number on a pad. Adding the international code, he punched it in and pressed send. The phone rang three times.

"I'm sorry, sir," another nearly indiscernible voice said. "You must—"

Sal pushed the end button, again scrolled his contacts, and compared Stosh's number to his copy. "Shit," he said. "That three should be an eight." As he wrote the correction and reentered the first number, the squalling from the street abruptly ended. He looked out the window and watched the mother leading her litter down the road and around the corner. He took his last gulp and looked at the phone.

"Fuck it," Sal said. "I'll call tomorrow."

***

Cory glanced at Stosh's face. He had never seen his dad look so defeated. He drove into the next town, stopping at the first of their two traffic lights. Stosh picked up his phone.

"Maybe I'll call Sallie now. I've yanked him outta bed for smaller crap than this." He tossed his phone back on the dash. "No, I'll wait."

The light turned, and Cory accelerated. "You're just anxious, Dad. When we get back, we'll sit down and script out exactly what to say. Think about that while we're driving. It'll keep your mind occupied."

The second light turned yellow. Cory sped up and almost made it through. He slowed and looked in his side mirror. "Shit," he yelled. He quickly checked traffic left and right and swung hard, throwing Stosh against the door and his cell phone to the floor as he pulled a U-turn and sped back.

"Jesum Crow!" Stosh yelled. "What the frick are you doin'?"

"That's Butch's truck," Cory said, pointing to an old orange pickup parked in front of a bar. Cory smiled. "Now we've got him."

Flashing red and blue lights raced up behind, and the blasting wow-wow of a state police car signaled Cory to pull over. "Shit," Cory said. "Why now?"

A Latina officer stepped out of the cruiser and cautiously approached Cory's pickup.

"Hands on the wheel," she told Cory. "Keep yours where I can see them," she directed Stosh. "Now slowly and in plain sight hand me your license and registration." Cory complied. "Any firearms in the vehicle?"

"No ma'am—I mean officer," Cory said.

"And what was your sudden need to change direction and risk the lives of everyone near you?"

"Officer, I looked to see if the way was clear," Cory said.

The officer smirked. "You sped through a red light and then performed an illegal and dangerous U-turn. That's two major moving violations. Do you understand why I pulled you over?" Cory nodded. "If the U-turn was to avoid my pursuit, this is more serious."

"It wasn't officer. I swear. I didn't see you."

The officer looked sternly at Cory. She looked at Cory's license. "Stoshowicz?" she asked. Cory nodded. "Any relationship to Yashu Stoshowicz?"

"Yes, my dad." Cory pointed at Stosh.

The officer stood silent and looked at Stosh. "Mr. Stoshowicz, you probably don't remember me. I'm Angela Rodriguez."

"Angela Rodriguez." Stosh paused. "Sure, I remember you. We did some work for your family. Your mom was studdin' to be a nurse. Too bad about your dad; he went way too young. You were the cutest little thing, and you have a brother—if I'm thinkin' straight."

"I'm flattered you remember."

"How's your mom?"

"Very well, she finished school and has been with a hospital in Tampa for—well let see—at least fifteen years now."

"And your brother?—Ritchie, wasn't it?"

"He's trying to straighten out. Took the easy path for a while—if you know what I mean. But, he's back in school and holding his own—I can't believe you remember us all."

"Sure. Nice family. Went through a lot a hard times when your dad passed. Well, at least, it looks like most a that's over. Jesum Crow, little Angela Rodriguez a frickin' trooper." Stosh took a deep breath, "Sorry, officer."

Angela laughed and handed Cory his license and registration. "You'll never know what your dad did for us."

"Aw, we just did some plumbin'. The house was in real bad shape, needed a lot of pipes, a new toilet, water heater—I think."

"And you wouldn't let Mom pay a cent."

"Your family'd been through enough. And your mom was broke."

"And at Christmas, all those wonderful things just showed up along with an envelope of cash. We all knew it had to be you."

Stosh smiled. "I grew up real poor. I know what it's like. Doin' stuff like that makes me feel good."

Angela wiped an eye. "Well," she said to Cory, "there must be some reason you made such a drastic turn."

"We're looking for a guy. It's all part of a big misunderstanding we're trying to fix. I saw his truck." Cory pointed at Butch's truck.

"Wait here," Officer Rodriguez said. Cory watched in his

mirror as she called in and returned. "That truck belongs to Byron Sneed—also known as Butch Sneed. There's a warrant out for his arrest. He's a suspect in an armed robbery a few weeks ago. Good thing you didn't confront him."

Cory shook his head. "No wonder he's been holed up at his cousin's."

"His cousin's?"

"Yeah, he's got a shack in the woods not far from here."

"OK, after we're finished, you'll show me? He's Bobby Sneed; he's wanted too."

Corry nodded. "What are we going to do?"

"I've called for backup. Then I'm going to arrest him. And before I take him in, you're going to work out your misunderstanding. OK?"

Cory grinned and nodded. "And the tickets?"

"Some days I hate this job. Today I'm thanking God I pulled you over. Today, I get to pay back a little piece of an old debt."

Two police cars rushed in and blocked the street in front of the bar. Officer Rodriguez joined them. Five troopers took strategic positions and entered the tavern. Within minutes, Officer Rodriguez marched out pushing a very drunk man in handcuffs. The man raised his head, and Cory smiled. Officer Rodriguez secured the prisoner in the back seat of her cruiser and signaled for Cory to come.

"You sit in the front. He's very intoxicated. I don't know if he'll make much sense. I have to listen in."

Cory nodded and hopped into the passenger side of the cruiser. Officer Rodriguez stood outside and listened.

"Butch, remember me?"

"Fuck no. This some kinda trick?"

"Butch, I'm Cory Stoshowicz. Remember? You did some work for me—helped fill in a bomb shelter. I gave you some tubs of food."

"Oh yeah. What the fuck do you want?"

"You were going to move it out."

"Fuck off. I'll get it; I told ya I would. That's not what this shit is about, is it?"

"You'll get it?"

"Yeah, when I get a fucking chance, I'll get the shit outta there and take it ta Bobby's. Fuck, if that's all this is about, I'll drive over and get it right now."

"Get it now?"

"Now or tomorrow, whatever the fuck works for ya. Now can I go?"

"Butch, where are the tubs?"

"Behind your fucking garage. Shit, I'm shitfaced drunk, and I know that much. I think *you* helped me stack all that heavy shit, remember? If you're the same fuckin' guy."

"You never picked them up?"

"I know I never picked the shit up. I didn't think you'd get the fuckin' cops after me for chicken-shit like that. Shit, I done a lot worse than forgettin' ta move some fuckin' tubs. Shit, me and Bobby robbed a fuckin' liquor store. Got thousands. I quit my fuckin' job, told the boss ta fuck off and eat shit."

Butch snickered and then dropped his head on his shoulder and passed out.

Cory stepped out of the cruiser. "He's out."

"Good. Then maybe he won't throw up. Find out what you needed?"

Cory smiled. "I hope so."

"Good, and thank you. We just got a confession as a bonus."

Cory pointed at his GPS and showed Officer Rodriguez the coordinates for Bobby's shack warning her of how Bobby received visitors. She thanked him, strolled over to Stosh's window. She stuck her head in and pecked his cheek. "You're a good man, Mr. Stoshowicz, and I'm glad our paths crossed."

Stosh nodded. "Say hi to your mom. Tell her I'm proud of her—not easy getting' through somethin' as tough as nursin' school, especially with two little ones to take care of on your own. And you be careful, Angela. There's a lotta nuts out this way."

Angela chuckled and was off.

"Let's go home, Dad."

"Did you guys make a plan to get the gold back."

"I think so."

"Whatta you mean *think so*?"

"You'll see," Cory said. "I hope," he whispered.

Cory followed every rule of the road as Stosh sat silent, continuing to compose his conversation with Sal. Cory pulled into the driveway, fetched Stosh's wheelchair, and helped his dad from the truck.

"Just get me the crutches," Stosh said.

"You want to deal with Mom?"

Stosh grunted. "Where the heck are you goin'?" he asked as Cory pushed him down the driveway.

"We need to check something, Dad."

Cory pushed Stosh to the back of the garage.

“I checked under all them tarps, Cory.”

“All of them?”

Stosh sat still, looking as if the answer was no. Cory rolled him to the far end of the garage where Butch and he had stacked the tubs. He set the brake lever on Stosh’s chair and flipped up the canvas. Stosh exhaled and grinned from ear to ear. Cory put his hand on his Dad’s shoulder; Stosh patted it.

“Now you can call the crew,” Stosh said. “First thing tomorrow, we visit the vault.”

CHAPTER XI

Caste

Sal's head smacked the ceiling as Munére drove through a cavernous pothole. "Are you OK?" he asked Sita.

"I am fine. I have sufficient distance, so my head does not make contact. You will be more comfortable soon. We will be back on the new road shortly, and we are only one hour from the Taj Mahal."

"Look at that," Ange said pointing to a three-story statue of a dark, blue-skinned god dressed in red and gold. The towering figure stood in front of a cow, smiling and holding a flute near his lips.

"Yes," Sita said. "We are in Mathura, the birthplace of Lord Krishna."

"Yes," Duke said from the front seat. "Krishna is the seventh avatar of our God Vishnu, the one that sustains the earth."

"No," Sita said. "He is the eighth avatar. Lord Rama is the seventh."

Duke exhaled. "Yes, of course, madam is correct." He turned his head forward and stared.

Sal gazed at rows of shacks dispersed between an occasional modern structure. As in Delhi, families with improvised shelters made from blue plastic tarps camped on all undeveloped spots. In front of a school, a group of young girls in tunics skipped down the dirt road swinging their books while a dozen or more boys pulled off their ties and crammed onto a small camel cart. In a garbage pile, a horse, birds, and poor women in saris rummaged for food. A few yards away, a bright yellow concrete building overspread with Hindi signs housed a small grocery store with chickens penned in metal cages and dozens of baskets filled with vegetables and peppers. Cows with long sharp horns roamed freely, occasionally stepping into traffic, forcing drivers to slam on their breaks. As Sal had seen before, packs of dogs ran loose everywhere, people in traditional Indian dress swarmed their way through the colorful disorder, and everyone seemed to be smiling.

After miles of countryside and thousands of potholes, Duke announced, "We are very, very close to Agra. We will be at the Taj in one-half of an hour."

Agra looked familiar. The same styles of buildings, streets filled with people and animals, and low hanging masses of electrical wire. Munére maneuvered through congested streets and crossed the bridge over the river Yamuna. "This is the holiest river in all of India," Duke said.

"It is a revered place, but it is not considered as holy as the Ganges," Sita corrected.

"The water looks filthy," Sal remarked.

"It is low at this time of year and looks more brown than

at other times," Duke said. "After monsoon, it is very clear and clean."

Sita looked out the window and shook her head. Duke pointed in the distance, "There it is, the Taj Mahal."

Sal struggled to lower his head and catch a glimpse. "What the fuck am I doing?" he whispered straightening up. "We'll be there in five minutes."

Munére pulled into the car park. Duke told the others that Munére had heard something grinding and would go for gas and have the Toyota checked. Sal wormed his way out and was immediately steeped in the sauna-like air. As he stretched, a pack of boys selling Taj Mahal booklets surrounded him.

"Sir, I have the very, very best book on the Taj Mahal, very, very cheap, sir. You must have one to take home with you," they said over and over. Sal ignored them. Duke waved them off.

"There will be many more of these boys," Duke said. "They skip school, buy these books at a cheap store, and try to sell them all day. If they can sell even four of five, they will make more than their fathers."

"And," Sita added, "they will have no education when they are older and can no longer get sympathy from the tourists."

Duke nodded and waved his hand forward. "This way, head um up and move em out."

The group joined a mass of visitors flowing through a gauntlet of hawkers and souvenir stands. Taj Mahal images on shawls, towels, and wall-sized tapestries hung from wires stretched above the heads of hundreds of vendors standing behind cloth-covered tables filled with Taj miniatures, mugs, glasses, framed pictures, and other trinkets, all with Arabic writing.

At the end of the street, uniformed guards separated the crowd. Sal noticed Duke waving to a guard and pointing at Sita as he walked behind her. Both were directed into the line for Indian citizens only. Sal and Ange fell in on the foreigner's side. Separated by a metal barricade, each line inched toward security.

Even with his head above the crowd, Sal was smothered by the compressed mass and the pungent smell of perfumes mixed with human body odor. Children in their best clothes clung to their parents. Foreigners in shorts and golf shirts chatted and laughed. Devout Muslims wore white and moved along in reverent silence.

After forty-five minutes, they reached the checkpoint. Guards searched bags, patted down a few randomly chosen people, and waved the others on.

Sal and Ange waited for Sita and Duke in a courtyard surrounded by more high stone walls. Monkeys jumped from rooftop to rooftop, grabbing tidbits thrown by children and tossing the remains onto visitors. Small groups stood about organizing their next steps and checking their cameras. Sal became concerned about Sita when he noticed the arrival of a family who had been behind her. Within a few minutes, Duke came.

"Where is Sita?" Sal asked. Before Duke could answer, Sita walked into the courtyard, silent and head bowed. She looked up at Sal and made herself appear normal.

"Are you OK?" Sal asked.

"We should continue on," she said.

Duke looked at her with a smile. Sita looked back with a stern face. Duke turned, waved his hand and said, "Forward ho."

"What does the calligraphy say?" Ange asked at the entrance to the enclosed red-stone hallway.

"It is a wish that we all be peaceful," Duke said.

"It is much more than that," Sita said. "It says, 'O soul, thou art at rest. Return to the Lord at peace with him, and he at peace with you.' You will see much more writing as we go along, many messages of judgment from the Qur'an, some Persian poems, and many more sacred tidings."

"Yes, madam is correct," Duke said.

The Taj stood framed by a three-story arch at the end of the great gateway. They stepped through and stood in a refreshing breeze. Sal looked at Sita, smiling as she gazed at the glistening white structure in the distance. She looks OK now, he thought. The crowd dispersed to the wide walkways running for hundreds of yards beside the long reflecting pool and through acres of lavish green lawns and carefully tended gardens.

"What are those?" Ange asked pointing at identical red-stone buildings standing on each side of the Taj.

"The one to the left is a mosque. The other one is there for architectural balance," Duke said. "Perhaps at one time, it was a guest house. Now it serves many, many purposes, mostly practical. We should go in this direction to the side. It is faster, and we will be able to take photographs without as many people in the way. We will be required to leave our shoes at a place next to the stairway to the terrace. It is over this way also."

"Slow down, Duke," Sal said. "It took us hours to get here, and you're moving us along like this is a cattle drive."

"Sure thing, Doctor," Duke said and smiled.

"And don't rush Mrs. Patil. Let her take all the time she wants to look and take pictures."

Duke nodded. "Certainly, madam will have all the time she wishes."

On the lower lawn, a dark man in green work clothes took their shoes and strolled out of sight into a maze of racks. Sal waited for a ticket. Duke marched to the terrace steps and waved the others on.

"They will have your shoes when you return," Sita said. "In India, we do not often use receipts. Do not worry."

A long queue wrapped around the glistening square terrace surrounding the mausoleum and extending nearly one hundred feet on all sides. White marble paving swirling with light brown highlights reflected the sun, frying bare feet, and baking those wearing socks. A few visitors stood by the mausoleum wall trying to snap vertical pictures of the fourteen-story marble minarets towering over each corner.

At the north side, Sal looked out across the Yamuna to the legendary Moonlight Garden where Shah Jahan walked and mourned the loss of his third wife, Mumtaz Mahal, who died just after delivering their fourteenth child and now lay beside him in the Taj. Just beyond the garden, a weathered wooden skiff with a small patched sail moved slowly through the water, passing three tarp camps shaded by a grove of trees. Sal shook his head and wiped his brow with his nearly saturated sleeve.

"Quite the contrast," Ange said. "But maybe they get the last laugh. They see the Taj Mahal every day for free, and I'll bet they're not sweating their asses off."

Sal smiled and thought of the old tarp he and Jimmy Eagleson found. He remembered how they designed their fort using the weathered canvas. They cooked over an open fire too, and he was happy there. Maybe some of these people were happy too.

Duke squawked into his cell phone and waved his free hand. Standing at the side of the queue, he looked down shaking his head. He snapped the phone shut. As he reentered the queue, a man with a German accent began to yell, "Hey the line starts back there!" Sweltering and dehydrated, Sal glared at him. The man turned away.

"What's up?" Sal asked Duke.

"Nothing of very much concern. Munére has found the problem with our vehicle and is working very, very hard to have it repaired. All is going very, very well."

"And if he can't get it fixed?"

"Oh, he will get it fixed, Doctor, no need to worry. All is going very, very well."

As they entered the mausoleum, Duke removed his Stetson, took a small flashlight from his pocket and began to explain *jali* inlay, the process used to insert thousands of small precious and semi-precious red and green stones into the pure white marble. Sal was impressed by the intricate floral design on the walls and sarcophagi. Duke demonstrated how reflection identified genuine jewels from the fakes sold in the streets and souvenir stores. The group gazed at the marble lattice and *jali* screen surrounding the tombs, one larger and on a higher platform. A guard yelled at the German man for taking pictures inside. The German snapped back at the guard and was escorted out.

"This is a very holy place," Duke said. "He should have been more respectful."

"These are only cenotaphs," Sita said. "They contain no remains. Mumtaz and Shah Jahan are in a chamber below in a place where they cannot be disturbed. After making people wait for over an hour in the very, very hot sun, there is no need to be so concerned about photographs taken of empty tombs." Duke looked away, silent.

After a half-hour of gazing at designs and bumping other sweaty bodies, even Sita had had enough. The group returned to the terrace.

"Munére is continuing to oversee the repairs on our vehicle," Duke said. "And I know that we had planned to visit the Red Fort today. But I am told that the fort is under renovation, so there is little for us to see there at this time. I would suggest that I arrange for another vehicle, and we visit a place where they handmake the finest handcrafted rugs in all of India. They will show you every step in the process. It is very, very informative and most enjoyable. Then we can go for some food and drink. Does this sound like a good plan?"

"NO!" Sita proclaimed. "This is a trick to take us to a store where you will receive compensation for delivering us. The Red Fort is always undergoing some sort of repair. I researched it last night. There are plenty of open areas and still much to see there. Please do not try to divert us again with this kind of dishonesty."

"You heard Mrs. Patil," Sal said. "Get a car, and we'll go to the Red Fort."

"Yes, certainly, madam is correct. However, please know that I was not trying to trick you in any way. I am only concerned with showing you the very most I can in the valuable time you have to spend."

Sita smirked. Duke led the group back to the shoe check. An attendant saw Sal, bolted to the racks, and returned with everyone's shoes. Sal smiled and tipped the man one hundred rupees. Sita shook her head.

"How did this guy know which are ours?" Sal asked.

"It is his job, and the amount you gave him is far too much. We should go in this direction where we can get some bottled water and then allow Jayanta the time to arrange another vehicle. He is a very poor guide. He does not know our history well, and he is full of tricks. *And*, he thinks that because he is of high caste, I am inferior to him and should keep quiet. I do not like him."

***

Sal's back ached from the jarring ride to the Red Fort in the cramped auto-rickshaw. But Sita was right; there was plenty to see, and they spent over two hours exploring. As they stood in the car park watching the sun set, Munére arrived in a small van with the faded logo of a hotel on the doors.

"I am very, very sorry," Duke said. "But our vehicle will not be repaired until the morning, and I have not been able to find another that can take us back to Delhi tonight. I have taken the liberty of arranging a hotel for us. Because it is late, most of the lodging is already reserved. We will need to stay just outside the city at a very nice, traditional Indian facility. It is small but very, very good and the food is excellent."

Sal looked pissed and shook his head. "Does it have a bar?"

"The owner will supply whatever alcohol you request. If you let me know your preferences, I will call ahead and make sure he has them ready."

The group crammed into the van and Munére sped away.

"This is just great," Sal said.

"I am glad you are pleased, Doctor," Duke replied.

"I'm not. That was sarcasm. We're stuck here overnight without a change of clothes or toiletries. Shit, we don't even have toothbrushes."

"I cannot help with the clothes, but someone will go for all of your other needs. There will be very good soaps and fresh towels."

"It is OK," Sita said. "We can manage for one day with our present clothes, and we will be back in Delhi tomorrow morning when we can properly wash and change."

"Will we, Duke?" Sal asked.

"What, Doctor?"

"Be back in Delhi tomorrow morning?"

"Yes, Doctor, most certainly."

Sal took the last swig from his flask, sniffed his armpit. "We'd better, for everyone's sake."

Munére swung into the dirt drive in front of a two-story concrete building painted turquoise with a small sign next to the door matching the print on the van. A few small trees in terracotta pots stood near the double glass doorway.

Duke hopped out and greeted a man rushing out from the lobby. Duke placed his hand on the man's shoulder and spoke to him. They both smiled and looked at the van. The others climbed out.

"Welcome, welcome. I am Sorab. We are most pleased we are able to accommodate you tonight. It is unusual that we have space at this time. You are very, very lucky. I will have a man run for any of your needs and have already obtained the beverages you requested. Please come."

The group walked into a small lobby with a wicker couch, two wooden chairs, and a squeaking overhead fan. Next to a doorway strung with hanging beads stood a wooden statue of a bare-breasted Indian dancer. Sorab plopped a guest book on a small worn reception desk.

"Please, if you will all sign here. Then I will acquaint you with the rest of our establishment and show you to your rooms. And please, I need your passports."

Sorab lead the group to a room with a six-foot bar and seven round tables each with four plastic lawn chairs. He strolled behind the bar to an old refrigerator.

"Would you like refreshment before we visit the upstairs?"

"I would like a beer," Sal said.

"And I will have water," Sita added.

"White wine," Ange mumbled.

"I know you requested Kingfisher beer, sir. But when Duke told me you were American I was able to get something much better." Sorab reached into the fridge and pulled out a twenty-ounce bottle of Budweiser. "I knew you would like this," he smiled and bobbled his head.

Sal closed his eyes and exhaled. "Next time stick to the order," he snapped. "But give me that anyway. Anything will do right now."

Sita saw Sal's irritation. "He is just trying to please you. We will not be here for long. Perhaps we should relax and make the best of things."

"It's not just that the place is a dump. It's the whole thing. I feel like I'm being played." Sal took a deep breath. "You're right, though. We are here, and we'll make the best of it."

After drinks, Sorab led the three guests up a narrow stairway to the second floor. Lit by small wall lights, the hallway served six rooms on each side.

"Your room is there," Sorab said to Sal and Ange as he pointed to the one farthest to the right. "And madam will be there." Sorab pointed to a door at the opposite end.

"You couldn't have put us farther apart," Sal said.

"I am sorry, sir; with this short notice these are the only rooms available."

"OK," Sal paused, "let's check them out and meet back downstairs in a few minutes."

Sal entered the room and shook his head. Two beds with three-inch mattresses were framed with finished two-by-fours and held twelve inches off the floor by wooden legs. They were jammed next to a closet-sized toilet, sink, and shower combination enclosed by a curtain. An empty plastic jug sat next to the toilet.

Sal cautiously sat on a bed. "Shit, the fucking thing is holding up," he said to Ange and laughed. "Sita's right; we'll get as good a nap as possible and be back in Delhi in no time. I'm going down to meet her. You make your calls."

Sorab rushed to the door holding a half roll of toilet paper. "Sorry, sir, you will be needing this. I should have placed it here earlier."

Sal met Sita downstairs. A half-dozen guests occupied three tables covered with bowls of Indian food. Sal watched them use their fingers to shovel naan, rice, and chicken into their mouths as they nattered and laughed. Sal and Sita took a table near the bar and waited for Ange.

"How is your room?" Sal asked Sita.

"It is acceptable. I have a chair and some space next to the bed. I was able to wash a bit. It will be fine for one night."

"Sorab brought me a bag with toothbrushes and some deodorant," Sal said.

"Yes, I have some also. It will be OK for one night. Remember to use only the bottled water to brush your teeth." Sal smiled and nodded.

Sal saw Sorab behind the bar. "Did you get the whiskey?"

"Oh yes, sir. I found the very, very best whiskey in all of Agra. Canadian, just as you requested."

"Crown?"

"Yes sir, it is called Supreme Crown, just as you ordered."

Sorab held up a green bottle with a white label. "I was told this is the finest."

"All right. Give me a small glass, no ice." Sal took a sip and winced. "This is scotch!"

"Yes, sir the very finest Canadian scotch whiskey."

"Just give me a beer and some water for Mrs. Patil."

Ange strolled in and sat. "Things are good back home."

Sal nodded. "Good. Shit, I forgot to call Stosh." He reached for his phone and then shoved it back in his pocket. "I'll call him later. Let's order some food, have a couple of drinks, and then get some sleep."

Sal was surprised at the meal. "This is good," he remarked as he adapted to using his hand. Sita chatted about the Taj and the Fort. Sal could see she was OK. He still wondered what had happened at the Taj, but didn't ask.

"It's almost midnight," Sal said.

Sita nodded. "Yes, I am very tired. Perhaps it is a good time to go upstairs."

Sal and Ange saw Sita to her door, walked to the other end of the hallway and turned in. After a half-hour of tossing and turning, they finally dozed off.

***

"Sir, sir, please, sir you must wake up and come!" a man standing next to Sal's bed pleaded.

Startled, Sal popped up and grabbed him by the shirt. "What the fuck—Munére?"

"Yes, sir you must come quickly, please, sir!"

"Why? What the fuck is going on?"

"Please, sir, it is madam. Please come right away."

Sal hopped out of bed in his shorts, ran to Sita's room, and kicked the door open. His eyes flamed. Sorab was behind Sita, clenching her by the waist and covering her mouth with his hand. Duke, naked, squatted in front, pulling down her pants and underwear. Sal grabbed Duke's neck, raised him off the floor, and hurled him on the bed smashing the frame into several pieces. Sorab pushed Sita into the wall, grabbed a broken end-post, and walloped Sal's shoulder. Sal spun, grabbed Sorab's hand, and squeezed until Sorab screamed and dropped the post. Sal seized Sorab and threw him on top of Duke, then grabbed the post and stood over the two would-be rapists.

"STOP IT!" Sita yelled, "STOP IT ALL NOW!" Sal turned and looked at Sita. "I cannot stand this violence; you are all so very, very brutal. STOP IT ALL NOW!"

"You know what they were going to do."

"Yes, and now you will kill them? Is that what must happen? And then what? Then do I become your—how would *you* say it—piece of ass? You will grab me by my hair and drag me off to your cave? IT MUST ALL STOP NOW!"

Sal pushed Sorab back as he tried to jump up from the bed. "Neither of you is going anywhere." He threw a towel over Duke. "Cover that pathetic thing before you make me laugh."

Ange stood at the door next to Munére. "She's right, Sal; don't hurt them. We'll be in deep shit, and it's not worth it."

"I'm not going to hurt them. But they're not going anywhere

until we have the car and our passports. Sal breathed hard. "And Duke's guide license. You won't be needing that anymore, will you?" Duke looked up and panicked. "That's right, little bandito, your rustling days are over."

Sita left the room with Ange. "OK, Munére, when can we expect the car?"

"Sir, I am very, very sorry. I have been lying. Jayanta told me I must do as he says, and I have not been truthful. I did not know they were going to do this thing. In my religion, this is a most bad sin."

"Munére, the fucking car?"

"Sir, the car is behind the hotel. It was repaired in the afternoon."

Sal glared at the shaking captives on the bed. "Where are the passports?"

"In a wooden box behind the counter," Sorab said. "It is not locked."

"Munére, check Duke's pants for his license." Duke started to protest but then saw Sal's eyes and stayed silent.

"Here it is, sir."

"Good, bring it with us." Sal looked at the post still in his hand and then stared at Duke and Sorab. "You two are real fucking lucky. I have a friend who's asked me not to use things like this anymore. But, if I ever see either of you again, I guarantee I'll return to my old habits and bash your fucking heads in. Munére, get the passports and the car. We will meet you in the front."

Sal stepped into the hallway. At the top of the stairs, Ange hugged and consoled Sita. Sal looked down and grinned. "So much for chivalry," he mumbled.

***

"How far?" Sal asked.

"About an hour, sir."

Sal looked to the seat behind him where Sita was stretched out, sleeping. "You still with us, Ange?" he whispered to the far back.

"Yeah, I'm good," Ange whispered back.

"Tell me something. How did those assholes think they would get away with that?"

"They probably would have—a woman in a room by herself with no witnesses. Some people here might think she had it coming. She probably would never have said anything anyway to avoid the shame. It's a different world here, Sal."

"Not all that different. All right, the sun's coming up, Munére. Let's stop at the next place we can get some coffee."

Munére pulled into a roadside stop. "I will fuel the car while you get your refreshments."

"We'll all stay together," Sal said.

"Sir, if I were going to abandon you, I would have done so at the hotel."

"Good point—we'll get you some coffee? You know, I didn't even know you could talk before tonight."

Munére smiled. "It is not my job to talk, sir."

Sal and Sita stood near the car. The rising sun filled the

trees with orange light. Sal looked into a roadside ditch filled with garbage. Sita looked up at the trees.

"Does anyone ever clean up this shit?" Sal said.

"Things look very good to me," Sita replied.

"How can you look at all this garbage and say that?"

"I am not looking down at the garbage. I am looking up at the flowers in the trees."

"Jesus Christ, you're one of those fucking people who see the good in everything."

Sita's head snapped around. "And perhaps if you opened your fucking eyes, even *you* would also see the good."

Sita wept. Sal handed her some clean tissue. She dried her eyes and quietly blew her nose.

"I am so very sorry. You have come here to a place you did not want to go to help me, and I am being so offensive toward you. I thank you for stopping that horrible attack, and I regret what I said then, too. Please forgive me. I have never used such language."

"There's nothing to forgive. I started it."

Sita smiled. "Well, I hope the use of your favorite words is not contagious." Sita and Sal chuckled.

"May I ask you something?" Sal said. Sita nodded. "What happened at the Taj?"

Sita hesitated. "I saw Jayanta smiling at a security officer. I'm sure he pointed to me. The officer took me behind a curtain and searched me. He placed his hands wherever he wished. It was Jayanta's reprisal for my corrections of his numerous mistakes. He knew what the guard would do. As I told you, he is of high caste and believed I should be subservient. But I could not let him have this satisfaction and corrected him even more. Perhaps that is why he arranged to stay in Agra. Perhaps the entire incident was my doing."

"It wasn't your doing. You did nothing wrong."

"I know this in my mind, but I am in India and also know what is expected of me." Sita paused. "Now it is over. Perhaps we should go inside and have something hot to drink. We will both feel better. I will get my scarf."

As Sita left for the car, Ange said to Sal, "Let me ask you something?"

"Yeah?"

"Would you have clubbed those guys? We both know they had it coming."

"No, I don't think so; I didn't feel it—like before."

"Before?"

"Something from the past, Ange."

"Sal ... why did you come here? You said just the thought of India repulsed you. We both know this jewelry thing is far-fetched. You don't need the money, and you've told me many times not to get into something you don't know. I don't get it."

"I came to settle up on an old debt, Ange."

Ange paused. "And how's that going?"

"I'll let you know."

CHAPTER XII

Hanuman

"That's four days from now," Ange said.

"Yes, I know, and I apologize," Sita said. "My uncle says he is also very, very sorry for the delay, but he has much business to attend to. He suggests that we meet in Varanasi. It is a good opportunity; he will be in a very good way there. It is our holiest city. He must be going there to meditate and will be in his most receptive state of mind."

"I expected another delay," Sal said. "All part of the game, and since we're here to win, we wait it out. But, we won't go to Varanasi until the day before the meeting. He needs to think we have other things going on too. But I don't want to stay here for three days either."

"I have a proposal if you wish to hear it," Sita said.

"Shoot."

"We are close to a nature reserve that my family has visited many times. It is very peaceful. There are many species of animals and birds, and the facilities are very modern and most comfortable. They provide safari vehicles and guides and have the kind of restaurant and bar that you would very much like."

"What kinds of animals?" Ange asked.

"Many kinds. There are tigers there. But in the many visits I have made, I have never seen one. Many people have seen them and say it was a wonderful experience to be able to watch them. I am told they keep their distance from the vehicles and are not a worry. And there are many other kinds of animals that the guides will show us, and very many monkeys."

"How far?" Sal asked.

"Two to three hours."

"Jesus, we've been here less than two days. We've seen most of Delhi, the Taj Mahal, one of the worst hotels in the world, and now we're off to hunt tigers."

"Not hunt, just watch if we are lucky enough to see one."

"Just a figure of speech. OK, what the fuck—sorry Sita."

Sita smiled and shook her head.

"I don't know about you two," Sal continued, "but I'm too tired to sleep anyway. Let's clean up, have something to eat, and go. Can you make the arrangements, Sita?"

"Most certainly, and I will contact a few of my relatives to see if any can join us. Of course, only the ones I think you would like."

Sal stood and stretched. "I'm going to talk to the management about our friend, Duke. Should I ask if they can hire Munére to drive us?"

"Yes," Sita and Ange said together.

"I don't think we need another guide. Besides, now I have one of these." Smiling, Sal pulled Duke's license from his pocket. The pin of Sal's brooch stuck to the case. Sita caught a glimpse before Sal slipped it back where it belonged.

"I did not know that you carried jewelry. May I see it?"

"It's nothing, just an old money clip."

"Oh, my eyes must be very tired. For a moment, the design looked much like my bracelet. May I see it again?"

"I'll show it to you later when our eyes are clearer."

Sita nodded and stood. "I will go to my room and make our arrangements. Perhaps we can meet in two hours?"

"Good," Sal said and looked at his Rolex. "I might be getting him out of bed, but I'll give Stosh a call."

Sal sat while the others walked to the elevator. He took out his brooch and gazed. "Not yet," he whispered.

***

"Stosh, how the hell are you?" Sal blared into his phone. "How's the hip, old man?"

"Sallie, it's good to hear your voice. The hip's gettin' better. I'm home now, no more hospital Jell-O and crap like that. How's it goin' in India?"

"We're playing the waiting game. Sita's uncle keeps putting us off. No big deal, I expected it. We'll be several more days, though. Hey, I'm sorry I didn't call you earlier. I tried, late the night before last, but I had a problem getting connected."

"No problem, your timin's perfect. I was real busy then anyway. Everythin' is good here. I moved the gold to the vault."

"You know, I'm glad to hear that. You must be more

comfortable now that it's not in your back yard. That's a hell of a lot of money to keep around the house."

Stosh laughed. "You don't know the half of it. I'll tell ya sometime over a beer."

"Or a vodka."

"Nope, no more vodka for me. It was startin' to mess with my head. But the beer still tastes mighty frickin' good and Deb's happier than a clam."

"Good for you. Listen, I'm going to let you go. I'm on my way to a nature reserve, or some shit like that."

"A nature reserve? Am I talkin' to Salvatore Esposito?"

"It's Sita's idea. She says they have tigers and a good bar." Sal laughed. "OK, Buddy, sounds like you've got everything well under control on your end. I'll report back when I know more."

"Yup, everythin's good here. Don't get eaten by one a them tigers, or nothin'." Stosh chuckled. "I'll be talking to ya."

***

Munére waited his turn to dart across a crumbling single-lane bridge. As he sped over, Sal took a swig from his flask. The dirt from the road left a low cloud as they passed through thick woods into a valley filled with well-attended fields spotted with uniform hay mounds. Munére slowed as they drove through a village of small concrete houses painted blue and saffron. People bustled about, stopping only to stare at the car full of visitors. Cattle wandered freely; a few others lay by the roadside chewing. In the center, a statue of the village idol—a guru from past generations—sat ornately honored with strings of colorful fresh flowers around his neck. Nearby, a boy stood naked in front of a small dwelling washing with water from a two-quart tin can while pictures from a color television projected through a window behind him.

After miles of more fields and woods, Munére pulled onto a paved drive, passed large red gates, and drove hundreds of yards to the covered entrance of a grand wooden building with a voluminous thatched roof.

"We are here," Sita said.

Sal stepped out and looked down the walkways at a dozen matching structures all meticulously maintained. On his right, a few sunbathers stretched out, laughing and sipping beer at a fifty-meter swimming pool with a clubhouse. Across the lane, guests played billiards in an open-air recreation room attached to a dining hall. Both areas had open bars.

"How the hell does a place like this exist here in the middle of nowhere?" Sal said.

Porters led the guests to two cottages at the end of a private walk.

"Only one of my cousins might be coming, and I don't think that is very likely," Sita said. "But, if we need additional rooms, they are available. I will put away my things and meet you back at the clubhouse."

Sal and Ange entered their cabin. A shared entrance led to bedrooms at each end separated by a common bathroom with a whirlpool tub and sauna. Near the couch in Sal's room, French doors opened to a patio with a round brick fire pit surrounded by six cushioned chairs. Sal tossed his bag on the king bed, checked the stock in the mini bar, walked through the bathroom door and saw Ange at a sink.

"Jesus, this is huge," Sal said. "There are three doors to this bathroom."

"Grab a sink, there are two more," Ange said. "And look at this cathedral ceiling. I've never seen one made from thatch before."

Sal looked at a map on his bedroom wall and decided to walk the trail around a nearby lake while there was still light. A couple of miles, maybe an hour alone, that will be good right now, he thought. He told Ange he'd catch up later and headed out.

The woods thickened at the end of the complex. Sal was surprised at how much the pines mimicked the Adirondacks. He wondered how Kate and Boozer were doing. It wouldn't be long before the ice was gone and Boozer could swim for his stick. He watched colorful birds dart from tree to tree as he hiked along the path. He thought of the loons on Lake Champlain.

The tarp camps across the Yamuna popped into Sal's head, and he saw the fort and Jimmy Eagleson. He spotted a group of trees, a perfect spot for the old tarp. Ray planned to put the boat in this year. Maybe they could find the place in the bay where Stosh and Ray scattered Jimmy's ashes. He smiled, put his hand in his pocket, and felt his brooch.

Sal thought of Johnny. Maybe, when he got back, he should see him. Maybe—if Sita's uncle ever showed—he'd be able to put the whole thing to rest. He wondered if just facing Mr.

Patil would be enough. Maybe he would have to confess, get it all out and over with?

Sal walked for over an hour, stopping to gaze at the lake and watch small animals scurrying about. He breathed in deeply through his nose and exhaled through his lips. He reached the trail's end and thought about making one more trip around but looked at his Rolex and headed for the cabin.

Sal removed his shoes and entered the cottage. He walked into the bathroom, took off his shirt, and twisted on the sink faucet. He splashed his face with cool water and looked into the mirror. He turned his torso and examined the black-and-blue welt on his shoulder from Sorab's whack in Agra. Those assholes got off easy, he thought. But at least he'd received a bit of penance. A whack from a club was always good. He smiled. He was proud he hadn't reacted—he'd fought his rage and won. He didn't need Sita to tell him to stop. He'd done that himself.

Refreshed and wearing a fresh shirt, Sal headed for the clubhouse. As he turned down the walk toward the pool, Sita and Ange came into view, sitting next to each other laughing. Sita waved to him and pointed to the chair across from her. He sat back, ordered a Kingfisher, and stretched out.

"I have arranged our tour for very early tomorrow morning," Sita said. "I have been told that some people from New Zealand have very recently seen a female tiger with two cubs. This is very exciting. But the tigers are nocturnal, and it is not likely that they will be about much during the daytime. So, we will leave at about five o'clock. Our breakfast will be ready for us, here at four-thirty."

Sal nodded and looked at a half-filled bottle of white wine sweating on the table. "That yours, Ange?"

"Mostly; Sita's had a glass. But she's switched to soda water."

"Yes, perhaps I will have a little more later, but for now, one glass was more than enough. They have your special whiskey if you wish."

"I think I'll take you up on that. Sal called a waiter and asked for whiskey. "So, we get up no later than four, right?"

"Yes, I think that would be very good."

"OK, we have time for a few drinks and some food."

As other guests gathered, a family in vintage Indian clothing arranged a small stage. Dressed like a raja, the man carefully placed his sitär next to a stool. His wife, dressed in a flowing red dress and covered in costume jewelry, spread a blanket next to him. She plopped down a baby wearing a clean but dingy diaper and began to play with her. The child giggled as her mother touched under her chin and sang rhymes. The father stood, introduced each family member, sat back down, tuned his sitär and began to play traditional Indian songs. The baby slapped the floor, almost in rhythm, and her mother began to sing. Sita grinned and hummed along.

"That is strange," Sita said after the third song.

"What?" Sal asked.

"I know that song. It is a very, very nice story about reincarnation. However, she chose to sing it differently."

"Yeah?"

"The words are 'where the eagle now lays, the dog *runs*.'"

"And?"

"She changed one word and sang 'where the eagle now lays, the dog *swims*.' I wonder why."

Sal shrugged. "Maybe she just improvised."

"Yes," Sita said. "That is most likely the answer."

The group ate, drank, and enjoyed the performance for nearly two hours. Sita smiled and laughed and decided to have another wine. Sal thought of the contrast with the night before. What a fucking country. He looked at his watch.

"OK, that's it for me," he said. "If we're up at four, I've got to get some sleep."

Sita and Ange nodded. "We'll catch up with you," Ange said.

***

As always, Sal awakened fifteen minutes before the alarm. In a fog, he stretched, switched the clock off, and stumbled into the bathroom. He stood in front of the toilet, raised the seat, and noticed the open door to Ange's room. He tip-toed over to close it. As he took the handle, he glanced in and froze in a stare. His cheeks flushed, and his muscles tightened. Ange lay spooned against a woman with long black hair. On her nightstand, a Patil bracelet glistened in the moonlight. Sal quietly shut the door. Bitterly stimulated, his need to pee fled and he stomped out to the patio.

I told that horny little fuck to leave her alone; Sal thought as he sat in the dark. What the fuck is he thinking? He shook and slapped his head. What the fuck am I thinking? Why should I give a shit about this? Shit, I should have seen this coming; it was obvious. He's the one comforting her. He's the one she's relaxed and drank wine with. And I have no interest in her anyway.

Sal looked down at his tented undershorts. At least, I didn't think I did. He chuckled, "Well, that's the biggest sign of life you've shown in a long time," he whispered. All right, they've paired up, and that's that. After breakfast, I'll tell them I'm tired and let the lovebirds look for tigers on their own. I could use some fucking sleep anyway.

Sal heard the faint buzz of an alarm clock. OK, they'll be getting up. Maybe I should grab the bathroom while I can. As he stood, a light came on in Sita's cabin. His eyes narrowed, he walked back to the bathroom and opened the door. A woman stood in Ange's robe examining her eye in the mirror.

"Oh, I'm so sorry," she said. "I should have locked the door. I think I have something in my eye. You must be Dr. Esposito. I am so pleased to meet you. I am Radha Patil, Sita's cousin. If you wouldn't mind, I will finish here quickly. Then I will lock the other doors, and you can use the room first."

Sal nodded and shut the door. In a moment, Radha yelled, "The room is ready for you now."

Sal trotted in and stood before the toilet, still seat up. Now he could pee.

***

The adventurers waited several minutes in front of the reserve for a ranger. Sal sat high in the back of their open-top vehicle and watched a man in uniform shake his head and point at him. The others—all in safari clothes—looked like the cast in a jungle movie. Sal stood out wearing a brightly colored shirt filled with shades of green and orange. The group's driver hopped down and walked to the gate. Bobbing his head, he stood listening to the guard rant, then he spoke and listened to the guard again. Looking discouraged, he returned to the vehicle.

"Sir," he said to Sal, "he is concerned about your dress. He believes some animals might be unnaturally attracted to you, especially given your very, very large size. He also thinks that you may be mocking the flag of India as you are dressed in those colors. I have assured him that you do not have this intention, but he is still reluctant to let you enter the reserve."

"Should I talk to him?" Sal said.

"I do not know if it will help, and his English is not very good. But, we can try."

Sal jumped down and, walking behind the driver, approached the guard. Standing eight inches over the man, he bowed and said a few words. The guard looked away a moment. Then he turned back, looked up at Sal, and nodded. Sal pulled out a wad of money from his pocket and peeled off two thousand rupees. The guard signaled for Sal to wait and sent the driver back for the others. The vehicle stopped. All stepped down to the road, and the guard checked passports.

"He says you will not all fit in one truck and must be separated. Each pair will have a driver and a ranger to guide you through the park. The visit will last for about three hours. You must agree not to leave the truck at any time for any reason.

The ranger will have bottles of water. He also says that because you required two vehicles, the cost will be two times."

Sal smiled at the guard and handed him another two thousand rupees. With no change in expression, the guard waved two safari Range Rovers to the gate. Sal and Sita climbed up to the raised, back seat of the first.

"There are no tops to these vehicles," Sita said. "That makes it much better for watching the animals."

"Unless they attack," Sal joked.

"Oh, do not worry. The guards are very well trained to manage any such situation."

"The Rovers will travel about ten minutes apart," the resort's driver said. "You can be sure the details here are now finished, but the drivers and rangers will expect some compensation following the journey. I will be here when your visit is finished."

The gatekeeper signaled the first group on. Their truck started slowly down the trail. Sal stood to look at a group of spotted deer. The ranger waved his hands downward and cackled in Hindi.

"He says you must stay seated," Sita said. "He will point out the wildlife as we go along, so you will not need to stand." Sal sat without fuss.

"I have not had the opportunity to speak to you since my cousin Radha has arrived," Sita continued. "While I do like her very, very much, I hope she is not an embarrassment. She is most liberal in her ways, especially for an Indian woman. As you have already seen, she is quite free spirited—although she took a most unusually quick liking to Mr. Costello, even for her."

"He seems to have that effect on women."

"Yes, there is something very kind in him, and non-threatening."

Sal snickered. "Yeah, so I've been told."

"Well, I am very glad to see Radha. Most of my relatives are very formal and do not like her. They think she is promiscuous and very unfit as an Indian woman. I believe she occasionally goes too far, but she is much fun. And I have not seen her in three years.

"As I am, she is also in the business of Asian carpets and has helped me on many occasions. I think she would like to join us in Varanasi also. She attended college there at Benares University and knows much about the city and Hindu tradition. I'm sure she would enjoy being our guide. That is, of course, if this is acceptable to you and you do not feel it will create a problem."

"No problem at all. Wow, a guide we can trust, that will be good." Sita forced a smile. "You know, from the back, you two are almost identical. But otherwise, she doesn't look much like you. Your complexion is darker, and your facial features are different."

Sita paused. "Ours is a very large family with many different looks."

The ranger interrupted to point out a pack of fox hurrying down the trail. His hands gestured and fingers pointed as he spoke. Sal didn't understand a word. Sita translated as quickly as she could.

They drove by more spotted deer, wild dholes, birds of all kinds, and tribes of monkeys playing in the trees and grooming each other. Through the wilderness, they observed dense and then thin sections of the jungle. They passed open clearings and several ponds bridged by dead trees and filled with crocodiles. Sal breathed in the musty air and began to sweat from the growing heat. The ranger held up a dog-eared guidebook and pointed to faded pictures as he tried to explain the habitat.

From time to time the driver stopped and turned the engine off so they could listen to the jungle's sounds. As the second hour ended, the driver halted. The ranger pointed out a perfect tiger paw print in the sand at the side of the road, and then at a pile of tiger dung a few feet away. He smiled and nodded as if he'd sufficiently proved that tigers *did* exist.

As they drove on, the ranger began to look concerned. He watched as a band of monkeys climbed high into the trees, clutched branches, and stared into the woods on the truck's right. He signaled for the driver to stop and for everyone to be quiet. The engine turned off and, like the monkeys, the group became silent. They heard rustling yards away in the thick underbrush. The ranger's eyes widened. Silence returned, and he exhaled. He turned to the driver and nodded.

As the driver reached for the ignition, the ear tearing screech from a monkey froze him. Scrambling from the woods the monkey darted under the truck. Eyes bulging and nostrils flaring, the driver tried to signal something to the ranger when a massive Bengal tiger roared and lunged over the brush. Everyone froze. Only their panic-stricken eyes moved to follow the tiger.

The tiger paced back and forth at the vehicle's side, eyes fixed on the monkey under the truck. The ranger's book fell from his hand and slapped the Rover's floor. Raising its head, the tiger stared and growled at the passengers, exposing bits of meat between its teeth.

The monkey bolted from beneath the truck and scurried up a tree. The tiger roared and began stalking the truck from end to end, its glare now set on its occupants. It let out a terrifying growl and swiped its claws at the front tire. The driver couldn't control his shaking. The tiger looked him over, swayed its head, thundered a roar, and crouched to leap. Sal sprang up and waved to draw the tiger's attention. The tiger locked eyes with Sal. Sal held his fists high and steady and glared back.

"GO AWAY!" Sal bellowed. Still staring, the tiger roared. "GO AWAY!" Sal repeated.

The tiger twitched its head and broke its gaze. It slowly circled, looked back at Sal, and snarled.

"GO AWAY!" Sal yelled again in a firm, commanding voice.

Again, the tiger circled. It stopped, gestured a paw swipe toward Sal, turned its tail-end to the front tire, hosed it with urine, vaulted into the woods, and dashed out of sight.

Sal lowered his arms and felt Sita's wet palm on his wrist. Breathing hard, she stared up at him. He plopped down and exhaled. The driver turned around and lowered his shoulders to Sal. He swayed his head up and down and repeated a phrase in Hindi; his palms pressed tightly together in worship.

"What's he doing?" Sal asked Sita.

"He is honoring you. And he is terrified. He believes you are possessed by the spirit of Lord Hanuman."

"Would you tell him to knock it off?"

"He will not. He is very serious and very afraid. He believes the spirit came to save one of his own. The monkey who escaped was of the *Hanuman Langer* species. It is thought to be protected by Lord Hanuman himself. Our driver is very, very superstitious and very, very afraid."

Sal looked at the ranger, also bowing. "And him?"

"I think he is not sure. He thought something was different in you when he saw your size and your shirt. I think he is not taking chances."

Sal stood again, placed his hands together and bowed to the others. "Namaste," he said. As they timidly looked up, Sal repeated, "Namaste, namaste."

Both men smiled and whispered, "Namaste." Gradually they turned and sat.

"Sir, I have never seen such a thing," the ranger said in a barely understandable accent.

Sal sat back next to Sita. "Are you OK?" he asked.

"I was very, very frightened, but you stood between the tiger and me, and I felt protected. I will be fine."

The second rover pulled up. "We saw from down the trail," Radha yelled. "Our guide says he has never seen a tiger behave this way. But there have been reports of an unusually aggressive one. It appears you have met it."

"You OK, Sal?" Ange hollered.

"Yeah," Sal said and nodded.

The driver started the Rover, and both vehicles drove on.

"Why did you behave as you did with that tiger?" Sita asked.

"I thought he was going to attack."

"Yes, but what made you stand and command him?"

"Ray, I guess."

"Ray?"

"Yeah, Ray always says if you're in the Adirondacks and meet up with a bear, your only chance is to hold your ground and take command. Put your hands up and growl right back. And don't turn your back. Try to think of the bear as a misbehaving pet. It was the only thing I could think of."

Sita paused and offered Sal a drink of water. Sal shook his head, pulled out his flask, and took a long swig. "Where did you get that shirt?" she asked.

"From a catalog."

"Why did you select it?"

"It fit. It's hard to find shirts that fit my shoulders. And I was going to Florida. I thought Stosh would get a kick out of the pattern."

"Why did you choose to wear it today?"

"It was the only clean shirt left. I sent all the others to be cleaned this morning."

"And, how did you know what would put our driver and guide at ease?"

"*You* told me on the plane."

"Very many coincidences," Sita whispered. She took a deep breath and smiled. "Well, Doctor Esposito, now I have seen a tiger."

***

The afternoon sun warmed Sal's face as he sat at the clubhouse bar and sipped Kingfisher. It was good to have time alone, he thought. Shit, I'm too wound to nap anyway. I don't know how the others can do it, even if we did all get up at four in the fucking morning.

Legends of Sal's heroic deeds had reached everyone in the complex. Several guests stopped and politely asked to have a picture with him. He graciously agreed although he didn't like it. Sal reached into his pocket and pricked his thumb on the brooch's pin. You had to remind me, didn't you? He thought. Yeah, some fucking hero. What would they think if they knew the truth about me, what I've done and why I'm really in India? Would they still want a picture if they saw what was left of that old man? Even a twelve-year-old is tried as an adult for that kind of shit. I was Hanuman then too. Hanuman the Hellkite, just like Ma said.

Sal saw Munére near the office. He asked the bartender to save two seats and walked over. Munére smiled and bowed. "I heard what you have done. I knew that you are very brave, but this is a very great act."

"It's all blown out of proportion. Come over and join me. I'd like to buy you a drink."

"Sir, thank you very, very much, but I am not allowed in that area. And I am Sufi. I do not drink."

"Sufi?"

"Yes, sir. We are a very peaceful form of Islam. Other

Muslims sometimes scorn us. They say we are too 'mystical' and do not follow the Qur'an strictly enough. But we are very contented.

Sal nodded. "You said, not allowed?"

"Yes, sir. I am in service here, not a guest."

Sal asked Munére to wait, walked into the office and spoke briefly to the manager. The manager bobbed and nodded, and Sal returned. "OK, let's go."

"Sir, I am very grateful to you, but I am not comfortable with these other people. They will not like being near me."

"OK, we'll take care of that." Sal escorted Munére to the bar. The bartender pointed to a table just out of sight around a corner. "What would you like?" Sal asked Munére. "The bartender will serve us over there."

Munére hesitated, "A Coca-Cola if that is possible."

They sat, and the bartender scurried over with their drinks. "That's the fastest I've seen anyone move since I've been here," Sal said. "Well, except for you, of course. You're the only hero around this joint. What you did the other night was the 'very great act.'"

"No sir, the situation was the result of my dishonesty. I should not be praised."

Sal smiled and shook his head. "We disagree on that point. What will you do now? Will they pair you with another guide?"

"No, sir. I have been released from my job."

"They fired *you*?"

"Yes, sir. It was done yesterday when we returned. I am only here because you specifically requested me. I will need to find other employment."

"I'll talk to management."

"Please, sir, do not. I can drive somewhere else, and I am to blame for the incident that occurred. If you interfere, management will be angry. When you leave, they will make things much more difficult for me."

"And Duke?"

"Jayanta has also been released. But they will return his license to him. He will go to another city for some time and then probably return to Delhi."

Sal sat back. Fire was in his eyes.

"Sir, India has her own ways." Munére paused. "Is this not true of America?"

Sal thought and then snickered. "Yes, have you been to America?"

Munére chuckled. "No, sir. Not everyone gets to go to America." Munére sipped. "Sir, is it true that everyone in America has his own vehicle?"

Sal hesitated and nodded. "Pretty much. Most people who want a car have one. Not all new, but still something."

"And, sir, is it true that most American people are fat?"

Sal laughed. "More than should be."

"I am from Kashmir. There are not many fat people, and very few have their own vehicle. But it is very beautiful. I will return when I have earned enough money. My wife and son are there. We will start a business. She is earning a guide's license. I will buy a suitable vehicle, and we will work together."

Munére paused. "When I first saw Mrs. Patil, I looked at her often. She looks much like my wife, who I miss greatly.

Then I saw I was being most inappropriate and kept my eyes to myself."

Sal grinned. "I noticed. How long will it take to earn enough to get started?"

"Two more years, I think. But I will need to secure another job."

"Listen, I've got a lot of money and for what you did, let me give you what you need. It's a drop in the bucket for me, and you earned it."

"Sir, I cannot. I would not be able to repay you. In my culture, one always reciprocates a favor."

"I will just be reciprocating what you did for Mrs. Patil. You saved her from enormous shame."

"No, sir. You saved her; I just tried to correct for my dishonesty. And, sir, it is important for me to make my life through my own work. Your offer is most generous, and many would gratefully take it. But I cannot. I must know that my success comes from my own sacrifice. Without that, it is of little value."

Sal sat and listened. "You see, sir, in India small things can make a person very happy. It is one of the things that is good here. From what I know, this does not often happen in the West. Jayanta wants the things of the West. He tries to take what he thinks he desires, but he will never get enough. What he acquires is soon no longer wanted. So, he is very unhappy, and that is his true reward."

Munére took another sip of Coke, closed his eyes and smiled. "In Agra, I was not honest. I did not expect Jayanta to do what he did, but I knew what he was doing was wrong, and I helped him."

Munére paused.

"Sir, have you found the world to be very complicated and at the same time very simple?" Sal nodded. "How can this be? What happens each day is created from countless decisions, each one affecting all others. I learned this from driving. It may look very much like chaos to you, but each driver knows what the other is doing. When I choose a space, it opens, and I open those necessary for others. Each of the thousands of vehicles on the road follows the same rule. Still, there *are* accidents. When I think of my future, I think of all the things that must happen to bring something about, and those things that can go badly."

Munére sipped, looked at his glass and licked his lips. "And I think of how only one wrong choice can change everything."

Sal looked away and exhaled. Right on the money, he thought.

"So, sir, in Agra if I had done what I knew was the right thing, the problem at the hotel would not have happened."

"But you were afraid to lose your job. Duke held the cards. He intimidated you. He made you lie."

"Sir, I was afraid to lose my job, and he did threaten me. But I did the lie. It was my act. And now I have lost my job anyway. But I have been reminded of the importance of my decisions. And I will find another job, and I will try not to make the same mistake."

Sal grinned. "You know, I didn't like you when I first met

you. But you're a good man, Munére, and you will do well, my friend."

"Thank you, sir. Sir, may I ask you another question?"

"Sure."

"Jayanta insisted on referring to me as a Huckleberry. I have come to learn that this is a small bluish berry. I do not know why he would call me this."

Sal chuckled. "In American slang, a huckleberry means the right person for the challenge. Calling you that was one of the few things Duke got right."

"Thank you, sir."

"Now listen, while you're taking responsibility for your lie, your honesty saved the day. And following your own tradition, you must let me return your favor." Sal reached into his pocket.

"Please sir, no. Nothing but the appropriate gratuity after my services have been completed. Please, Sir."

"Munére, somehow I have to return the favor."

"You already have, Sir."

"What? I've done nothing for you."

"Sir, you bought me a Coca-Cola."

***

Seated close together in the packed dining room, Sita and Radha giggled and chatted in Hindi while Ange filled Sal in on the business at home. Other guests stared and pointed as they swapped stories about the giant man *Salvatore* and his ability to tame tigers with the power of Hanuman. The manager strutted in wearing the gift Sal had given him. The now legendary shirt draped over him like a poncho as he walked from table to table showing it off. Sal nodded and smiled to his fans.

"It's a good thing we're out of here in the morning," Sal mumbled. "I can't take much more of this shit."

The servers placed platters of rice, fried vegetables, and chicken pieces cooked in a spicy red sauce in the center of the table. One server handed Sal a knife and fork, and then bowed and smiled in reverence.

Sal sipped his Kingfisher and scanned the room. Seeing he was the only one with utensils, he put them down, reached with his right hand and took rice with his fingers. He looked for something to wipe his hand and grabbed a wet paper napkin. He pinched another lump to his mouth and picked up the napkin again. He chuckled, put the napkin aside and let his hand feel the food. He relaxed and, watching the others, used his fingers to mix his food before scooping a portion. The spicy chicken nipped, and he licked his lips. After several successful mouthfuls, he joined the conversation, now feeling comfortably skilled in hand-to-mouth dining.

"Tomorrow we can sleep in before driving back," Ange said. "We fly out in the afternoon."

"Good, we will have some time to tour Varanasi," Sita said.

"What about the meeting?" Sal asked.

"My uncle will arrange the meeting for late in the afternoon. It will be his way of saying that it is not of great importance and other business must come first."

"Of course, there will be no other business," Radha chimed

in. "Uncle Amol is quite old-school and still thinks that no one sees his games. I worked for him for two years. He is a very difficult man. But he would not meet with you if he did not see some gain for himself."

Sal listened intently trying to envision what his face-to-face with the old man would be like.

"Radha is less positive toward my uncle than I. I believe he can be reasonable and quite fair."

Radha chuckled. "Those would not be my words. But, I am interested in seeing the outcome of your venture. While Uncle Amol will not show it, he will be intimidated by Doctor Esposito. I wish I could be at the meeting."

"That is most definitely not possible," Sita snapped.

"Yes, Cousin, I know. Forgive me for speaking so bluntly."

Sita paused. "I am sorry, Radha. I am so pleased you are with us and did not mean any offense. It will be difficult enough with one woman at the meeting, and you and Uncle Amol have a history that would not be of benefit."

"Yes, Sita, you are right, and I was only jesting. And before your meeting, we will have all of tomorrow afternoon and the morning to explore Varanasi."

"Yes, we must go to the river for sunrise. It is the festival of *Parvati*; it will be very exciting. The Ganges will be full of worshippers bathing and praying near the ghats."

"Parvati?" Ange asked. "Consort of Lord Shiva?"

"Yes, she shows herself in many forms and ways and is a most beloved goddess. And, of course, *Ganga* is always present. Many will bath in her water believing they are washing away all of their sins."

“I could use a bath like that,” Sal whispered.

“What did you say?” Sita asked.

“Nothing. So, if we don’t have to rise early, let’s go back to our cabin and light a fire on the patio.”

All nodded. “Good. I’ll have someone bring over whatever anyone wants, and we’ll get away from this crowd. Let’s go.”

Sal smiled and waved to the guests as the four left the dining room and headed down the walk. Radha and Ange held hands. Sita and Sal kept a respectful distance. On the patio, Sal inspected the wood and began arranging a properly tented fire.

“A man will be here to do that,” Sita said.

Sal shook his head, “I’ll take care of it.”

Sal found a small stack of newspapers, twisted several sheets to the perfect firmness, and split kindling with an old hatchet he found near the wood pile. He slipped the paper, some shavings, and kindling under loosely stacked chunks of dry beech wood.

Three men arrived with two bottles of wine, four Kingfishers, and more wood. One offered Sal a container of kerosene. Sal shook his head. He leaned in and struck a match. A small flame popped from the paper’s edge. The flame grew and spread to the shavings and kindling. Within a minute, it climbed the inner sides of the wood and was blazing. The delivery men stood cackling in Hindi and nodding. One snatched up the kerosene can, and they bowed and left.

Radha opened a bottle of wine and poured two glasses. She looked at Sita, held up the bottle and raised her eyebrows. Sita nodded and smiled, and Radha poured a third glass. Radha and Ange sat in seats out of earshot, chatting and making eyes at each other. Sal popped the cap off a Kingfisher and sat back in a chair next to Sita.

"Where did you learn to build such a good fire?" Sita asked.

"My friend and I had a place where we camped when we were kids. We built a lot of fires there."

"Is this your friend Jimmy Eagleson?"

"Yes." Sal looked down and smiled.

"You always speak of him with such affection."

"He was the best. When we camped, we'd stay up half the night solving the problems of the world, and then sleep like logs."

"I hope not like those logs," Sita said, pointing to the fire and giggling.

Sal chuckled. "No, like dry, safe ones. I remember one time. It had been a warm day, but that night we got a freak frost. We'd left our sleeping bags and only brought blankets. I woke up freezing. The fire had died down, but it still had some good embers. I wrapped my blanket around myself; my teeth chattered, and I was shaking from the cold. But I stoked the coals and piled on some wood. Jimmy woke up and joined me. He was frozen too. The fire grew slowly at first, but then it flamed and roared, and we stood as close as we could. I turned my back to the fire and dropped my blanket. Then I turned around again and put my palms close to the flames. I'll never forget the warmth from that fire. I don't think I've ever felt a greater comfort." Sal paused. "Tell me about your uncle."

Sita's eyes widened, and she took a sip of wine.

"My uncle is a very wealthy man. He became that way

because he is very, very strict in his business. When my grandfather allowed him partial management of the company, it was not doing well. Because of my uncle's determination, it grew very, very rapidly. When he decided to move to Canada, many were against the idea. But, for the short time they stayed, he and my grandfather made it very successful. When my grandfather became blind, my uncle accepted complete control, and they returned to India. From that time, he has had no active business outside of India. So, we are here because I am hoping he remembers his success and will support our plan. But, I am not as naive as Radha might suggest. If my uncle accepts our plan, it will only be because he knows it will be very, very profitable and he will share in the wealth."

"I'm sorry," Sal said.

"About what?"

"What happened to your family, your grandfather."

"The West can be a very violent place. My family was surprised that such a thing happened in Canada. But, some people have a liking for physical confrontation there too. That was a very long time ago, and grandfather is at peace now. Part of him is in the Ganges where we will go tomorrow. Ganga provides for him."

Sal gazed at the fire, "I'm still sorry."

Sita's eyes narrowed, and she took a long sip of wine. "Have you always been rich?"

"Where did that come from?"

"Where did your question about my uncle come from?"

Sal nodded. "My father wasn't rich. He was a tailor. We

were comfortable but not rich. My mother was an entertainer. She could have become rich, but she gave up her career."

"And you?"

"Well, I wasn't born rich." Sal and Sita chuckled. "But I always thought I would be. I don't know why, but I never doubted it."

"Then in some ways, you are like my uncle," Sita said after a pause. "He also never doubted it."

Sal noticed the fire dying. He stepped to it and began stoking. He brought the flickers to a blaze and stood staring into the flame, before returning.

"There, that should be good."

Sal and Sita talked for nearly two hours. Radha and Ange continued to spark. Ange ordered another bottle of wine. Sita had had enough, so Ange and Radha drank it themselves. The clouds slowly revealed a bright moon, and the lovebirds left.

Sita shook her head. "Well, at least they are taking their activities somewhere private." She and Sal broke into laughter.

"I must say goodnight," Sita said. "I am not as liberated as my cousin, and it would be improper for me to be alone here with you at this hour."

Sal nodded and stood. Sita smiled and left. Sal popped another kingfisher and sat staring into the fire, thinking of their conversation. If she only knew... He thought of how the meeting would be, then grinned. One thing was sure; in less than forty-eight hours Salvatore Esposito will finally face his demon. He placed his beer on a table and sat back. Gazing at the clearing sky, he dozed off.

In an hour, Sal woke, shivering. The fire had turned to embers.

CHAPTER XIII

Ganga

"There must be two or three thousand people on this street," Ange said.

"I'd say five or six," Sal replied.

"Come this way," Radha said, pointing to a stream of bodies flowing in the dim light toward the Ganges River. "The sun will rise in one-half hour, and we must try to get a boat and be on the Ganges by that time."

One by one Ange, Radha, Sita, and Sal merged into the current of bodies. After fifteen minutes, the bottleneck ended, and the compressed humanity was released onto an open area of hundreds of feet bordering the river.

"This way, please," Radha said. "I will arrange a boat for us."

The group hiked toward the waterlogged planks used as makeshift docks for the lines of weathered wooden rowboats. Sal stopped near a man with long weedy hair and a scraggly gray beard. He wore a saffron kurta shirt and painted on his forehead were uneven yellow stripes. Their eyes met, and the man put his hand out. Sal looked at Sita. She shook her head.

"He is not real. He dresses as a holy man to fool visitors into paying him."

The man's eyes flared, and he waved his fingers toward his palm for his handout. Sal shook his head. The would-be holy man spat on the ground in front of Sal.

Sal waited near the river's edge. The screeching and yowling from a band of feral dogs seized his attention. He watched as the young pack members ganged-up to depose their spent leader, biting and chasing the skinny old top-dog with half an ear and white fur around his mouth. They mercilessly tore at his legs and ears, sinking their teeth deep before viciously jerking their heads and ripping his flesh. He fell onto his back. They continued to tear at him. He bled and yelped helplessly.

Sal looked around; no one else was paying any attention. Finally, one dog pulled back and howled. The others left their victim, jumping and barking as they swarmed around their new kingpin. The pack ran off. The old dog struggled to his feet, licked an open wound and limped away, alone.

"The strongest mongrels end the cruelest, old dog," Sal whispered.

Sal looked at the Ganges and scanned the shoreline. A baby girl sat in the water slapping and laughing. Her mother tickled the baby's belly, and she screamed with glee. Sitting above them with legs crossed, a young man wearing purple pajamas sat meditating. Around his neck hung a string of prayer beads made from chestnut sized bodhi seeds inlaid with blue and red stone fragments. Seeing the young man's reflection, the baby joyously yelled out. The young man opened his eyes and flashed a scolding stare at the mother. She smiled, moved the child several yards and set her back in the water. The child looked about, splashed, laughed, and continued her play.

With a stern face, the meditator closed his eyes and forced himself back into his devotions. Sal watched the baby and grinned. Then he glanced at the meditator's grimace and recalled Sita's plea on the way back from Agra: "Open your fucking eyes."

"Come, Doctor," Radha yelled. "We have a boat, and the sun is rising. Come quickly. I don't want you to miss seeing anything."

I've already seen plenty, Sal thought, making his way to the boat. Ange and Radha stepped carefully to the boat's back bench. Sal stood behind Sita as she stepped aboard. She slipped and fell backward. Sal quickly clutched under her arms and lifted her into the boat. Then he stumbled into the water himself. Wet to the knees, he laughed hysterically, the others chuckling and grinning. Still smiling, he motioned for everyone to sit close to the port side, grabbed the starboard edge and hoisted himself in.

"I think Ganga likes you," Sita said.

"Look, the sun has risen above the shoreline," Radha said and pointed. "It is most bright and red this morning. It is a good sign."

Sal watched passengers in other boats snapping their cameras.

"It is said that a photograph of the sun rising over a boat on the Ganges will bring good luck," Radha said.

Ange took a small camera from his shirt pocket and began clicking. Sal smiled.

The rower pulled slowly on his oars twisting the boat's path and helping Ange get good photo angles. Then he pulled away from the dozens of other boats and headed up the river.

"The Ganges is narrower than I expected," Ange said.

"Yes, here," Radha answered. "But there are places where it is well over a mile in width."

"Why is the east side undeveloped? There's nothing there but some abandoned boat-wrecks."

"Perhaps to keep the sunrise pure. Others claim it is reserved as a place of penance or meditation. I remember being told when I was a child that if I abandoned my Hindu responsibilities or became a Buddhist, I would be reincarnated there as a donkey." Radha chuckled. "They told me many silly stories then trying to scare me into being a devout Hindu girl—to most carefully follow *all* the rules."

Radha looked toward the west. "You see the wide steps leading into the water," she pointed out. "They are called ghats. There are about ninety of them, and each has its own color. You will see many murals of Lord Shiva, for this is his city, and the goddess Ganga, for this is her river. We entered at the Dasashvamedha Ghat where many ceremonies are held. Varanasi is the city of light, so most ceremonies take place at night and use much fire. We will travel to the Manikarnika Ghat where the sacred flame has burned for over two thousand years. This is a most holy place, and there are always cremations occurring on the ghat. An ember from the holy flame is used to light sandalwood to purify the remains of one who has passed on. Then a bit of the ash is placed in the river. It is hoped that the deceased will have earned a better life in their next incarnation, or even better, *moksha*, the release from *samsara*—the continuous cycle of life and death. This is the most desired accomplishment for a Hindu."

"This water is filthy," Ange said.

"Yes, it is very much polluted mostly from the waste dumped into it," Radha said. "India is a place of much inconsistency. In the same waters where holy remains are spread and people bathe to cleanse their souls, untreated sewage flows." Radha pointed to on open drain pipe oozing brown muck into the water. "But it is said that there is a special gift in the river that keeps it free of disease."

"This water would need a major endowment," Ange said.

"They're called *bacteriophage*, Ange," Sal said. "They are microorganisms that live on bacteria. This river is one of the few places where they replicate on demand. The bacteria in this water are over fifty times what is considered safe. But there are nearly equivalent bacteriophages to reduce their effect."

"This is the first time I have heard you speak like a doctor," Sita said.

"My mistake," Sal said and grinned. "You see, Ange, it's like American business. For every little piece of shit, there's a little shit-eater waiting to gobble it up."

Radha and Ange broke into laughter. Sita looked away and shook her head in disgust.

"Well, that's what they told me in med school," Sal said.

Sita fought the humor, lost, and cracked up.

Hundreds of people bathed and played in the river. Children

floated on their backs. Their parents dunked themselves and washed their hair. Others scrubbed clothes, kneading, rinsing, wringing and beating them on rocks. Sal scooped water in his hand and wet his forehead. Sita saw and smiled.

Captivated by the bustling, they passed ghat after ghat where crowds celebrated. By nine o'clock the sun was becoming uncomfortable. Radha had explained more than could be digested and the group was ready for land.

The boatman pulled for the last time, and the skiff ground onto the gravel shore. Sal insisted on helping the others before hopping out. His white pant legs had dried leaving light brown residue up to his knee. He didn't bother to brush it off.

"Where to now?" Sal asked.

"This way," Radha said and led the group to a narrow side-street. Sal turned sideways to fit between eight-foot stacks of sandalwood waiting for their turn in the sacred fire. Beyond were several small temples, pottery stalls, and storefronts packed with flowers. The group squeezed around donkeys, cows, and camels, Stepping carefully to avoid their excrement.

Eventually, shops appeared. Radha led them into one specializing in fabrics, incense, and icons. A short man behind a counter greeted them. He smiled with palms pressed together, bowing and repeating "namaste, namaste." He offered them chai in small dried mud cups. Radha accepted for the group, and he poured four.

"It is his gift to us, and it would be impolite to refuse," Radha said. "But," she whispered to Sal and Ange, "be sure not to agree to any prices he says without bargaining. You should convince him to reduce the cost by at least twenty percent."

Radha and Sita looked at shawls while Sal and Ange surveyed the trinkets on the shelves. A second man appeared and started to take items down and flash them in their faces.

"This is very, very good quality, and I have a very, very good price for you," he said several times. Sal reached for a six-inch bronze statue of Hanuman. "Oh yes, Lord Hanuman. The gentleman reminds me very much of him. You are very, very big and powerful in your stature."

The man smiled and stated a price. Sal shook his head. The man repeated with a slightly lower offer. Sal had already calculated a twenty-five percent discount from the first figure and—pretending little interest—offered it. The man countered. Sal smirked, shook his head, thanked the man, said he no longer wanted it and walked outside. The man followed and made another counter offer. Sal shook his head. The man went lower. Sal smiled and bobbled his head as if he might be interested. Then he said no. The man opened his hands and pleaded his case—he'd gone as low as he could, at this price he was giving it away; it was a very special piece, and Sal would regret passing it up. Sal smirked. Then he looked the man in the eyes and repeated his offer. The man shook his head and began to recap his previous argument. Sal interrupted him.

"Would you charge Lord Hanuman himself more than I am offering?" Sal said and smiled.

The man laughed, placed his palms together, bowed several times, and agreed. The satisfied bargainers stepped back inside.

"Should we find a place to eat?" Ange asked.

"I think it is better to return to the hotel," Radha said.

"Most of the food we will find here will not be kind to your stomachs. I am accustomed and would be fine, and I like it very, very much. But it could make you very, very sick. Even Sita has been away too long to be sure."

Radha phoned the driver, and they made their way back through the main street to the car park. The crowd had subsided, and the store fronts were visible. Sal looked inside a fabric shop where a Brahma bull lay in the center of the floor. Customers stepped around as if he were a fixture. Sal gazed at the clothing, bags, tapestries from various religions and hundreds of brass icons. He spotted another six-inch Hanuman. He asked the price and smiled. He'd done well.

The group stopped to let a colorfully painted elephant pass. The elephant tapped Sal's shoulder with his trunk.

"That is very good luck," Radha said.

Sal watched a crippled beggar on the other side of the street. The young man lay prostrated in the dirt, pulling his lifeless lower body with one arm and pushing a tin plate with the other. The plate rattled from a few coins. Sal looked at Sita. "Is he for real?"

"I believe so. But if you put much money in his dish, someone might steal it. Some Hindus would believe taking from him is a necessary part of his curse from some very evil actions in a previous life."

"What do you think?"

"I think they are wrong."

"Come this way, I see our driver," Radha said.

***

Sal sat in his room bolstering his courage. His mind replayed the night in Montreal over and over. He'd never seen Amol Patil. Radha said the old man was short and plain and cagey. Sal looked at his Rolex. Who the fuck starts a meeting at five in the afternoon, he thought.

Finally, the phone rang. Sal hesitated and then picked it up.

"OK," Sal said. He straightened his tie and brushed a hair from the sleeve of his suit coat. He looked at Hanuman standing six inches tall on the dresser. "Here we go, big guy. In one way or another, I've been waiting forty years for this."

Sal walked across the hall and tapped on Sita's door. She stepped out wearing a soft blue sari and modest makeup. Her Patil bracelet gleamed on her forearm. "How do I look?" she asked.

"Very professional," Sal said.

"I hope so. Remember it is very, very important for my uncle to believe he is dealing only with you. Talk to him only, never to his man. I thought of creating an excuse and not attending this meeting. But Radha said it would be a very big mistake, and she knows him best."

Sal nodded. "Yeah, she gave me a good prep session too."

Sita smiled. "OK, Doctor Esposito, it is time."

Ange waited by the elevator in the lobby. A hotel attendant walked over from the desk and led them down a hallway to one of several small conference rooms. The attendant opened the door. Two men stood just inside.

"Hello and welcome to India. I am R. G. Gogte." R. G.—a medium height man with thick black hair and a pleasant face—bowed and said, "Namaste."

The new arrivals bowed and repeated, "Namaste."

R. G. pointed his open hand to his right, "And may I introduce you to Mr. Amol Patil." Patil nodded without speaking.

Finally, there he was. Radha was right; he did not make a strong first impression. Only five-foot-one and less than one hundred pounds, he wore a loose fitting black business suit with a plain black tie. His white hair lay pasted across his head in a bad comb-over. His stern face and pale brown eyes gave him the appearance of a skinny mortician.

"Let us sit," R. G. said and pointed to a rectangular table with eight chairs. R. G. led Mr. Patil to the chair at the table's head—the only chair fitted with a terrycloth cover and pillow. R.G. pulled the chair out and seated the old man. He adjusted the pillow until Patil nodded and pointed for Sal to sit to his left. R. G. took the chair to Patil's right. Ange sat at Sal's left. Sita sat next to Ange, out of her uncle's gaze.

"Let us begin," R. G. said. "We are very pleased to be here with you today to consider the very well-prepared proposal you have graciously offered to us. As you may know, Mr. Patil has had some very, very unpleasant experiences with his business endeavors in North America and is somewhat reluctant to participate in such ventures again. However, as his presence would not be required and the financial benefits offered are very generous, he is interested in hearing what you have to say. Doctor Esposito, perhaps you could explain why you have chosen *us* for your project and how you see our relationship working."

Sal directed his palm at Ange. "We believe," Ange began, "that the Patil name and craftsmanship are essential to the success of this prospect."

Old man Patil turned his head slightly toward Ange and stared, expressionless. Ange laid out the essence of the business plan being sure to include the Patil name often. After a half-hour, he turned to Patil and asked if he had comments or concerns. R. G. popped in, and the game continued until Ange and R. G. had spent an hour and a quarter exploring details and projecting profits. Patil nodded occasionally. Sal sipped from a bottle of water. Sita sat quietly with her hands folded. Finally, R. G. leaned back, and the room was silent.

R. G. bobbled his head and looked at Patil—still sitting without expression. He turned his head to Sal and pronounced, "You have presented us with a very comprehensive plan and a very attractive partnership. We believe this plan will work and will be very successful. We are very pleased that you have asked us to join with you. Mr. Patil is honored to have this opportunity."

R. G. stood and reached over the table. Ange stood and shook his hand. Sal and Sita stood as R. G. helped Patil to his feet. Patil looked at Sal and made a token nod. Sal nodded back. Sita stood looking down at the table.

Patil directed his attention toward Sita and for the first time spoke, rattling off a few words in Hindi with a squeaky nasal voice.

"Gentlemen, we are finished," R. G. declared. "Mr.

Patil would like to spend a little time with his niece if you don't mind." Sita looked at Sal and smiled as the three men left the room.

"It was most pleasant meeting you both," R. G. said as they stood outside the door. "Mrs. Patil will meet you in the restaurant area a little later. I believe they will want to talk for some time, at least a half-hour. I will remain here to assist Mr. Patil when he is finished, and then we must leave immediately. Mr. Patil has an early morning meeting in Delhi. I speak for us both when I thank you for bringing us such an excellent opportunity."

Sal and Ange nodded and walked toward the lounge. "Good job, Ange," Sal said.

"Thanks, Sal. That was strange. But R. G. sucked the whole thing up."

"Strangest fucking meeting I've ever been in. I didn't say one word."

Sal stopped and exhaled. He took the brooch from his pocket and stared at it. Decades of waiting to say something to this guy. Now they finally meet, and he doesn't once have the chance to open his mouth.

"You coming?" Ange said. "We've got some celebrating to do."

Sal nodded. "It's probably safe to call Radha and let her know where we'll be. But wait until we get to the restaurant. I need a drink."

***

Radha and Sita arrived from different directions at the same time. Sal and Ange sat at a round table sipping their third drinks. Sal looked relaxed; Ange was fired up.

"Well, we did it," Ange announced as the ladies sat. Expressionless, Sita looked down and folded her hands. "You put together one fine proposal, Sita," Ange continued. "That guy couldn't put a dent in it. He sucked it up like a cat with a bowl of milk." Sita exhaled and closed her eyes. "What's the matter?" Ange asked.

"We have not succeeded," Sita said. Sal's eyes narrowed, and Ange opened his hands. "Mr. Gogte's comments were all empty praise for the plan and the *opportunity* it offered. At no time did he say we had reached an agreement or present the possibility of another meeting. The proposal has been rejected."

"He brought R. G.?" Radha said. "Then he was never serious. R. G. is his man for saying no. The meeting was a waste of time."

"But the guy shook my hand," Ange said.

"He was only thanking you for your participation, just being polite. The arrangement was not to be with you. An affirmative decision could only have come from my uncle, and it would have been with Doctor Esposito alone."

"Welcome to India," Radha said and laughed.

Sal's serious look evaporated, and he joined her. "Welcome to fucking India," he toasted.

Sita's eyes welled. "I'm sorry. I know there is humor in this for you, but I have failed, and I have wasted much of everyone's time."

Sal touched her hand. "You haven't failed. There are a lot of different ways we can make this work. This is just a setback. It is probably best for you not to work with your uncle anyway."

Sita looked at Sal and forced a smile. "You are right about my uncle, but I believe this plan is finished." Sita turned to a passing waiter. "Could you bring some white wine, please?"

"And a bottle of your best Champagne," Sal said.

"That would be very expensive sir," the waiter said.

"Do you have Dom?"

"Yes sir,"

"Bring a bottle now and put another aside for after dinner." Sal quieted Sita's protest. "We've done well on this trip in many ways, and if the jewelry plan isn't going to fly, better to know early. Besides, it's probably karma, right?"

Radha laughed. Sita smiled, sipped her wine, grew a grin, and nodded.

"Sita, you're a brilliant woman," Sal said. "And one thing I know for sure, there is always another opportunity."

The waiter popped the Dom and filled four glasses. Sal and Ange each proposed a facetious toast to their might-have-been partners. Everyone laughed and drank. Sita held up her glass. "To Uncle Amol. May he live long and find *moksha*."

Radha eyes opened wide. "And to my cousin Sita's forgiving soul," Radha added.

The flutes raised, they drank.

The waiter returned and covered the table with platters of chicken, rice, prawns, and vegetables. Sal filled plates and passed them. With his right hand, he tore off a piece of naan and dug into the food. With the pre-meeting jitters, he'd forgotten to eat and was starving. He leaned over the table, drew in the smell of curry, swayed his head, and smiled. Sita and Radha laughed as they nibbled and sipped. Ange was off his leash and becoming drunk.

A duet with a small drum kit and electric guitar set up in a nearby corner and began to play traditional Indian songs mixed with a few American standards. Sal got a kick out of the combination. Once the food was cleared, the waiter brought the second bottle of Dom. Ange could barely hold his glass. After two flutes, Radha announced, "I'd better get him to the room, or he will be useless tonight." Sita looked appalled and then giggled.

As Radha led Ange away, Sal looked into Sita's eyes. "May I ask you a question?" he said. Sita nodded. "What did your uncle say to you?"

Sita looked away and then turned back. "He said I should remember my place. I should go back to America and marry another Indian man who can make sure I live as I should. He said he did not like Angelo, and he said he did not like you. He said you were a man who could never have conceived of this plan."

Sita sipped and smiled.

"We did not secure a partnership, but you did not let him win the meeting. You never addressed him. That bothered him very much. I am very glad."

"Just what does he think your place is? What you should remember?"

Sita looked down and then back up. "I was not born a Patil. I do not know my birth family name. My father adopted me when I was a baby against the wishes of most of his family. My father was a very kind man. My real family could not afford me. He and my mother accepted me and raised me as *their* daughter. I did not know I was adopted until I was twelve. When I was fourteen, my father and mother died, and I went to live with my uncle. He continued my education but never accepted me. In his eyes, I am and always will be *Dalit*.

"When I was sixteen, he betrothed me to my husband. He was forty. I was married to him for twenty-six years. He was a good provider. When we moved to America ten years ago, he was very worried that I would become like the women he saw on television. For that reason, we lived in the closed community I have told you of. It was when he died that I became independent for the first time. It was very difficult. But I met others, and I studied, and I learned about many good Western ways."

Sita paused. "It was not fair for me to bring others into my wishes as I did. After being away from India for ten years, I had forgotten how many old ways are deeply fixed here. I believed my uncle would accept me now. I was stupid."

"You were not stupid," Sal said. "He's the one who is stupid."

"He has had a hard life with the things that happened to my grandfather and his needing to leave Canada."

Sal sat back and closed his eyes.

"I thought he could see me in a different way," Sita continued. "However, I am still the untouchable baby his brother forced him to care for."

Sita looked down again. "You have been so kind and understanding, and I should have never brought you into this situation. I have criticized the way you behave and the words you like to use." Sita paused. "All of this has cost you much money and time. I am ashamed."

"OK, let's stop that. I'm glad I came, and I have more money and time than I know what to do with these days. Thank you for telling me all of this. It could not have been easy for you."

Sal paused and thought, maybe, someday, I'll be able to be as honest with you. He poured two fresh flutes of Dom. "Here's to honesty," he toasted. "Now I know why you like Radha so much."

"Yes, she has always been good to me. I very much admire her spirit."

Sal and Sita chatted and laughed. Sita told stories of Radha's defiance. Sita gazed into Sal's eyes, smiled, and nodded.

"What are you thinking?" Sal asked.

"Many have said they see the strength of Lord Hanuman in you, and it is true you are very powerful. But I see the heart and courage of Lord Rama. You have a truly noble essence, Salvatore."

Sal looked down and began constructing his rebuttal. Then he looked up at Sita and, for a moment, forgot about Montreal.

They finished the bottle. Sal suggested another, but Sita declined. "I should go to my room now. I have enjoyed this evening very much, even with the results of our meeting. And again, I thank you for all you have done."

Sita stood, touched Sal's wrist, placed her palms together, bowed, and said, "Namaste."

Sal reciprocated, and Sita left.

Sal debated another drink as he listened to the duet finish their night. Finally, he gave in and asked for a Kingfisher. Yeah, Salvatore Esposito with the noble essence of Rama, he thought. Sal smirked. If she only knew the truth. Maybe I'd better tell her.... But after tonight, I'll barely see her.... Best leave it alone. Old man Patil seems like a hunk of shit anyway. At least I faced him. I guess that's something.

***

Sal butted the door shut, stripped off his clothes, and pulled on a robe. He looked at Hanuman. "Well, big guy, that's the end of that—on to bigger and better deals. I didn't like the old man anyway. It would have been hard to trust him." He brushed his teeth, hung his clothes, stretched, and sat on the corner of the bed. "Good night, big fella," he whispered.

Sal heard tapping on his door. "May I come in?" Sita asked, holding a bottle of Dom. Sal nodded. She placed the bottle on the dresser next to Hanuman and turned to Sal. She smiled and slowly approached him cradling his head in her hands leading his lips to hers. She pushed the robe over his shoulders and to the floor.

"Sita," Sal said. She put her finger over his lips, stepped back, smiled, and gracefully unwrapped her sari.

***

Sal woke stretched out on his back. He slowly opened his eyes, yawned, and looked at the fuzzy numbers on the alarm clock. "Jesus, it's ten o'clock," he whispered.

He looked at the empty space and ruffled sheets beside him. The night before flashed back into his head. Sita was gone. He cleaned up, dressed, and sat looking at Hanuman standing beside an unopened bottle of Dom Pérignon.

"What the fuck did I do?" he said. He looked back at the disheveled bed and back at Hanuman. "She'll think I took advantage of her. I have to talk to her."

Sal looked at the ceiling fan and then down at the floor. He noticed a piece of paper peeking from under the door. He smiled and exhaled, no doubt a so-long Sal letter. He smelled it. Yup, he thought. He opened a Kingfisher from the mini-bar and began to read.

Dear Doctor Esposito,

I wish to thank you for all you have done for me. I will never be able to repay you. Last night I believe I behaved in a most improper way. I have embarrassed myself and you. But it is an act I will have to move beyond. I have decided it is best that I return to America by my own means. You are a good man, and I regret that our venture was not successful. I have enjoyed your company and the company of Mr. Costello. It is best now that we do not see each other again.

Sincerely,

Mrs. Sita Patil

Sal put the note down. “FUCK,” he said.

A ringing phone startled him. “Yeah?”

“Sal, it’s Ange.”

“No shit.”

“Wow, you’re in a good mood.”

“Sorry, a little too much champagne last night. What’s up?”

“We’re going to meet in the restaurant if you want to join us. Radha has a flight this afternoon. Have you seen Sita?”

“I’ll be down in a few minutes.”

Sal hung up and whispered to himself. “OK, we’re out of here first thing in the morning, back to Camp, back to reality. She’s gone, and that’s good—quick, clean, no worries. Jesus, this was about the dumbest idea I’ve ever let myself get involved with. Now it’s dead. I’m glad. I came, and I saw the old son-of-a-bitch—time to put that shit in the past, too.”

He gulped the rest of the Kingfisher, bid ado to Hanuman, and strutted out the door.

***

“Well, Doctor Esposito,” Radha said, “I will be leaving in a half-hour for Delhi. It would be nice to sit here by the pool with you and Angelo, but I must get back.”

“Where is Ange?”

“He will be along shortly. You are a most interesting man,

and I hope we see each other again. I am very surprised at Sita's decision, but she is a woman with her own ways. She may have had some business to attend to that required her to return as she did."

"Would you like some wine, Radha?"

"Thank you. I believe I have time for one." Sal signaled the waiter. "I am curious about something, Doctor." Oh shit, here it comes, Sal thought. "What did you think of my Uncle Amol?"

Didn't see that coming, Sal thought.

"I didn't say one word to him. I haven't much to base an opinion on."

"Well I do," Radha declared as the waiter handed her a glass of chardonnay. "It is good that you will not be doing business with him. He is mean and very, very greedy. I know it is not proper for me to say so, but he is what Americans describe as an asshole."

Sal almost spat his beer and laughed. "Did he greet you saying 'namaste'?" she asked.

"No, R. G. did."

"Well, at least Uncle Amol hasn't sunk that low, and R. G. is a snake. To say 'namaste' when you do not mean it is very hypocritical."

"We all said it back."

"That is not the same. It would be impolite not to. And it is perfectly acceptable to say as a greeting if you genuinely intend friendship and kindness. But to begin a business meeting by saying 'namaste' when my uncle's only goal was to berate Sita is despicable."

"You think that was your uncle's only purpose?"

"Yes, now that the meeting has happened and Angelo has described it to me. I am certain of it."

"That—"

"Asshole?"

Sal laughed. "Yeah, asshole."

"You know, 'namaste' has many levels of meaning. But the deepest is the most important and should only be used when it is meant." Sal remembered Sita's lesson but let Radha continue. "It means 'I see the divinity in you.' Many Hindus take it further also to mean 'I *see* all that you are and all you have been.' I am glad my uncle avoided blasphemy."

"You speak very openly, Radha. I'm glad. I didn't like your uncle or R. G. It's good we didn't do business."

"Yes, but poor Sita had her heart set on it so very, very much. She believed the old man would change. She was very, very wrong." Radha grinned. "I find it curious how often things begin and end at this holy river—Sita always believed in the power here. It has been the source of her dreams. Now it becomes the place where her heart is broken."

Radha stood. "Well, Doctor, I hope you have good feelings about your time in India. You have had quite an adventure. I wish you a safe journey home. And, Doctor," Radha placed her palms together and bowed, "namaste." Sal smiled. "Oh, I must go quickly; my driver is waiting."

Radha jogged off to her car before Sal could respond.

Sal put the chaise lounge back a notch and let his thoughts flow. Just how do I feel about my time in India? I don't know. He remembered a trick a professor taught him in law school—if you can't identify what something is, start by eliminating all the things it is not. OK, how do I *not* feel? I'm not disappointed. Sal thought a moment. I'm not love-sick. I'm tired but not whipped. I'm not sorry. Now, what am I? I'm fucking pissed at that old cocksucker, and I'd like to find that fucking Duke and shove his cowboy hat up his ass. I'm fucking—

"Hey Sal," Ange yelled as he strolled from the hotel door. "Where's Radha?"

"She left, Ange. She had a plane to catch, remember?"

"Shit, I thought she'd a least wait long enough to say goodbye." Sal shrugged. "Son of a bitch, Sal, I feel like I've been dumped again. Kind of hollow. And, I feel like there's more to do, something's left undone. This can't be the end. Shit, Sal. How do you feel?"

"I was just working on that, Ange." Sal took a sip of whiskey and a long drink of beer.

"Well?" Ange probed.

"I feel like getting drunk and saying 'fuck' … a lot."

CHAPTER XIV

Johnny

The moon shone brightly over Lake Champlain as Sal drove down the drive to Camp. He fought to keep his eyes open and yawned as he pulled into the garage. He looked at a clock as he slogged through the door. Four in the fucking morning, shit, he thought. I'll catch a few hours anyway.

Sal flipped on the bedroom light, placed the brooch and Hanuman on his dresser, stripped off his clothes, and clicked off the light. The mattress had become familiar after six months. Sal smiled as his head hit the pillow.

The dream came quickly.

Sal stood on a street in Varanasi. The paralyzed beggar crawled on his belly. Only a few people strolled about. One tossed a baby on his plate. Another glanced around and bent to steal it. A tiger appeared, roared in the thief's face, took the baby in his mouth, leaped over a Howdy Doody doll with a bright red cowboy hat and bounded away toward the Ganges.

Now Sal sat in the back of a Land Rover speeding toward the river. He held the broken leg from a bed frame in his right hand and a pen in his left. The rover became a rotting boat and flew through a circle of fire before plunging into the water and sinking. Sal swam in the murk unable to see. A stroke of his hands cleared the silt, and Lord Shiva appeared. Shiva looked deeply into Sal's eyes. His four arms and legs became long and slimy, and he transformed into a giant squid. He grabbed Sal with his tentacles, pulled him toward a ghat where a crowd bathed and washed clothes, and pushed him deep into a sewer pipe.

Sal crawled through excrement toward a clean, well-lit space. A wave of raw sewage threw him back. The tiger appeared behind him and tossed him and the baby onto the unsoiled area. Sal was spotless and neat; the baby was strapped to his back; his pen and bed leg lay in front. He picked them up and crawled to a grated opening. He looked down into a conference room where a small man with a white comb-over stirred the familiar caldron of lentil dahl.

As always, the dahl turned to gold and boiled over spitting and bubbling. The man dipped his finger in the gold and tasted it. Sal pried the grate with the bed leg and held the pen like a dagger. The grate burst free and—still grasping the pen—Sal and the baby slipped forward through the opening and into a free-fall.

Sal awoke, his eyes opened wide. It had been months, and he knew it was long overdue.

He showered longer than usual. His robe felt soft and smelled fresh. Kate must have washed it. He sat looking out on Lake Champlain.

This dream had been different. He wasn't alone. He hadn't realized how Sita's story had hit him. He'd thought about it on the plane, but it didn't seem like that big a deal. Now he knew it was. Her uncle had crushed her. What would it be like to be a sold-off child and always kept as an "untouchable baby"? Radha was right; Patil was an asshole.

Sal made coffee. No sense trying to sleep now; maybe a nap later. As he returned to his chair, the sunlight peeked over the Vermont horizon. He sipped his coffee. He watched the orange sun grow as it raised to a full sphere and cast a trail of saffron light across Lake Champlain.

***

Boozer's tail wagged furiously as he jumped and slapped his paws on Sal's open hands. "I missed you too, Buddy. But it's only been a few days."

"Productive trip?" Kate asked.

"Yeah, in many ways. No deal, but that's for the best."

"No deal? Sita must be disappointed."

"Yeah."

"Oh, let me show you something." Kate led Sal to the garage and pointed to a stack of rolled carpets, each wrapped in thick plastic. "They're from Sita."

Sal exhaled, "When did they come?"

"The day you left. I called some guys to put them down, but I need to know what you want to do with the old ones."

Sal nodded. "I'll think about that. How much were they?"

"The guys?"

"The rugs?"

"The invoice said paid in full. I think she sent them as a gift."

"That's just fucking great," Sal whispered. He paused and smiled. "Anything else going on?"

"There's a letter on the bar."

"Johnny again?"

"It's from the prison."

Sal nodded and yawned, "Want some coffee?"

"I'd love some, but let me get it. You look exhausted."

Sal sat on the porch rubbing Boozer's ears. He smirked and tore open the envelope. His face remained expressionless as he read. He laid the letter on an end table and went back to Boozer's ears. Kate brought fresh coffee, and he took a long sip. He sat silent. So did Kate.

Sal stood and stretched and looked at Champlain. The open lake was alive with waves and free of ice. What little remained in the bay was cracked and melting. In a few weeks, he'd put the dock in, and Boozer could swim. He'd have Ray bring the boat and show him where Jimmy's ashes were. On his toes, he caught a glimpse of Turtle Rock's outer edge. Finally, Kate spoke. "Any change?"

"Not in Johnny."

"You do look exhausted, you know."

"Yeah, I'm whipped. I'll try to get some sleep this morning. Would you call the carpet guys and see when they can come? If you don't want any of the old ones, let's ask Ray. If he doesn't, we'll just send them to Goodwill. Jimmy would want that."

"I think the guys can probably come this afternoon."

"No, not this afternoon. This afternoon I have to see my brother."

***

"Jesus, Sallie it's been a long time," Johnny forced out in a raspy, weak voice.

"Yeah. I won't ask how you're doing."

Johnny chuckled, "Seen Ma?"

"Last week. She's okay. Doesn't know who anybody is."

Johnny exhaled. "I kinda miss the old bird, you know? I put her through a lotta shit."

Sal snickered and nodded.

"She still singing?"

Sal shook his head. "Not much, she's nearly forgotten all that."

Johnny looked away, his eyes misty. "Too bad, I loved that voice. Worse thing about being in this fucking prison, I couldn't see her or ask her to sing."

Sal chuckled. "It's a little late to think about that, Johnny."

Johnny looked away and paused. "Still knockin' the shit out of anything that gets in your way?"

"I'm trying to quit."

Johnny chuckled. "You were fucking good. Do you remember how Ma said you had the strength of Hanuman? But you had something more. You had that hair trigger temper. The littlest thing would set you swinging. I used to get a kick outta that."

Johnny struggled to lift a glass, then sipped water through a straw. "Why'd you wait so long to come?"

"I've been busy—out of the country for a while."

"Yeah, I heard about your club in Saratoga." Sal's eyebrows rose. "Sounds like quite the joint. And you've got some kinda shit going on in Florida. All that must keep you real busy. Don't look surprised—I'm still in touch." Johnny looked into Sal's eyes. "Why'd you come now?"

"You're my brother."

"You mean *half-brother*, don't you? Weren't you always careful to point that out? You're still pissed aren't you? Still blame me for the fuckup in Montreal."

Johnny turned, coughed for several seconds, wiped the phlegm from his chin, and weakly tossed the tissue to the side of the bed.

"No one else to blame," Sal said.

"I thought you'd be grown outta the little woe-is-me Sallie shit by now."

"Fuck you, Johnny."

"Good one, Sallie. I see you still got your wit."

"You know what I did to that old man, Johnny. I was twelve fucking years old. You're the one who told me to use that club and keep swinging."

"Whoa, Sallie. You never needed to be told to keep swinging. For you, that was instinct. Hanuman in rage, just like Ma said. You had that long before Montreal."

"You talked me into that fucking job. You—"

"Oh, wait a minute there, Little Brother. You couldn't wait to get into my business. 'Come on, Johnny, I can do it, I'm tough, take me along, I'll show you.' You badgered me for months to let you get involved in my shit. You knew what it would do to Ma if she found out. And you knew it was risky. And I wouldn't let you. I didn't want you involved in anything *like* my business, *ever.* I wanted you to go to college and use that enormous fucking brain of yours, just like Ma did. Then one easy little fucking job came along, and I gave into your taunting."

"I was twelve fucking years old!"

"That didn't occur to you then. How many fucking times did I point that out to you? But you just kept pestering and pestering. And when the one thing you could be useful for got fucked up, you blamed everybody else."

"It was your fault, Johnny. You and that fucking Buzzy Kline."

Johnny chuckled, then coughed. "Buzzy Kline, there's a name I haven't heard in years. Always liked that name. Clever, you know, and it's got a ring to it, Buzzy Kline."

Johnny coughed again and spat into a Styrofoam cup. He struggled to take a breath, then he continued. "Listen, Sallie; maybe the *whole* thing wasn't your fault. But if you'd stuck to the plan, everything would have worked. But you didn't. You couldn't do one simple little thing, open one window—one fucking window—and it all got fucked up. That's what happened, Little Brother."

"Fuck you. I knew I shouldn't have come here."

"Ah, that's the Sallie I remember. Run away from it. Hide in the corner—someone else will take care of it and make all the bad things go away. You got that shit from Pop."

Sal darted a stare into Johnny's bloodshot eyes. "Bullshit, Johnny. Pop was as solid as it gets. He worked his ass off in that shop until he could build his house. He didn't steal for it. And even with my scholarships, I could never have finished college without his help. Don't start in on Pop. You're full of shit."

Johnny laughed, bending forward and hacking into a tissue. He wiped his mouth and grinned.

"You really think Pop built that house? You really think a fucking tailor in Plattsburgh, New York, with a fix for the ponies put away enough money to build that fucking house? Let me tell you something, Little Brother. I built that house! He didn't steal for it; he let me do that. And something else you shoulda figured out by now, I gave him the money to send to you. Between their trips to the city and his time at the track, he barely made ends meet. Shit, I had to bail him out on stupid bets, twice. You have no fucking idea how much he was into Pencil Nick for.

"No, Sallie, when he wanted something he came to me, his *stepson*! You were the chosen one, his *real* boy, and I'll bet he never asked you for a fucking dime. You made up some fucking fantasy in that head of yours. Maybe that's from having too many brains. You're so fucking smart you can't see what's right in front of your face."

Sal's eyes flared, and his cheeks reddened. "You're full of shit!"

"Think about it, Little Brother. Am I?"

Sal snatched his hat and stood.

"OK, Sallie, run off for the last time. Hate my fucking guts all you want. You have for forty years, why change now? But I'm glad you came. And now at least you know a little of the truth. Call it all bullshit if you want. And, Sallie, I barely scratched the surface."

"Goodbye, Johnny. I hope things aren't painful for you."

"Looks like less for me than you," Johnny chuckled and coughed.

***

Sal slammed the bag, again and again. After more than an hour, he dropped his arms and sat on the stack of rugs. He looked at his swollen fists and breathed hard.

He stood—leaving a puddle of sweat on the plastic—and staggered into the great room. He made his way to the sink and drank two glasses of water. He stood silent and then poured a tumbler of whiskey and drank half in one gulp.

He stared at the player piano, put the glass on the bar, and stormed to the piano. He thwacked his butt onto the stool, hooked the roll, smacked the keyboard cover back, and slammed the pedals to the floor. He started furiously pumping. "Moon River" bellowed out, first the intro and then the opening stanza. Sal pumped harder, grabbing the ridge under the keyboard to increase his leverage. The volume grew, and the roll tightened. Sal's eyes turned red, and he began to sweat again. He pumped as if possessed. Then he heard a deafening WAABOOM followed by the hiss of escaping air.

The pedals lay flat. Sal pulled one up, but it fell back. He jumped up, shoved the stool away and glared at the half-played roll. "FUCK YOUR BUSTED BELLOWS, POP!" he yelled and slapped his hands on the keyboard.

Sal grabbed his whiskey and sat on the porch looking into the north woods. The door squeaked as Kate and Boozer walked in. Sal didn't turn.

"We heard the piano. Everything OK, Sallie?"

"Don't fucking call me that," Sal blurted. "...Shit, Kate, I'm sorry." Sal turned his head, and Kate saw tears. She hugged his head. Boozer licked his hand, and sat.

"I'm sorry, I'm fucked up right now," Sal wiped his eyes.

"It's OK, Sallie. Let it out, or you'll be the next thing to explode."

Sal looked up and forced a smile. "Yeah," he said. "OK, anyone want a drink? Boozer would you like a little beer and maybe a Nutter Butter?"

Kate and Boozer didn't respond.

"I saw my brother. I don't know, Kate—forty years of the same shit. I thought I had it fixed in India, or at least under control. But ten minutes with Johnny and I want to tear the fucking world apart, again."

Sal stood and sipped his whiskey.

"OK, here it is. Maybe you should sit down; it's not a short story."

Kate sat by Boozer. Sal paced.

"I was twelve years old. I idolized Johnny. I used to tell

other kids, 'You think I'm tough, you don't know my brother.' I don't think any of us knew then how rotten he was.

"I knew he was breaking into places. To me, that seemed like a big-time adventure. I bugged the living shit out of him to let me go with him. Shit, I was like a kid begging to go to an amusement park. Then something came up, and he had a use for me.

"We met downtown near my pop's shop. It was past midnight when a guy pulled up in an old white panel van. His name was Buzzy Kline. Buzzy was older than Johnny and gave the orders. I rode in the back. Before we crossed the border, Johnny gave me a blackjack—you know one of those leather-covered clubs. I can still hear him barking at me, 'Nothing better than a good *two-by-four* in a fucking jam. And if you need to use this, don't stop until the job is done.'

"After we had crossed into Canada—in those days, it was no big deal, you remember—they told me the plan. We were going to hit a jewelry store. They knew a soft spot in the security. I never asked how. A ventilation shaft led to a grate in a closet wall on the second floor of the business next door. It also fed the ceiling of the jewelry store. It was just large enough for me to crawl through. Once I got in, I was to open a security window in the back; Buzzy said the alarm there would be disconnected. That was it for me; they'd take care of the rest. The van would be parked two streets over. We'd all meet there.

"We got in without a hitch—it was an old building with a lot of substandard retrofitting. Johnny found the closet and opened the vent. I crawled in. Johnny had a shit-eating grin.

He started clapping quietly and nodding his head. I actually fit; I think he thought that was a crapshoot until that moment. Then Buzzy signaled Johnny, and they left.

"I knew something was fucked up as soon as I started crawling. The vent reeked of curry, and I could hear some rustling around in the room below. I crawled along, as quiet as I could. I saw light and crawled to a grate. When I looked down, an old man was at a workbench eating a bowl of rice and some vegetables. On a hotplate next to him was a pot of boiling lentil dhal. He reached to turn it down and heard me. He looked up and started yelling in some foreign gibberish. I didn't know what to do, I froze for a second and then jerked on the vent until it gave way and I fell onto the workbench splattering the dhal and scalding my arm.

"The old man stood over me screeching meaningless words. I yelled at him to shut up, but he slapped my head and kept on. I jumped to the floor and grabbed the blackjack. I whacked him on the side of his head, but he kept squawking. I hit him a second time, and then again and again. He stopped, but I didn't. I was out of my mind. I struck and struck and struck.

"He was bleeding from his nose and ear when I stopped. I lifted his arm, and it dropped back, lifeless. I was convinced I'd killed him. Kate," Sal paused. "For those few seconds when I couldn't stop beating him, I felt absolute hate … I was *pure* evil. I remember thinking in a flash that he had no right to be there fucking things up. I'd show that old fuck. He had no right to be in my way; he had no right to be alive."

Sal looked off to the woods and took a drink.

"I looked around. I saw a bandanna and wrapped it around

the burn on my arm. I smacked away a big bowl of rice to see what was on the bench behind it. It flew all over and spattered my shirt and pants. I tried to brush it off, but it stuck everywhere.

"I searched the room. There was nothing of value except one gold brooch on the work bench. The old man must have been working on it. I grabbed it, and then—for some fucked up reason—realized where I was and what I'd done.

"I panicked and forgot the plan. I yanked off two open padlocks, one from each side of the steel back door, then crashed the escape bar and fell through to the street. The fucking alarm blasted, ringing and whooping. I ran. I don't know what direction. I stopped at an alley, hid just inside, and gathered my wits.

"I crouched behind a garbage can and brushed off most of the rice. Then I remembered where the van was and started walking, trying not to look suspicious. I could still hear the alarm and saw police cars race by one block up. The van was gone. I stood there cursing Johnny and that fucking Buzzy Kline. I didn't know what to do. Why did those fuckers leave me? I remember thinking it must have been that fucking Buzzy Kline—Johnny wouldn't have left me if Buzzy didn't make him.

"I pulled together and walked on. It started to rain, hard—then sleet. I walked toward the highway and followed it for a couple of miles. I was fucking drenched and freezing, but I had to keep walking. I saw a produce truck stopped at a light with a sign on it—*Lacolle Vegetables*, or something like that. I jumped on the back and tried to get between some crates to cut the wind. I was so fucking cold, and some rice must have gone down my collar. My chest was itching like it was covered with maggots.

"The truck drove for forty minutes until it stopped just north of the border. When I jumped off, the driver saw me and ran after me yelling in French, but I made it into the woods. He must know, I thought. He must know I'm the one who killed the old man in Montreal. By now, it would be all over the radio. By now, everyone would know.

"I found a spot to hide. I took off my shirt and rubbed rice from my chest. I got most of it and put the wet shirt back on. There was a stream, and I soaked my burned arm in the cold, dirty water. When I pulled it out, a leech was sucking just below my elbow. I jumped up and yanked the bastard off. Blood squirted on my pants and its teeth stuck in my skin. I scratched and scratched until I'd dug them out, then rewrapped the bandanna.

"I sat in the woods shivering. For hours. The rain turned to sleet again, and I tried to cover up with some leaves—Kate I've never been so fucking cold—and thought of giving myself up. But I didn't. Just before sunrise, the freezing rain stopped, and I snuck across the border near Rouses Point.

"Once the sun rose, I wasn't as cold. I walked a few more miles. I was almost dry when a guy in a pickup gave me a lift into Plattsburgh. I was so tired, and I thought he must know I was the murderer everyone was searching for. I didn't care. But he just chatted away about chicken-shit and drove on.

"I got home about an hour later. My mother was furious when she saw me. She saw bits of rice on my clothes and blood on my pants and stared into my eyes. I just stood expressionless. She removed the bandanna and saw the burn and sore from the leech. She didn't say a word. She washed my arm, rubbed on salve and disinfectant, and wrapped it in clean gauze. She slipped a plastic bag over the bandage and sent me to shower. From the bathroom, I heard her on the phone with Pop. She kept yelling, 'That Johnny! That Johnny!'"

Sal paused with a wry smile. "I guess I was still her favorite."

Kate asked, "Was this the Patil jewelry store?"

"Yeah."

"Did the old man die?"

"No, but I blinded him for life."

Kate pondered. Her eyes opened wide. "Sallie, was this Sita's grandfather?"

"Yes."

Kate took a deep breath. "My God. Whoever said it was a small world made one hell of an understatement."

"Kate, I thought I'd killed him. But there was nothing about it on the radio. Even the local paper didn't cover it. My guts churned and churned on it—the guilt was destroying me. I knew I should turn myself in—until almost a week later when I saw a Montreal paper in a pile behind the barbershop. It reported the burglary but barely mentioned an assault. And, it said Patil had lost over two-hundred thousand. Shit, we took nothing; but the fucking guy was cashing in on his insurance. A month later, a friend of Ma's who shopped there said the business was closing. The old man was blinded in an attack, and his son wanted to go back to India. I didn't know until then what I'd actually done."

"And Johnny, did he ever say why he left you?"

"I saw him a couple of hours after I got back. He started yelling at me. 'You stupid little shit, you couldn't even open a fucking window. This total fuckup is on you.'

"I took a swing at him, but he grabbed my arm and laughed. I screamed to know why he left me. He said he knew I'd find my way back, and since it was *all* my fault, it would be a good lesson.

"From that day, I've hated him. Ma wouldn't let him near me any longer, but I'd see him around, and he'd taunt me about 'Little Sallie's fuckup.' And today, forty years later, lying in his bed, coughing up chunks of his lungs, he blamed me again. He had to do that—and set me straight on my pop. That's the only reason he wanted to see me—to fuck with little Sallie's head one last time."

"Your pop?"

Sal shook his head. "Not now."

Kate nodded. "Sallie, may I ask you one more thing?"

Sal smiled, "Why not, Kate."

"Does Sita know?"

Sal shook his head. Kate stood and hugged Sal again.

"Thanks for listening," Sal said. "I've never told anyone about this."

Sal let out a deep sigh.

Kate stood back. "You know, maybe a drink wouldn't be such a bad idea. And then, maybe we could go for some hot dogs."

"Sounds damn good to me." Sal smiled. "What do you think, Boozer, a little beer and then some Michigans?" Boozer woofed.

***

"That was the best sleep I've had in years," Sal said as Kate placed a plate of eggs and Canadian bacon in front of him.

"I'm not surprised. You've been carrying a lot of stress around, Sallie."

"Speaking about carrying around," Sal reached into his pocket, "ever seen a genuine Patil brooch?"

Kate held the brooch in the light. "It's beautiful. Too bad it comes with such horrible memories. Sallie, yesterday you said you became pure evil. Have you ever felt that again?"

"Not as bad—until recently."

"Recently?"

"In London. I was trying to save a friend and completely lost myself again."

"How bad?"

"I stopped before I almost killed the Son of a Bitch."

"Why?"

"My friend asked me to."

Kate smiled and nodded.

"And almost, in India. With a couple of fucking bastards; but I stopped myself."

"You stopped yourself. Sallie that's wonderful. What did they do?"

"They were trying to rape Sita."

"RAPE SITA?"

"Yeah."

Kate looked down and shook her head. "That must have been some trip."

"We were almost attacked by a tiger too." Sal recapped the India adventure. Kate stared wide-eyed, and Boozer held his head up.

Kate refilled Sal's coffee mug. "So, you saved Sita from rape and a tiger?"

"Yeah, sort of."

"Sallie, that's bonding. From a woman's perspective—even without physical contact—that's a significant tie."

Sal looked at his plate. He'd chosen not to mention the last night in Varanasi. "I guess so. Where are you going with this, Kate?"

"I think you have to tell her—for your sake. It sounds to me like your old curse may be broken, but if you're not completely honest with Sita, you'll carry that around in its place."

Sal licked his upper lip. "Any more bacon?"

Kate chuckled, took Sal's plate, and filled it with a second helping. "You are feeling good," she said.

"I know you're right about Sita. But, I can't see her. We didn't part on simple terms. Maybe I should send a letter. But, I need time to process everything." Sal patted his chest. "I need to get to know what's going on in here. I don't know if I'm making any sense. Now isn't the time for more contrition."

Kate grinned, "You're one smart man, Salvatore Esposito."

***

"It's been a calm couple of weeks, Boozer," Sal said. "I don't know that I've ever been as relaxed."

Sal heard a knock and opened the back door. "You up for female company?" Kate strolled in with a bag of groceries. "I thought you bachelors could use a good home-cooked dinner."

"Welcome back," Sal said. "How was your retreat?"

Boozer jumped off his couch, ran to Kate and licked her hand. "Great, but three days is enough. I don't know how these guru types do it every day. But it was good—oh, Sallie, the new carpets look fantastic."

"I hope the rug guys put them where you said."

"They're perfect. My, Sita has exquisite taste."

Sal smiled. "Yeah, I thought I'd write her a note to thank her. it's a good opening. I thought I'd attach a letter." Kate smiled and nodded. "Would you like to read it?"

Kate shook her head. "No. What you say to her is for her only, from you only. I'm sure what you've written is consummate."

Sal nodded. "That's what I thought you'd say. I sent it yesterday."

Kate grinned, and the house phone rang. "Yes," Sal said and listened. "OK, I'll let you know. Thank you."

Sal poured a drink and smiled. "And that is that."

Kate tilted her head.

"Johnny is dead," Sal said. "They cremated him. Said they'd hold the ashes for next of kin. Since I'm next of kin…."

"How do you feel?"

"I feel nothing."

"Well, you knew it was coming."

"Yeah."

"Still want dinner?"

"Sure—you know, they said he died last week. I wonder why they called me now."

"Bureaucracy."

"I guess." The house phone rang again. "Hello—what's up, Ange?"

"Sal, I couldn't reach you on your cell—"

"It's dead. What's up?"

"Listen, we've got a problem. Mindy called me—"

"Who's Mindy?"

"Frankie Napoli's wife."

"Ange, I thought you were going to—"

"Sal, please listen. She said she overheard Frankie and some other guys. They're coming after us. She said Frankie made it clear that he was going to really fuck us up."

"Us?"

"Yeah, *US*, that's what she said."

"What's his grind with me?"

"I don't know, but that's what she said, *US*. Sal, I'm scared shitless. She said these guys are dangerous. Son-of-a-bitch, you were right. He was never going to let it go."

"But why now and why me?"

"Sal, how are we going to deal with this? He's sending a pack of tough fucks—pros, Sal—we got nobody who can stand up to that shit."

"All right, Ange, I'm coming down tomorrow. Tell Robert

to meet me at the club around noon. Tell him to have the other bartenders and the bouncers there. You disappear. Get out of town. I think Frankie's wife got it wrong—she's not the brightest bulb on the string. I don't think they're after me. Frankie probably just popped for some reason. But I'll get as many guys together as possible, just in case."

"Sal, I'm telling you they're coming after both of us. You don't have the guys for this."

"Ange, I'll handle it. You disappear. Get lost any way you can."

"All right, Sal, I'll let you know where I am."

"Don't! Just disappear. I'll call you when it's fixed."

Sal hung up and gulped down his whiskey.

"Trouble in Saratoga?" Kate asked.

"Yeah, I'll have to go down tomorrow."

The phone rang again. "What? ... Please excuse me; I thought you were someone else ... Yes ... How? ... Well, that's what he said he'd do. I'm very sorry ... Two weeks? ... I'll let you know."

Sal hung up and exhaled. Kate looked at him, concerned and silent.

"That was a guy from a place I visit in London. My friend Colin died. They're having a service for him in a couple of weeks. He wasn't religious; they're just doing a reception at his club."

"Was this expected?"

Sal shrugged. "He took himself out. He was a true Stoic. The crash must have hit him harder than I thought."

Kate paused. "You still want dinner?"

"Yeah, but let's take everything to your house if you don't mind."

"No problem."

"Good, I need to get away from this fucking phone."

***

"Yes, Robert, still no sign? Well, it's been several days. If he were going to do something, he would have moved by now. Maybe Frankie sobered up and came to his senses. Yeah, I'll be down after you close. Leave the receipts in the back room. Did you get the jukebox fixed? ... OK, good. The fucking music turning off and on, on its own really pisses off the customers ... All right, I'll catch up with you tomorrow."

Sal moved to a rocker and looked at the Hudson. It looked like a false alarm. Frankie probably just had a loose screw for a couple of days. But, at least Sal'd had time to pack what little was left. The realtor said the place would sell fast—even in this economy. He looked around and thought of his pop. Johnny was right—how did Sal ever think a small-town tailor could afford a house like this.

Sal looked at the six-inch statue of Hanuman on the bar. "Looks like I didn't need you after all, big guy," he said and chuckled.

Around midnight, Sal left for the club. He picked up coffee and a donut and took his time. When he arrived, the lights were off and the lot empty, as expected. He opened the back door to the office, flicked on the lights, and locked the door behind him. He sat at his desk sipping his coffee and looked down at the night's receipts. Not bad for a weeknight, he thought.

Sal sat back and thought of what Johnny said. He wondered just how much Pop *had* been into Pencil Nick for, and how many times. He remembered the money he needed in college and how relieved he'd be when it arrived. Would have quit if he knew it was from Johnny? He shook his head, looked back at the receipts, and started counting.

Sal heard music from inside the club.

"That piece of shit jukebox turned itself on again?" Sal thought to himself, "Probably a song someone punched in three hours ago. Robert said he had the fucking thing fixed. Next time the service brings a new one, or we're done with those assholes." Sal unlocked the inner door and walked into the club. Two men grabbed his arms. From behind, a voice said, "Nap time."

Sal came to barely coherent, flat on his back in the middle of the dance floor. With only moonlight from the small windows, he squinted and tried to see as he struggled to reach the pain at the back of his skull. On the jukebox, Dean Martin sang "Arrivederci Roma."

"Frankie thought you might enjoy a little entertainment," a man said. "He said you were tough, but so far all I see is a pussy."

Sal saw fuzzy images of four men standing over him—one slapping a blackjack into his palm.

"How'd that feel? You like the throbbing from a club cracking your thick fucking skull?" The man smirked. "You fucked up, big fella. Now you pay up.

"Frankie wondered how you'd like a wheelchair for a while. Then you'd have some time to think about when he'd finish you. And taking out the legs is his favorite anyway. First, we'll crush the ankles. Then, the knees. You see, if it's done right, you can't fix them. The idea is to crush as many bones as you can."

One assailant grabbed Sal's ankle and turned it sideways. The spokesman grinned and raised his steel toed boot. "This is going to smart some."

The jukebox went dead and the dance-floor lights popped on. The intruders gazed into the bright colors as the disco ball speckled the room with illuminant dots. "WHO THE FUCK'S THERE?" the head thug yelled.

The bar lights snapped on. A man behind the bar set down a portable sound box and carefully aimed the speakers at the dance floor.

"Sorry ta keep ya waitin'," he said. "Be with ya in just a sec."

The attackers stood astounded as the man casually reached down to plug in the box and stood up smiling. Standing at around five-foot-nine, he wore a 1930's style leather football helmet with the fighting Notre Dame leprechaun on the front.

"Sorry ta show up so late, boyos," he said. "But there's still time fer some fun."

The thugs stepped toward the bar. "Listen, asshole," the lead intruder said. "I don't know who you are, but this is none of your fucking business. Get your nose in this, and you'll be pushing your chair alongside this fuck."

"Ah, I see. In every gang, there's a Gob—ah sorry, that'd be a *mouth* here in America. You must be him. And a big one ya have, Mister Mouth. Yes, yours is a mouth in need of a slappin'. And ya brought along yer gurriers—*punks* 'ill work fer a translation. And a sorry group a punks ya are. And a private fight is it? But so unfair, no fun in that."

The intruders stepped forward. "Ah, I'm bein' rude," the man behind the bar continued. The exit lights flipped on. Three identical, stout men with crossed arms and flaming red hair stood in front of the doors.

The advancing thugs froze on the dance floor.

"Gentlemen, may I introduce Mathew, Mark, and Luke—the synoptic brothers. Oh, and I'll be bein' your master of ceremonies fer tonight's entertainment—ya did say there'd be entertainment—Danny Flannigan is the name."

Danny chuckled and flicked off the disco ball. "Won't be needin' that feckin' thing no more." He adjusted the floor lighting and nodded. "This is much better fer the show we'll be havin'."

Danny reached over to the sound box and fumbled with some knobs. "Be just a second. Gotta figure out the feckin' thing—ah, there we go." He held his finger on a button.

"And now it'll be time ta fix the odds. Open up yer ears, boyos, here's the rules. If ya can win the contest at hand, ya can go on your way with no interference from us others." Danny snickered. "Good luck to ya, you'll be needin' it.

"And now, may I introduce your opponent for the festivities. For the first time in America, please be greetin' the meanest, the most ferocious, the most terrifying hardchaw in all a Dublin. The pride of Ireland. The one, the only—Seeaaamus Clancy!"

The boom box blasted-out Dennis Day singing, "Clancy Lowered the Boom." Seamus Clancy stepped into the light wearing a brown vested suit and a bowler hat. He stared at the intruders sternly as he casually removed his coat, hung it neatly on the back of a chair, and placed his bowler on the table in front.

"Look at this little fuck," The Mouth said and laughed. "Well, at least the little cocksucker has balls!"

Shamus stepped toward the gang, raised his fists, and began to bob and weave. One punk slapped his knees in hysterics. Seamus shuffled over and like lightning riveted the thug's kidneys with half a dozen blows. Seamus sprung back, then bolted forward again and struck a smashing blow to the jaw. The punk's head jerked to the side, and he dropped flat. "The first one's always the easiest," Seamus yelled to Danny. "Now these gougers 'ill start fightin' fer real."

As Dennis Day's powerful tenor voice rhythmically crooned warnings, the remaining three punks circled. Seamus popped about strategically changing positions to block his opponents' moves. The combatants maneuvered for over a minute with one punk or another occasionally tossing out a close punch.

Then Seamus spotted an opening. In a whirlwind move, he bent his knees, leaped, and with flying scissors slapped his legs around one punk's solar plexus. He squeezed like a vice, whacked with a side head-butt, vaulted back to the floor, joined his hands, spun and slammed the punk's back with his joined fists.

The punk screamed, bent backward, and grabbed for his

back. Seamus swiftly slammed the punk's chin. The punk cried out and fell next to his friend on the floor.

As quickly as the remaining two moved forward, Seamus moved back, repositioned, and regained his wind. After more than thirty seconds of pacing off, the third punk lost his patience and lunged, swinging wildly. Seamus ducked, but a punch smacked his ear. Seamus darted slightly out of the fray, shook his head, and raised his eyebrows. "Lucky one," Seamus announced. "I'll have ta be more careful."

The enraged punk started swinging again and dropped his guard. Seamus bobbed and weaved and struck a quick blow to the face.

"MIND YOUR HOUSE!" Danny yelled from the bar as The Mouth shifted to grab Seamus's arms from behind. Seamus shuffled out of reach just as The Mouth pounced and stumbled. Seamus saw his chance, double chopped the wild puncher at the neckline, and rammed his knee into the into the punk's belly. The punk grabbed his stomach and staggered away, trying not to throw up.

Only The Mouth remained. He grasped the blackjack and swung at Seamus's head, missing by a hair.

Seamus skipped out of range. "I never liked them things," Seamus said, breathing hard. "Only a coward needs one a them. Now you're makin' me mad."

Seamus inched in teasing, prancing in step with the music, and ducking as The Mouth swung the blackjack. Seamus stood, pretending to be winded. As the Mouth moved in and swung fiercely, Seamus darted to the side. The Mouth missed and lost his balance. Seamus spun and kicked the blackjack from The Mouth's fist. As The Mouth grabbed his stinging hand, Seamus snatched the blackjack and hurled it to the bar.

"Here, Danny boy," Seamus huffed, "a keep-sake from America fer ya."

Seamus continued taunting, popping in, slapping The Mouth's face, and bouncing back. The Mouth stood like a boxer and swung again and again, desperately struggling to land a blow. Seamus continued suckering; The Mouth continued swinging and began to stagger.

After dozens of wild swipes, he bent forward, parked his hands on his thighs, and fought for breath. Seamus swept behind The Mouth and walloped the back of his knees with two rapid strikes from his foot. The Mouth fell. In a fetal position, he covered his head and gasped for air.

Panting, Seamus surveyed the three bodies on the floor and one in the corner still hurling.

"Savage," Seamus said. "I come better than three-thousand miles fer just a five-minute go with these ejets. But, 'twas fierce. I'm breathin' hard and got a bit of a drip goin'."

Seamus looked at his wet armpit and laughed. He patted his ear.

"And one bucko got in a grand puck, though a mighty feckin' lucky one. Hope this ear don't puff much."

Seamus laughed again. "And there's Guinness—and the whiskey's fierce—shite, I think I'm likin' America."

Still dizzy, Sal managed to sit up on the floor. "I've never seen anything like that," he said.

"I thank ya fer yer appreciation," Seamus said and bowed.

Sal felt a hand under his arm and looked up to see Ange

bending over him and smiling. "I didn't know what else to do, Sal. I hope you don't mind. I used the plane."

Ange helped Sal to his feet. Sal grinned and looked at Ange. "Thanks, Ange," he said. Sal gingerly shook his head and, with Ange's help, staggered to the bar.

"Well now," Danny said. "What are we ta do with these naughty boyos?"

Sal looked at the intruders—three still on the floor and one vomiting in the corner. "First, I need to know what this was all about," Sal said as Danny handed him a whiskey and an Ice pack. Sal formed the ice pack to the back of his head and stepped over to The Mouth, still lying on the floor. "Why are you here?"

"Frankie Napoli sent me. Didn't say why."

"And these other fucks?"

"Picked them up in Vegas. Couple of bouncers and a security guy from one of the joints. They don't work for Frankie, regular."

"I suggest we behave like civilized gentlemen and offer our opponents a post-thrashin' beverage," Danny said.

The triplets gathered The Mouth's punks and seated them at the bar. Groaning, The Mouth wriggled from the floor and sat.

"Are you the one who clubbed me," Sal asked The Mouth. The Mouth hesitated.

"Now speak up, boyo," Danny yelled over. "Answer Doctor Esposito's question."

The Mouth's' eyes widened, and his jaw dropped. He looked up at Sal and shook his head, "Esposito? You're Johnny Esposito's brother?"

"What's that got to do with anything?"

"That fucking Frankie. Listen, Mr. Esposito, I woulda never come here if I knew who you were. Frankie never said."

"I'm not following. What are you talking about?"

"It's hands-off Johnny Esposito's brother. Everyone on the street knows."

Sal's eyebrows lowered. "Why?"

"I don't know. Always been that way. I'm sorry, sir, I never woulda come."

Sal helped The Mouth stand and escorted him to the bar. Danny began handing out ice bags and pouring drinks. The gang members looked at each other dumbfounded as cocktails were set before them and Seamus slapped their backs.

After the first round, Danny held up the blackjack. "Ah, there's still the little matter a this," he said. "Salvatore, I believe you have one penalty strike comin' to ya. Ya know, for the sneak attack?" Danny looked at The Mouth. "It's a very bad habit ta get inta fightin' dirty, laddy."

"No, we're square," Sal said and grinned as he held an ice bag on the back of his head. "I've seen too many of those in my life." Sal looked at the club. "What went around just came around," he snickered. "Now I know what it feels like. Let's have a couple more rounds in honor of my aching head. And when we're finished, our guests will go back to Vegas and inform Frankie Napoli it's over."

Sal looked at The Mouth, then pointed at the security cameras and the microphone hanging behind the bar. "This whole event is on record. Any more trouble and it's clear who's responsible. Whatever bug's up Frankie's ass, he's had his shot, and it's done."

***

"Angelo did a fine bit a work findin' us this hotel," Danny said from a wingback chair next to Sal in front of the lobby's fieldstone fireplace. The early American décor, rich in pine accented with hunter green, reminded him of Ireland. He placed his coffee on the oak sidetable and gazed at the antlers above the mantel. "That's a grand deer that carted *them*."

Sal looked at his Rolex. "We've got an hour or so before we leave for the train station. Ange has everything set up for the city. We'll be right in Midtown Manhattan close to everything you want to see."

"Savage," Danny said.

The friends sat and sipped. Danny broke the silence. "What's yer thinkin' on Colin?"

"I don't really know. He did things his way to the end, I guess. Hard to put myself into someone else's head."

"Yeah, yer right on that. I'm not one for the offin' out. But, he said it was his way, and he was true ta his word. Ya goin' to the gatherin' for 'im?"

"Yeah. You?"

"Na. Don't figure a bold Dub like Danny Flanagan would fit in at one a them high Brit clubs. Didn't get a true invite anyway. And shite, I only knew 'im a few days. Quare though, seems longer. Like with you. Never set eyes on ya till a few months ago. Seems donkey's years."

The friends paused.

"Thanks again for saving my ass," Sal said. "Those fucks meant business; I'd be crippled if not for you guys."

"And me dead, but fer Salvatore Esposito," said Danny, chuckling. "And I can't think of a better reason ta visit the States than ta help a friend while watchin' the likes a Seamus Clancy. 'Twas grand."

Sal looked at the fire, grinning and shaking his head.

"How's yer hatin' been?" Danny asked.

Sal paused. "Better ... The main source is gone. Now ... just trying to put things in perspective."

"Perspective takes time. But, ya seemed settled last night when ya had the chance ta bash that boyo. Ya never even give it a thought."

Sal sat silent a moment. "Yeah, I'm working on it." Again, Sal paused. "OK, Danny, in a few minutes we're off to New York City and one hell of a week!"

"Yeah, the two of us driftin' about, seein' all we can a the world. Oh, and with the others, a course."

Sal grinned. "There's a lot of world, Danny. We'll start with New York."

"Now you're suckin' diesel."

***

Sal sat looking at Lake Champlain. Boozer sprawled out on

the couch next to him. Sal smiled as he thought of the last week in New York City. Danny and the boys had the time of their lives, and the bartenders at two of the Irish pubs recognized Seamus Clancy. The four saw all the tourist sights and—when he could sneak away—Sal made a point of walking by Jimmy Eagleson's old place in Soho. Danny liked Saint Patrick's best. He visited four times.

Before Sal had the boys flown back, they all made a pact to meet again in the fall. The plane turned out to be a good investment—and gold was continuing to climb, and the market was at least stabilizing.

All in all, the spring was starting well. Still nothing from Sita, but Sal didn't expect that.

Sal hopped up to open the garage door. "Come in, Ray," he said.

"I'm surprised those kegs lasted as long as they did," Ray said.

"I've been out of town. I'm flying out again in the morning for a couple of days."

"Where to?"

"London, I'm going to a service for a friend."

"Sorry—should I wait to change the kegs?"

"No, I won't be gone long. Say, Ray, have you ever heard of Kingfisher beer?"

"No."

"Could you ask the distributor about it? I'd like a couple of cases."

Ray wrote a note. Boozer jumped down and joined his pals as they sat at the bar, sipped, and chatted.

"Ray, remember our talk on those snake men?" Sal asked.

"Yeah, the nagas."

"I read the book you found. It said they're unpredictable, show up on their own."

"Yeah, that sounds right."

"So, you don't find them; they find you?"

"Yeah, usually, but I think it can work both ways. I'll have to look again, but I thought they could be sought out on occasion. Yeah, I think in the East, it's all related to karma. You can't find them for bad purposes, but they might turn up for good ones. Why?"

"Just something that popped into my head."

"Well, tell me about India. You must have seen some interesting shit."

Sal spent an hour recapping his trip. Ray soaked it in.

"I'd love to see the Ganges," Ray said. "You know, Sal—about what we were discussing before—please don't think I'm nuts, but I think I might have met one."

"One what?"

"A naga. I was in the mountains by myself. I'd been hiking for several days and hadn't eaten much. I remember I felt kind of light-headed. This guy came from nowhere and started a conversation. He must have gone six-six, and he had an enormous head. And his voice, Jesus, that loud bass shook the woods. It was just after Jimmy died. I was still feeling guilty about the whole thing—you remember. This guy seemed to know all about it. He never said anything specific but it all sort of … fit, you know?"

Sal nodded.

"I guess I'd filed it in the back of my mind until you brought them up. It's funny how we think we see something—you know, like we've talked about with Champy? People are convinced they talk to ghosts, have guardian angels, see ancestors in animals and the like.

"Most of the books I've borrowed tell myths of one kind or another—hundreds of them about spirits and avatars. I used to be totally skeptical—there always seems to be a logical explanation. But, now I wonder. It's hard to believe that so many people in so many cultures could all be having the same hallucinations. Even if they are, I wonder if their reality isn't just as sound as Einstein's or Aristotle's. This all probably sounds like bullshit, but the guy I ran into seems beyond simple coincidence."

Sal sat thinking. "I wonder too," he whispered.

CHAPTER XV

Karma

"Good to see you, Pal. It's been a few months," Sal said as he looked up at the painting of Hanuman. His London suite looked the same as he'd left it. He checked the mini-bar and smiled. The hotel found Kingfisher. He heard a knock and answered the door. A porter rolled in his suitcase, put it in the bedroom, and stood waiting for a tip. Where's Sita when I need her, Sal thought and grinned.

"Your tuxedo will be pressed by three o'clock," the porter said.

Sal nodded and closed the door. He popped a Kingfisher. He sat in his favorite British chair and looked down at the courtyard. New leaves covered the trees and shrubs. Guests sat chatting at the wrought-iron tables sipping tea and crunching biscuits. Sal glanced at his Rolex, three hours before the limo comes, plenty of time to visit the bar.

Sal strolled by the helmets and ballcaps. He stopped and stared at the new additions. Miami and Notre Dame next to each other? He would have to talk to someone about that. He took a familiar stool at the corner of the bar and ordered a Crown Royal XO. The bartender searched until he found a half-filled bottle in a back cabinet.

"Sorry, Doctor," he said as he poured. "You came on short notice this time. I'll have more by tomorrow."

Sal smiled and sipped.

Sal noticed a few new pictures, but everything else was the same. He thought about drinking there with Colin, just six months ago. He remembered their talk with Danny in Amsterdam about family and ex-wives, and about fate. Colin had been true to his word. Too bad—Sal could have helped. But Colin was proud. Today Sal would have to visit the club without him—or Ange for that matter. He patted the full flask in his breast pocket.

Sal looked at one of the new pictures—three drunken frogs. He thought of Stosh and Jimmy Eagleson, and a young Salvatore Esposito, sitting on Turtle Rock drinking beer and solving the world's problems.

"Doctor Esposito, your tuxedo is ready and has been placed in your closet," a porter said as Sal finished his drink.

"OK, here we go," he whispered.

***

"The service was largely a waste of time, Ange," Sal said into his cellphone and listened. "No, Este wasn't there, I'm surprised you'd ask after the way she dumped you at Covent Garden. She's in Paris with—well, you know, some guy. I spoke to the lord for a minute. I think he has developed some dementia. He was so sharp in October; it's amazing what six months can do. He kept saying 'Colin was barking mad, I conjure.' He must have repeated that twenty times. I stayed about an hour—talked to people I didn't know—as I said, it was a waste of time."

With his phone on speaker, Sal sipped his coffee and cut his bacon. Ange filled him in on things at the club. All quiet on the southern front.

"Good," Sal said and took the phone off speaker. "I'm flying back tomorrow. I'm going to wander around today, see if I can find someone ... No, no one you know ... Yeah, I should be back by mid-afternoon. Talk to you then."

Sal took his brooch from the mantel and slipped it in his pocket. "See you later," he said to Hanuman. "I'm going for a walk while I still have some daylight."

The hotel seemed busier than usual as he strolled through the lobby to the street. You'd never tell from the bar last night, he thought. He'd had the place to himself—not a bad deal.

He hiked to the tube stop, pushed through the turnstile. A short, elderly woman dressed in her Sunday best and using a cane carefully hobbled to the edge and stepped onto the descending escalator. Forgetfully, she stood to the left—the side reserved for hurried walkers. A young man in a black suit and overcoat darted from the newsstand through the gate and sprinted down the moving escalator grates. Forced to stop behind the old woman, he cursed, pushed her aside, and ran on. She struggled to regain her balance and stabilized just before the landing where she carefully stepped off. She stood out of the way straightening her hat and slowly walked on.

Sal's instincts told him to chase the asshole. But, impressed by the woman's composure, he walked behind to keep an eye on her. As they reached the train platform, the rude, hurried man paced and looked at his watch. Sal kept his cool and watched as the old woman approached him and demanded he stand still while she calmly gave him a scolding. The man shook his head and snickered as his leg shook from nervous energy. As the train doors opened, he jumped in and sat before others could depart. Waiting their turn, the old woman and Sal carefully boarded and stood. The hyperactive rattlebrain looked away, his leg still bouncing. Sal paused and then approached him.

"Would you mind moving?" Sal said. "You're in a seat reserved for the elderly, and this lady would like to sit."

The man ignored him. Sal tapped the man's shoulder. The man flinched as if punched and jumped up. He flashed his index and middle fingers in Sal's face and pushed his way through the crowd to the other end of the car. Sal helped the old woman sit. She nodded, thanked him and said he was a good boy. Sal smiled, he hadn't heard *that* in many years.

"Too bad that young man is in such a hurry," the old woman said. "He won't get there any sooner by behaving badly. You know, son, he will reap what he sows. He will be shoved aside himself someday."

Sal helped the old woman to the street. She smiled and looked up at him with bright blue eyes. "Thank you, son," she said, "I can make it from here. And, God bless you."

Sal nodded and watched her waddle off, one careful step at a time.

Sal strolled through the park, looking at familiar sights and thinking of Colin and Danny. He chuckled as he recalled Colin's run-in with the transvestite. He stopped chuckling when he remembered Colin's description of his ruinous marriage. Since their trip to Amsterdam, Colin was gone, Danny's head was bashed for good, and Sal—well he'd faced a tiger. Sal stepped into the bicycle lane, and a rider flew by him yelling obscenities. Sal moved aside and strolled on.

Sal saw a coffee shop on the corner and after two hours of walking the idea of a hot cup pulled him in like a magnet. He ordered an American-brew black and sat near the window. A man in formal business attire with an alligator briefcase sat near the wall tapping his foot and rolling his fingers as he stared into space and gulped his jumbo latte. Sal looked at his blank eyes and knew he was struggling with something—Sal had been there, many times.

A young woman carrying a heavy backpack trudged in. Sal watched her count change from her pocket and smile when she saw she had enough. She carried her gear and small cup to a table where she placed her pack out of the way and began to mix her coffee. She slowly poured in milk and carefully shook just the right amount of sugar. She stirred twice and raised the cup to her nose, closed her eyes and smiled as she drew the aroma into her nostrils. She sipped slowly and curiously glanced around the room before opening her lips for another taste. Sal thought of Munére, his Coca-Cola and "the little things."

The streetlights flashed on as Sal took his last sip—time for his other mission. He hoped it wouldn't be another waste of time. As soon as he raised his hand, a cab pulled in. "Prévoyance," he told the driver.

The streets bustled with the evening crowd heading for drinks and dinner. Prévoyance was packed. Sal worked his way to the bar and asked about the mysterious Jesse—the real reason Sal had come to London. The bartender shook his head and said he thought Jesse had returned to Paris, or wherever he was from.

Sal drank a quick beer and left. He walked a few blocks, watching people and looking at signs. In the distance, he noticed an Indian restaurant. Some good curry chicken and saffron rice, he thought. He strolled on and crossed the street, carefully dodging the evening traffic. He smelled the curry a block away.

As the greeter led him to a table, he glanced at the bar and froze. It can't be, he thought as he gazed at the familiar back side of an Indian woman with knee length black hair. He hesitated, then stepped over and tapped her shoulder. As she turned, he stepped back surprised.

"Doctor Esposito, what in the world are you doing here?"

"Radha, how are you?" Sal replied.

"I have just left a meeting and am very much in need of a glass of wine. But I needed to wait for the others to leave before I could sneak away to this bar. It is very important that these people see me as very conservative. I am very, very close to a very successful arrangement. And you, Doctor, why are *you* here?"

"Looking for a friend."

"Well, you have traveled a very long way to look for a friend."

"Yeah, I've been doing that lately. Radha, would you join me for dinner?"

"What about your friend?"

"I haven't found him. I'm sure he won't be coming."

"Well, most certainly I would love to join you, Doctor. And, I have some news that might interest you. This is quite a coincidence."

"Yeah, the coincidence faucet seems to be wide open these days."

"I do not understand."

"Neither do I."

They sat at a table near a window where they could watch the evening activity on the street. Radha insisted on ordering for them both as she knew the specialties of the place. They talked about the food in India. Radha assured Sal the food here would be almost as good.

"So, Radha, what news do you have?"

"Well, in one way it is tragic, and in another, it is karma at work. My uncle Amol is in a very bad way. He has had a most horrible accident and can no longer manage his business. While I take no pleasure in his condition, I have watched his ways for many years. He is neither a kind nor generous man. He has treated Sita as a servant and me as a minor employee. And now that he is incapacitated, he has no one in the Patil family to take over.

"What happened?"

"It was a most tragic error on R. G.'s part. He was filling Uncle Amol's car with gasoline. You know how very short my uncle is. He was—for some unknown reason—standing very, very close to the nozzle when ash from R. G.'s cigar ignited the fuel. My uncle was very badly burned. His face is most disfigured. Many Hindus believe such things come from very bad karma, and Uncle Amol is most ashamed. He refuses to go out into the public and will not meet with others outside of our family."

Sal exhaled and thought of the asshole smoker near Stosh's boat and Stosh's words of wisdom, "The fire always cooks an S-O-B like him, when it's time."

"When did this happen?" Sal asked.

"Only a few days after your meeting. He has contacted Sita. He begged her to reconsider the arrangement you presented and to assume his representation."

Sal looked down and shook his head.

"She told him she had decided he was right and she should go back to being a traditional Indian woman. Participating in a business like his should be the work of men. He knew her real meaning immediately. He then contacted me. I also rejected his offer."

Sal's smile grew to a grin. "Good for her—and you too."

"Yes, while we both regret his suffering, his situation has given us the opportunity to carefully assess our own lives. We are both doing well. We have formed our own import business specializing in fine carpets. This is something we both know well. My uncle was very secretive about his jewelry business. I learned very little from him, and I have come to see that one should not become involved in enterprises where one's expertise is lacking."

Sal broke into laughter and nodded vigorously.

"I see you agree, Doctor. So, we felt that accepting his offer would be a very, very bad idea. Besides, I cannot imagine the *real* condition of the Patil jewelry business since R. G. has been there. I have no confidence in its future."

"I'm proud of both of you."

"Thank you, Doctor. I will tell that to Sita."

Sal paused and looked out the window. "I wrote her," he said.

"Yes."

"OK, enough said."

"She told me. Sita is confused. She is not angry. As I have said, she has come to appreciate that she can do well on her own and is very much enjoying her independence."

The waiter brought the food, strategically arranged it, and poured Radha more wine.

"*Dhanyavād,*" Radha said and looked at Sal.

"Yes, I know; it means 'Thank you.'"

"Yes, Doctor. But let me continue. Both Sita and I are amazed at the conflux between you and our family—I am still amazed to be with you here, at this moment. And, there is a most important part of it that you should understand. My grandfather was a kind man and was very good to us. But he was not always that way. My mother told me that before he became blind, he was much like my uncle—perhaps worse. Sita and I were eleven when he died. We remember him saying, many times, that he had to lose his sight to find his heart. Your attack on him was the very, very brutal act of a boy. And I imagine, in your own way, you have suffered greatly for it—I see you as a very good man. You could not have known the true results of your action. Again, perhaps there is karma at work here too."

Sal's eyes welled as he looked at Radha. "Dhanyavād," he said.

Radha and Sal ate and talked for two hours before she asked the waiter to call for a cab.

"I am so sorry to have to leave, but I have a very early flight tomorrow. Doctor, thank you for dinner and for being so honest. It has brought us comfort to know what happened was an awful mistake and not the act of an evil person."

Sal saw Radha her cab. He stood a moment and then flagged one for himself. Gazing out the window, he breathed deeply through his nose and exhaled through his lips. He felt guilt respiring away.

Sal walked into the hotel's empty bar. He saw that the Notre Dame and Miami football helmets had been appropriately separated.

The bartender held Sal's bottle to the light. "Looks like one more glassful, Doctor. Sorry, they didn't deliver more this morning. Maybe we can find something else you'll like."

Sal nodded and sat on his favorite corner stool.

"If you could excuse me for a few minutes, Doctor, I have business in the office. I'll be back before you're ready for something different."

"Take your time."

Sal sat alone and sipped. He gazed at the drunken frogs and thought. As when he confessed to Kate and Boozer, his relief came with an uneasy lack of purpose, like after a fight. He wondered what to do next. He exhaled and pursed his lips. There was still Johnny. What to do with fucking Johnny?

"I had an older brother," Sal heard a deep voice declare from a back booth. "I thought the world of him—wanted to be just like him. Later, when I grew, I found he wasn't so hot—just another man who happened to be my brother."

A tall, thin man with an enormous head stood and stretched. "How are you, Salvatore? Do you mind if I join you?"

Sal nodded, and Jesse took the other corner stool.

"You sound very Midwestern, Jesse," Sal said.

"Yes, it's one of my favorite accents. So, you've taken a liking to curry?"

"Yeah, how did you know?"

"You smell of it."

Sal sniffed his sleeve and chuckled. "Yeah, I do."

"It's a good smell—you know I *did* have a brother," Jesse continued. "He got me into some trouble. It took me a while to get over it. But at least I learned something."

"What did you learn?

"That everyone lives with one delusion or another. As a kid, I wanted his. When I got older, I found plenty of my own and saw that his hadn't been all I thought. But, as I've told you, I'm full of shit."

Jesse took a swig from a Budweiser. "I like this beer," he said and smiled.

"You said he got you in trouble."

"Seemed like a big deal for a while. We do stupid things when we're kids—some more stupid than others. He's gone now. I can't blame him for anything anymore—that sort of pisses me off, you know? I miss that—blaming him."

Sal smiled and nodded. "Yeah."

"I guess a lot of us go through that shit. But, you know, one brother goes and another—of one kind or another—seems to show up. Say, how's that beautiful clear lake of yours? I hope the monster doesn't nibble your toes." Sal's eyes opened wide. "And you've seen some intriguing rivers lately." Jesse took his last swig. "Did you take my advice about the water?"

"Jesse, who the fuck are you?"

Jesse stood and straightened his back. "I told you, Jesse—the shit-filled loudmouth."

Jesse walked slowly and stopped under the hanging baseball caps. He looked up and grinned.

"Look, Salvatore, here's a Yankees hat. I always liked the Yanks, even though I root for the Cardinals.

"It's the top of the ninth, Salvatore. Remember what they say, 'Be ready for the curve ball when you're facing a lefty.' Goodbye, Salvatore."

Jesse strolled through the exit, raised his hand and yelled back, "BATTER UP!"

CHAPTER XVI

Casey

"They lost Johnny's ashes?" Kate said, "How?"

"I don't know. I called before I went to London and told the guy I'd pick them up when I got back. He said no problem; he'd call when they were ready. It's been three weeks, and I still hadn't heard. I called, but no one knew what was going on. So, I went up there this morning. Some dumbass said someone had claimed them two weeks ago. I asked who, he checked his papers and said it was Mr. Esposito's brother. I told him I'm Mr. Esposito's brother. He checked again and looked baffled. He called some other guy in— they talked—they looked like a pair of dumbfounded fuckups—they said they'd have to get back to me."

"Bureaucracy—even so, how do you lose someone's ashes?"

Sal's phone buzzed. "Yeah," he said. ... "Tonight, it has to be tonight? ... All right ... Yeah, I'll see you then."

Sal looked at Kate. "Fucking partners. We had a meeting set for tomorrow afternoon to settle the sale of the club. I was going to go to the house in the morning and grab the last things left there. Then I planned to meet with the boneheads, and after, explain the details to the staff—I want them filled in before any rumors fly. I thought I'd be back before dinner. Now one of them can't make it. His son has a T-ball game—a fucking T-ball game. He's called the others, and they want to meet at six o'clock. Tonight.

"Ah, fuck it." Sal punched a number in his cell. "Robert, listen, I want you to get the staff together first thing in the morning. The partners' meeting has been changed to tonight ... Yeah, I'll stay at the river house ... No, I won't need anything, but thanks for asking."

Sal popped open a Kingfisher. "No big deal." He sipped. "I can leave in a couple of hours and be there on time." He paused. "My last night at the river house."

***

Route 87 was free of traffic, but it would be an hour to Saratoga even at Sal's speed. He thought of Pop's precious riverfront house. He hoped never to stay there again. But he *was* getting rid of it—now that he knew how Pop paid for it. But he got through college with the same money. And Ma must have known; she knew everything that went on. Maybe big bad Johnny had a soft side.

He recalled what had Jesse said about missing the hate. He'd hit the nail on the head. The hate *was* slowly leaving, and, as with his missing guilt, Sal didn't know how to replace it. He thought of his talk with Radha. If she and Sita could so quickly forgive the man who blinded their grandfather, why was his contempt for Johnny still there at all? He'd spent hours talking to Kate about it. She'd said he needed to let it go. Maybe in just a little more time.

He was full of questions that Johnny could no longer answer. What had Johnny meant when he said he'd only scratched the surface?

Everything else was so calm. He'd felt more at ease than at any other time he could remember. Just the one lingering thing between Sal and his brother.

***

The meeting went as expected. Everyone seemed satisfied. One more pain-in-the-ass, out of the way. Sal pulled into the driveway, parked to the side, and hopped out of his Mercedes. He stood and looked at the moon shining on the Hudson. Someone will really enjoy this place, he thought. But the sooner I'm out, the better.

As he strolled toward the door, he heard a voice.

"You can stop right there, Sallie," a man said. Sal turned. Frankie Napoli stood with a gun several yards behind. A cylinder was attached to the gun's barrel. "I should have come myself the first time. You really buffaloed those dumb fucks."

Sal exhaled. "How so, Frankie?"

"One punch and you were on the floor whining, they told me. 'I'm Johnny Esposito's brother. He'll kill you—you fuck with me you fuck with him,' you squealed like a scared pig."

"I thought you were tough, Sallie. But you curled up like a baby and pissed your pants."

Frankie laughed. "Well, they didn't know Johnny was dead, and all bets were off." Frankie grinned and shook his head. "Yeah, I really thought you were tough. I shoulda known you were a pussy all along."

"Frankie, your wife was fucking someone else. What's your grind with me?"

"None, Sallie. But you fucked over some guys in Phoenix a few years back, and they're still pissed—you shoulda known they wouldn't forget. So, I got the call. It's what I do, Sallie. And tonight, I like my job."

Sal looked up the driveway and saw The Mouth from the club and another stooge standing near the road. No escape there. As he looked back, another man stepped next to Frankie.

"Remember these fucking things?" said Robert the bar manager, smirking and holding out the marbles from his gas tank. "I listened to these fucking things for months. You thought that was funny, didn't you? Now I'm going to stuff them down your throat. We'll see if they rattle in your corpse. By the way, I let Frankie's boys in the club. I *saw* you piss your pants. Oh, and Sal, somehow the video of that night just disappeared. I wanted to watch you snivel one more time and must have hit the wrong button. Oh well, what the fuck?"

Sal smirked and raised his hands. "OK, Frankie what's holding you up?" Sal pointed to his crotch, "You see piss, Frankie? Be careful with your new boy here; he's not only a bad thief, he's also a pathetic liar. I'm surprised you'd buy his bullshit. But you never were known for your brains."

"Fuck you, Esposito!" Frankie shouted. Robert grinned and rolled the marbles in his hand.

Frankie smirked, "So long, little Sallie. Say hi to big brother Johnny for me."

Sal positioned to rush him as Frankie raised the gun.

"That's enough Francis, point your pistol down," a voice ordered.

An old man with full head of bright white hair, wearing a Yankees jacket stepped from the dark. Frankie's eyes bulged, and he lowered the gun.

"What the fuck! What are *you* doing *here*?"

"Francis, you do remember the rules? There is a proclamation on the streets; you *know* the penalty."

Frankie quavered. "But Johnny is dead, sir." He tried to clear his throat.

"Francis, you are among the most challenged of those I have been associated with. But even you couldn't think *Johnny Esposito* had that kind of authority? Who did you think he was, the reincarnation of Charles Luciano?"

"But when the Phoenix guys called—"

"You accepted without permission."

"I've seen this old asshole at the club," Robert said stepping forward. "Who the fuck is he?"

"Shut up, Bobby Sox," Frankie barked.

Robert looked up the drive to see two men had replaced The Mouth and his associate.

"Bobby Sox?" the old man said. "That is one of the most ridiculous names—Francis, please explain."

"He's Robert," Frankie stuttered, "and he loves the Red Sox. So, one of his old girlfriends called him Bobby Sox."

The old man glared. "Loves the Red Sox?" Frankie nodded. "Bobby Sox, I don't like you. But this is your lucky night. Frankie, you like Vegas? Good. You won't be needed in New York. And your young friend will be joining you."

The old man looked at Robert. "You'll be packed and out of the East Coast in forty-eight hours."

"Fuck that," Robert said. "I like it here."

"You're going to Vegas," Frankie said. "It's a good deal."

Robert grimaced. "Shit," he said as his eyes widened and he stood straight. He looked at Frankie. "Is he …?" Frankie nodded.

"I'm sorry, sir," Robert said to the old man. "Vegas will be fine—thank you."

"And, Bobby Sox—that really is a ridiculous name—there is one condition. You are holding three marbles. Place them back in your gas tank. Doctor Esposito was correct. You are one who needs reminding."

Robert stone-eyed the old man.

"Do not push your luck," the old man said quietly, staring into Robert's eyes. Robert's expression disappeared.

"After all, the Red Sox needs all the fans it has," the old man said, winking at Frankie.

"Francis," the old man said holding out his hand, "before you go, very carefully place the butt end of your pistol in my hand."

Frankie handed over the gun, looked at Robert, and pointed to the end of the driveway. They trudged past Sal into the dark.

The old man looked at Sal and exhaled. "I'm not involved in this kind of activity often and must admit I resent having to be tonight. But, I'm told it is very difficult to secure competent associates these days, and Francis is clearly among those most problematic. He's something of a dinosaur. Things are not done now as in the past, and he has never really adapted. But, he has influential relatives."

The old man looked at the pistol and sighed. "You were not in as much danger as you may have thought. Francis is best known for his skills in physical injury. He is *not* a marksman. Under the best conditions, he would have difficulty hitting an elephant from the distance he was standing. With one of these sound attachments added to his pistol, the moon was in as much peril as you."

The old man smiled. "Salvatore, perhaps a chat would be appropriate."

Sal had stood rigid as a statue since the old man appeared. "Yeah, that would be good," he said.

"Salvatore, may I ask you a question?" Sal nodded. "Would you have any chilled Budweiser?" Sal shook no. "Michael," the old man yelled up the drive, "would you please bring some cold Budweiser—oh and the other thing too."

The associate left and quickly returned with the old man's request. Sal led the old man into the house.

The old man placed a six-pack and a paper bag on the bar. "May I sit?" he asked.

Sal pointed to a stool and brought him a bottle opener and glass.

The old man popped off the bottle cap and sniffed the

escaping vapor. Then he slowly poured half into the glass, creating a one-inch head. He took a small sip and smiled.

"I like this beer," he said. "I've been drinking it for over sixty years and never had the urge to try anything else. To me, it always tastes just right."

Sal poured a drink and sat across from the old man.

"Sir—"

The old man raised his hand, "I don't mean to be rude, but it's a long story." He looked at the six-inch statue still guarding the bar from Sal's last visit. "Hanuman, one of my favorites. Ma used to read the *Ramayana* to John and me when we were young. You know, Salvatore, Hanuman reminds me of you."

Sal turned rigid and glared into the old man's eyes.

"I'm not your brother, Salvatore."

"Then, what are you saying?"

"I'm your brother's brother." The old man smiled at Sal's confusion. "John was my younger half-brother. A year after my mother passed, my father married a beautiful young singer he'd fallen for, Ma. She became my stepmother. I was only four, so, you see, she was the only mother I ever knew. John was born when I was twelve. My father was killed a few years after. Then Ma married your pop. By the time you were born, I was out on my own, learning my trade—you might say. I never left New York.

"Your folks felt it was best that you didn't know about me, probably because John had made me his hero and insisted on trying to follow in my footsteps. He was eleven or twelve when they moved to Plattsburgh, and his die was already cast. They didn't want a second son aspiring to my profession. Neither did I. Your pop formally adopted John so our names would be different. It didn't have much effect."

"What *is* your name?"

"Well, Ma calls me Casey—she thinks I'm the mighty Casey from the old poem—I kind of like that. Why don't you call me that too?"

Casey stared into Sal's eyes. "You and I met only once. That night John introduced me as Buzzy Kline."

Sal sat back, still stiff.

"Yes, that was a difficult event."

Casey took a sip and smiled again. "You know, we came up with that name while we were driving to pick you up. Remember Kline's barbershop, the guy who lost a son in Vietnam?"

Still stone-faced, Sal nodded.

"Remember his sign 'Free buzz cuts for all servicemen in uniform'? Well, we saw that and came up with Buzzy Kline—strange how names come about."

Sal remained expressionless. Casey took a deep breath.

"I didn't know *you* were the young man we were picking up. John just said he'd found someone the right size. In fact, I didn't know who you were until we were back from Montreal. I was furious with John. He said not to worry, you were only twelve; if you got caught, you were just a juvenile, and the Canadians were notoriously lenient on juveniles. But … he also said his little brother is far too smart to ever get caught. You'd find your way back. And he was right."

"You both said there wouldn't be anyone there," Sal

snapped. "But there *was*. The old Hindi was there, and I almost *killed* him!"

The old man exhaled and nodded. "You have a right to be angry. And I can see John has never explained any of what actually happened. He should have told you everything years ago. Your brother was a hard person to understand. He was prouder of you than you'll ever know. But when he saw you, when he was in your presence, he just wanted to hurt you. Salvatore, the whole thing was an inside job. The old man's son, Amol Patil, set it all up."

Sal's eyes widened.

"He'd already moved most of the gold from the store. All we were supposed to do was make it look like a robbery, not that hard in those days. But he double-crossed us. John told him you would be carrying a club and told to use it, so Patil *knew* he *had* to make sure the place was empty. But *instead*, he made sure the old man was working that night. Salvatore, he wanted you to kill his father."

Sal sat dazed. He thought of Amol Patil with his bad comb-over. Then he imagined his newly burned face.

"It almost worked. But the old man lived, and there wasn't enough evidence of a robbery. When the police searched the son's house, they found the gold and filed charges for insurance fraud. The easiest thing for the authorities was to deport him."

"Deport?"

"He was thrown out of Canada. A major disgrace in his culture."

Sal shook his head and smirked. "Why would he want his father dead?"

"Who knows? Probably to get the entire business. A man like that will go to any means for what he is after. Not like us. I'm one hundred percent Sicilian. To us family is sacred. And you are seventy-five percent, you know well what I mean."

Sal eyes narrowed. "Seventy-five percent?"

Casey shook his head. "Shame on John—there is so much you should have been told."

Casey poured another half glass. "Your grandmother, on Ma's side, was not Italian."

"What?"

Casey paused. Then he reached for the paper bag on the bar and pulled out a package of Gold Fish cheese snacks. He opened the bag, smelled the contents, and took a few. "Gold Fish, Salvatore?"

Sal nodded, and Casey shook some into Sal's palm.

"I like these," Casey said. "There's just enough cheese, and they have a good crunch. They make them with extra flavor now, but those are too much for me. A little overwhelming, you know? These are just right. I don't know why they have to fool around with something they already have right, you know?"

One by one Casey savored three of the tiny crackers and sipped his Budweiser and smiled.

"Your grandfather," he continued, "was quite the character. He sailed in the merchant marine. Just before the first war, he was working on a German boat. When the war started, they were in port and your grandfather—a very smart man I should add—jumped ship. He was the only Italian on board and wanted nothing to do with a German boat heading for the Fatherland. He was resourceful—you know, one of those men who was going to make it regardless of what was thrown at him. He met your grandmother on the streets—horrific slums, far worse than we see here. She was much younger, maybe fourteen—that was old enough in those days. They were a good team. Made enough to get out and start a business."

"Where was he?"

"When?"

"When he jumped ship, where was he?"

"Bombay."

Sal dropped his hands to his knees. "This is one fucking night for surprises," he whispered. "So, she was—"

"East Indian."

Casey snacked on more Gold Fish while Sal sat silent.

"She was a stunning woman—jet black hair and beautiful smooth skin," Casey said. "You know, some Eastern women look much like Sicilians. You never knew her, but she lived with us in New York until she passed. She was a hoot, and ageless. She looked young until the day she died. She and your grandfather encouraged Ma's singing. After what they'd been through, nightclub performing probably sounded like a dream job. He died when I was young. As I said, he was much older."

"What had they been through?"

"They went to Italy for a while. But she was never accepted there, so they came here. Your grandfather played some violin and—what is the name of that little accordion?—the concertina. He opened a small music store and did some other things on the side. She cooked for a while but became a house mother when Ma was born. Ma was their only child, and they wanted to spoil her."

"What did they do in Bombay?"

Casey shrugged. "I'm not sure, whatever they had to, I guess."

"What did she do before she met him?"

Casey snickered. "Whatever she had to, I guess."

"Do you think she had to—?"

"I never asked," Casey said. Sal looked down and nodded. "The days of doing what one wants—choosing one's own way—they are relatively new, Salvatore. You and I—and even John—had many options. And you chose well. You know, we were all proud of you. And we've helped when needed."

Sal looked up. "You, too?"

Casey nodded. "Your deals were almost always straight, but you wandered into some dangerous territory a couple of times. Like a few years ago, in Phoenix—although that wasn't completely your fault. But that's all done now—oh, just a second. Let me write something down. I'm getting to that age where I need notes."

Casey took a pen and notebook from his pocket and began to write. "Let's see, Phoenix and Costello," he mumbled.

"Costello?"

"Yes, your friend Angelo won't have any more trouble as long as he keeps his nose clean. You know, you really should speak to him about his choices in bedmates."

Sal grinned and nodded.

"I'll call Dominic and have him make the orders very clear. Francis isn't the only incompetent we have to put up with."

"Dominic?"

"Yes, now there's a perfect example of what we were talking

about. One little habit and Dominic Scardaccione becomes forever known as Pencil Nick. And Ma, your grandmother named *her* Maafi."

"Maafi? That wasn't her name."

"You knew her by her second name, but you—and almost everyone else—always called her Ma. Most people thought it was short for mother—an understandable mistake; it's a quite common contraction. She wouldn't have told you. She was secretive about her origins once she moved to Plattsburgh—most people thought she was Sicilian and she preferred that—East Indians were often looked down on. At least Sicilians were feared."

Salvatore exhaled, "Maafi."

"Yes, I was told it's either Marathi language or Hindi or a combination of the two. They're the most common languages in Bombay. Roughly, it means forgiveness. Not all that different from your name, Salvatore." Casey paused to crunch another goldfish. "You see, when Ma was born, your grandmother saw it as proof she'd been forgiven."

"What did she need to be forgiven for?"

"I never asked."

Casey savored another sip.

"You would have liked your grandmother, Salvatore. She taught us all many words in Marathi and Hindi, mostly bad insults—I recall them coming in handy from time to time. Now I'm rambling."

"So that's it," Sal said.

"That's what?"

"Lately, when I call her Ma, she insists I don't know what it means."

"Maybe not technically, but your understanding was genuine. You always took good care of your ma, and your pop."

Sal pondered and sipped his drink. "Back to Pencil Nick?"

"Yes, he said he ran into you in Tampa. He's been ill. Diabetes—he's gained a lot of weight. Dominic is not just involved in gaming, you know—although I won't go into details. I've asked him to look in on you from time to time."

"In Phoenix?"

Casey smiled and sat silent.

"Tampa?"

"Now that was pure coincidence—he was vacationing. Interesting, that occurrence—I don't usually believe in coincidence."

Sal chuckled. Casey sipped his beer and watched the bubbles.

"I think, Salvatore, there is often something unseen that's working in the background. I was bailed out when I was young. I still don't know why or by whom, but it seems the natural order. Most of us have unknowingly had our backs covered on some occasions."

"Johnny?"

"At first. But some people are beyond help. The last time I worked with him was that night in Montreal. He'd become careless and vicious—almost perverted. He was moving drugs and acting like a bigshot. Did you know when he killed that man—the one he felt the need to castrate—he got the wrong person? He didn't care. I kept an eye on him but had little contact after that. It is a good thing he ended up in prison. Violence for its own sake is wrong. Evil.

"That reminds me." Casey reached for the paper bag. He looked inside and lifted out a plastic package. "Here, this is your half."

Sal examined the bag and nodded. "Thank you," he said.

"I thought each half-brother should have half the remains and half the responsibility. I have already taken care of mine. Do what you will with yours."

"May I ask you a personal question?"

"One can always ask."

"You speak very well."

"Thank you, I try. Ma always stressed education. John never listened. But you and I benefited from her advice. I never accomplished what you have, but at one time I thought of changing careers and teaching English. I attended NYU part time—earned a bachelor's degree and part of master's. But, as much as I enjoyed school, I found my profession hard to leave.

"I've never regretted the education, though. I find it most useful—when people actually listen. And you, Doctor—MD, JD— you never used your degrees either—at least not directly. We do have a few things in common."

Sal and Casey continued talking. Casey told stories about Ma and their grandmother, and Sal filled Casey in on a few of his escapades.

After his third beer, Casey looked at his watch. "Well," he said, "this has been most enjoyable, Salvatore. Three beers are my limit. I'm afraid I must leave."

"Will I see you again?"

Casey smiled and shook his head. "Probably not. And, Salvatore, for the record, you didn't see me tonight." Casey stared into Sal's eyes, and Sal nodded. "I don't think you will need me again."

"One more personal question?"

"Certainly."

"What's your real name?"

Casey smiled. "A good attorney never asks a question he doesn't already know the answer to."

Sal smiled and nodded. Casey brushed Gold Fish crumbs into his hand, dumped them into the paper bag. Then he rearranged the three bottles left in his six-pack to better distribute their weight.

"Thank you," Sal said and extended his hand.

Casey took Sal's hand and pulled him into a hug. "Goodbye, Salvatore," he whispered before grabbing his beer, walking out, and quietly closing the door behind him.

Sal stood in his living room looking out onto the Hudson. His mind spun—so many new actors. Casey the lost stepbrother, his grandmother on the streets of Bombay, Sita the untouchable baby, Colin the stoic, Danny the loyal friend, Jesse the snake man, Radha, Munére, Duke, Seamus—the whole cast danced in his head.

And Jimmy Eagleson, where was Jimmy Eagleson, the only one Sal could ever fully confide in? What Sal would give for one more night at the fort with Jimmy. They'd light a fire, cook some hot dogs, and drink a few beers. Together they could sort all of this out.

Sal looked at the package on the bar. Oh yeah, and then there's Johnny. He picked it up and stared at the ashes and pieces of bone through the clear plastic. How could this small pile of soot cause so much pain? He thought of his talks with Jesse and Kate. He turned the bag and examined what was left of Johnny from the other side. "So, this is what's left of big, bad Johnny Esposito," he said and exhaled. "Not worth hating a bag of ashes."

He carried Johnny's remains to a chair and sat. Was it all that bad? He remembered a time when he was seven. Johnny bought him a toy gun for his birthday, one Ma and Pop wouldn't get for him. And Johnny snuck him other things. It was Johnny who always gave him the forbidden candy and soda. Ma would have exploded if she'd found out.

Sal chuckled. Even then, the only real bond he had with his Johnny came from breaking the rules. And what to do with Johnny now?

Sal looked at the river and smiled. Any attorney knew what he was thinking was illegal in New York. But, what the fuck, this was Johnny and *everything* Johnny did was illegal. And this was the house *Johnny* built on the spot *Johnny* found for Ma and Pop. Any good Johnny had ever done revolved around this place.

Sal strutted to the side door with Johnny in his hand. The moon cast a trail of light on the Hudson's rapids. In a few hours, the sun would rise. But now, when it was still dark, was the time for a spirit like Johnny Esposito's.

Sal looked about and sneaked to the riverbank. He hopped out onto a rock surrounded by flowing water. He pulled a pen-knife from his pocket, squatted, and carefully slit the plastic. Bit by bit, he sprinkled Johnny onto the water and watched the river take him. Sal smiled at the thought of Johnny finally set free in a place where he could do no harm. He slowly turned the plastic inside out and submerged it to let the Hudson wash away all remaining specks. He paused to say his last goodbye. He wondered what judgment waited for Johnny Esposito around the river's bend. He hopped back to the shore. Looking at the empty bag, he suddenly felt lonely.

As Sal walked back to the house, he thought of his pop and Johnny and the days in Plattsburgh—before Montreal. He pulled the brooch from his pocket and Rubbed it with his thumb. He smiled and reverently laid the plastic bag in a trash can. He turned toward the Hudson, closed his eyes, thought of Ma, and listened to her sing "Moon River." Tomorrow, he'd visit Maafi Esposito.

***

"Sal, I wish you'd let me pay more for this place," Ange said. "I know I'd be able to afford it. Business is good."

"The price is fair, Ange, and I want away from the club business as fast as possible."

"I'll look for a new bar manager right away. Strange how Robert just quit. I thought he was doing well. You're sure he isn't coming back?"

"Yeah, I'm sure."

"Say, I might have a buyer for your house." Sal's eyebrows

rose. "Yeah, a young doctor and her husband. They drove by the property yesterday and loved it from the outside."

"Fantastic, but tell them to contact the agent. It's his job to show them around. Once was enough for me."

"When it's gone, how often will you come to Saratoga?"

"It's only a ninety-minute drive, Ange, and we still have other business to manage. You'll be seeing plenty of me. And day trips are easier if Boozer wants to ride along."

"You know, Sal, I think the shit with Frankie might be over. Since the night with Danny and the boys, things around here have been real quiet."

Sal grinned. "Yeah, Ange, I think you're right."

"You going to Camp this afternoon?"

"After I visit Ma."

"How is she?"

"I'll find out."

***

The attendant saw the doors open. She quickly finished on the phone and straightened her back.

"Good afternoon, Dr. Esposito," she said. Sal nodded as he strolled by and through the open door to Ma's room.

"Hello, Ma," Sal said.

"Who are you?" she replied. "And don't call me that; you don't even know what it means."

Sal smiled.

"Are you here for the wedding?" Ma asked.

Sal shook his head.

"Well, if you're delivering something you can leave it at the front desk. It's a good thing you're not late; the ceremony is this evening. I'm wearing white. I've never been married before. Neither has my fiancé. We're looking forward to having children. I've always wanted a family. Why are you still here? I told you to leave whatever you have at the front desk."

Sal wiped the corner of his eye. He knew it would happen eventually but didn't expect it to be today. Ma was gone. He looked at the dresser. No stereo. He exhaled and pulled together.

Sal felt a hand on his shoulder and turned to see the head nurse.

"Can we talk in the hall?" she said. Sal followed her out of the room. "It's always hard when after so long of just a little bit; there's nothing. She stopped singing two weeks ago. She has a beau down the hall—Johnny Mercer's old room. That's all she thinks about now. Doctor, you know how horribly Alzheimer's ends. But for now, she wakes up each morning thinking it's her wedding day. In her world, it's a wonderful time of life."

Sal looked at Ma as she watched a kingfisher in a tree outside the window. He stepped back in the room. He knelt next to his mother on one knee and touched her hand. "Dhanyavād, Maafi," he said gently.

Eyes sparkling, Ma turned. She gazed at her son, smiled and whispered. An empty face reappeared. She turned back to the window.

"What in the world did you say?" the nurse asked.

Sal sighed. "It means: thank you, forgiveness."

"Can you tell me what *she* said?"

Sal paused, smiling. Then he nodded. "She said, 'You're a good boy,... Salvatore.'"

CHAPTER XVII

Namaste

Ray and Sal sat on the porch watching Boozer play with Kate on the beach.

"You know, I never thanked you for rebuilding the docks and getting them in the water," Sal said.

"Yeah, you did, twice already. I'm sorry I couldn't get to them sooner. I'll put Jimmy's old Lyman in soon. I've got a few repairs to do to the hoist first. But I've refurbished the entire boat. I've got to tell you, Sal, her new finish makes the old girl just shine. Jimmy would be pleased. Hey, you know, there's a classic boat show in Vermont we should enter. We'll be crossing to Malletts Bay in style."

"On the way, maybe you can show me where you spread Jimmy's ashes."

"It's funny, Sal. With the Lincoln in the garage and the Lyman in the water, it will almost be like Jimmy's back."

Sal exhaled. "Yeah … almost."

"Summer solstice, today—longest day of the year," Ray said. "It's a holiday in many places. Lots of celebrations and festivals all over the world. I always wondered why it's not celebrated here. Maybe it's too close to the Fourth of July."

"That reminds me," Sal said. "Stosh is coming for the Fourth. He'll be here for a couple of weeks. Why don't you come down and stay? He'll want to spend time with you."

"Sure, if you don't mind. I'd love to stay with you guys for a few days. When does Kate leave?"

Sal looked at his Rolex. "In about an hour. She's really into her yoga shit. These workshops have become a regular thing. She gets away for a while and always brings home some new contortion." Sal chuckled. "I tried a couple of them myself—almost stuck like a pretzel once. This retreat's the longest she's ever done. She'll be back just before Deb and Stosh come. It will be just Boozer and me for a while."

"Sounds like a good time. OK, I need to get going. I've got a lot of shit to do at my place. With this fantastic weather, I've been able to work outside a lot." Ray smiled. "The lean-tos on the Adirondack trails are full. It's been a great spring for camping. And this should be a perfect night—clear skies, almost zero chance of rain, and black flies aren't as bad this year."

"I hate those little bastards," Sal said.

"OK, Sal, I'm off."

"See you next week, Ray."

***

Sal hoisted Kate's suitcase into the back of her microbus. "Jesus, she has a lot of shit for a 'Buddhist,'" he mumbled. Sal walked to the driver's window. Kate adjusted her rearview mirror and fastened her seatbelt.

"Everything here will be fine," Sal said.

"Remember, don't let Boozer drink more than a splash or two," Kate said. Sal nodded and Boozer woofed.

Sal and Boozer watched Kate drive off. Sal looked at the north woods. "Come on, Buddy, let's go for a walk."

As soon as they reached the trail, Boozer darted after a squirrel. Sal breathed in the warm summer air and pushed from his face branches loaded with new maple and oak leaves. At the clearing, he sat on his rock and waited for Boozer.

Sal thought of Jimmy Eagleson. Funny how Ray brought him up. Jimmy had been on Sal's mind a lot lately. Life had somehow become uncomplicated. With nothing grinding in the back of their heads, it would be the perfect time for Sal and Jimmy to sit and talk.

Boozer bounded out of the trees, twirled twice, and licked Sal's hand. Sal looked at Lake Champlain. Jimmy must have liked this spot. Their fort had been a great place too. He remembered the day Jimmy found the stick. They must have picked off a thousand bad guys from behind the old stone hedgerow that day. What would they be doing now—if Jimmy had lived? One thing for sure, *tonight* they would be sleeping at the fort. He remembered how it looked before the trees were cleared and the pole barn was stuck there. He'd never gone back. He wondered if there was anything left there from the old days.

"Shit," he said. "Come on, Buddy, let's go for a ride. There's a place I want you to see."

Boozer hopped in the back of Sal's Mercedes. They sped up the drive to the road, barely looking both ways. He passed a half-dozen new houses and a small strip mall. How did all this shit wind up *here*, he thought.

Sal bore right. Just before a fork in the road, he drove a few yards and pulled off. There it was, less than a mile from Camp, the ugly fucking baby-blue pole barn where their fort used to be. A pickup was parked near the pole barn's open door.

Sal hopped out of the Mercedes and opened its back door. "Come on, Buddy," he said. They strolled to the door.

"Hello!" Sal yelled.

"Yeah, whatcha want?" A man hollered back. In his seventies, he wore bib overalls.

"Mind if we look around inside? I used to camp out here when I was a kid."

"Well, I don't suppose it would hurt. Just don't touch nothin'."

Sal walked around the dirt floor trying to imagine the place before the trees were cut and the knoll bulldozed flat. "Look at all the shit this guy's packed in here," he mumbled as he surveyed decades of accumulated junk. He started to chuckle.

"What's so funny?" the old man asked as he walked over.

"Nothing really, I just haven't been here in years. I thought I might recognize something, but it was a long time ago."

"Well, I built this barn near forty years back. Use it for storage mostly. Don't know what you'd find after all them years."

"Yeah, I guess—OK Buddy let's go!" Sal yelled to Boozer. Boozer sat still at the far end of the barn staring. "Come on, Buddy!" Sal repeated. Boozer sat firmly.

The old man chuckled. "Yer dog's sorta stubborn."

"Come on, Boozer, there's nothing here!" Boozer barked twice.

"Prob'ly sees a squirrel or such,"

Boozer looked at Sal and began to bark repeatedly. He got up, circled several times, sat back in his place, and again stared.

"I'll get him," Sal said. "I've never seen him act like this."

Sal walked over. "Come on, Bud." Boozer just sat. Sal glanced where Boozer was staring. Nothing but a worn canvas tarp covering a rusted old tractor in the corner. Sal's eyes followed as squirrel bolted across the dirt from behind the tractor and scurried out through a hole in the barn's wall.

"It's just a squirrel, Buddy. Now let's go."

Boozer barked twice, looked at Sal, and snapped his head back to the corner.

Sal looked back in front of Boozer and then stood stiff, dazed.

"Holy shit," Sal whispered. "That ours. That's *our* fucking tarp."

"What is it?" the old man yelled."

"Just a squirrel, like you thought," Sal said. He wiped his eyes. "Listen, how much for this old tarp?"

"Why would ya want that damned thing? I found that on the

ground when I bought this lot. Frickin' thing's shot. Been cut in a couple places and got some holes in it. Prob'ly mice and such in there too."

"I'll give you a hundred dollars."

The old man looked stunned. He turned to look at Sal's car. "That your Mercedes?"

"Yeah."

"Say, this ain't one of them things were ya go out and find things that don't look like they're worth nothin', but they are, is it? I seen them shows on T. V. Let me think a minute—well, I'd have ta buy a new one, can't leave a machine like that uncovered or nothin', and that one *is* canvas. Hard ta find real canvas anymore."

"Two hundred, cash right now."

"I don't know, might be worth more."

"All right, five hundred. The things not worth a cent to anyone but me. Grab it while you can."

The old man pondered. "OK, if ya throw in one a them new plastic ones, but you'll have ta climb back there ta get it—and put the new one on too."

"Deal," Sal said and quickly peeled five one-hundred dollar bills from his money clip. "I'll take this one now and be back with your new one this afternoon."

"Well, I s'pose that'd be OK. How you gonna get it out a here? You ain't gonna strap it to the top a that Mercedes are ya? It'll scratch the b'jesus outta the paint." Sal nodded. "Shit, I knew it was worth more."

"What color do you want?"

"What?"

"What color tarp do you want?"

"Well ... I'm partial to blue, yeah blue."

Sal grinned. Five hundred dollars and one blue plastic tarp—a year's pay and basic shelter in India. But today, to Salvatore Esposito, worth the world. He smiled like a kid on Christmas morning as he loaded Boozer's find onto the top of his car and strapped it down.

"Thanks, Buddy," Sal said to Boozer. "You don't know what this means to me."

Boozer woofed.

Sal and Boozer raced back to Camp and unloaded the tarp. Sal laid it out in the driveway and inspected the damage from the last forty years. Sal counted the holes and made a list. He tied a line between two trees and hung the lost treasure to air out in the breeze.

"OK, Buddy, I think we have a handle on this. Let's go."

They sped off to a hardware store. Sal parked at the side.

"Hey, I'm sorry, but you'll have to leave your dog in the car!" a cashier yelled.

"Service dog!" Sal yelled back.

"Yeah, sure—OK," the cashier snickered.

Sal pushed a cart up and down the aisle loading it with repair fabric, rope, two sleeping bags, a lantern and other assorted camping gear.

"Where are the tarps?" he yelled out.

The cashier pointed to the back. Sal and Boozer strolled to a rack filled with plastic tarps of all sizes and colors. They took their place waiting behind a woman holding a baby and an old fellow on a motorized cart. In front of the line stood a man grumbling to himself in French as he sorted through the tarps, occasionally stopping to read a label and then standing back, brooding. Sal, the old fellow, and the mom waited patiently for ten minutes. Then the baby began to cry.

"Excuse me, ma'am," Sal said and approached the Frenchman. "Sir, could you please step aside a moment and let these people get what they need. You've been looking at these for a long time, and this lady has a baby."

"Wait your turn," the Frenchman barked back.

Sal smiled and placed his hand on the Frenchman's shoulder, "Sir, please step aside," he gently ordered.

The Frenchman jerked. His eyes flared. He looked about for help but saw none, so he grudgingly moved out of the way. Sal helped the fellow in the motorized cart and the woman with the baby before turning back to the Frenchman and pointing to the rack. "Your turn, again."

"You think because you are so big you can boss me around," the Frenchman whined.

"No sir, we all waited patiently. You were *very* inconsiderate. It was time for you to get out of the way."

The Frenchman turned and paraded off waving his arms and mumbling obscenities. Sal smiled and added a large blue tarp to his cart.

After a quick visit to the pole barn, Sal's stomach began to rumble. He looked at the dashboard clock.

"Shit, it's almost six," he said to Boozer. "Let's grab a couple of hotdogs. We still have time to put this all together for tonight." Boozer woofed.

Sal ordered two Michigan hot dogs with onions. "You want

onion too? Kate says they give you awful gas." Boozer woofed. Sal ordered two more Michigans with onions and two sides of onion rings.

"Shit, we might as well really do it up with the onions, Buddy. We're celebrating the solstice."

Sal cut Boozer's hot dogs, placed the pieces and some onion rings on waxed paper, and laid Boozer's dinner on the back seat. Boozer slowly savored each bite. He continued munching for minutes after Sal was through.

"You are one polite eater," Sal mumbled as he watched Boozer finish up.

Sal raced down the drive and parked next to the tarp. He watched it sway on the line. The smell of musty canvas filled his nose. For an hour, he ironed patches and reinforced the cuts and holes he and Jimmy had made to fit the tent posts through, years ago. He looked in the garage and found four twelve-foot oak rods left from the rolled carpets Sita sent. "I knew I'd have a use for these," he said to Boozer.

Sal carried the tarp, rods, and rope into the woods to the fort's new home. He slipped the rods through the old holes, rested the wood frame on tree bows and tied them in place.

"These four trees are perfect for this. They're spaced apart at just the right length—shit the bows are even the right height." In no time, the new fort was ready.

Cut canvas flaps hung in the front for doors, and the oak rod frame supported a pitched roof. Three walls extending snugly to the ground on the back and sides. Sal secured the walls' bottoms with stones while Boozer twirled around inside clearing the floor of imaginary snakes. Finished, they stood back and inspected. Sal smiled and nodded. Boozer woofed.

As the sun began to set, Boozer ran to Kate's porch and grabbed his stick. Sal arranged a stone circle and found wood for a campfire. After two trips to Camp for their gear, Nutter Butters, and beer, Sal reached for a pack of matches and squatted to light the fire. Boozer began to bark.

"What's the matter?" Sal said.

Boozer picked up his stick and dropped it.

"There's not enough room to play here, Buddy. Let's wait until morning, and I'll throw it from the shore."

Boozer barked twice, picked his stick up again and dropped it.

"I don't get it, Buddy."

Boozer picked up his stick, took it into the fort, dropped it on his sleeping bag, moved to Sal's bed and pawed it.

Sal thought a moment and laughed. "Oh, I need a stick too. Well, I just happen to have one."

Boozer woofed.

Sal and Boozer jogged back to Camp and Jimmy's study. Looking at the prized stick resting on its wall mount, Sal said, "I don't think it has been out of this room since Jimmy was alive."

Sal held the stick by the barrel. He no longer felt a need to aim at Johnny, or anyone else.

"You're right, Buddy. This is the finishing touch."

After half a bag of Nutter Butters and some beers, the busy day caught up with the campers, and they began to yawn. Sal stirred the fire and thought of the tiger reserve as they watched it reduce to a low flame. Sal and Boozer climbed into the fort and plopped down on their new sleeping bags. Their sticks lay between the beds. They quickly dozed off.

Sal slept soundly before the dream came.

Sal felt warm. He stood alone on the west bank of the Ganges. He watched an empty boat rock against a dock and heard a pack of feral dogs far in the distance. He looked up as the sun began to rise and saw Hanuman standing on the east shore. Hanuman's club rested on his right shoulder. He held a range of mountains high over his left. Hanuman grew into a monstrous giant. He lowered his left arm and gently spread the mountains over the flat east shore scattering a few pieces into islands.

The Ganges swirled and transformed into Lake Champlain. In the center, a snake-like creature raised his oversized head high out of the water. The creature turned to look into Sal's eyes. It smiled, exposing a large rack of teeth. It laughed in a low bellowing voice before diving out of sight and creating a wake that rippled to the beach and tickled Sal's toes.

Hanuman threw his club into the air. It exploded into a billion bits of lit phosphorus and fell over Champlain in glowing saffron flakes like perfectly detailed fireworks. Covered with radiant speckles, the lake glimmered. Hanuman waved goodbye and marched out of sight.

Sal now sat in bright moonlight on Turtle Rock next to Jimmy Eagleson. Jimmy smiled and nodded. Sal reached for him, but he disappeared into a foul-smelling haze.

Hovering among states of consciousness, Sal started to wake. "Jesus, Eagleson," he grumbled, "You did it again. You cut those wicked farts every time you eat those fucking onions. You're driving me out of the fucking fort, *again*!"

Sal reached for the front flap, threw it over the fort's top, and waved his arms to fan out the stench. He turned, started to grouse again, and saw Boozer holding his head up staring back.

Sal rubbed his face to clear his head, and a strong, warm rain burst from the sky. He looked back at Boozer. Boozer gazed into Sal's eyes and smiled, then flopped his head back down, took a deep breath, exhaled a long sigh, and went back to sleep.

Sal wiped the corner of his eye and grinned as he turned to watch the rain showering Lake Champlain. "OK," he whispered. "I get it."

***

"This is excellent," Ray said.

Sal nodded and took another sip from his mug.

"It was hard to find. Kingfisher isn't exactly a household name. But with these new, smaller kegs a lot more brands are available. You know they're brewing this in Saratoga?"

Sal grinned and chuckled.

"You know, Sal, I've been mulling over your story. The whole thing in Montreal must have been devastating. Shit, you were only twelve. I remember how I felt after Jimmy died. I thought *that* was my fault. I can't imagine the guilt *you* carried around. You going to tell Stosh?"

"Yeah," Sal nodded. "Then my confessions are over. Ray, each time I tell the tale, it seems less important. Confessing to Kate and Boozer was one of the hardest things I've ever done. Now, after telling Sita and you, I wonder if it's even worth talking about."

"Funny how guilt can own us," Ray said. "And I know *well* what you mean about looking back and scratching our heads wondering what the big fucking deal was anyway. I miss Jimmy terribly. We all do. But what happened, happened. I couldn't have stopped it." Ray paused. "As Jimmy always said, it is what it is." Ray took a sip. "You said you had nightmares?"

"Yeah, nothing to tell there. You know how dreams are—hard to recall and even harder to interpret."

"Yeah," Ray said. "You never know what they really mean."

Sal grinned and gazed at Lake Champlain. "They're over now." He looked at Boozer sacked out on his favorite couch and chuckled.

"I noticed a little statue of Hanuman in Jimmy's study on a shelf below your stick," Ray said. "And a gold brooch. Is that the one you carried?"

"Yeah, keepsakes—you know—fetishes you pick up along the way—so you won't forget."

"I always liked Hanuman—one of those gods who is always around when you need him."

Sal smiled and nodded. "Yup—well, not to change the subject, but the place looks great. Thanks for the help. How's your room?"

"Very comfortable, as always." Ray looked at the clock. "Stosh should be landing in an hour or so. Is Kate back?"

"No, said she was delayed. She'll be here about the same time as Deb and Stosh."

"Good. Everyone will be together again, like Thanksgiving. I still miss Jimmy at these gatherings, though."

Sal glanced back at Boozer and smiled. "I think Stosh will like this beer," he said and nodded.

***

Sal sat with Boozer on Turtle Rock while Ray puttered in the garage. The afternoon sun baked the back of his neck. He stood, stretched, and watched small waves lap over the rocks. Boozer snapped to attention, his tail wagging, and bolted up the stairs to the top of the bank. Sal looked over his shoulder. Kate was home. He watched her rub Boozer's ears.

"Who's a good Boozer?" Kate said. "Are you a good Boozer? You're a good Boozer, aren't you?"

"Stosh just pulled in," Kate yelled down. "Can I talk to you a minute before the party begins?"

Sal nodded.

Kate and Boozer stepped down the stairs to the shore. Kate gave Sal a hug. "I don't want you to be mad at me, Sallie, but you told me not to ask when I had a plan, just do it. Remember?"

Sal nodded and smiled.

Kate patted Sal's hand and pointed toward Camp. Beside the porch door stood Sita Patil.

"I think you two should talk."

Sal exhaled and nodded.

Kate jogged back up the steps and spoke to Sita.

Sita slowly trod to the shore and approached Sal. "How are you, Doctor Esposito?"

Sal smiled and gestured for Sita to join him. She sat on Turtle Rock beside Sal.

"It is difficult for me to know where to begin," Sita said. "First, I apologize for leaving India so very abruptly. I felt it was best."

Sal opened his lips to speak.

"I do not wish to be impolite," Sita said. "But please let me finish. I have rehearsed my words in my mind, and if I do not say what I am thinking now, all at once, I might not be able to do this."

Sal nodded.

"I did not know the twelve-year-old boy who struck my grandfather. That was many, many years ago, and young people often do bad things they later regret. I know a man I met last autumn who swears too much, drinks too much, and often displays much aggression. But *this* is the man who took me to India—although he did not want to. I saw *this* man save me from a brutal attack without becoming brutal himself. I saw him reason with a tiger, and remain composed when faced with my uncle's insulting behavior." Sita paused. "*This* is the Salvatore Esposito *I* know.

"My husband was not a kind person. While he did not often want me, when he did, it was humiliating and painful." Again,

Sita paused. "This is not easy to say … I never experienced intimacy until our time in Varanasi."

Sita looked down blushing. She looked at Sal and smiled.

"I must be very, very clear that I do not wish for another husband. I do not want the responsibilities that come with a domestic relationship of *any* kind. Radha and I are growing a very successful carpet business and are planning for much expansion. I have very much enjoyed my independence and the time I have had to put into my work. I do not wish to change any of that part of my life. But I have a deep fondness for you, and—perhaps I have watched too many American stories—I would like to be a 'special' friend if you find such a relationship appropriate."

Sal looked stunned.

"I am very, very sorry," Sita said. "I have been far too forward—I told Radha that speaking so openly would be a mistake. If you are uncomfortable with my being here—" Sal vigorously shook his head. "I could stay with Kate tonight and return to Florida tomorrow."

Again, Sal shook his head and smiled from ear to ear. Sita grinned.

"May I stay in the room I enjoyed so much last fall? I can only be a week, then I must return to my work."

Sal nodded and grinned. "And, perhaps, if we both find it desirable, on some evenings we might visit one another's room?"

Sal chuckled and nodded.

"And perhaps tonight might be one of those nights?"

Sal reached for Sita's hand and nodded again.

"I would very much like to touch here in the open on this lovely beach," Sita said. "But, while my views on many things have changed very, very much, I continue to have a repulsion for public affection."

Sal let Sita's hand go. Sita picked his hand up and smiled.

"We will have private opportunities," she said.

"What a surprise!" a voice yelled. "Two a my favorite people!" Sita and Sal turned to see Stosh standing at the top of the bank. Boozer darted up the stairs, jumped up and slapped Stosh's open palms.

"I'm just on my way up to unpack my things," Sita shouted.

"Take your time, no hurry," Stosh yelled back. "Look at this beautiful lake. There's lots a beautiful water ta look at in the world, but nothin's like Lake Champlain."

Boozer ran down the stairs and out into the lake.

"Boozer should be careful," Sita said. "Remember, there is a monster in this lake."

Sita began to laugh as Boozer swam.

"But then Champy *must* be a nice monster," she said. "Look at him swim, Salvatore. One would believe he has fins. That's what you should call him, Fins."

"Did you say Fins?" Stosh hollered. "That name's already taken. I'll tell ya about it."

Sita patted Sal's hand, jumped up, and trotted to the top of the stairs. "And I have many things to tell you," she told Stosh as she walked with him to the porch. "You would have laughed so very, very hard. When we were in Delhi, Salvatore was very, very startled by our driver and he yelled ..." Sita's voice faded from Sal's earshot.

In a moment Stosh's belly laugh broke the silence, followed by music as a soothing female voice began to sing "Moon River."

"Is that too loud?!" Stosh bellowed from the porch window. Sal exhaled. He raised his hand and signaled a thumb up.

Boozer shook, splattering water on Sal. He grabbed his stick and tossed it at Sal's feet. Sal stood and hurled it far out into the lake.

As Boozer bolted for the dock, Sal glanced down the shoreline and squinted to see a man and woman sitting on a large rock. The man visored his eyes with his hand as he watched Boozer leap from the dock, explode into the water, and swim frantically to retrieve his prize. Snatching it in his mouth, Boozer started a casual paddle back to shore.

Sal smiled and looked out onto Lake Champlain and Vermont's Green Mountains. He breathed in deeply through his nose and exhaled through his lips. As he watched his buddy glide through the water, he couldn't imagine anything happier. He looked into Boozer's eyes, placed his palms together, and bowed his head. "Namaste, my friend," Salvatore whispered.

DG

To the reader,

Thank you for joining Sal on his odyssey. I believe when one reads a story, they give the author a little piece of their life. I thank you for that gift. As always, your Amazon review would be much appreciated and you can contact me directly at JeffDelbel.com.

The tale goes on in…

Kate's Gift

COMING IN 2018

Namaste my friend,

Jeff Delbel

ACKNOWLEDGEMENTS

Those to whom I owe my gratitude are many.

David Connelly, my editor mentor, and coach through three novels. David shared a Pulitzer prize leading a team covering the eruptions of Mount St. Helens in 1980. His skill is immense and his ability to bring one along, invaluable.

Ryan Z Bartlett, whose superior publishing skills make a difficult process, enjoyable.

David Henry, whose patience and artistic vision produced a perfect cover.

Patricia Killoran, whose insight and support are cherished.

Elizabeth Haydon, author of more than 200 books whose council is invaluable.

Moreen Austin, Bill Canale, Aggie Crothers, Kathleen Connelly, Claudia Conway, David Conway, Glenn Dalton, Lonnie DeCavallas, Mary DeCavallas, Victor Garlock, David Henry, Karen Henry, Rich Kavanaugh,

Kimberly Miller, **Mitch Pajonas**, for their acute and honest content analysis.

Keith Batman, **Bruce Baird**, **Judy Baird**, **Judi Campagna**, **Patrice Case**, **Amy Casella**, **Tom Casella**, **Steve Keeler**, **Chuck Medoro**, and **David Raymond**, the rest of my diligent readers whose clear criticism led to much improvement.

Each of those listed contributed to making *Salvatore* a much better book.

Two additional recognitions are paramount.

Rebecca Anne and **Nathaniel Preston**. It is beyond my ability to express how much pride, respect, and love I have for you.